'*All the Painted Stars* is wonderfu
heartbreakingly tender. I wanted to
world for another thousand pa

'A delightful friends-to-lovers slow burn romance.
I absolutely loved meeting Lily and Jo, watching them
explore their feelings, find their voices, and discover
what happiness can truly be like!' **M.N. Bennet**

Praise for Emma Denny

'Road trips and secret identities … a beautifully
thoughtful and deliciously sweet romance about
getting lost in order to find oneself. I loved every
moment spent with Penn and Raff.' **Freya Marske**

'A heartwarming tale of forbidden love that captured
my heart from its opening page… Unputdownable.'
Sarah Ferguson, Duchess of York

'*One Night in Hartswood* is a thrilling, heart-stealing
historic romp and achingly romantic.' **M.A. Kuzniar**

'A beautiful love story and journey of longing until
your heart is torn apart and rebuilt.' **Liz Fenwick**

'A heart-wrenching, spellbinding love story, and I couldn't
turn the pages fast enough to find out if Raff and Penn
would get their happy ever after.' **Cressida McLaughlin**

'*One Night in Hartswood* is an utterly bedazzling novel,
a compulsive page-turner rich in historical detail, and
a heart-stopping debut romance.' **Kirsty Capes**

Emma Denny submitted her first manuscript to a publisher when she was eight and a half, and was astonished when it was rejected. Thankfully, that didn't put her off. After completing a degree in English & Creative Writing, Emma became a professional copywriter and now spends all day – literally – writing. Living on the edge of a forest, Emma enjoys exploring the wilderness while thinking through her latest plot tangle, scouting out exciting craft ales and indulging in historical romances. *One Night in Hartswood* was her debut novel, followed by the heart-stealing *All the Painted Stars*.

ALL
the
PAINTED
STARS

EMMA DENNY

ONE PLACE. MANY STORIES

HQ
An imprint of HarperCollins*Publishers* Ltd
1 London Bridge Street
London SE1 9GF

www.harpercollins.co.uk

HarperCollins*Publishers*
Macken House, 39/40 Mayor Street Upper,
Dublin 1, D01 C9W8, Ireland

This edition 2024

24 25 26 27 28 LBC 5 4 3 2 1
First published in Great Britain by
HQ, an imprint of HarperCollins*Publishers* Ltd 2024

Fragment 31 from Rayor, D. J. Sappho: A New Translation of the Complete Works, Edited and translated by Diane J. Rayor, Introduction & notes by André Lardinois © Diane J. Rayor and André Lardinois 2014, published by Cambridge University Press. All rights reserved.

UK ISBN: 9780008622435
US ISBN: 9780008673390

This book is set in 11.8/16 pt. Centaur by Type-it AS, Norway

Printed and Bound in the United States

For everyone who took a little while to figure it out.
With thanks to all the Mabels of the world.

To me it seems that man has the fortune
of gods, whoever sits beside you
and close, who listens to you
sweetly speaking

and laughing temptingly. My heart
flutters in my breast whenever
I quickly glance at you—
I can say nothing,

my tongue is broken. A delicate fire
runs under my skin, my eyes
see nothing, my ears roar,
cold sweat

rushes down me, trembling seizes me,
I am greener than grass.
To myself I seem
needing but little to die.

Yet all can be dared, since . . .

SAPPHO

(TRANS. DIANE J. RAYOR)

Prologue

My Jo,

You must stop apologising in your letters. I do not find them dull. I find them very interesting, in fact, because they are from you.

I miss you very much. I know it has not been so long since you were last with us, but it seems as if an age has passed. The blackberries growing near the lakes are so close to ripeness: if you were here, we could walk to the water's edge and pick them. Perhaps there may still be some berries left after your brother's tournament.

I must once again ask you to pass on my displeasure to your steward at his refusal to invite my family. Does he fear that we will cause even more scandal? Have we Bardens given ourselves such a fearsome reputation in the South?

The tournament would have given us an opportunity to fix that. Ash is passable at the joust and very good with a sword, although no doubt he would have caught the eye of some southern beauty and then caused even <u>more</u> scandal when he inevitably cursed at her to leave him alone. Raff <u>was</u> fair with the sword, but with his arm as it is I am quite sure he will never duel again. He refuses to take better care of himself, and is always off wandering up mountains or through forests with Penn. I am often forced to remind him that if he does not do as the physician says then his arm will fall clean off.

I told him that when this happens and it is eaten by wild dogs I shall laugh at him. I do not think he found it amusing.

I could ride in his stead. I have always wished to take part in a tournament, ever since I was small. It sounds _thrilling_. And I would not have cursed at any southern beauties. Quite the opposite, in fact.

I wish I had more exciting news for you; although nothing rivals the excitement of a tourney, I am sure. I eagerly await your next letter, and even more eagerly await your return to Dunlyn Castle.

Yours,
    Lily Barden

✳

Dearest Cecily,

Thank you a hundred times for your latest letter. I, too, wish that I could visit Dunlyn Castle once more. I would love to return to the lakes and pick berries and enjoy the sunshine. I cannot imagine anything I would like to do more.

But I cannot, even after the tournament is over. I have discovered at last why the steward, Edmund, has been behaving so peculiarly. He took me yesterday morning to my ~~father~~'s brother's solar to inform me that they intend to find me a worthy husband amongst the tournament's attendees.

I suspect Edmund feared that I would react strongly, but in truth I felt very little. I know that I cannot remain in the keep forever, and now the time has come when I must leave.

I should not allow myself to slip into doubt or worry. Certainly, I do not have time to do so. It is not as if I am being married _today_.

I do not wish to burden you with these thoughts. It should be a time to celebrate Ellis's new title. This is what I remind myself every day: that all my pains are for him. When he is a man grown, I hope he will remember, and be a better earl than our father was, God save his soul.

Please send my love to Penn, and tell him I miss him every day. Please also send my regards to your brothers, and inform Raff that I quite agree with you on the matter of his arm, and that if he loses use of it (I do not agree with you that it will fall off and be eaten by wild dogs), then that is his own fault for not taking better care of himself.

I hope I will see you again soon.

All my thoughts and regards,
  Johanna de Foucart

Chapter I

Oxfordshire – 1362

Long strands of vibrant red hair caught on the brambles of the blackberry bush, snagging in the thorns and twisting in vivid dashes across the plump berries. A few were picked up on the breeze, dancing over the dark green leaves and away, scattering into the air.

Lily lowered her knife and shook her head, sending yet more strands flying. They floated up and over the bramble she'd camped behind, spinning upwards like the folks of the seelie court in their woodland groves. Beside her, shoved haphazardly beneath her pack and unravelling swiftly, were two long red plaits.

She tugged her remaining hair over her shoulder and set to hacking at it again with the knife. It was horribly uneven, but better to be uneven than long enough to raise suspicion. No knight sported waist-length hair, and certainly not a knight in attendance at a tournament. It was also far too risky: too easily grabbed in a fight.

When she was finally done, she placed the blade atop her pack then combed through her hair with her fingertips. From the other side of the clearing, her dun palfrey peered up at her where she was drinking from the stream, her ears twitching as hair floated past.

'Do not look at me like that, Broga,' Lily said, standing and stretching out her arms. 'It is better than being recognised as a woman or tumbling during a tilt after getting entangled.'

The horse did not respond, simply ducked her head once more. Lily dropped to the bank beside her and cupped her hands in the cool, clear water. She splashed it messily over her face, slicking back her hair. Cutting it was a small sacrifice, and she was already enjoying the feeling of the breeze on her now-bare neck. She had never been overly attached to her hair, and had often envied her eldest brother's short, messy crop.

As a child, she had been subject to her nursemaid's daily hair-brushing, and while she had enjoyed the tingling feeling it elicited, she had resented how *long* the process had taken. When Lily had demanded her hair be cut short like her brothers', the nursemaid had lectured her about *beauty* and *glory*, and she had not asked again.

When she had taken the first of her thick plaits in hand and sliced through it with her knife, her only regret had been that she hadn't sharpened the blade beforehand. She had expected to grieve as her long hair, grown since she could walk, tumbled to the ground and slipped away on the breeze. But instead she felt relief – like releasing a breath held for too long.

Without a mirror to see herself in and with the water too fast to reflect her face, she would have to hope that her work was acceptable. Truthfully, it was unlikely anyone would question her dishevelment, but she needed to be seen as a travelling knight or squire, *not* a runaway noblewoman.

As she stood, rolling up the sleeves of her stolen tunic, she wondered if her family in Dunlyn Castle had realised she had vanished yet. The younger of her two brothers, Raff, was beyond the Scottish border with his companion, Penn. They were visiting the family of the Barden siblings' late mother before carrying on north and would likely be gone for months. No doubt they were halfway up some blasted mountain, entirely unaware that she had gone.

She was less certain about her father, Earl Griffin Barden, and her eldest brother, Ash. After finally embracing the role of heir that he had managed to shirk so effectively for so many years, Ash was travelling across Barden lands with their father, visiting neighbouring vassals and allies. Where Raff had headed north, they had headed east, and with any luck would be away for several more weeks.

She had even seen to the steward and servants, telling them that she wished to visit the local convent to pay her respects to the women who lived there. The steward had found this perfectly acceptable. It had been assumed that Lily would one day enter the convent herself, a common fate for any woman deemed unmarriable. This was no great hardship: she could certainly think of a worse fate than living amongst only women. She had no desire at all to be married, and being publicly jilted the morning of her own wedding had granted her a freedom she had grasped with both hands. Nobody wanted a forsaken bride whose first failed betrothal had brought so much scandal with it.

Perhaps her brothers would not even return to an empty keep and a well-placed lie. With any luck she could see out the tourney and be back home before anyone else. She had certainly made good time: by her estimations, she would arrive at the de Foucart keep before midday, and the tournament would begin the day after.

She reached mindlessly towards the brambles, pulling off a plump blackberry and popping it into her mouth. It exploded on her tongue, rich and flavourful. As she grabbed for another, her fingers caught on the tiny thorns and with a curse she snatched her hand back, squeezing the berry too hard. It burst beneath her fingertips, staining them a vibrant, bloody red.

She stared at her fingers. The sunshine turned cold. She wiped her hand on her stolen breeches, staining *them*, too, the marks clinging to the wool and to the pads of her fingers.

Forcing the unsettled feeling away, she reached for her pack and pulled out Jo's letter. She'd read it dozens of times – hundreds – since the messenger had handed it to her at the gates of Dunlyn Castle. She was sure, now more than ever, that Jo's measured, polite words hid terror beneath.

I hope I will see you again soon.

It was a cry for help which Lily was determined to answer.

While she had met Jo several times, much of their friendship had been built on these letters. Lily herself had written the first: a sincere message that expressed her sorrow that they would not be made sisters. Penn – the man with whom her brother was stomping around Scotland – was Jo's brother, and Lily's once-intended. After their betrothal had fallen apart, she assumed she would never see Jo again.

But she *had* seen her again, even if it was not as often as she would have liked, thanks to the unexpected union of their brothers.

Lily carefully folded the letter, now smudged with pink fingerprints, put it away, then swung the pack onto her shoulders. At her feet the pair of plaits tangled on the dry earth like an accusation. Before she could move on, she would need to hide the evidence of her transgression. She certainly couldn't leave them where they lay, easy for anyone to find, but there was scant room in her pack as it was, and anyone who looked inside would surely question why a lone knight carried such trophies with him.

She could burn them, but while she had been lucky thus far to meet very few people on the road, the stink of burning hair would be sure to rouse the suspicion of anyone who *did* pass. She reached down, picked up the plaits without bothering to shake the dirt from them, and looked around.

Beside the stream, Broga snorted at her, apparently just as keen to move on as she was.

And then an idea struck her.

The breeze blew against Lily's neck, ruffling the oversized collar of her tunic, kissing her nape. Broga tossed her head as they picked their way back towards the path through the brambles, still adorned with strands of long hair, floating upwards in a slow, twisting dance.

Tossed on the surface of the turbulent water behind them, rushing downstream and picking up speed, were two vivid red plaits. They drifted for only a moment, before vanishing silently beneath the deep, dark water.

✳

Johanna stood with her arms folded in the middle of the armourer's yard and regarded her tiny half-brother.

Earl Ellis de Foucart was seven years old, painfully stubborn, and gripping a shining sword nearly taller than he was in both hands.

'But it's *my* sword,' he whined.

Marshal Brice lingered nervously beside him with the young earl's nursemaid. Both were frozen with indecision: the earl was still the earl, even if he *was* only a child.

Jo had to concede that Ellis was correct. The sword had been forged for their father — taken to war with him in service of the king – and had been but one of several heirlooms Ellis had inherited along with the title when Earl Marcus de Foucart had died. It was an enormous, two-handed broadsword, the steel glinting dangerously in the sunlight.

Ellis had accepted the role of Earl with excitement, if only because he had no true notion of what the title entailed beyond the ability to tell others what to do. Despite Jo's best efforts to teach him, Ellis had shown very little enthusiasm in the running of the keep. This was fair: he was still young, and far more interested in the spider he'd somehow captured in the stables than he was in politics.

Jo had heard stories about young sons who had inherited titles far too early making outrageous demands which their new courtiers were obliged to see out. Ellis's most extravagant demand since becoming Earl had been that they allow him to keep the spider.

'Ellis.' Jo resisted the urge to kneel in front of him, partly to avoid patronising him, and partly because she had no desire to bring her face so close to the blade. 'We understand that this is your sword. But as the Earl, you must be sensible when you choose your weapon, yes?'

'But it's *mine*,' he repeated, pouting.

'Very well,' Jo said. 'Demonstrate it to us. Take a swing.'

Ellis narrowed his eyes at her. 'Truly?'

'Of course,' she said. 'You *are* the Earl, and it *is* your sword. If we are beset with invaders then I wish to know that you will keep us safe. Go: swing the sword. Marshal Brice will observe and assess your form.'

She took a step back, praying that Ellis would not injure himself – or one of his audience. The nursemaid went to speak – 'Ellis, are you *quite . . .*' – when the tiny Earl heaved the sword up, swung it as high as he could, stumbled, and embedded the tip several inches into the soft earth at his feet.

All three adults leapt back.

Ellis stared at the place where the sword was lodged in the ground.

Jo took a moment to steady her breathing, then finally bent down so she was eye level with him.

'What must you know, if you are the Earl?' she asked.

Ellis tugged at the sword. It didn't move.

'You must know your own strengths and limitations,' she continued calmly. 'Your sword is very impressive, but what would have happened if you attempted that swing in a tourney?'

Ellis considered this. 'I . . .' he started, working it out. 'If my sword were stuck, I would have been hit.'

'Exactly. If your sword had not been so heavy, you would have been able to right it and defend yourself against an opponent's blow. But now—' she gestured to the ground, 'you cannot.'

Ellis tugged harder at the sword. Still it did not move.

'Come,' Jo said, doing her best to appear put-upon. 'We need to make the final preparations for your guests. Marshal Brice needs to ensure the armoury is ready for use, which *includes* your sword. It must be sharpened and polished so it can be displayed.' Ellis made a face, so she continued. 'And someone must head to the kitchens to see if the cook has found a solution for their beetle infestation . . .'

That caught Ellis's attention. He paused in his efforts to remove the sword from the ground. 'Beetles?'

'Yes,' Jo said, distractedly. 'One of the kitchen girls moved a basket of vegetables to find a whole nest of them beneath.'

Ellis's eyes sparkled. 'Are they very large?'

'*Huge*, to hear the kitchen girl speak of them,' said Jo. 'Although I have never seen beetles of the size *she* described in these parts. The cook is furious, of course, for they've *ruined* all those vegetables, and her staff have been set to clearing out the awful things instead of preparing for the tournament.'

She pretended to think for a moment, then looked back down towards Ellis.

'Perhaps your nursemaid could take you to speak to the cook?' she asked him. 'As the Earl, it is important that you know of all threats to our keep. They can be the first invaders you vanquish.'

'Do you suppose there are many left?'

'I am sure there must be *some*,' Jo said, 'given how many there were earlier.'

The sword was immediately forgotten as Jo directed Ellis towards the nursemaid with a smile.

'Ensure you tell the cook that I sent you,' she said to him. 'She will be pleased that you have seen fit to deal with the matter yourself, my Lord.'

Ellis gave her a wide grin, grabbed the hand of the long-suffering nursemaid, and dragged her across the yard.

Jo let out a long breath as she watched his departing figure. His little adventure had pulled her from the laundry, where she had been instructing the maids on where to take fresh linens for those arriving for the tournament. She would have to hope that they had managed without her.

The upcoming event was supposed to be a celebration of Ellis's new title, but it felt more like one for the death of her father. For many, it would be: they cared little for Ellis but had loathed the late Earl. Now he was gone.

Her father's death should have been a loss. Dressed in mourning clothes, she had lingered beside his casket in silence, watching the flickering light of the torches against the rough stone wall. She had felt very little. She still did.

She had completed the requisite mourning period. The keep had been unnervingly silent. And then – like clouds lifting, like the first light of spring – a change came over the castle. It was not happiness, not quite, but the air felt fresh and hopeful.

Without her father, they all lived less in dread, although it often seemed as if the anxiety they had all felt was built into the stones of the castle itself; the mortar saturated with blood and fear. But it was growing less every day, the eerie sense of unease washing away like grime in the rain.

They hoped that the tournament would finally expel that sense entirely, even if it was a celebration in name alone. The council that had gathered to rule before Ellis came of age saw it as a keen way to display the family's status without making themselves – or the young, vulnerable earl – look like a threat. Jo's father had kept power through force and the promise of violence. But like this, they could rely on good faith and familiarity while still ensuring that any who saw fit to push against the new earl would be treated to the sight of their wealth, power, and sizeable army.

It wasn't just their father who had tarnished the family's reputation. Her brothers' behaviour, too, needed to be atoned for. Henry, the eldest and most dutiful son, had died years ago, leaving the family with two unsuitable heirs. Leo, the next in line, had been dismissed and removed from the keep when Jo was only fifteen after becoming attached to one of their servants. Jo had never been privy to all the details of the affair, but the arguments between Leo and their father had rung through the castle. Leo's disavowal and removal had been swift and merciless.

Even now, when she closed her eyes, she could still hear the sound of the dogs.

It had been a dark time for the remaining de Foucart children – still reeling from the sudden death of their eldest brother only to lose another sibling. It had been worse for Penn, her remaining brother. Younger than Jo and struggling under the weight of a title far too heavy for him, he had snapped.

He had fled the keep, ruining the betrothal which would have granted their father the ancestral power he craved, as well as destroying the reputation of Penn's once-intended.

Her brothers' disastrous legacies had set a precedent for her own behaviour. She had to make up for their crimes. She had to be *good*, be a dutiful daughter like her elder sister Rosalind and buff out the stains that Leo and Penn had left.

Her upcoming marriage would do that. It would make it clear that the family's reputation was not entirely in tatters, and besides: the tie to another noble family would secure them even more allies.

It wasn't a surprising development: Jo had been training for marriage for twenty-seven years. But now the expectations were greater than ever. She was more valuable as a bride than a sister.

She was approaching the matter practically. Her mother had been so *young* when she wed, forced to marry a tyrant against her will, and Jo had been terrified that her future would mirror the late Countess Eleanor's. It was what had, in part, encouraged her to learn all she could about the running of keep: a pleased husband would be less likely to treat her cruelly.

But with the support of her stepmother, Isabelle, and Ellis's council, she hoped that she would not be tied to a cruel man at all. As the second wife of Jo's father, Isabelle especially was aware of the pain of *that* sort of marriage, and Jo trusted that she would do her best to prevent it.

Jo was not unhappy to wed: a good match would free her from the de Foucart keep. Even without her father, the castle was full of ghosts. It would be good to move on and move away, just as her siblings had, in one way or another. She was clever and capable, as she so often tried to remind herself. She would flourish away from the keep, if she was granted the chance to do so. She was not walking into a prison, but escaping one.

It was what she had been born to do, after all. What one *did*, as a noblewoman. And she would do it well.

Incredibly, the tournament really *was* mending the divide. Most of the invitations they had sent directly had been accepted, and as word spread they had received news every day of more people who were attending. People loved entertainment, and it was clear that many were willing to forget, if not forgive, the actions of her father in exchange for a week of jousting and fighting and good, strong ale.

And all of it was to celebrate a boy not even eight years old with a sword too large for him to swing. She would miss her little brother when she left the keep, and had hoped that he really *had* taken on at least some of her lessons. She could not bear for him to grow up into the shape of their father.

Giving brief thanks to Marshal Brice, who was now inspecting the tip of the sword for damage, she smoothed her skirts and headed towards the gatehouse where she had promised to meet Countess Isabelle.

Jo had fallen into an easy rapport with her late father's wife.

When Isabelle had married Earl Marcus de Foucart, Jo had felt uneasy at best and cautiously hostile at worst towards the woman who was replacing her mother. After he had died not six months ago, Isabelle had relaxed into the role of widow with an ease that Jo hadn't expected of her, and she had realised, belatedly, that her father's temper and cruel nature had been a spectre over Isabelle's life, too. Closer in age to her new children than her husband, Isabelle's lot had been the same as most noblewomen – the same as Jo's was now – a marriage bartered for profit and power and little else.

Isabelle was determined, stronger than she appeared, and fiercely protective towards her own children, Ellis and Ingrid. Without de Foucart, Isabelle and Jo were now closer to sisters than mother and daughter, and Jo had found surprising security in her. But as Jo approached the gatehouse, Isabelle was nowhere to be seen. Instead, lingering beneath the open portcullis was a rider on a horse.

He greeted her as she approached. They had become close over the past year or so – this was the messenger who carried letters to and from the keep. Often, he brought letters from Cecily.

Jo had been re-reading Cecily's latest missive that morning, within which Cecily had expressed her desire for Jo to return to Dunlyn Castle. She spoke of lakeside walks and summer sunshine and blackberry picking, long days with no end, full of sweetness and laughter. Jo had read the letter with her chest squeezing. She wanted it so much it *hurt*.

The northern keep felt farther away than it had ever been. It was a two-week ride between the two castles when travelling with a retinue – a long but manageable journey. Now it seemed an impossible distance.

The first trip to Dunlyn Castle had been an act of diplomacy. Penn was by law the family's hostage – a prisoner for peace, as part of negotiations made after de Foucart's temper and violence had nearly ruined them all. But Penn was a prisoner in name alone. It was a ruse, allowing him to stay with Raff: Penn's lover, and Cecily's elder brother. Jo had journeyed to Dunlyn to confirm he was being treated well, thus ensuring the terms of the agreement still stood.

He *was* well, as she had known he would be. The Barden family had embraced him as one of their own, and they embraced her, too, for the short time she was there.

Away from her father's iron rule and explosive temper for the first time in her life, she was happy. She could breathe. Cecily had declared her a friend, and by the time she was packing the carts for the journey home she had spent more time with Cecily than she had Penn.

Her trips since then had been diplomatic in name alone. She longed for that lightness and laughter, and had never found companionship like she had in Cecily. She was so free, so entirely wild and confident, and that wildness had been near-intoxicating. Cecily had taken her on grand walks of her father's grounds and lands, visiting villages and beautiful scenic lakes. Jo's time with Penn often amounted to little more than shared meals or long evenings gathered beside the fire. Once, she had arrived to find that Penn and Raff had taken themselves off on an excursion to Cumberland, and he had only arrived home the day she had left for Oxford.

She longed to go back, but now she was to be married. Another visit north may not happen for months – perhaps years – if her husband even allowed it. She had spent weeks grieving the fact that she would not return north before the tournament was upon them.

She had told Cecily of her upcoming marriage in her last letter, and had still yet to receive a reply.

A letter from Cecily would go some way to buoying her spirits. She was not *unhappy* to be married, and far too busy to be miserable, but she was desperate to hear from her again anyway. It felt like a fragile friendship – one which Jo had never had before, and one which she was keen not to lose.

'Good morning, Lady Johanna.' The rider smiled down at her. 'All is well?'

'Very well,' she said, with a short curtsey. 'You had no trouble in the grounds?'

He laughed, looking over his shoulder. 'It's furiously busy out there,' he said, 'but I got through unharmed.'

He passed her a bundle of parchment tied with twine. She tugged the tie away and quickly skimmed through the letters, but realised with a leaden feeling that none were for her. She would have recognised Cecily's messy handwriting anywhere, and today – as it had for over a fortnight – it was not to be found amongst the missives.

The rider noticed her disappointment. 'Everything all right, m'Lady?'

Jo set herself, fixing her face back into a smile. 'Quite all right,' she said, quickly. 'I was expecting a letter. Perhaps it has become waylaid.'

The messenger gave her a sympathetic look.

'Perhaps tomorrow, then,' he said. 'I hope the tournament goes well, m'Lady.'

Jo thanked him, and watched as he turned the horse around and made his way back through the gatehouse, weaving around people.

She gripped the bundle of letters in her hands, rubbing the rough parchment between her fingers.

It was unusual to go so long without hearing from Cecily. It was very likely that a letter *had* been waylaid or lost on the long journey between their homes, but a dark little voice at the back of her head told her that this was not the case.

You are too dull, it said. *She has grown bored of you.*

Jo wasn't sure why it hurt so much. Perhaps it was for the simple fact that Jo had never *had* a friend like Cecily before. She had never even *met* someone like Cecily, and none of the dozens of women who flitted in and out of her life could hold a candle to her flame.

Even during their first meeting Cecily had been bolder than Jo had expected. She couldn't tell if Cecily didn't realise how strict de Foucart was, and so had not known the need to rein herself in, or if it was simply in her *nature* to be bold, no matter what.

The more they spoke – both in person and in letters – the more Jo suspected that it was her nature. She feared that she was boring in comparison.

'Johanna?'

Jo turned. Isabelle stood behind her, wearing a dazzling light-blue gown and a curious expression. When she spotted Jo's face, the expression slipped into concern.

'Are you all right?'

'Oh— Yes, I am quite well.' Jo handed her the pile of letters. 'I was lost in thought.'

Isabelle regarded her with a pointed look. 'Nothing from the north?' she asked. 'Or *Cecily*?'

Jo swallowed. There was an odd lilt to the way Isabelle had said Cecily's name that she couldn't quite understand. Did Isabelle find their continued friendship inappropriate? Her expression, though, was teasing – eyebrows raised, lip quirked.

'No,' Jo admitted. 'Nothing.'

Isabelle gave her a soft, slightly sad smile. 'I am sure you will hear again soon enough,' she said. 'Did you inform . . . *her* of the tournament?'

'Of course.'

'And of the arrangements we are making for you?'

It took Jo a moment to realise what she meant. 'Of my marriage?' she asked, brow furrowing. 'Yes, I mentioned it in my last letter.'

'Oh.' Isabelle looked surprised. 'I had not expected— Well, that may go some way to explaining it, I suppose.'

Jo was lost. 'I . . . am not sure I understand.'

Isabelle chose her words very carefully. 'It may no longer be . . . appropriate,' she said at last, 'to continue the friendship? Considering that you will soon be wed . . .'

This was even more confusing. Only a cruel man would forbid his wife from having female friends beyond the confine of their keep, and Jo knew that Isabelle was keen not to tie her to a man like that. Isabelle read the confusion on her face, then to Jo's shock, ducked closer, lowering her voice.

'I understand that you found happiness in the north, Johanna, but he must—'

'Countess Isabelle!'

Isabelle cut herself off with a sigh then swept forwards to greet the man who had shouted to them from the other side of the gatehouse.

'It is wonderful to see you again, Lord Thomas,' Isabelle called. 'I am so glad you could attend . . .'

Jo watched as she welcomed Lord Thomas and his wife. It had been a strange conversation. Isabelle had been treating her oddly since Jo's first visit to Dunlyn Castle, and she could not place why. It had not been the first time she had spoken about Cecily with raised eyebrows and an exaggerated expression.

'But he must . . .' It appeared that Isabelle hadn't been talking about Cecily at all, or had misspoken. Jo sighed to herself. She would have to unpick the matter *later*: right now, Lord Thomas's wife, Lady Ava, was approaching. Jo pulled her face into what she hoped was a welcoming smile and embraced her.

'My Lady,' she said, with a curtsey. 'I hope the journey was fair?'

'Very fair,' Lady Ava said. She shot a look over her shoulder to where Lord Thomas and Isabelle were still talking, then took Jo's arm and led her away from them. 'I have been quite desperate to ask,' she said, voice lowered. 'Have you had any luck with your search?'

Jo knew at once what she was talking about. Leo.

After Penn had vanished and Jo assumed him dead, she had decided that she would not lose anyone else and had set out to find their elder brother. Leo had always been strong – stronger than Jo – and he would not have simply given up.

She sent letters to the courts of those who were familiar with the family, begging for old allies to inform her should they hear word of him. Lady Ava had been one of the many noblewomen she had asked; once a close friend of their mother's and sympathetic to her plight. Jo had trusted her to ensure word of the hunt never reached Jo's father.

It had been a huge risk. Jo had felt her father's eyes bearing down on her, positive that he *knew*, somehow, every time she sent a letter or whispered a word into the ear of a woman she could trust. She waited for weeks – *months* – for discovery and punishment.

But discovery never came. Nor did she hear anything back. Leo – and the girl he had left with – had vanished. The steely sense of certainty that had made her seek him out had been blunted. Now, she had all but given up.

'I have not,' she said, matching Ava's whispered tone. 'I fear it has been a futile search.'

Ava gripped her arm. 'I am so sorry to hear that,' she said. 'You may hear yet.'

Jo didn't have the heart to tell her she was wrong. 'Perhaps. Have you many men in the tourney?' she asked instead, keen to move the conversation on.

'Oh *yes*.' Ava's eyes sparkled. 'We've several of the younger boys keen to enter, you know how they are, and of course Thomas has decided he simply *must* enter the joust and nothing I say will dissuade him . . .'

Jo slipped into easy conversation with Lady Ava before directing the party inside. She had no time to speak plainly to Isabelle about their aborted conversation: more guests were arriving, all of such rank that it would be improper for at least one of them not to greet them personally.

Many of their guests had brought sons whom she was introduced to with raised eyebrows and knowing looks, or were unmarried men of rank seeking a bride themselves. The hairs on her nape prickled unpleasantly as another man old enough to be her grandfather placed a damp kiss to the back of her hand, his eyes lingering on her for far too long as Jo gave him a dutiful, forced smile.

She needed a suitable reason to remove herself. Looking through the still-open gates, she could see the tourney grounds beyond, alive with people far too unimportant to be allowed entry to the keep itself. She made her way over to where Isabelle was talking animatedly to an older woman and her tall, slender daughter.

She edged forwards as soon as the conversation appeared to be over. 'My Lady, if I could?'

'Yes?'

'There are quite a number of lower-ranking men attending,' Jo said. 'More than I had anticipated. Would you give me leave to head into the grounds and greet them? It would do to welcome even the wandering knights.'

Jo had ensured that such men had suitable places to sleep, choosing the patch of land for rows of empty tents herself, and so it would be fair to welcome them, too. She did not want anyone in attendance to feel as if they were *lesser*. A tournament was supposed to be a leveller, after all.

'A keen idea,' Isabelle said. 'It will let our guests know that we welcome all of them, not just the nobility. But please, do find Brice or Edmund to accompany you. We've no idea what kind of men have seen fit to attend.'

Jo paused. Yes: there were more likely to be rogues or bandits amongst travellers, but she was well aware that noblemen were just as likely to be cruel or violent. Moreso, given their birth right and power. Perhaps beyond the walls of the keep, away from money and influence, was a *better* kind of man.

She gave her stepmother a dutiful curtsey.

'Of course, my Lady.'

Chapter 2

Lily stood in the shade of Hartswood Forest, staring at the castle that loomed ahead and the neat rows of tents that flanked its walls.

This was the third time she had found herself on the edge of the de Foucart keep, and each time had brought with it a greater sense of fear than the last. The first had been for her own wedding. The second, weeks later, had been to retrieve her brother, so horribly wounded that no one even knew if he was alive. And now, here she was again, wearing stolen clothes with stolen armour strapped to her horse, ready to enter once more in search of someone she—

Someone she cared for.

She set her shoulders, pulled her cap low, then walked forwards, tugging Broga beside her. As she picked across the tourney grounds, a thrill coursed through her body. This would be where she would make her mark, where her plan would come to fruition.

She was going to enter the tournament disguised as a man, embarrass the other competitors, and save Jo from a life of shackles. She was going to pull her from the keep and the arms of a husband and gift her the most precious thing Lily could: her own freedom.

Lily was not so bold to assume that she could beat *all* of the well-practised lords and knights in attendance – men who had ridden into battle as much as they had ridden at each other in these mock-wars. But her years training at her yielding brothers' sides had given her skill enough to be confident that she could hold her own against them.

Besides, she didn't need to win outright. Jo's letter had not mentioned that the *winner* of the whole affair would be granted her hand – just someone who was worthy. And who was more worthy than a nameless travelling knight with no familial ties who defeated a host of rich noblemen and their lackeys? There was *no one* worth more than that: it was the stuff of courtly romances.

She would best the competition and embarrass the other attendants. She would knock her opponent from his horse, swing from Broga's saddle, and kneel at Jo's feet as a man with no name and no titles. There would be negotiations, of course, and no doubt there would be scandal. And in the chaos, Lily would reveal herself to Jo, take her hand, and whisk her away to a future that was entirely her own. Lily would stand by her side each step of the way, guiding her, and letting Jo guide *her* in turn.

And perhaps Jo would even stay. Perhaps she would not only take Lily's hand, but accept it, too.

Beside her, Broga whinnied. Lily realised she'd been tugging too hard on the reins. She loosened her grip with an apologetic pat. She'd drifted into fantasy; unachievable and deadly in its inevitable ending.

'My apologies,' she murmured to the stamping horse. 'I fear you are the wiser of us, today, Broga.'

Broga sniffed in reply, nudging Lily with her nose. Lily sighed and peered around, trying to find a suitable spot to make camp. At the far end of the grounds were a sparse number of empty tents which had been set up for travellers like herself: knights-errant and wanderers, men who had no one to journey with and nowhere to go.

It was a thoughtful touch. Lily wondered if the decision had been Jo's or the steward's. Providing accommodation for the lowest competitors — even if that accommodation was no more than two dozen simple tents — was a conspicuous demonstration of the family's hospitality.

And, of course, of their wealth. Lily was unsure just *how* wealthy the family remained, but clearly the expense of the tournament was worth it to mend the divides between the de Foucart family and their allies. The money would be recouped in the future, should the tourney be a success and their station restored.

It would also be aided by whichever man left with Jo as his prize should Lily fail. The cost of the grand event and even Jo's dowry would pale in comparison to the significance of an important political and financial union with a wealthy lord.

She tried not to think too hard on the more painful realities of Jo's marriage as she led Broga to one of the empty tents. She could not allow herself to linger on it, instead thinking ahead to the excitement of the tournament. Her plan to scupper Jo's betrothal was an enormous risk, one which she could not let overwhelm her.

She had very few things with her, and she quickly unloaded the packs from Broga's back and her own shoulders, tossing them haphazardly inside before seeking out the stables that had been set up on the edge of the grounds for competitors.

Keeping close to Broga, Lily observed the other attendees. Many of them were in groups, and spirits were high. Several men greeted her as she passed — some sincerely, some poorly disguising their mockery at one so young. Some attempted not to disguise it at all: as she walked past a huge tent with luridly coloured banners fluttering outside, the gaggle of lords lingering within stopped their conversation to stare at her.

They burst into laughter before she had even rounded the corner.

No matter. Better for them to think her a young, useless boy than a woman. Mockery she could stand. Discovery was far more dangerous.

And besides, she thought, setting her shoulders. Perhaps she would have a chance to best one of them in the field. Only *she* would be laughing, then.

The stables were well stocked, and the stablehand she passed Broga's reins to seemed attentive enough. She returned to her tent, greeting the man who had occupied the one beside it in her absence, tightly knotted the flap shut to ensure no one would enter and, finally, peered around.

It was a simple space, with rushes on the floor and a straw mattress to one side. It was another reassuring touch, and she quickly saw to her things, few that they were. She pulled her stolen armour from the sack she'd slung it in, laying it out upon the rushes so she could better assess it.

She had been lucky to find it: a full set of armour, hidden away at the back of the armoury. It had belonged to her brothers when they were young; both of them, in fact, made for Ash then passed to Raff when he outgrew it, although it had never fit Raff particularly well.

She held the chest plate, the metal cool against her fingers. It must have been a sense of nostalgia that had made her father keep it all these years.

She placed the chest plate down and picked up the shield that

26

she'd found in the same dusty back room. *This* she could remember very well: it had been one they had all shared while her brothers trained and she had forced herself into their games. At some point, it had been painted a vibrant blue with tiny white dots: a night sky speckled with stars.

It had been a fanciful scene, even then. Traditionally her shield should have borne the colours of her house, but as this had been for little more than training and play, they'd been given the choice to paint it however they deemed fit. She couldn't even remember who had chosen the stars, now, although she was sure there had been an argument about it.

Spread out on the rushes, it all looked very passably like the garb of a knight-errant. She'd tried it all on a few nights before she had absconded, and found it fit fairly well, especially with the padding of a gambeson and tunic beneath. The shape of the chest plate and the hang of the tunic had the additional bonus of obscuring her silhouette, making her look less like a young woman and more like a youthful lad.

It was enough. It *had* to be enough, for what she intended to do.

There was nervous energy thrumming beneath her skin, making her fingers tingle. It was not even midday. If she were to spend the rest of the day and the long evening hidden away in this tent, she would go mad. She needed something to *do*.

She grabbed the armour and began to tug it on. She'd led Broga past a training yard on her way through the grounds, which had been teeming with squires. She could easily find someone willing to spar with her. Anything to channel the tumbling in her stomach and rushing in her blood: anything to stop her thinking of what she was about to do, and who she was doing it for.

She clasped the final buckle, strapped her sword to her hip, and strode back out into the teeming noise of the tourney.

✳

The grounds outside the de Foucart castle were a hive of activity. Jo dodged servants with baskets of linens and food, pairs of boys carrying lances three times their size between them, an endless number of horses being urged towards the stables, and dozens of dogs bounding and barking as they wove through people's legs. Marshal Brice had agreed to chaperone her, and together they were exploring the training ground, where Brice was keen to ensure that all was running smoothly before the tournament began the next day.

Jo recognised a handful of the colours on display around them – either hanging from horses, splashed across shields, or on the gambesons and tunics worn by those practising. Lower-ranking sons, squires, and green boys, all keen to make a show of what was for most of them their first tournament. Many of them recognised her as she approached, immediately removing their helms and bowing low in deference as she greeted them.

At least their deference was just that. None of these lads would be permitted the chance to take Jo as a bride – she was a prize for their elders and betters – and so without the barrier of fear and flirtation, conversation came far more easily. Excitement buzzed about the place like summer bees, and it was clear that all the men she spoke to were excited for the event and endlessly thankful for the chance to compete.

As she was speaking to one of Lord Thomas's boys, they were interrupted by a cheer from the far end of the grounds. They both turned to see a man raising a practice lance triumphantly in the air with a wooden hoop spinning around the base. He was wearing finely made but old armour, rusted around the edges. Not *cheap*, but well used, and a little dated. From beneath his tarnished helm stuck strands of vibrantly red hair. He turned the horse, holding the lance higher, hoop rattling.

This was a popular training method – catching hoops on the end of a lance to practise form and ensure one could land a precise blow. As they watched, he twisted his palfrey around, steadied it, then nodded towards a lad at the far end of the stretch of grass.

Jo only realised what he intended to do when there was a whistle, and suddenly there was another hoop spinning up into the air. With a shout, the man kicked his heels into the horse's flank and dashed forwards, lance readied. He caught the hoop on the very tip of the lance and then – to the delight of both the gathered crowd and the boy Jo had been talking to – it slid down towards his hand.

It was clear that Jo would find no further conversation with the young squire, and even Brice's attention had been caught by the performance, so she walked over to watch. A few of the crowd bowed or nodded towards her, but many were too enraptured by the knight on horseback to pay her any mind.

She wondered if the young man was unsettled by the growing crowd. It appeared not: he whirled the horse around again and called over the noise – '*Again!*'

Another wooden hoop was flung into the air. Again, the knight sped forwards, horse snorting, weapon raised—

And missed. The hoop bounced from the shaft of the lance and spun away across the grass. The excitable crowd burst into jeers and laughter. The knight didn't appear to pay them any mind, merely shrugged, threw the lance down to a waiting boy, and swung himself from the horse.

He hitched the animal to the post at the far end of the field then stooped to grab a shield leaning against the fence. It was wooden and battered, painted to replicate the starry sky. He must have been a wandering knight, not attached to any single family.

He chatted for a moment to a handful of men who had watched his performance. Jo lingered, waiting for him to be free, before heading across the field to greet him.

'That was well performed, sir.'

At her voice, he gave a jump, spinning to face her. Through the visor of his helm was pair of handsome blue-grey eyes. He was shorter than her, but when he spoke, laughing through his own shock, he did not sound *young*, just surprised.

'My Lady – I had not realised you were watching.'

He gave her a low bow. That appeared to be where his formality ended: unlike the others she had spoken to, he did not remove his helm.

'It was an impressive display,' Jo said, smile fixed. He was a knight-errant, after all: she could forgive his lack of etiquette.

The man shrugged, tapping out a tattoo on his vambraces with his fingers. 'I missed the final throw.'

'To catch two is still very impressive,' Jo said. 'I assume you will be competing in the joust?'

'Of course,' the man said. 'And single combat, too.'

'I am pleased to hear it. What is your name, sir?'

It took him a moment to respond. 'William, my Lady. William Dale.'

She did not recognise the name, but something about him

seemed familiar: the flash of his eyes, the tone of his voice. He was from the north, that much was clear.

'I wish you luck, then, Sir Dale.'

William gave a sharp, ringing laugh. 'Not a sir,' he said. As he laughed, sunlight glinted off his helm. 'Not a knight. Not *knighted*, in any case. Just a wanderer, my Lady, keen to compete.'

Jo knew what *that* meant. Brice and Isabelle had ensured hefty prizes for the winners of certain competitions. Some were golden coins, some jewels and precious goods, a few simple wares or weapons. Any would be immensely valuable to a wandering knight.

'And to take home a prize?' she asked.

There was a flash of *something* in his eyes. A sudden shift in his tone.

'Perhaps,' he said. 'I hope to rob someone less deserving of one, if I can.'

Jo blinked. That was bold. *Very* bold, for a man with no name and no retinue, speaking to one of the ladies of the house.

'Less deserving?'

William gave a one-shouldered shrug, causing his armour to clang together. 'I should not speak so plainly of my competitors. *Yet . . .*'

She shouldn't be allowing this. She should be removing herself from the conversation, and this strangely familiar man.

She raised an eyebrow. 'Yet?'

He shrugged again, and through the slit in his helm his eyes were sparkling, as if he was laughing beneath the metal. There was a squeeze in Jo's stomach.

'I would wager that few of the noblemen competing here deserve *all* that is on offer. Perhaps I can ensure *those* prizes go to ones who have truly earned them. There are some rewards here far too precious to be awarded to just anyone.'

The squeeze expanded, a hot pit. Everyone in attendance knew that someone at the tournament would leave with her hand: it was the grandest prize on offer. But why would a knight-errant have any opinions at *all* on the topic of her marriage? She blinked away the thought. He was no doubt bitter that one of their valuable trophies would likely go to an already wealthy man.

'I—' She swallowed, throat tight. 'Indeed, sir.' Behind her, she heard Marshal Brice bidding goodbye to the lads tidying away the lances. She snatched the opportunity. 'It has been very interesting to speak with you, William Dale. I hope I will get to watch you compete.'

He gave her another bow, eyes crinkling.

'As do I, my Lady.'

Jo was the centre of attention as they walked back towards the keep. She could feel eyes on her as she passed the stands, and was called to and greeted more times than she could count. She had memorised the names, faces, and stations of the men vying for her hand, hoping to ensure she was at least aware of the one who would eventually become her husband.

She felt calculative, assessing them all so thoroughly, examining them from afar. She hoped that anyone who caught her gaze would assume she was just staring — staring, she thought with an odd twist — in the way many of them were staring at *her*: in the way a lover might stare at the object of their desire.

Truly, she desired none of them. Many of them were handsome, many suitably aged, but none stirred anything more powerful in her than acceptance; than the notion that *this* potential suitor could be a better match than the previous.

All but one. She didn't even know his face, yet still she thought of William Dale as she walked. All she'd seen of him was a pair of sharp, sparklingly intelligent blue-grey eyes. Beneath the shadow of his helm, he had looked as if he was laughing – as if the tournament was a grand joke; one that they were both privy to.

He had been interesting. Far too free with his words, far too bold for someone with no connections. And there had been something else, something she couldn't name.

Jo was *sure* she knew those eyes. Even his voice had felt oddly familiar, although she couldn't place why. He'd been easy to talk to, and Jo had slipped into rapport with him despite his boldness. It was no doubt because he was only a knight-errant. With him, she wasn't forced to perform, holding herself to an impossibly high standard. It was a cruel thought, but he was no one very important.

She had never even heard of William Dale, and he certainly wasn't a regular fixture at any local courts. It wasn't as if he would be easy to miss: not with his obvious accent and shocking red hair.

That was why he was so intriguing, she told herself. His familiarity made him a mystery; a question that she needed to answer.

He was a *distraction*, of that much she was entirely sure. If she could seek out Edmund, perhaps she could learn more about him, and finally put this strange feeling to rest.

She attempted to shake the image of tarnished armour and laughing eyes from her head and headed back towards the castle.

Chapter 3

'So you know nothing of him? At all?'

Edmund shrugged as he strode through the keep, Jo hurrying by his side.

'He is a knight-errant, a wanderer,' he said. 'It would be more worrying if we *did* know of him, my Lady. That would mean there was some *reason* for him to be known, and very rarely are those reasons good when it comes to travelling knights.'

'You must have *something*.'

Edmund stopped. With a beleaguered sigh, he opened the ledger he was carrying, flicking through the pages. Every individual who intended to enter the tournament was listed here, along with their retinue. Each was marked with the man's signature: a sign of good faith and agreement to compete fairly.

'Here,' he said, pointing.

Jo peered over his shoulder. William's name was listed amongst those of the other wandering men.

William Dale, knight-errant. No retinue. One dun palfrey.

It was a simple entry for a man who was – at least in Jo's mind – all but simple. And there, scrawled beside it in a messy hand, the man's signature – *William Dale*.

Jo hesitated. She looked closer. The name itself was as unfamiliar as ever, and the entry gave her no clue at all to who he could be. But the scribble of his name . . . *that* sparked a memory.

'Is that all, my Lady?'

'Yes, Edmund,' Jo said, distracted. 'Thank you.'

She watched him as he walked away. She had learnt nothing at all about William, but there was something familiar in that smudged scrawl. It was the same familiarity she had seen in his eyes, and heard in the lilt of his northern accent.

She thought she knew his eyes, and his voice. But she was *sure* she knew that handwriting.

William Dale. A man from the north, with red hair, and handwriting worse than even Cecily's—

Jo's heart stopped. She knew that handwriting because she had spent hours poring over it. She'd searched for it with every stack of letters that had arrived at the keep. It had branded itself into her memory through reading and re-reading.

No. Surely not. It was impossible. She was imagining it – her desperation to see Cecily again was mingling with anxiety about her upcoming marriage and her strange, unexpected interest in William Dale. It was her overtaxed mind clinging to something familiar.

She was being absurd. Attempting to distract herself, she headed towards the kitchens. She needed to be certain that enough food had been supplied for these first few days of the tournament, and that the beer that was arriving every day had been properly divided between the tents.

'There you are!'

She spun on her heel. Ros – for once, without her flock of children – was standing just behind her.

'Isabelle and I have been waiting for you for an *age*,' her sister said, looking reproachful.

Of course: Jo had promised to meet Isabelle to try on the new dresses that had arrived for her that morning. She had entirely lost track of time, too distracted by the puzzle of the knight-errant.

'Oh, Ros – I entirely forgot,' Jo said. 'I am so sorry . . .'

Ros shook her head at her, not unkindly.

'You take on *far* too much work,' she said. 'You will be gone from here soon. You know they will manage perfectly well without you.'

Jo concealed a wince at that. Until now, Isabelle had been content to let Jo see to the practical running of the keep. While Jo saw to servants and supplies, Isabelle saw to the children or hosted local noblewomen – or was hosted by them. While Jo ensured the kitchens were running smoothly, Isabelle was busy convincing the women who were once their friends that the family was one they wanted to be tied to once more. Jo didn't resent this: she *enjoyed* the work, and she was good at it.

But she had become replaceable. Her upcoming marriage was proof enough of that. It was why she needed to ensure she made a good wife. Isabelle was keen to help – whether through altruism, a sense of romance, or even a desire to be rid of her, Jo wasn't sure. Ros, too, found unmatched glee in the prospect of her little sister's wedding.

She let Ros lead her up to Isabelle's chambers, nodding along to Ros's chatter. She had already seen the dresses, and was rhapsodising on their style and beauty and the fineness of the fabric.

Jo understood her eagerness, but she felt like she was being dressed and paraded like one of their knight's horses with a plaited tail and fine caparison.

'My apologies, Isabelle,' Jo said, as they finally made their way into her rooms. 'I was waylaid—'

Isabelle waved away her excuses. 'You are here now, which is what matters. Let's see what we have, shall we?'

She got to work immediately. Jo's skin felt hot and ill-fitting as Isabelle and Ros bustled around her, pulling the first dress over her head and tying the fastenings in place as she awkwardly stood in place. But this was Isabelle's realm, not hers. She could hardly complain.

'There,' Isabelle said, stepping back as Ros wrapped a belt around Jo's waist.

'Oh, *Johanna*,' Ros breathed. 'You look wonderful.'

Jo regarded her reflection. The gown was made of deep orange linen with a low, scooped collar embroidered in a dark red. The belt matched the collar, pinching in her waist. The sleeves were tight around the arms before opening up at the elbows, dangling so low they nearly touched the floor.

It fit her very well, that much she was sure of, hugging her curves and emphasising her hips. It was a colour she wouldn't have usually chosen herself, but it paired well with her dark eyes and hair.

'What do you think?'

Jo looked at Isabelle's reflection in the mirror.

'It's lovely,' Jo said, which was not a lie. 'It is quite beautiful, Isabelle.'

Isabelle's smile melded into one of relief. Jo was pleased; she did not want to hurt her stepmother's feelings, or make her think her efforts were wasted. And it *was* a lovely dress, but as Jo watched herself in the mirror, she felt again like she was being groomed, dressed, and made beautiful so she would better win the attentions of a suitable man.

Ros placed a hand on Jo's shoulder. 'You must wear one of the new gowns at supper.'

Jo turned. 'At supper?'

'We have invited Lord Adam to join us.' Isabelle put down the gown she was folding and gave Jo a pointed look. 'He is keen to get to know you better.'

Jo remembered Lord Adam Wyck. He had arrived a few days previous with a huge retinue, and his tent numbered amongst the largest of all their guests'. She had been watching with Ellis from the wall walk as he approached, where she had been attempting to teach her brother to recognise the coats of arms of his allies.

Lord Adam's were simple yet eye-catching, perfect for such a lesson: a red field bisected with a golden chevron. Beneath the chevron, also picked out in gold, a flaming heart. The design splashed across their shields, too, and a few men – those closest to him – wore surcoats and cloaks dyed in that same red and gold, split down the middle. It was an impressive sight, and of the dozen families they had watched arrive, Lord Adam's were the only banners Ellis could recall later.

The man was a little older than her, recently established as the lord of a keep some way away. He was well respected, and would be competing with the more seasoned knights. Ellis had found him supremely charming when they had met him upon his arrival, which was not overly surprising: he embodied all the elements of knighthood that Ellis had come to admire.

It was immediately clear why Isabelle had seen fit to formally introduce Jo to him so early in the tournament. She *was* being dressed to please a man after all.

'Oh—' She wasn't sure what else she could say, so added, dutifully, 'I shall be glad to properly meet him.'

She had hoped that once they had deemed the dresses suitable she would be free to return to work, but it was not to be. After choosing one of the gowns, Ros took her arm and led her on a turn of the castle and the grounds beyond. Jo assumed that Ros was just keen to catch up after so long apart, but as they walked, she could sense an odd sort of tension in her sister.

'Johanna—' Ros said finally, as if she had been building to this for some time. 'I . . . that is . . .'

When Jo glanced at her, she realised Ros was blushing. 'Yes?'

Ros heaved a sigh, peering around them.

'Oh, I am behaving like a *maid* . . .' she said, shaking her head. 'Johanna, I simply wanted to ask if you are prepared for marriage. If you know what to expect.'

'What to expect?'

'From a husband. In your . . .' Ros hesitated again, and then, finally, let it out in a whisper. 'In your *marriage bed.*'

Oh. Jo had been half-expecting a conversation like this, although she was surprised it was coming from Ros and not Isabelle.

'I am aware of the, ah, *details*, yes,' she said, matching Ros's blush.

'I know it can be a little overwhelming.' Ros gripped her arm tighter. 'But if you have any questions, any fears . . . I would like to think you can talk to me. It is not *just* about begetting children, of course.'

In truth, those finer details of marriage had been something Jo had been happily ignoring. Now, she realised, she could no longer do so: *when* she became a wife, she would need to do *all* that was expected of her. The marital bed was the one area in which Jo was woefully inexperienced: she had never even *kissed* someone, a fact that until now hadn't seemed very important.

'It helps, of course,' Ros was saying, speaking over her own embarrassment, 'if your husband is handsome. Lord Adam—' She faltered, as if she had spoken out of turn. 'Well, *he* is very handsome. There are worse people to kiss.' She laughed.

Jo considered this. Lord Adam *was* handsome, everyone said so, but in the brief moments they had spent together he had seemed wholly unremarkable. He had thick dark hair, a square jaw, and broad shoulders – but Jo struggled to describe much else of the man. Ros was *giggling*, now, leaving Jo feeling afloat. She thought of *kissing* Lord Adam – in the way she had seen other couples kiss – and it made her feel prickly and unsettled. It was not an image she wished to linger on.

No matter. Whoever she married – be it Lord Adam or someone else – she was sure she would get used to *all* the aspects of a marriage, including those confined to the marital chamber. Through time and practice she would grow to want her husband like that, she was sure. And if she needed to, she *could* talk to Ros about the finer details, even if the prospect of such a conversation made her blush.

Having said her piece, Ros deftly moved the conversation on. Jo engaged her as much as she could, but there was an odd feeling in her chest, now, a tight grip of anxiety.

Not for the first time, she felt a sharp pang of loneliness. Isabelle was something of a friend, and Ros meant well, but still Jo could not help but feel alone. They both took it all so *seriously*. There was no one to take her hand and make light of the situation; no one whom she could speak to about her doubts or anxieties without feeling like a failure.

This was why she was so fixated on William Dale. She *didn't* know him, but his northern accent and red hair and disastrous handwriting made her long for someone who would have been able to soothe her anxieties through the trials of matchmaking.

Cecily would have treated all of this – the tournament, the marriage – as a farce. She would have pulled Jo along into the absurdity of it, and the clouds hanging over her would have broken into summer sunshine, bright as Cecily's hair. No wonder Jo saw her where she wasn't – seeing her in William mirrored the way she'd seen Henry's face everywhere after they'd had word of his death. Desperation – be that from grief or loneliness – played tricks on the mind.

As she walked through the tourney, greeting noblemen and pausing to watch practising knights or trilling musicians, Jo couldn't help but peer around, looking for those blue-grey eyes and bright red hair. She *did* want to see William again. He intrigued her, playing on her mind like a tune one couldn't be rid of. That, too, made anxiety knot her stomach. The idea of seeing him again made her heart beat quicker, a strange feeling she wasn't familiar with.

Ros chatted beside her, her words mingling with the noise of the tournament. She mentioned Lord Adam again, and Jo thought once more of what it would be like to kiss him.

But now Lord Adam melted away, and in his place was a man with messy red hair and laughter on his lips, his face no more than a half-imagined blur.

The image was so sudden and so strong that it made Jo stop in her tracks, causing Ros to ask if she was all right.

'Yes,' Jo said, the thought fading as quickly as it had come. 'Yes, just – thinking.'

She was blushing. Ros gave her a knowing look as she led her on through the grounds.

As it transpired, William was nowhere to be seen. Jo was unsure if this annoyed or relieved her; she had no way of telling how she would react to meeting him. It was still with that flushed sense of uncertainty that she headed back to the keep for their evening meal.

Lord Adam and his party were already there when they arrived, along with Isabelle and Ellis. He sat with a choice few from his retinue: Lady Anne, his mother, and a handful of his men. Next to him sat Sir Lanval, a well-respected knight who had been sworn to the Wyck family since his youth. Sir Lanval was a little shorter than Lord Adam, his strength more concealed compared to Lord Adam's broadness, but he had a reputation as a fierce fighter. His light brown hair was slicked back from his head, making the pinched expression he was watching her with even more pronounced.

As the family entered the room, Lord Adam immediately rose from his seat. He bowed deeply towards them, then took Jo's hand and pressed it to his lips in a kiss, meeting her eyes over her fingers.

'It is wonderful to finally meet you properly, my Lady.'

Jo gave him a dutiful smile as he rose. 'And you, my Lord.'

They sat to eat, Jo listening to Lord Adam as he spoke of the tournament, the competitions he was entering, and his plans should he win. He told her of his lands, which were vast, and his power, which was ever-growing. As he talked, he compulsively swept his dark hair out of his eyes.

She watched him as he ate: his manners were good, and his face *was* handsome, as everyone said. She observed as he spoke to her brother, and to the servants, both of whom he treated a little stiffly. Throughout the meal she could feel Isabelle, Ros, and the steward staring at them, and felt quite silly at how closely the party was observing each other, all with one thing in mind.

Lord Adam spoke of the melee on the final day of the tournament, and how keen he was to enter. Before then, he would be taking part in the single combat competition.

'You will attend, of course,' he said. 'For luck. I am sure I will strike a good victory with you there.'

It had not really been a request, but even if it were, Jo would have been unable to refuse. The demand disguised in courtly language irked her. She swallowed the feeling down with a vapid smile. Lady Anne was soon drawn in to the conversation, and swiftly the three of them were discussing the Wyck keep and lands, as well as the rest of the family and Lord Adam's late father, who had died not three months prior. At the mention of his name, Lord Adam's face fell. Jo felt a pang of sympathy for him. She had heard of his father, and he had seemed a fair, kind man. She did not know Lord Adam's grief, not exactly, but she understood the loss.

As he spoke of his father, his voice low, she spotted Sir Lanval – who had been oddly quiet – watching him closely. She realised that he, too, must still be reeling from the man's death, having trained and squired beneath him. At the mention of the late Lord, a cloud had covered them all. She wondered if his passing had been the thing that spurred Lord Adam to seek out a marriage.

She quickly moved the conversation onto lighter topics. Lord Adam complimented the food and ale that they had provided, and

Isabelle immediately launched into effusive praise for a brewster in Astmere. Lord Adam took it all into account, and Jo suspected this was because it would behove him to know where he could find the best food and drink for his *own* keep without being forced to rely on his steward or housekeeper.

Despite the easy conversation, the evening still passed slowly as Jo kept one close eye on Lord Adam, unable to truly relax as she tried to form an idea of the sort of man he was.

Before his party left, Lord Adam bowed to Jo and kissed her hand once more. His hair fell into his eyes.

'I look forward to seeing you again,' he said.

She gave him a deferential nod. 'Thank you, my Lord.'

She watched him stride across the yard, Sir Lanval at his side. They appeared to be locked in animated conversation, Sir Lanval placing a hand to Lord Adam's arm as he spoke. As she watched them go, she realised again how lonely she was. How much she longed for someone who would ease her fears and let her speak without judgement.

She was considering removing herself to her rooms when Isabelle appeared at her side. There was a small, pleased smile on her face.

'That was—'

'I think I will retire,' Jo said, cutting her off, aware that she was being terribly rude. 'It has been a long day. My apologies, Isabelle.'

There was a hand around her wrist. 'Wait, Johanna—'

Jo hesitated. 'My Lady?'

'I understand that you may not, perhaps, wish to marry, but – if you wish to talk about it . . . ?'

Jo had not realised her mood was so clear on her face.

'Oh, I – no, it is not that. Not *quite* that.'

Isabelle frowned at her, so Jo continued.

'It is just . . .' She couldn't find the right way to describe it: the loneliness, the sense of loss. The aching desire to have someone *for her*. She settled on something that Isabelle would understand. 'This event has made me realise how much I miss my brother,' she said. 'I had hoped that after the tournament I would be granted leave to travel north again and see if he is well.'

Sympathetic understanding spread across Isabelle's face. 'Oh,' she took Jo's arm, 'I see.'

Isabelle took a breath and peered around. They were not quite alone; the yard was still teeming with servants, and the steward was lingering nearby with Ellis and Ros's family.

'Would you come with me?'

Curious, Jo let Isabelle lead her deeper into the keep. At first, she thought Isabelle was taking her to her chambers, but she moved onwards to a tiny side room. Isabelle fished a key from her skirts, unlocked the door, and pushed inside.

Piles of boxes and discarded furniture emerged from the gloom. Isabelle stepped in, shut the door, then gestured to a pair of crates stacked near the window.

'I was able to search your brother's chamber, before . . .'

She trailed off, eyes low. Less than two weeks after Penn had been removed from the keep, her father had emptied his old room, stripping it of everything that had been his. Many of Penn's things had once belonged to their mother, or to one of their brothers: books, clothes, hand-carved trinkets. Removing Penn's memory was as good as removing *their* memories, too.

When she'd found an empty chamber and a loaded cart swiftly trundling away, she'd been overcome with a hot, sudden surge of anger. But her father's gaze had been a warning, and she had said nothing. She *always* said nothing. She regretted doing so every day.

Isabelle's voice broke her from those thoughts.

'I saved a few items,' she said. 'Too few, in truth, but I made sure they were put aside. If we claim you are returning them to him, I can ensure that you are granted leave to return north before you are wed.'

There were tears suddenly stinging in Jo's eyes. 'Isabelle . . .'

'I am sorry I did not inform you sooner,' she said. 'I dared not, while Marcus was alive.'

Jo took her hand. 'Thank you, Isabelle. Truly.'

'It is only a small thing . . .' Isabelle sighed. 'I understand the pain of it, Johanna. To give one man your heart when you know your hand will be promised to another. To know that you are leaving behind love and safety and comfort for—' Her voice caught. 'For the unknown.'

Jo frowned at her. Once again, Isabelle appeared to be talking in riddles. Surely she wasn't talking about Penn?

'I . . . do not think I understand?'

Isabelle gave her a long, hard look.

'I understand that my coming into the family was difficult,' she said, 'but I think — we are *friends*, now? I do not want you to feel you have to lie to me. Certainly not about matters of the heart.'

'Truly, Isabelle — I am not lying . . .'

Isabelle shook her head. 'You are very clever, Johanna, and very sure, but I fear you are not *so* keen at hiding your feelings. When you returned from your first visit to Dunlyn Castle you were so *bright* . . . I had never seen you so happy. It was clear what had happened. You had found someone. And with each letter that arrives from the north, that happiness grows. It is obvious that you are receiving notes from a lover and claiming they are from Cecily . . . or using her as a way to send messages between you without arousing suspicion. You do not need to lie to me about missing your brother if you wish to return north.'

Jo's own words stuck. This explained Isabelle's behaviour at the gatehouse. It was a bold assumption, and Jo had not even realised that her shift in mood had been so clear. Isabelle spoke on, taking Jo's shocked silence as confirmation that she was correct.

'I may not have loved your father, but I *have* loved,' she continued. 'I know that feeling. I recognised it the moment you were home. I thought at first that it was likely one of the Barden family's allies, but if that had been the case, why lie? Why not inform us that you had made a suitable match yourself? So, I thought . . .' She looked away, blushing. 'Well, the Barden brothers *are* very handsome . . .'

Jo realised what she was implying. It made her head reel.

'Isabelle, *no*—' she spluttered.

Isabelle laughed. 'No?' She shook her head in disbelief. 'Johanna . . . I understand that whoever your love is, you cannot take him as a husband. Whether that is because he is unsuitable through scandal or birth or class, I do not know, and I will not force you to tell me. But until you wed you are under Ellis's rule. And Ellis is under *my* rule, until he comes of age. I cannot give you and him a lifetime together, but with this' – she gestured again to the meagre pile of Penn's things – 'I can give you a few more weeks. It is more than what many people get.'

Jo's heart lodged in her throat. Isabelle was granting her respite before she was tied down. She was giving her all the things she had been so desperate for: lakeside walks and long evenings and the tart sweetness of blackberries. A chance for true companionship, true *friendship*. Isabelle hadn't even realised what she was doing, so caught up in the romance she'd entirely imagined.

Jo's first instinct was to attempt to correct her again. To tell her that there *was* no secret lover, that Isabelle's romantic nature had caused her to see things that were not there. But not only did Jo suspect she wouldn't believe the truth, she also feared that the chance to return north depended entirely on this imaginary man.

'I—' She struggled with the words. 'Thank you, Isabelle. This is far too kind.'

'It is all I am able to give,' Isabelle said. 'And you must ensure I can reach you if needed. If I were to send a letter to Dunlyn, would you receive it?'

'Of course.' Jo appreciated that this, at least, was not a lie.

'I wish . . .' Isabelle sighed. 'Often, I wish there was some other way. But . . . we must do what we can.'

She looked very small, and very sad.

'I am so sorry, Isabelle,' Jo said. 'For the man you left behind.'

Isabelle's eyes shimmered. 'I . . . miss him tremendously. But had I not married Marcus, I would not have been blessed with Ellis or Ingrid. And I love them more than I ever loved him. More than it is possible to love anyone else.'

Jo took her hand. Beyond the single tiny window of the store-room, the sun was setting.

Chapter 4

The sword glinted in the air, cutting through the sunlight in a sharp, dangerous arc.

Lily met it above her head with her own and a *clang* that rattled through her arms, eliciting a gasp from the sparse crowd and a grunt of shock from her opponent. Using his surprise, she forced him back, pushed his blade down, spun around him, then ducked low and beneath his arm. The man took another swing, but she was too quick, dancing out of the way, and spotting how he was now unbalanced she smacked her painted shield against his back.

He stumbled. She took the opportunity, kicking out at his ankle, and he collapsed, his sword skittering away across the straw. The crowd, small though it was, cheered, and she could finally breathe again.

The single combat matches were not as popular as the joust, especially not so early in the tournament, but they had still managed to amass a few onlookers. She reached down and helped heave her opponent back to his feet. The announcer had introduced him as Sir John.

'You fought very well,' he said, tugging off his helmet to reveal his sweaty pink skin, dark brown eyes, and messy hair plastered to his head. 'I fear I may have underestimated you.'

Lily grinned, opening the visor of her helmet without removing it. 'Many do,' she said. 'Will you be in the joust this afternoon?'

Sir John laughed. 'I am not *quite* ready for that,' he said. 'Are you competing in the lists?'

'I am.'

'Then I wish you luck, Knight of Stars.'

He gave her a brief bow, then headed out of the ring. Lily watched him leave, still catching her breath. *Knight of Stars.* She had fallen entirely accidentally into the sobriquet, yet it had stuck.

She had entered under the false name William Dale, but had forgotten it entirely when asked at the start of the first fight. The announcer, who clearly thought her a young, nervous boy, had spotted her painted shield and declared her *The Knight of Stars* before pushing her into the ring.

She'd been placed against the youngest son of a nearby lord, defeated him easily, and the decisive win had meant the name had stuck. Lily had been unsure of it at first, but it was easier to remember than the false name, and besides, it was attention-grabbing. With luck, it would make her plan even more successful, especially if she could embarrass titled men with nothing more than a sobriquet.

Sir John had been the third man she had defeated that day. Three wins, two draws, and two defeats. She was doing well.

She would have to prove herself that afternoon during the first joust of the tournament. It was a smaller affair than those that would come later, but even so, the thought thrilled her.

As she slid her sword back into its sheath, she remembered the play-jousts she and her brothers had enjoyed. As children, they had often tilted at each other with broom handles, and as soon as Lily had been old enough she had insisted that they allow her to join instead of just waving the flag and declaring a winner.

They had all seen their fair share of injury through such games. She could still vividly remember Raff sprawled unconscious on the floor, blood spurting from his nose as she had run to find their father. Raff's nose had never healed properly, but even *that* had been unable to stop them.

She would be a fool to think such games had adequately prepared her for a real joust. But she had practised as much as she could, both at Dunlyn Castle and on the road during moments of rest, tilting with fallen branches at low trees. She had spent the day she arrived and that very morning, up before dawn, riding in the practice yard.

She did well against wooden rings or straw-stuffed soldiers on sticks, but she was poorly prepared to face off against another person. She would have to hope that her first few tilts would be against equally inexperienced men, and she could treat them as she had the dummies in the yard: just practice.

'Sir!'

Lily turned at the intrusion to her thoughts. Ellis — *Earl* de Foucart, she reminded herself — was perched on the fence, stood on the lower rail so he could better see. Standing just behind him was Jo.

She had seen Jo from a distance throughout the day, hurrying back and forth with her family wearing a deep orange dress that billowed up dry dirt around her as she walked. The overall impression was that Jo had been striding on a cloud. It put Lily in mind of the valleys in the mountains near her home, the way they filled with mist.

She had wanted to rush to her, to embrace her and greet her

as a friend. But disguised as she was, it was impossible. It was an urge she had been forced to suppress yesterday, when she realised Jo had been watching her train, entirely unaware of who she was.

When Jo had first approached as she was practising in the yard, Lily had nearly swallowed her own tongue in shock. She had not expected to see her again so soon, and had warred with indecision. She wanted Jo to know who she was, but understood that if she *was* caught, Jo would be implicated in her crime. Lily needed to wait until she'd seen her plan through, until the so-called Knight of Stars was the obvious choice for Jo's hand. Only then could she tell Jo who she was, and whisk her away.

Until then, Lily was only able to watch from afar as Jo mingled, chatting to nobles, smiling vaguely at their jokes. She looked not *miserable*, but certainly not happy, and each time Lily caught her from the corner of her eye being forced to tolerate some lord or breaking into false laughter at a joke, it made her push harder, fight more fiercely.

'My Lord.' Lily deeply bowed towards Ellis. 'I had not realised you were observing our fight.'

Ellis grinned. 'I enjoy duelling,' he said, voice remarkably sure for one so young. 'You performed well. But your weapon is rusty.'

Lily tugged her blade from her sheath to look at it. Ellis was correct; it was speckled with corrosion.

'You must forgive me, my Lord,' she said. 'I journeyed very far to attend this tourney and celebrate your new title. I admit that I have neglected to take proper care of my sword.'

Ellis gave her – and the sword – an assessing look. 'You should take it to Marshal Brice,' he said. 'He will see to it. How far have you come?'

Lily shrugged, pushing the sword back away. 'Fourteen days' ride?' she guessed, adding on a few more days' travelling time to obscure her real home.

'You sound as if you are from the north,' Ellis pressed, with all the tact of a child, as Jo watched on.

'That is because I *am* from the north,' she said, addressing the tiny Earl directly.

'I am surprised that word travelled that far.'

It was the first time Jo had spoken. This close, Lily could see that the dark orange of her dress made the brown of her eyes even deeper.

'The news came with a trader,' Lily said, cautiously.

'How interesting,' Jo's eyes bored into her. 'I am happy you came all this way for us, William. I am sure there must be equally fine tournaments in the northern counties.'

Lily held her gaze. 'Not quite so fine.'

'No?' Jo raised her eyebrows. She stepped forwards, hands lightly pressed against the fence. 'I hear the north is very beautiful this time of year. I have often been recommended to visit in the summer, so I might walk the lakes and taste the wild blackberries. I have been told they are much sweeter than those in Oxfordshire.'

Lily smiled. She wondered how Jo would look back on this conversation later, when they were free from the keep and able to talk.

'I agree,' she said, terribly amused. 'They are *much* sweeter than those I have found here.'

Jo nodded, almost solemnly.

'Although I have heard some truly *awful* things, too.'

'Oh?'

'Oh yes; I was told a quite dreadful tale about roaming packs of wild dogs ravaging the country.'

Lily paused. Something prickled at the back of her head. 'Oh?' she repeated.

'*Indeed*,' Jo continued, looking surprisingly smug for one apparently discussing the horrors of the north. 'I have been warned that they are prone to eating men's arms clean off.'

Lily blinked. She thought of their latest letters, and the way she'd teased Raff. The buoyant sense of victory died in her chest. She couldn't speak – she couldn't *think* – and still Jo just watched her with that careful, calculating expression.

'Although of course they may have just been *rumours*. No more than fairy stories spread by the mad. Would you not agree, *William*?'

She knew. Jo was sharp – her sharpness came across in her letters – but to be subjected to it in such a scrutinising way was more than a little thrilling, despite the shock of discovery.

'I—' She swallowed heavily. 'That . . . may be an accurate assessment, my Lady. Yes. Quite mad.'

Jo's expression flicked, just a moment, into one of triumph. Lily began to regret being so free with her words. Of *course* Jo had worked her out. It would have been impossible for her not to.

It was impossible, too, to acknowledge the sudden shared secret, not with so many people milling around and Ellis still leaning on the fence watching them both with interest.

'What did you think of my performance?' she asked, keeping Jo's gaze. 'Did you enjoy the duel?'

'I did.' Jo nodded. 'You are very . . . bold.'

Lily knew Jo was not simply speaking of her swordplay.

'I would describe myself as reckless and chaotic,' she said. 'But I thank you for the compliment.'

Jo laughed at that – a genuine laugh, Lily thought, unlike the fake smiles she had seen on Jo's face while talking to the other attendants.

'It would not behove me to be so rude about one of our guest's technique,' she said. 'Although I concede that it is perhaps a *little* chaotic.'

'Better to confuse my opponents,' Lily said, cheekily.

'Or better to be beaten by them,' Jo countered. 'Is this your first tournament?'

Lily swallowed. 'Yes, my Lady.'

'And,' Jo pressed, 'you have come here alone? You are not part of a retinue?'

'I am not,' Lily said, wondering what Jo was leading to. 'I ride only with myself, my Lady.'

Jo nodded at her, as if she were considering this.

'And is that not foolishness too?' she said at last. 'To come so far and risk so much entirely alone? Perhaps . . . with respect, sir, it would be *wiser* for you to go home?'

Ah. But Jo didn't look angry – she was not *chastising* Lily. Not yet, anyway. Just warning her. *Worrying* about her.

'I am sure that *would* be wiser, yes.'

'Then—'

'But I have no intentions to leave.'

'*Sir Dale.*'

'In fact,' Lily continued, rather enjoying the way Jo was staring at her, 'I think it would take those ferocious wild dogs you spoke of to drag me away.'

'And what if you are wounded?'

Lily shrugged. 'I must endeavour to not be.'

Jo stared at her. Lily had the advantage, if just for the moment: to insist Lily leave would be to give her away, and she knew that Jo couldn't.

'So.' Lily leant against the fence, attempting to move the conversation on. 'Are you enjoying the tournament?'

Jo sighed at her, plainly aware that there was nothing she could do. 'I am enjoying it quite well, yes.'

Lily thought of the lords and knights she had seen Jo talking to. She had no idea if Jo's hand had already been won – and no way to ask plainly. But she needed to know, or her coming here was for naught. She kept her words vague, hoping Jo would understand.

'And have you a champion yet?'

Jo looked put out at the question. 'I have had some offers,' she said. 'When one is the unwed sister of an earl, *everyone* wishes to win for you.'

'Or for your hand?'

Jo's lips twitched. 'Quite,' she said. And then, bolder: 'Are you putting yourself forward, *sir*? Do you also wish to declare yourself my champion? Do you intend to win this tourney in my name?'

Lily laughed again. It was so easy to slip into camaraderie with her – to forget she was supposed to be William.

'My Lady, I am more likely to become King of England than I am to win this tourney. I believe we both know that.'

'I had thought you would be more confident in your abilities.'

'Confident I am, but foolish—' Lily paused, considering where she was and what she was doing. 'I admit that I am foolish as well. But not *so* foolish.'

Jo looked as if she was about to agree, when she was cut short by her brother. Lily had almost forgotten he was there.

'Johanna says that one must know one's own ability, if one is to succeed,' he said.

Jo looked surprised. 'That is true,' she said. 'Very well remembered, my Lord. Yes: confidence is important, but *overconfidence*,' she said towards Lily, with a glint in her eye, 'will get you killed.'

'Only if it is unwarranted,' Lily countered, with a smile that Jo couldn't see. 'You should count yourself very lucky to have such a clever sister, my Lord,' she said, turning to Ellis. 'Perhaps I *should* declare myself her champion, if just so she can better guide me to be less foolish in the future.' She bowed towards Jo. 'And if I cannot win the tourney for you, I am sure I can embarrass a few men in your name, if it pleases you.'

Jo flushed.

'I am not sure that is the behaviour of a champion. Aren't you supposed to uphold knightly virtues?' she asked.

'Ah, but the virtues of self-betterment, and determination, and valour? One could argue that those virtues are more impressive when found in a lowly man such as myself. It is easy for a rich man to be virtuous, or to be skilled, when he has wealth to fall upon should he fail and a lifetime of training behind him.'

'Is that so?'

'It *is* so. And anyway,' Lily added without thinking, 'a promise to win this tournament for you is a worthless one.'

'And why is that?'

'Because winning only proves that these men are champions over each other. Champions of their own pride. If they were *your* champion, they would be fighting to give you something you truly want.' She realised she had been speaking too loudly. She lowered her tone, keeping Jo's gaze. 'Or fighting *beside* you, so you could take it yourself. If I were your champion, I would fight for *you*, not for the accolades of a dozen boring old men and a bag of coins. I would fight for whatever you would have me fight for, my Lady.'

The ensuing silence was heavy on Lily's shoulders. She had not meant to say so much – she certainly hadn't intended to declare herself Jo's champion. But the idea had flooded her head and spilled from her tongue before she'd even had a chance to stopper it. Her heart pounded beneath her armour, her skin prickling with a renewed sheen of sweat.

Jo seemed to be rendered speechless. Her lips were slightly parted, her skin pink around her ears and cheekbones. Lily only had a brief moment to take her in – to realise that it was *her* words that had caused such a reaction – when Ellis once again spoke up.

'You must give him a favour!'

'My Lord?' said Jo, frowning.

'If the Knight of Stars is to be your champion, you must present him with a favour,' Ellis insisted. 'That is how it is done.'

'Oh—' Jo's eyes had gone wide, and there was a charming flush creeping up her face. 'I had not *really* intended—'

Lily attempted to cut in. 'That is not—'

'But he offered to be your champion!'

Both women fell silent. Ellis folded his arms across his chest, looking for all the world like a miniature lord. Lily understood Jo's hesitation: giving a favour to a knight-errant with no name and no title would send a clear message to all of those in attendance who were true suitors. It was an insult for her not to choose one of them. It would be one thing to accept Lily as her champion as a jest – a shared joke between them when only *they* knew who Lily really was – but quite another for her to seal the arrangement so conspicuously.

But Ellis was glaring at Jo, now. Jo would struggle to refuse him, both as her earl and as her little brother. He had no idea what he was suggesting. No doubt he had heard stories of knights and favours and courtly love and thought it amusing.

'I do not think it would be appropriate, my Lord, for your sister to name me her champion,' Lily said, carefully attempting to save Jo the pain of refusing him. 'I am only a knight-errant. There are many men here more suitable for such an honour.'

'But she wants *you*.'

The blush had reached Jo's hairline, now – although one could easily dismiss it as a flush from standing in the sun for so long.

'Ellis, I *cannot*—'

'But you *must!*'

A ringing silence fell. Jo looked between her brother and Lily, eyes wide.

'I will not ask for anything my Lady does not wish to give,' Lily said.

Jo's expression shifted. Lily's pulse thrummed in her neck.

'I—' Jo began.

'My Lord!'

The moment shattered. Lady Isabelle was approaching, tightly gripping the hand of little Ingrid with a nursemaid close behind. Ellis rushed towards her.

'Mother!'

He grabbed her, nearly sending her toppling down.

'Are you enjoying your tournament, my Lord?' Isabelle laughed.

'Very much so, yes.'

'I am pleased to hear it.'

'Johanna has been talking to the Knight of Stars!' Ellis proclaimed.

Isabelle looked up, eyebrows raised. She glanced from her son to Jo to Lily, still leaning against the fence.

'Is that right?'

'My Lord and Lady have been complimenting me on my wins,' Lily said smoothly, as Jo burnt under Isabelle's curious gaze.

'Very good,' Isabelle said, with a deferent smile. 'Come, my love, your food is waiting for you.'

This was Lily's cue to leave.

'Thank you for your time, and your kind words, my Lord,' she said, giving Ellis a deeply exaggerated bow, which delighted him. 'And you, my Lady.' She reached across the fence to take Jo's hand. Her heart battled itself beneath her chest plate. 'Thank you.'

She bent low over Jo's fingers. Jo's skin was soft, and warm. Lily suddenly regretted wearing her helm: it meant she couldn't press a kiss there.

When she rose, Jo's face was pink. Lily didn't want to let her go. But remembering the role she was playing, she forced herself to release her. With a final nod she went to walk away, settling again into the sure stride of a victorious knight.

'Good luck, Sir Dale.'

Jo's words, quiet though they were, struck her like a blow. Lily stumbled – her feet suddenly too large, her limbs too awkward. But when she turned around, Jo had her back to her.

It took more effort than it had to win the duel to walk away.

Chapter 5

The sun, suspended at its zenith above them, warmed Jo's skin as she followed Ellis and Isabelle back towards the keep. Around her, the world was alive. The constant clash of steel and the neighing of horses filled the air. Dogs and children rushed past, barking and squealing. A troupe of musicians had struck up near the ale tent, singing a bawdy song with a crowd of onlookers around them, many singing along. On the air she could smell roasting pork and trampled hay.

Ellis was chatting excitedly about the tournament, the fight they had just watched, and the prowess of the other knights, but Jo wasn't listening.

Her suspicions were correct. She had no idea how she hadn't seen it before.

At least she now finally knew why Cecily had never responded to her letter. Depending on when she left Dunlyn Castle, she may not have even received it. She had mentioned her desire to ride in a tournament, but Jo had never even considered she would see that desire through. It was madness.

Engaging Cecily in conversation for so long had only been a way to tease her, to tell her *I know who you are.* To make herself part of the joke. Yet every time there was a lull in conversation

Jo's mind drifted back to a pair of sky-grey eyes and a shock of messy red hair.

As they returned to the keep, she thought of Ellis's insistence that she take the Knight of Stars – take *Cecily* – as her champion. Cecily had even offered so herself. She had told Jo she would fight for her, and Jo knew that it was true.

She had mused last night about William Dale and his interesting nature and striking eyes. She had thought it typical, then, that the only man who had ever stirred anything in her stronger than begrudging acceptance was a man of no name and no rank, completely unsuitable.

And now she realised he was not even a man. What Jo had taken for interest was just familiarity: the safety she felt around Cecily, the friendship they had built together, and the relief that it had not toppled as she feared.

Yet when the Knight of Stars had bowed over her hand, her taking Jo's fingers in her own, Jo had forgotten how to breathe.

She wondered what would have happened had Isabelle not interrupted them. She had been so close to allowing it, to slipping her hand into the pouch at her hip and passing Cecily her handkerchief: the only thing on her person even *slightly* suitable as a favour. Cecily deserved it. She certainly deserved it more than any of the men Jo had met these past few days.

It was something in the sparkle of Cecily's eyes, her confidence on the field, the *foolish* thing she was doing.

And it *was* foolish, horribly so. Cecily was taking an enormous, dangerous risk. Jo wished she had been able to pull her away. After their midday meal – during which Ellis had told his mother of the so-called Knight of Stars in great detail – Jo had attempted to remove herself from the family party to do just that, but Isabelle had stopped her.

'There will be time for that *later*,' she had said, and Jo was forced to stay, feeling as if Isabelle had made a joke she couldn't understand.

Insisting Cecily leave would have ended in disaster regardless. Cecily herself would never be convinced, and while it was in Jo's power to demand *William Dale* be removed from the grounds, Edmund would want to know why. There would be ramifications, and rumours, and worse: Cecily would never forgive her.

There had to be *something* she could do to keep her safe. She remembered Ellis chastising Cecily as they lingered by the fence, telling her that her sword was rusty. Jo knew nothing at all about blades, but she *did* have an entire armoury at her disposal.

A good sword was useless in the joust, but if Cecily intended to enter more of the single combat competitions, it would serve her well. It would also better protect her if the need ever arose for her to *be* protected.

The squire arrived in the gatehouse flushed and out of breath half an hour later, carrying with him a long canvas-wrapped bundle. The boy was one of the younger lads squiring with Brice, which was why Jo had chosen him: he was less likely to recognise the gossip, or to tell anyone else of the task he had been given. The coin she had pressed into his hand would ensure that, too.

Jo's palms were warm where she gripped the letter. She'd rewritten it several times as she waited for the boy to arrive, keenly aware that if it was read by anybody else it could damn both her and Cecily. She'd even signed it vaguely, to allow her more deniability if it *did* land into the wrong hands.

William—

I hope this gift finds you well. While I fear I cannot encourage you to be less foolish in this tournament, I pray that this can go some way to keeping you safe. The Earl commented on the state of your blade, after all. It would not do for a family favourite to be so poorly armed.

I also enclose a token for good fortune. And my acceptance of your offer, if it is one you stand by.

Good luck.

J

The letter was bulky in her hands. The handkerchief gave it an odd sort of weight, even though it was made of no more than silk. She'd folded the whole thing in another sheaf of parchment and sealed it crudely, forgoing the family mark. The sword was reasonable. The favour was not: it was a desperate attempt to grant Cecily luck and keep her safe should her sword fail her.

She handed the letter to the boy then watched as he dashed off back into the tourney grounds. Jo released a long breath, praying he would not be waylaid, and headed back inside.

There was a low, buoyant sensation in her stomach. Cecily was *here*, a fiery answer to Jo's silent prayer for an end to her loneliness.

As she made her way into the hall, she found that they were once again beset with guests. Isabelle, Edmund, and Ellis were seated at the long table, joined – much to her surprise – by Lord Adam and Sir Lanval. Sir Lanval looked flushed; he must have only recently come inside, his cheekbones sun-kissed.

'My Lady—'

Lord Adam rose as she entered. He greeted her swiftly and courteously, presenting her with a bow and a kiss to her hand. Jo wrenched her thoughts away from Cecily's duel and the favour as she greeted him in kind.

'My Lord.'

Above his back, she caught Isabelle's eye. She shot her a brief, apologetic expression.

'Lady Johanna,' Edmund said. 'How fortuitous you are here. We have been discussing the union of Lord Adam and yourself.'

Jo realised what was happening. It had not even been a question: just a statement.

She was to marry Lord Adam. She felt . . . nothing.

Lord Adam gave her a brief smile as he rose. He looked relieved.

'Most of the arrangements have been seen to,' Edmund continued. 'The dowry has been set, and we have begun discussions on, ah, trade, men . . . and the ceremony, of course.'

Jo blinked at him. 'Of course.'

Lord Adam took her hand. 'I am very pleased to have you as my wife, Lady Johanna.'

Johanna felt his rough fingers beneath her own. This was what she had been working for. This was her freedom from her father's keep, still haunted by his memory.

She stood a little straighter, tilting her chin. 'It is an honour, my Lord.'

Another smile. From the table, Sir Lanval watched them impassively.

'Wonderful,' Edmund said, placing his hands together. 'Lady Johanna and Lord Adam will wed as soon as the arrangements can be made.'

Lord Adam gave her fingers a brief squeeze before letting go. Jo flexed them instinctively. There was an unpleasant clench in her chest which she could not name.

The rest of Jo's morning was a blur of wedding arrangements, seated by Lord Adam's side. Most of the formalities of the thing had already been set, and when Edmund mentioned in passing how pleased the Chaplain was to hear of the match, she realised that she had been the last person informed. It made her reconsider Ros's chatter about Lord Adam and *marital expectations*.

She wondered how long ago they had planned this. If their match had been set from that first meal, or if Lord Adam had *always* been the man who would leave with her hand, before they had even been formally introduced. That thought made heat build in her chest, tightening her shoulders. But there was no room for anger, no space for it. She pushed it away as they continued to discuss the wedding plans.

She was thankful when Lord Adam returned to his own camp to spread the good news and prepare his men for that afternoon's joust. It seemed that even a betrothal could not stand between a lord and the lure of the tournament.

Jo, too, returned to the tourney grounds – although her position in her family's seats above the jousting field was far different to Lord Adam's out amongst his men. She sat in their raised box in the stands beside Ellis, who was squirming excitedly in his oversized seat, propped up on a mountain of plump cushions. On his other side, Isabelle was nodding dutifully along while he described his favourite horse to her for the third time that afternoon, and on her other side sat Ingrid, more interested in the nursemaid in attendance than the joust. With the family occupied, it left Jo alone with her thoughts as she observed the proceedings below.

She leant against the railing, barely paying attention to the announcer who was doing his very best to excite the crowd. Her thoughts, until now, had been on Lord Adam and the future that lay ahead of them both. He seemed a fine man, although she struggled to describe him as anything more interesting. But now, listening to the squires and knights milling about them below and straining her ears for a familiar laugh, she had sunk into anxiety.

Cecily would be riding in the joust. As William Dale, she would be tilting soon – likely paired off against another travelling knight or a low-ranking son. Jo was *terrified*.

It was a dangerous competition, even for seasoned knights. The first tournament Jo had ever attended, barely older than Ellis was now, she had watched in confused horror along with the rest of the crowd when the young son of one of her father's allies had been roughly struck and fallen awkwardly from his horse, sprawled unmoving on the ground. Afterwards, they'd told her that he'd broken his neck.

Leo had taken her hand and reassured her that it was an accident, little more than poor luck. That hadn't stopped her from hiding behind her hands and burrowing into his side when it had been Henry's turn to ride, convinced that he, too, would perish on the field. Leo had held her close, wrapping his arms around her shoulders until it was over.

'It is all right,' he had whispered into her hair. He had smelt of wool and smoke. 'I will look after you.'

That had been years ago, and she'd attended numerous

tournaments since then, never once seeing the same tragedy. Yet it still gnawed at her, and as the announcer clambered over the dividing fence and swaggered towards the stands, she stared to either end of the field, looking for tarnished armour and red hair.

The first three jousts were predictably uneventful. The men tilting were unschooled, unpractised, and riddled with nerves. They held their lances loosely, gripped their horses too tight, hesitated when they galloped forwards. Their tilts were rushed, messy, and over quickly, the crowd cheering without particular favour towards either rider.

And then she saw him. Saw *her*. William Dale, the Knight of Stars, was already atop his horse, one of the many squires who had been milling about walking beside him with his lance. He – *she* – appeared to have forgone her painted shield for one more suitable for the joust, but the patina of her armour and the tufts of vibrantly red hair that stuck out from beneath her helm identified her easily.

Cecily seemed nervous, one of her feet bouncing in the stirrup, but she quickly fixed herself, straightening her shoulders and settling herself more sturdily on her horse as she looked around. She glanced only briefly towards her opponent at the opposite end of the track – the fourth son of a lord – then peered around the stands.

Jo wondered if she was about to show off for the crowds, as many of the younger knights did in an attempt to win favour and fame. But she didn't, simply glanced around the seats as if searching for something. And then, at last, she looked towards Jo. From such a distance Jo could only see the flash of her eyes. Blue-grey, like a summer storm.

Cecily held her gaze.

She *winked*.

The packed stands fell quiet, as if all the sound had been sucked from the world. The sun was burningly hot on her cheeks. Jo's fingers, which she realised were clinging to the railing, tingled.

There was a scrap of white fabric hanging from the front of Cecily's chest plate. Jo's handkerchief, she realised. She was wearing her favour. Jo's mouth went dry.

'—of Stars. Johanna? Johanna!'

And then the sound rushed back all at once. Cecily took her lance from a squire, raised it in the air, then bowed towards Jo before finally looking away.

Ellis was tugging at the sleeve of her dress.

'You are not *listening*,' he whined.

'My apologies,' Jo muttered, blinking away the sudden strangeness. 'I was quite distracted. What were you saying?'

Ellis gave her a critical look in the way that only little brothers could, before continuing.

'I *said*, there is the Knight of Stars!' He paused, peering down at the field. 'Although his shield is different now.'

Jo attempted to find her way back into the stream of conversation.

'Ah,' she said, 'yes, earlier he carried the painted shield, I remember.'

'That's because you need a different shield in the joust,' Ellis went on, with all the authority of a knight five times his age. 'When fighting with a sword, you need to block blows from above, but in the joust you must be sure to . . .'

Jo blithely nodded along, barely listening as Ellis launched into a description of the shields and armour used for different competitions. Over his head, she spotted Isabelle watching her. Isabelle said nothing, but glanced towards the Knight of Stars then back to Jo, eyebrows raised. Jo flushed, willing that she wouldn't. Isabelle's lips quirked into a smile.

'Do you think he will win?'

The question jerked Jo back into the conversation.

'I . . .' She looked back towards the field, where Cecily was preparing to ride. 'I think he may, yes.'

She hoped she was right. She *needed* to be right. If Cecily lost, it was a blow to her pride more than anything. But if she was *wounded*, she would be found out. She would be punished.

If she was hurt, *really* hurt, or killed like the young man Jo had watched as a child . . . Jo didn't know what she would do. Her stomach lurched sickeningly as Cecily and her opponent took their places on either side of the rail.

The inches of wood between the riders seemed no more substantial than a ribbon caught between two branches. As Cecily moved her horse, a spot on her armour caught the sun for just a moment, flashing in a silver burst. Jo leant forwards, her arms pressed against the railing, unable to look away.

There was a trumpet blast. A shout. A flag cutting through the air like a whip cracking.

And then the flurry of hooves as both riders spurred their horses forwards. The squire who had handed Cecily her lance leapt back as she shot forwards, her opponent only a second or so behind. Next to Jo, Ellis was bouncing on his pillows, squealing. The crowd, now roused, cheered. Jo's heart thundered in her chest, rising up her throat. The two knights collided in a shower of splinters.

The crowd equal parts hissed and cheered as they rode on. Cecily's lance was no more than a jagged mess in her hand, and her opponent was sagging, but still on his horse. It had been a decisive blow. Jo breathed again, lungs burning. Both riders quickly righted themselves, picking up new lances and preparing to tilt again.

There was a new set to Cecily's shoulders that could not be missed. She held her back straight, her fingers gripped tight around the lance. One apparent victory had been enough, and now she held herself with a swagger as she shifted her mount around and raised her lance to the crowd. Jo's first response was to roll her eyes – such bravado was so *typical* of Cecily – but she realised that she didn't just want her to be safe.

She wanted her to *win*.

The flag cut through the air again, and once again the two knights charged at each other. Jo's heart was in her mouth now, her pulse thrumming in her teeth. As they collided, Cecily thrust the tip of her lance against the shoulder of her opponent. It shattered, sending him toppling messily into the dirt below.

The crowd, now fully engaged, burst into cheers. Jo was cheering, too, on her feet, ears ringing. Cecily had *won*, easily and swiftly. Good God, she was magnificent.

Cecily threw aside what was left of her ruined lance, circling around the barrier. Her opponent's men were hurrying towards him, helping to pull him from the ground where he struggled in his heavy armour. Cecily paused for a moment, enjoying the applause, then threw herself from her horse, passed the reins to a lingering squire, and quickly made her way towards the fallen knight.

She reached for him as if to help, but the man snatched his arm away and quickly strode off, sending servants scattering in his wake. For a moment, Cecily only watched as he stalked away. And then her shoulders lowered. Jo was sure she shook her head.

Beside her, Ellis had burst into wild applause. Finally coming back to herself, Jo lowered herself back to her seat.

In her walk back to the end of the field, Cecily turned, and looked at her.

Chapter 6

The crowd roared. Lily's ears throbbed with the sound of hoof-beats and shattering wood. It had been another swift and thorough victory. Her name was on the wind, yelled from two dozen pairs of lips.

Not *quite* her name. *Stars*. But it was enough to thrill her anyway.

She passed Broga's reins to the squire with a word of thanks. He nodded to her, looking a little in awe, then led the horse away.

The roar of the crowd was intoxicating. Addictive. It was easy to forget, with her skin aflame and her chest pounding and her stomach flipping, that she was doing this for Jo.

She quickly checked that Jo's handkerchief was still tucked beneath her chest plate. Really, her joy and the chance to win Jo's freedom were one and the same. The more successful she was, and the more impressive her performance, the more likely she was to unsettle proceedings. She had tried not to imagine too hard what success might feel like, fearing that it would never come to pass, and now it filled her, making her burn. Her victories had been swift and many.

It was late afternoon. Lily collected her things—sword and shield—and with no other tilts that day was preparing to return to her tent and rest when there was a shout from behind.

'William!'

Sir John, whom she had bested in the sword fight that morning, was hurrying over. To her surprise, he was dressed in what was clearly a second-hand surcoat, the red and yellow colours faded through use. He was a large man, tall and strong, probably around thirty years old. Now he was no longer dripping with sweat, his hair had dried into a mop of curls.

'Are you joining us to eat this evening, William?'

'Ah—'

'Come,' said John. 'You must be exhausted, and your performance truly was impressive. Join us for a drink, at least.'

Lily hesitated. 'I am not—'

'Come on, lad.' Another man approached. Lily recognised him as one of the men who had managed to beat her that morning in the sword fight: Sir Rhys. 'None of us will be eating in the castle tonight.'

'You came here alone,' added John. 'It would not do to eat alone as well.'

'Thank you,' Lily said, relenting. 'I will, but I must change and rest. I am sure beneath this armour I am *covered* in bruises.'

'Do you need to see the physician?' John said, looking concerned. 'Alsen, from the keep, has taken residence in the infirmary tent.'

Lily frowned. She recognised that name. 'Did he—' she started, the memory surfacing and bubbling out before she could stop herself. 'Ah, that is—'

Sir Rhys raised his eyebrows. 'Did he what?'

Damn. Lily couldn't back down now. 'I heard . . . no doubt just a *rumour* . . .'

The older man's puzzlement morphed into a knowing expression.

'Ah,' he said. 'This is about that Barden lad, isn't it? You are from the north, I forgot. You must know Lord Griffin and his family?'

Do not panic, Lily warned herself. *Do not let them see you panic.*

'I . . . yes,' she said, slowly. 'Rather, I know *of* them. I heard of their troubles when I was last near Dunlyn Castle.'

'But you did not know if the rumours were true?'

She gave the man a half-hearted shrug, unable to say anything else. She noticed that Sir John, too, was watching closely. He also seemed keen on the gossip.

'Aye,' Sir Rhys said finally. 'It *is* true. At least, the part where the Earl – God save his ruined soul – shot that lad. Alsen treated the wound. Healed nicely, from what I heard. His arm was better than before!'

Raff was still battling with the wound a full year and a half later. It would *never* heal, Lily knew; he still struggled to even dress. She plastered a false smile on her face, attempting to hide her true feelings.

'He must be very talented. But I do not think I need his attentions. Just some rest, and to get out of this armour.'

Both men laughed. 'Very well,' said John. 'Go, I will not delay you. But I intend to see you at sundown at the mess tent!'

Lily grinned, bid them both goodbye, and made her way across the grounds. Before heading back to her tent, she stopped at the stables to ensure that Broga had been properly seen to. The horse snorted when Lily approached, recognising her despite her helmet. She gave Broga a quick pat down, assessing her, then fed her a handful of oats as she scratched her nose.

Pleased that her horse was being well cared for, Lily left

the stables and walked straight into another knight, dressed in expensive armour with his helm held beneath his arm.

He gave her a sharp look as she collided with him. She recognised him as Sir Lanval: a high-ranking knight who had come to the tournament with the retinue of one Lord Adam Wyck. She had seen them competing in both combat and the joust, and both men were confident, powerful fighters. Sir Lanval was tall and sturdy – not a large man, like Lord Adam, but strong. She swallowed as he stared down at her, his eyes flashing.

'The Knight of Stars,' he said, coolly.

For a moment, she wondered how he knew her name. Then she remembered the shield that still hung from her arm, and how quickly her reputation had spread in just a single morning.

'Sir Lanval.' She gave him a curt bow, befitting her lower status.

'An odd name?' The statement curled into a question as he raised his eyebrows.

'Not one I chose myself,' she said, her pulse quickening under this sudden examination. 'My true name is William Dale, sir, if it pleases you.'

He did not seem pleased. His gaze slid down, taking her in. It caught on the favour still hanging from Lily's chest plate, lingering there too long. She snatched it up and shoved it into her pocket.

'I have heard much about you,' Lanval said, meeting her eye again. 'Lord Adam's retinue is buzzing with word of the young knight who came alone yet performed so well.'

Lily blinked. 'Thank you, sir,' she said, although his words did not sound like a compliment.

He only stared at her. 'I am honoured to finally meet the man who has caused such a sensation.'

'I . . .' Lily floundered, unsure what would make a suitable response. 'I am grateful to meet you, too, sir. It is always a blessing to meet a man so well-practised. If you tell Lord Adam that we spoke, send him my regards.'

His impassive expression did not change under the flattery. 'Indeed.' He frowned, as if having a sudden unpleasant thought. 'Good luck in the tournament.'

And with that he stalked around her and towards the stables. Feeling like she'd failed a test, Lily waited until he had disappeared inside before quickly hurrying away.

She made her way to her tent blissfully unimpeded, leant her shield against the canvas, then stepped inside. She tied shut the flap of the tent tight behind her.

Alone at last, she released a breath, and pulled off her helmet. Her hair was plastered to her head, and she winced as she pushed her hands through it.

She placed the helmet carefully aside, followed by her armour, stripping off the sweat-sodden clothes beneath. She had been right: there were bruises on her arms and chest, some from blows and some from the armour itself, along with dark red marks where it had pressed into her skin. She quickly got to work checking for more serious injuries.

Thankfully, she was largely unharmed, and she sprawled in her stolen braies on the straw mattress with throbbing limbs. It was a good feeling: it was a sign that she had fought hard, and won. It was a satisfying pain that left her exhausted but proud.

She had done well. She had done *very* well.

Lily had dreamt of this for as long as she could remember – since the first time one of her brothers had allowed her to hold a sword. Her father, so scared of pushing her away after the death of their mother, had allowed her training and her insistence on being included in her brother's games. He did not approve, but neither would he deny her.

However lenient her father had been, she would never have been allowed to enter a tournament or train with anyone beside her brothers or their marshal, sworn to secrecy. But it had come so easily – far easier than her activities at court as a noble lady, where the other women abided by rules Lily didn't know and couldn't understand. They were effortlessly competent, always able to say or do the right thing. Lily felt as if she had been born to ride and fight and joust, and was only now able to do so. She was like one of her father's hounds, released to run in the fields for the first time.

Lily couldn't think ahead to what would happen after the tournament, not while Jo's fate still rested in her hands. But she was realising that soon she would have to. Entering had given her a sense of purpose, one which she had never had before and was keen not to lose. For now, she would continue to direct it towards her goal: saving Jo from the cage of marriage.

It was the same cage that Lily herself had escaped, and she could still remember the feeling of dread in her stomach when her father had announced she was to be wed: as well as the fragile, desperate elation when her would-be husband had vanished. She'd grabbed the chance to be free with both hands. Now she would give that chance to Jo, too.

She reached across to the messy pile she had left her clothes in, scrabbling in the heap until her fingers brushed against something silky and soft. The handkerchief. She pulled it up to her face so she could better see it.

It was very simple, and no doubt the only thing Jo had to give. The stitchwork was a little thick, the lines imperfect: embroidery was not Jo's strongest suit. Lily herself was very skilled at the work, finding it a calming way to keep her hands busy when her mind raced. Besides, being able to invisibly mend tears in her dresses was an invaluable skill if she didn't want to be chastised by the housekeeper.

She ran her fingers over the uneven lines. There was a — *creature* embroidered in the corner. Lily smiled fondly at the wonky shape, unable to quite tell what the animal was supposed to be. It was so painfully charming that she held the fabric to her face, grinning.

It smelt faintly of lavender.

Lily's heart stuttered uncertainly. That particular organ had been betraying her since she had arrived; since Jo had complimented her, and teased her, and challenged her with that sharp wit.

When the lad had handed her Jo's letter — along with a *sword*, of all things — it was like Lily's heart had swelled. It became a star itself, too bright to be contained, burning her up from the inside out.

She would have to douse it. That was not why she was here. That was not what mattered, not when the chance to help Jo find her freedom was so close.

It would be foolish of Lily to deny that she felt anything more than friendship towards Johanna de Foucart. She had been half in love with her since the day they met. Back then, it was a passing infatuation, one that Lily had suffered through dozens of times before. She knew it well: a fleeting, flighty feeling that would never bloom into anything stronger but was no less intense for its brevity.

It should have guttered out. If Jo had never replied to Lily's first letter, it would have. But Jo had replied, and here Lily was, back at the keep she had vowed never to enter again.

Regardless, she reminded herself, she had no indication at all if Jo's preferences mirrored her own. Jo was aware of the true nature of their brothers' relationship, but acceptance of their brothers did not mean that she, too, harboured such feelings. Jo's letters, and her actions in the moments they had spent together, were *kind*, but Lily had mistaken kindness for something more too many times. It always stung.

She wondered if this was how other women like her always felt – always balancing on an edge between friendship and something more. She couldn't tell if this – like her love for women – was something that was part of her, something baked into her bones, or if it was simply her own foolishness. If she should *know*, or somehow learn, the difference between camaraderie and attraction.

But she didn't know. And here she was, fighting in a tournament, disguising herself, putting herself in danger for—

For Jo. That much she could be certain of. The rest didn't matter.

She wished she could have been able to respond to Jo's note. To thank her, for both the favour and the sword. To hold Jo to her word and call her *my Lady*, if Jo really had accepted her as her champion. But there had been no time. All Lily had been able to do was wear Jo's favour, and hope she saw it.

She dozed for a while on the pallet, rubbing the handkerchief between her fingers as her limbs began to settle into a true ache. With a groan, she finally stood, quickly wiped herself down with a scrap of linen from her pack and some water from her canteen then pulled on a fresh set of clothes.

She had no idea who the clothes belonged to. She was fairly

certain that the breeches had been Raff's: she didn't have to turn them up so many times. The tunics and undershirts could be *anyone's*. She had taken all she could fit in her pack from the laundry, some of the clothes still damp.

With the baggy undershirt and bulky tunic, she looked once more like a young, awkward man. It took her a moment to find her knife – which she was sure she had only just placed down – then strapped it to her belt. She wished she had a mirror with her so she could assess her appearance. As it was, she would just have to hope that no one scrutinised her too closely.

Thus far, no one had questioned her. She suspected she had been saved by little more than expectation. No one expected to see a woman in the lists, therefore they didn't. It was far more reasonable to see a young man who had bluffed his way in despite being underage than a woman in disguise. Many of the competitors no doubt had similar stories of their own youthful exuberance, and instead of finding her appearance shocking or concerning, saw it as a reminder of their own foolhardiness when they had been boys.

She paused as she went to leave the tent, then grabbed Jo's handkerchief and shoved it into the pouch hanging from her belt.

Lily weaved her way among the tents, the sun now setting behind the forest, heading towards the sound of noise and laughter. As she approached, she spotted Sir John sat at the edge of the proceedings, whittling something with his knife. When he spotted her, he rose, calling over Sir Rhys as he did.

'My God,' Rhys exclaimed as she walked towards them. 'You *are* young. That, or I am getting old to be nearly beaten by no more than a babe.'

Lily scoffed at him. 'I am twenty-three,' she countered, one of the first true things she had said about herself. 'But I have been blessed with a youthful face, I admit.'

'Oh yes, and you managed to achieve so close a shave with that blade, did you?' Sir Rhys said, glancing disbelievingly at her knife.

'He may look like a babe, but he fights like a wolf,' said John, laughing. 'Leave him be, Rhys. I'd rather have two dozen beardless youths in my army than a single seasoned knight if they've all got his spirit.'

Rhys chortled, and the three of them headed towards the bonfire that had been set up beside the mess tent, away from the crush of the tournament on the outskirts of Hartswood Forest.

An enormous pig was on a spit above the fire, crackling as its juices dripped onto the logs below. It smelt *delicious*, and Lily's stomach rumbled. As she sat on a tipped log, John pressed a cup of mead into her hand before settling next to her.

'Drink,' he said. 'You look as if you need it.'

Soon, the pig was ready, and silence fell as they began to eat. The meat was rich and perfectly cooked, and Lily ate greedily, happy for a good warm meal after so many days of making do. As she tore at the meat, a boy approached. It took her a moment to realise that it was one of the de Foucart servants.

'Yes?' she muttered, mouth full, as he stared down at her with wide-eyed awe.

'I, um . . .' the boy stuttered.

Lily felt slightly sorry for him. 'What is it?'

Without another word, the boy thrust a neatly folded piece of parchment towards her. Lily tossed the bone aside, wiped her hands on her breeches, and took it from him.

'Thank you.'

He stared at her for another long moment before finally spluttering: 'I watched you in the joust. You were very good.'

Before she could thank him again, he hurried off. John laughed at his departing figure as she unfolded the parchment. Written on it in a neat, familiar hand were two words.

Well done.

Lily's heart beat faster. Her stomach swooped – dangerously, considering the meal and mead she'd just consumed.

'What's that?'

She quickly folded the parchment again and shoved it into her pouch. 'Nothing.'

Sir John gave her a disbelieving look but did not press the matter as another man walked past, nose in the air. Lily immediately recognised him – he was the knight she had unseated that morning, who had refused her help. He scowled at her as he strode towards the other side of the bonfire.

Sir Rhys appeared from the tent behind her, a bottle in his hand.

'You,' he said, watching the knight angrily hurry away, 'are unsettling things.'

Lily looked up at him. 'Is that right?'

'It *is*. Do you know who that is?' He gestured towards the man, then seated himself on the ground at their feet.

'All I know is that I beat him.'

Rhys snorted through his nose. 'That is Sir Walter. Newly knighted, too. He's the fourth son of some lord, and this was his first chance to demonstrate his skills to his master, and – I have been told – his master's exceedingly beautiful daughter. And you' – he gestured towards her with the bottle – 'made a fool of him.'

'I merely beat him,' she said. 'He made a fool of himself by refusing my help.'

'Hah!' Rhys slapped his leg. 'I am forced to agree with you, there. None of us here' – he looked around to the camp, at the men eating and carousing – 'have any chance of winning this tourney. Yet along comes this green lad, with no title, who embarrasses such a great number of men that his name spreads throughout the grounds, *and* is so bold as to speak to Lady Johanna. If you're here to make a name for yourself, boy, you're doing so.'

'Will spoke to Lady Johanna?' John looked up, interested.

'Indeed he did. I saw him talking to the good Lady and the Earl after your fight.'

John scrutinised her. 'Is that so?'

'Aye,' Lily said. 'The young Earl and his sister complimented me on my win. She is very—'

'Beautiful?' Rhys cut in.

'I was going to say *gracious*. Furiously clever, too.'

Rhys laughed. 'They all are, I swear. Got that from their mother, of course, the late Countess Eleanor. You should have met her brothers, sharp as knives, the lot of them. Especially William.'

Lily made a soft, startled noise. Sir Rhys laughed.

'Of course, another William amongst us. Seeing how *that* ended I cannot tell you if that is good fortune or not. Likely not,' he concluded, darkly.

Lily gave a nervous laugh. When she had chosen the name several days ago, it had seemed hugely funny: taking her would-be husband's cast-off name to rescue his sister. Now, it seemed like a horribly foolish decision, and one that would surely get her found out.

'Anyway,' Rhys continued, handing around the bottle, 'I reckon he did more than just talk to the lady.'

John's eyebrows raised. 'Oh?'

Rhys turned to Lily. 'Whose favour is that you've been wearing?'

Lily was suddenly the subject of several scrutinising looks. John was staring at her. But there was no way Rhys could know.

'What do you mean?' She was going red. *Damn it* – that would give her away.

'You rode with a favour in the joust,' Rhys said, smugly. 'Who gave it you?'

Lily sat straighter, attempting to ignore her blush. 'I don't see that it matters,' she snapped.

Rhys and a few of the other men laughed. Someone pointed out Lily's flushing cheeks, which only made them burn hotter. Rhys clapped his hand to her shoulder.

'Calm yourself, lad. Don't give yourself apoplexy, I mean nothing by it.'

'Who *is* the favour from, then?' John was still watching her.

Lily took too long to respond, and there was another raucous laugh from the other men.

'That's as good as a confession.' Rhys chortled.

'I—' she started uneasily, then sat straighter, squaring her shoulders. 'And what if it *is* from her? That is between myself and Johanna.'

'Not if word spreads,' said Rhys. 'Giving a favour to a lad like you? People will talk.'

'She was only being polite,' Lily said desperately. 'Ell— The Earl urged her to accept me.'

'He urged her to accept you?' said John, now frowning. 'So you offered to be her champion, then?'

' . . . only in jest,' she muttered, feeling like that was a lie.

'Jest or no, she still gave you a favour,' John pressed. 'That, you cannot deny.'

'I cannot.' Lily sighed, immensely regretting admitting to it.

'Come then, boy,' Rhys said. 'Show us what she gave you.'

Something hardened in her.

'That *is* between Lady Johanna and myself,' she said. 'Perhaps it was out of turn to speak to her, but I will not allow your attempts to embarrass me. Embarrass us *both*. If you were so curious, *you* should have declared yourself her champion. Perhaps she likes older men.'

That elicited a snort from their onlookers.

'Yes,' someone said, laughing, 'or she may feel sorry for you, Sir Rhys.'

'You are both out of luck.'

Another man approached. He wore a red and gold surcoat, although the fine fabric was stained. It took Lily a moment to recognise the colours: a man from the Wyck retinue.

'And why is that, Andrew?' Rhys pressed.

Andrew took a deep drink from a wineskin he was carrying. 'The Lady Johanna is to be wed. Have you not heard?'

It was like a stone in Lily's stomach. The meat and ale curdled there, solidifying. *No.* Before she could press for more information, John spoke over her.

'To who?' he demanded.

Andrew looked shocked at their collective ignorance.

'To my Lord Adam, of course,' he said. 'You truly have not heard? The tents are ablaze with the gossip.'

Sir Rhys shook his head. 'Word always reaches us last,' he said. 'Lord Adam, is it? He's a fine man.'

'He is,' Andrew agreed, dutifully.

Lily couldn't tell if he truly believed that, or if it was loyalty to his lord moving his tongue. Her brief encounter with Lanval had soured her towards his master already, that sourness only ripened by this sudden news.

She wondered if the others could see her displeasure on her face. She hoped not: to look like a jealous, defeated suitor would only make them tease her more. She was *not* a suitor. She never had been.

Yet still the announcement stung. She swallowed back the dregs of her mead, trying to push that feeling down. It was the failure that hurt most, she told herself. She had been scuppered before she had even had a chance to do what she had set out to achieve.

She roughly wiped her mouth with the back of her hand before reaching for the bottle at Rhys's feet.

'Come,' she said, topping up her cup. 'You invited me to celebrate, drink, and share your food, yet here you all are, gossiping like old women.'

John snorted, shaking his head. He took the bottle from Lily. He, too, seemed on edge as he filled his cup.

'You truly have not spent much time around knights,' he said. 'They are worse than washerwomen when they get to gossiping.'

'Then let us gossip about someone *else*, for a while. One of you must have a more exciting story than Lady Johanna's betrothal.'

'Here, Andrew,' Rhys said, turning back to the man. 'What happened with that squire you were telling me of? With his baker?'

Andrew's eyes widened. 'Well remembered,' he said, then stood and shouted to a youth across the way. 'Bran! Come over here a moment, I've something to ask you—'

Plied with yet more food – some, apparently, a gift from Bran's baker – Lily forced herself to relax. The sting of defeat and the undeniable pang of jealousy still loomed over her shoulders, but she was enjoying the company of the men who had gathered from miles around for the tournament. They were all lower-ranking, and as night drew in, they were joined by several squires and servants, sneaking away from the keep after finishing their evening duties.

She felt *free*. At home, she could only be this unguarded around her brothers and Penn. An event like this in Dunlyn Castle would have found her acting as her father's daughter, entertaining guests and dutifully obeying Lord Griffin, as much as she ever *did* obey him.

But like this she could do as she pleased. She laughed too loudly, ate messily, and spat out crude jokes as good as any of the older men in attendance. No one had worked her out, and there were still several days of the tournament left. She could compete, as she'd always wanted to. She could pick up the role that was expected of one of her brothers, and perform it better than either of them would have done.

That was its own kind of thrill – one that had come second to the goal of saving Jo. But now that goal had shattered, she really *was* just William Dale, the Knight of Stars.

When Lily had left Dunlyn with her heart in her throat and her good sense nowhere to be found at all, she had been content with her own uncertain future. She had accepted the suggestion that she would one day enter the convent, as so many unmarried women did.

Now, with her limbs aching and her chest puffed with pride, that wasn't enough. She had all but failed in her quest to save Jo, but the urgent need to do *something* still lingered, ringing in the void between her ribs. She would give her all in the tournament. She would win where she could, then head home and begin to examine her future. Perhaps if she returned victorious and confessed what she had done, her father and brothers would be so impressed that they would be forced to reconsider her role in the keep.

And perhaps not all was lost, either. There could still be a way to save Jo – just not one she had seen yet.

When the moon was high above the bonfire in a sky full of sparks, she unsteadily rose to her feet. Someone called after her before she had even made it halfway towards the treeline.

'And where are you going, Will?'

'For a piss,' she yelled over her shoulder. 'Or is *that* a competition, too, amongst noble knights?'

This was met with even more laughter, and confident that no one was following her she headed into Hartswood Forest. She walked until she could no longer hear their voices, despite the darkness: of all the ways for her disguise to be discovered, she *refused* for it to be while relieving herself.

When she was finished, she pulled up her breeches and headed back towards the flickering lights of camp. She was feeling light, filled with success and acceptance and strong mead. She didn't notice the hand that darted from the shadows until it was gripped around her arm.

'William Dale.'

Lily spun around. Sir Lanval. He was alone. She had not

seen him around the campfire; he must have left his retinue to seek her out.

'Sir Lanval?'

'What do you think you are doing?' He did not let go of her arm.

'Going for a piss.'

She spoke without thinking, the mead loosening her tongue. She regretted her words instantly. Lanval flung her around, throwing her against the nearest tree. Lily gasped as she collided with the trunk, the air knocked from her lungs.

'What are you—'

'You spoke to the lady of the house.' Lanval pressed her against the tree. His eyes were red and unfocused. He was drunk.

'Countess Isabelle?'

'Don't be an idiot. We both know I mean Lady Johanna.'

'We merely spoke—'

'She gave you a favour. How dare you even *ask* that of her. You have no title, no lands, and no money. You are *entirely* unsuitable.'

How did he know about the favour?

'I – what?'

Something flashed beside Lily's face. It was a knife, glimmering in the moonlight.

'Cease your attentions on Lady Johanna.'

'But—'

'Cease. Your. Attentions.'

Lily swallowed, keeping her eyes fixed on Lanval's face and not on the blade.

'Lady Johanna is *not my concern*.' The lie was heavy on her tongue. 'I am *no one*, as you have informed me. If my presence here risks your lord's arrangement, then I am afraid the fault lies with *him*, not me.'

Lanval leant even closer. He looked furious – but beneath the expression was panic. He was acting rashly in his drunken state.

'You will not pursue her,' he said. It was not a question or a request. He was not *bartering*. It was a command.

He twisted the tip of the knife into the bark beside Lily's face. She thought of the handkerchief in her pocket, bunched next to the congratulatory note that the boy had slipped into her hand only a few hours ago.

But she had no choice.

'I will not pursue her,' she said, hating herself.

They were so close that their noses nearly brushed. She could smell wine on his breath. She didn't blink. She had her own knife at her hip, but she didn't want to use it. Not unless she had to.

'I *know* what you are doing,' Lanval said.

Lily froze. *No.* Had he caught her relieving herself? Or had he just *known*, instinctively, that she was a woman? She swallowed, but pressed against the tree, there was nowhere she could run.

'I do not—' she started, desperately.

She was cut off by a crash between the trees. Footsteps.

'Lanval?'

Lanval immediately released her, taking a swift step back. Behind him, from the direction of the keep, a figure had emerged. Lord Adam, silhouetted hugely against the moon, framed between the trees. Lanval blanched.

'Adam—'

'What is this?'

'I just—'

'*What is this?*'

Lanval's expression melded into fear. He took another step away from Lily, staring only at Adam. Lily wanted to run, but Lanval was still hovering close by with the dagger in his hand, and Adam's broad form was blocking the easiest path back towards camp.

'My Lord—' she began, taking a step forward.

'Leave.' He still hadn't taken his eyes from Lanval.

'But—'

'I am *commanding* you to go, boy! I need to speak to Lanval. Alone.'

Lily's stomach lurched. She stepped around Lanval, then paused as she approached Adam. She hated being so suddenly power-less – she was *not* a knight, she was forced to remember. She was a woman in disguise.

And if Lanval knew that, then surely Adam did as well. An attempt to challenge either of them would be disastrous.

'I—' Adam glared at her. She felt very small. 'I think, my Lord, it would be best if . . . if none of us discussed this. If word did not spread.'

He looked again at Lanval. Lanval had not moved. When Adam turned back, his expression was stony. He nodded, once.

'Go.'

Lily didn't need telling again. Without looking back, she dodged around Adam and hurried back towards the dancing light of the bonfire.

Chapter 7

The de Foucart keep had never been so busy. Jo made her way across the yard, dodging out of the way of servants and guests. She had arranged to meet Ros on the far side of the tourney grounds, where together they would be walking to the final duel of the day to watch Lord Adam. That evening they were holding a lavish banquet – the first event where she and Lord Adam would be presented as a couple.

She had hoped that once the match was made public she would be less busy, yet somehow she was in more demand than ever. As a member of the de Foucart family, she needed to be seen watching the tournament, entertaining nobles, and creating new allies. As Lord Adam's betrothed, she had to be seen with him and by him, attending his or his men's matches, dining by his side.

She wanted to seek out Cecily, but there was no time, and even fewer moments of solitude. Jo was always with someone, or expected by someone. She'd been approached by a girl from the stables that morning, who had pressed a torn-off scrap of parchment into her hand before scampering quickly away. She'd read the note quickly before hiding it in her pocket.

Thank you, my Lady.

It had been signed not with a name, but with a scribbled star. But Jo had been taking the morning tour of the tourney grounds with Ellis and Isabelle – then on to Lord Adam's encampment where they broke their fast with him – and there had been no opportunity to respond.

Even when they bid Lord Adam farewell, she had been needed. She'd spent the rest of the morning making the final preparations for the feast, and had finally been released that afternoon.

As she hurried across the grounds to where she would be meeting Ros, she could hear that the final joust of the day had begun. It was a smaller affair, where a winner would be chosen from the lower competitors: young lords, knights-errant, the squires of the men competing in the real lists.

Cecily would there, too. Jo could only hope that she would not get hurt, and pray that her favour really would bring her luck.

Deeper down – a feeling that had sparked during the first joust and had grown stronger since – she hoped Cecily would *win*. There had been something thrilling about watching her performing, knowing who she was. It was a shared secret, a hot little thing they held between them, a pinprick star like the ones on Cecily's shield.

So many years surviving her father had forced Jo into politeness and pliability. But Cecily's cynicism about the noblemen attending and her boldness in assuming she could defeat them was *addictive*. It spread, like weeds.

When Jo heard other men talk in shocked tones about the Knight of Stars, be they praising him or cursing him for beating them, she could not help but feel pleased. Several of Lord Adam's retinue had been discussing him – how he had *beaten* them – and she had only realised she was smiling at their unconcealed jealousy when Isabelle shot her a pointed look.

She was walking away from the jousting field when her thoughts were broken by a mighty crash, the scream of a horse, and the gasps of the watching crowd. The sounds mingled into a horrible cacophony, and Jo reacted without thinking, dashing towards the field where a crowd had already gathered near the centre of the fence. Just beyond, a terrified-looking squire was attempting to calm a panicking dun palfrey.

She knew that horse. With a sickening jolt in her stomach, she pushed through the crowd to see Cecily flat on her back upon the dirt. Her already tarnished breastplate was horribly dented, her right vambrace hanging on by the strap. Jo stumbled to her knees beside her, hands hovering over the sun-warmed metal.

'Has anyone fetched the physician?' Jo looked around at the surrounding crowd, all unmoving. 'Well? Has *no one* thought to fetch Alsen? No one at all?'

No one spoke. Clearly not.

'You' – she pointed at a young maid who had been staring at the scene with wide eyes – 'fetch Alsen. He is likely in the infirmary with—'

There was a sudden grip around Jo's wrist. She froze, warring against the instinct to snatch her arm away. Cecily had grabbed her. Through the slit in her helm, her pleading eyes shone bright grey.

'Do not fetch the physician,' she said, hoarsely.

Jo did not move. She barely breathed.

'You are injured,' she muttered, unable to say much else.

'I am merely winded,' Cecily said. 'I simply must—'

'Unhand the lady!'

Jo spun around as Cecily winced at the voice, immediately releasing her wrist. She was not the only person who had been attracted by all the noise: Lord Adam had appeared, flanked by his men and half a dozen other nobles, all peering to see what had happened. At his side stood Sir Lanval, looking furious.

Lord Adam's face was bright red. He must have rushed over at the sudden sound and the gathered crowd. The colour blotching his cheeks mingled exhaustion, rage and – Jo thought, as he glared down at Cecily prone on the ground – embarrassment: here was his bride on her knees in the dirt for a knight-errant.

'My apologies, my Lady,' Cecily wheezed, lowering her gaze as one of the nearby squires heaved her into a sitting position. She hissed as she sat up, whispering a brief curse beneath her breath low enough that only Jo caught it, and colourful enough that it made her blush.

'It is . . .' Her tongue was heavy. 'It is quite all right.'

'And apologies towards you, Lord Alfred. I acted without thought. I had not intended to impede upon the honour of our most gracious lady.'

'It is Lord *Adam*.' Lord Adam's scowl deepened. 'See that it does not happen again. My Lady Johanna, if you would allow me—'

He reached down one mailed hand. Jo was being watched. She swallowed, resisting the urge to look back, and allowed Lord Adam to pull her to her feet. Beside her, a pair of knights hauled Cecily up as well, where she swayed unsteadily. Before Jo could ask if she was sure she was all right, Lord Adam strode forwards, one hand outstretched.

For a moment, Jo thought he meant to strike Cecily. For a moment, she nearly threw herself between them.

But he didn't – and Jo's legs had turned to stone, buried in the ground, keeping her stuck. Lord Adam reached out and snatched at the mud-stained scrap of fabric tucked into Cecily's chest plate.

Jo's handkerchief. Lord Adam barely glanced at it, just pulled it violently away.

'I believe this belongs to you, my Lady.' He placed it in Jo's hands.

Jo's fingers tightened around the fabric. 'Thank you.'

Behind Lord Adam, Cecily was watching her. The squire had finally regained control over her horse, handing her the reins. Cecily leant against the creature, breathing heavily. A thin, delicate stream of blood trickled across one of her eyebrows and over the corner of her eye, forging a scarlet path down her cheek like a tear.

Jo could not leave her. Not like this. But Cecily had been right to refuse the physician: she would be discovered.

'William,' Jo said, as Lord Adam looped his arm through hers, keeping her carefully back. 'Are you quite sure you are well?'

Cecily waved away her concerns once more, shaking her head with another wince.

'It is just shock, my Lady,' she said. 'The force of the blow, and—' for the first time, Jo noticed hesitance in Cecily's voice. It trembled, slightly, turning a little pitched before she quickly fixed herself. 'I will return to my tent to rest and clean my wounds, with your leave.'

Jo wanted to refuse. She *could*. She could have her *dragged* to Alsen, if that was what it took. But Cecily's gaze through the helm was pleading, and Jo relented. It *was* too dangerous.

'You have it,' she said. 'Rest and heal well, sir. I hope I will see you again soon, at this evening's feast.'

Something flashed in Cecily's eyes. She said nothing, just bowed, then pulled her horse around and limped away towards the rows of tents that flanked the walls of the keep.

'What *youth*.'

Jo had all but forgotten Lord Adam.

'My Lord?'

'The impertinence!' he scoffed. 'But it is to be expected, in one so young and so green. He is lucky he did not find himself in the lists against a knight with any true fortitude or strength.'

A knight like yourself? Jo kept the question in her mouth, simply gifting him an agreeable smile.

'I pray . . .' Lord Adam continued, leading her away, 'he did not hurt you?'

Jo frowned. 'No, my Lord. Why would he have hurt me?'

'Your wrist.' Lord Adam gestured. 'He was gripping it so tightly. And you appear quite pale.'

Jo blinked. Her skin still tingled where Cecily had grabbed her so hard, where her glove had dug into Jo's skin. She flexed her fingers instinctively, her pulse still fluttering in her neck.

'No, my Lord.' She allowed him to lead her away, her mind racing with the memory of that tight grip, those grey-blue eyes, and the neat line of scarlet blood. 'He did not hurt me.'

Lily stumbled through the flap of her tent, her legs trembling. It felt as if the only thing holding her up were her greaves. With a groan, she tugged off the helmet and tossed it aside. The ringing *clang* it made when it landed set her teeth on edge, sending a shooting pain through her temples. The pain *spread*, tightening around her nape and sparking sharply around the cut above her eyebrow, her whole head throbbing.

She pulled off her gloves, throwing them aside, too, then spat at the ground and wiped her mouth with the back of her hand. Her knuckles were bruised. Her spit was pink. Her stomach lurched. When she had fallen, there'd been a pain in her mouth and the taste of iron; now the rush was wearing off, she could tell that she'd bitten the inside of her lip as she'd crashed to the floor.

She turned next to the vambraces. One had almost been ripped off, hanging only by a half-severed strap. She attempted to unfasten it, but her hand was shaking and she couldn't find purchase. With a grunt, she grabbed the vambrace and *pulled*, snapping the fastening away from the arm guard and throwing it to the floor. Heart pounding and head reeling, she peered down at the other arm.

God curse it all.

Everything hurt. She had pushed herself too hard before, had been thrown from horses more times than she could count. She had been battered and bruised when training with her brothers, insisting always that they go harder on her than either of them had been comfortable with. But this was a new sort of pain – it flared in her head, across her chest, down her legs.

She had won – her opponent had fallen first. But she was beaten, too. She pushed her hand through her hair, wincing as it tugged at the cut above her eyebrow. If Jo had managed to send her to the physician, she would have been ruined. No doubt she *should* have been sent to the physician – even breathing made her chest twinge – but it was impossible. She could only pray that she would be able to return to Dunlyn Castle in one piece.

Her plan had failed. She couldn't maintain the ruse, not like this. She'd lost both her chance to save Jo, and these few, bright days of true freedom.

She would leave a note for Jo and return home at dawn. If she was lucky, she would heal enough on the slow ride back that her family would never question her. If they learnt the true extent of her injuries, they would put an end to all of this: to her training, to her games, to the bright hope that she could continue to fight once the tournament was finished.

She took a step forward. The greaves around her legs were suddenly too tight, digging into the backs of her knees. She couldn't breathe. She stroked her hands over her armour, desperately looking for the straps, but she could only skim her nails across the surface. She took another step towards the pallet.

She took a rattling breath, her palm skimming over the dent in her chest plate, and gracelessly collapsed onto the mattress.

Chapter 8

Lord Adam led Jo back towards the keep in careful silence, handing her over to the housekeeper, giving her a brief explanation of what had happened and asking her to stay by Jo's side.

'But what about the competition?' Jo asked, aware that it was expected of her. 'My Lord, I would see you fight—'

Lord Adam took her hand.

'You have had a shock, my Lady,' he said, not unkindly. 'The excitement of the duel would not be good for you. Rest, and I will see you this evening.'

Jo couldn't help but feel like he was patronising her. But her head still rang with the scream of Cecily's horse, and the horrible crash that had rung out as she'd fallen.

'Then I wish you good fortune,' she said. 'I am sure you will do well.'

He smiled at her, squeezed her hand once more, and set off back towards the grounds, hand pushing through his hair. The housekeeper led Jo up to her chambers and sat her on the bed. Jo hated the attention, but she knew that she must look shaken.

The fall had been terrible. Jo had been flung back to that moment so many years ago, the poor boy with his broken neck, the way he'd sprawled on the dirt with his limbs at odd angles. The thought of that happening to Cecily made her feel sick.

She needed to get out and find her. But the housekeeper was hovering, sending one of the maids to fetch cool water. However much Jo insisted she was fine, she would not relent. When the housekeeper *finally* left, Jo was on her feet and at the door in an instant, only to find the way blocked by Ros, red faced and anxious.

'Johanna—' she breathed. 'Are you quite all right? Lord Adam told me all about it . . .'

Jo was trapped until the evening. However stubborn the house-keeper had been, Ros was more so, refusing to leave Jo alone for even a moment. As the sun beyond the castle walls set, any chances to leave were entirely scuppered when they were joined by two local ladies to prepare for the banquet – women Jo was friendly with but thought more of as acquaintances than anything else. They were daughters of her late father's allies; Winifred, who still lived in her family's keep, and Clara, recently married to an earl from the west.

Their chatter and buoyant moods only went a little way to relieving Jo's anxiety, even if none of them noticed her silence as they helped her into one of the new gowns, this in a deep blue. She had insisted upon this fabric: it reminded her of the colours her mother had favoured.

Like Isabelle, the other women were invested in the prospect of Jo's marriage, and it was the topic of much-animated discussion, as were the other men who were in attendance.

'Lord Adam was the obvious choice, of course,' Ros was saying, threading bangles up her arms. 'Although I think Lord Hughes's son John is just as fine to look at.'

'What about the Knight of Stars?' Winifred responded, fiddling with the ties of her gown. 'He is surely handsome.'

Ros shook her head. 'Winifred,' she said, her tone severe despite her smile. 'He never removes his helmet, how can you be so certain that he is handsome?'

Winifred shrugged slyly. 'It is in the way he carries himself,' she said. 'He seems very sure, even for one so green.'

'Perhaps he is scarred.' Clara was standing behind Jo, brushing out her long hair. 'Perhaps he was in some battle . . .'

'Or a deserter?' Winifred put in, eyes wide. 'Didn't you speak to him, Johanna? How did he seem?'

Jo felt every eye in the room upon her.

'I did, on the first day of the tournament. Ellis was impressed by his single combat performance and we congratulated him on a good win. He seemed . . . very fair. And *exceedingly* sure of himself.'

She thought of the rest of the story – of the way her pulse had thrummed in her fingers when Cecily had taken her hand, the flush that was already creeping up her face just for thinking about it. Of accepting Cecily as her champion.

She thought of how the story ended – with Lord Adam snatching Jo's favour away and thrusting it back into her hands. It was now tucked at the very bottom of the pouch on her belt.

It was not a tale she wished to spread.

'You are blushing!' Clara giggled. 'Was he so charming?'

'He was . . . interesting,' Jo said. 'Very interesting . . .' and then, because she could not help it, 'and quite unlike the other men I've spoken to these past few days.'

'In any case,' said Clara, standing and brushing down her skirts, 'I hope he is well. Did you hear the fall he had in the joust today?'

Ros looked up sharply. 'Jo—'

'No, it is quite all right.' Jo cut her off. 'I was nearby when it happened,' she explained. 'He was able to stand and walk away, but I fear he was more injured than he wished me to realise.'

Clara rolled her eyes with a snort. 'In that way, then, he is very much like other men. No doubt it is little more than bruised pride.' She cut a sly look at Jo. 'He will be in attendance this evening. You can check on him then.'

Jo considered this. Perhaps Cecily *would* attend the banquet. She could not be sure — would Cecily risk revealing herself? Would anyone else even recognise her if she did? Only a handful of people in the keep had met Cecily when the Barden family had visited; with luck none of them would recognise her with her short hair and bruised face.

'Yes,' Jo said, keeping her eyes low. 'I suppose I can.'

'But you must ensure you entertain Lord Adam, too,' Ros added. 'He *is* a good match, Johanna. You make a very fine pair.'

'Of course,' Jo said, placatingly.

Jo was aware that she should take Ros's advice seriously. She was the perfect role model for Jo's future. She had entered a marriage with a stranger happily and dutifully, and if she *had* felt any nervousness about the match, she had never spoken of it: certainly not to Jo. Jo couldn't deny that luck had played into it, too — both Ros and Lord Peter had been enamoured from the first time they had laid eyes upon each other.

Jo had felt no such connection with Lord Adam. Nor, for that matter, any of the men who wanted to win her hand. The only one who sparked anything within her was William Dale — and that was a thought she was trying to ignore. Besides, many marriages that began as a union with a stranger blossomed over time into real, genuine feeling.

It would take *work*, and she supposed in that sense she *was* lucky: she enjoyed work, and was good at it. Growing to care for Lord Adam was just another task delegated to her, one at which she was determined to succeed.

It wasn't as if there were anyone else she *wished* to marry. She was not like Isabelle, pulled away from a true love and forced to marry another.

Jo was thankful for that. She had *seen* the ruin that came in the wake of love. Leo had fallen in love with a servant and was now as good as dead. Penn's more tumultuous affections – ones which were not just improper, but *dangerous* – had nearly killed the man to which his heart really belonged *and* had caged him, taking him away from her forever. Penn, at least, was happier now – but Jo could only assume that Leo really *was* dead. It was not worth it.

Jo prided herself in her ability to control her own feelings, managing them as effectively as she did her late father's keep. It was a skill she had learnt even before her mother had died, and one that she had learnt *from* her, as well. Any unsuitable feelings – anger, grief – were buried, forgotten, and forced into nothing. Part of her worried if she would even be able to recognise love when it *did* come after a lifetime of ignoring any feeling stronger than polite acceptance.

Finally ready, Jo headed into the great hall to stand beside her brother as he greeted each person entering the room. Many of them congratulated him on the success of the tournament. Ellis only laughed as Isabelle and the steward graciously accepted their thanks with dutiful smiles. No one passed similar praise on to Jo.

The only people who acknowledged her properly were allies who had known her since she was a babe, and Lord Adam, who bowed low and kissed her hand.

Ellis took to the task of welcoming guests fairly well, enjoying the novelty, but soon he grew tired of the parade of strangers, keen to get on with the far more engaging matter of eating. She watched as Isabelle gave his hand a squeeze behind his back, where no one else would see it.

She felt a pang of grief. She wished that *her* mother could have been at her side, holding her hand. Ros was seated at her own table, too far away to bring her any comfort. She remembered Leo's promise to look after her. If he were here, he would have put an arm around her shoulder and told her to be strong. Were it *Penn* at her side, he would have been whispering in her ear all night with gossip about their guests, or, more likely, teasing her about Lord Adam. She would have felt less alone for either of them. She would have given all she had for both.

She stared around the packed hall, hands clutched in front of her. It was so *loud*. The room was hot and crowded, full of bodies and noise. Dogs lounged on the floor or begged at their masters' feet, musicians lingered in corners plucking at their instruments, and servants sped to and fro carrying jugs of wine and ale, dancing between each other.

Jo scanned for Cecily among the press of people, but she had not appeared.

Trying not to let herself worry, Jo attempted to enjoy the banquet. The servants brought out great dishes of food, the tables groaning under the weight of it: whole roasted pigs, swans with elegantly twisted necks, tiny plucked birds, bowls of wine-soaked pears garnished with nuts. When the cook led in a serving girl carrying a whole peacock to the top table with its feathers in full display, Ellis gasped in delight.

Even Jo could not help but appreciate the feast, especially when a platter of blanched almond fritters was placed in front of her, glistening with a honeyed wine sauce. Almond fritters had been a favourite of hers for as long as she could remember. They had been the cause of her one and only youthful indiscretion, when Leo had goaded her into stealing a batch of them from the kitchens. The guilt of the crime, which had made her stomach lurch and her heart race, had been soothed by their honey-drunk laughter as they'd demolished the whole plate under a tree on the edge of Hartswood Forest.

As she licked the sauce from her fingers, peering around, she realised that Cecily had not made an appearance. Fear began to gnaw at her. What if she had been so badly injured that she was not able to attend? What if it had been worse than even Jo had feared, and she was out there, alone, and—

She tried to swallow that thought down. The meal took an *age* to finish, and by the time it was finally over and Cecily *still* hadn't arrived, Jo was so nervous that her leg was bouncing beneath the thick wooden table.

She cleaned and replaced her eating knife to her belt just for something to do. She had owned the knife since she was a girl – carved from bone with a dainty heart punched through the handle – and was very fond of it, if only because it had been with her so long. She fiddled uselessly with her plate and empty goblet, wishing there was more she could do; any way to keep herself occupied.

Taking her leave from Ellis, she rose to her feet. She would have to engage with her guests and betrothed, no matter how anxious she was. Perhaps that would go some way to distracting her. Several men asked her to dance – including Lord Adam, who looked in fine spirits, and even, to her great surprise, Sir Lanval, who did not.

But still her fear grew. She refused any further dances, unable to concentrate on her feet, her legs unsteady. She lingered at the side of the hall, watching the others laugh and celebrate.

She could not wait any longer. Cecily was not coming.

Jo could sneak away. She could even go through the kitchens and find food to take to Cecily, too: she was just as much a competitor as any of the other knights, and as such she deserved their hospitality.

At the top table, Ellis was playing with a handful of peacock feathers. Isabelle was dancing with Marshal Brice. Lord Adam was absent: he must have retired outside with his men to catch some air. It was as good a chance as any. She slid from the hall and down the empty corridor beyond, making her way to the kitchens.

A sudden, raised voice caught her ear. Just ahead was a rarely used side room. The door was slightly ajar.

'—nothing to worry about, I have told you.'

She recognised that voice. It was Lord Adam.

Jo took a single, silent step back, pressing herself against the stone. She shouldn't be listening.

'You *told me* you had it in hand—'

'I did. I *do*. I swear it, Lanval. He is not even here! He is no true suitor if he has not even shown his face at this feast.'

'I know. I know! But his presence at the tournament is enough to unsettle things. I will not have our plans ruined because of some green boy who has decided to try to woo the nearest available lady!'

'Our plans are *not* ruined. The match has been made. There is *nothing* to fear from the boy.'

It was obvious what they were talking about. *Who* they were talking about. Jo swallowed back the surge of fear she felt at being spoken about so casually – about her *marriage* being spoken about as if it were a secret, conspiratorial thing. She needed to focus on finding Cecily and making sure she was not too badly hurt. Lord Adam – whatever he was planning – would have to wait. She would have a lifetime married to him in which to find out.

Yet she could not force her feet to move as the argument continued.

'You are too trusting, Adam. He—'

'—is not here!' Lord Adam shouted. 'He is *wounded*. No doubt he is preparing to slink back to whichever northern kingdom he hails from. We have *nothing* to fear from him. Lanval. I need you to trust me.'

A long pause. 'I do trust you. But what about *her*? You *know* she sent him a gift. And everyone has been saying that he is wearing her favour!'

Acid rose up Jo's throat. She nearly choked on it.

'It does not matter,' Lord Adam said, coolly. 'I ensured she did not seek him out after that fall, and with any luck by the morning he'll have returned home. She will never see him again. Johanna is just as keen to be wed as I am, you know that. She needs this marriage. The whole family does.' There was a small yet heavy silence. 'I will ensure she agrees to a speedy match. William will be forgotten. He is merely an *amusement*.'

'But I don't—'

'Lanval.'

Jo's hands shook. She thought of Lord Adam. The wealth he possessed, the land under his rule, the power he wielded. The power he would *need* to wield to maintain it, and the power he already had without her even knowing. He had insisted on the housekeeper staying with her. He must have sent Ros to her too, knowing she would not leave her be.

She thought of the meals they had shared, and for a brief, terrible moment his face contorted into that of her father's.

'Come. They will have noticed our absence. If we can—'

The door burst open. Jo jumped back, but there was nowhere to flee: Lord Adam had already seen her.

'My Lady?' He looked pale.

'Why are you not at the feast?' Sir Lanval's words were clipped.

'I—' Jo needed an excuse. *Any* excuse. She thought of Cecily, and of Isabelle's proposition. 'I received a letter—' she spluttered, the lie hot on her tongue. 'There was a rider—'

'This late?' Sir Lanval looked suspicious.

Jo bundled up the fear in her chest and let it spill over. She took a shaking step forward. Both men looked alarmed.

'It was from Dunlyn,' she continued. 'Where they are keeping my brother. He has been taken ill, but they do not say if he is wounded, or if it is a sickness . . .'

She had never lied like this before. She had concealed truths or hidden secrets, but never lied so boldly. She tapped into what she knew: her love for her brother, her desire to return to Dunlyn, and her horrible fear that something awful had happened to Cecily without her there to stop it. She released a single, choking sob.

Guilt clouded Sir Lanval's face, the expression deepening as Lord Adam pushed him aside to take Jo's hands.

'My apologies, my Lady. Are you all right?'

She shook her head. She desperately hoped that Lord Adam would not question her further – she had no idea if she could maintain the lie.

'I – I simply need some time to decide what I must do, my Lord. I cannot enjoy the celebrations while I do not even know if he is well.'

'Of course.' He was treating her kindly, but the overheard conversation was still ringing in her ears. 'Do you need escorting to your chambers?'

No. She could not allow him to trap her again.

'That is extremely gracious, my Lord, but I will manage. Please, do enjoy the feast.'

She gave him her best, quivering smile. He squeezed her hands once more, bowed towards her, and with another farewell headed back towards the sounds of the hall and the feast, Sir Lanval close behind. Jo waited until their footsteps had died away before finally allowing herself to breathe, then rushed on towards the kitchens.

They were busy, as she had expected, but thankfully no one questioned her sudden arrival. The cook was distracted, and a maid was more than happy to assist her as she quickly packed a basket with food. She paused before snatching up a bottle of wine, too, placing it in amongst the rest. With a word of thanks to the maid, she hurried on.

She was nearly through a rarely manned side door when there was a voice.

'Johanna!'

Her first, horrible thought was that Lord Adam had changed his mind and would insist on escorting her to her rooms after all.

But as she spun, the basket gripped in white-knuckled hands, she saw Isabelle standing in the darkness. She was alone. Isabelle ran forwards, skirts gripped in her hands.

'Johanna, are you all right? I have just spoken to Lord Adam, and he—'

She spotted the basket in Jo's hands. She paused. She treated Jo to a long, hard, penetrating stare. Jo had been able to lie to Lord Adam not easily, but surely. She would not be able to do so with Isabelle.

'He told me there was a letter from Dunlyn. But he was mistaken, wasn't he?'

Jo felt a surge of guilt. 'I – I had to ensure he did not follow me.' She swallowed. 'Or stop me. I did not—'

Isabelle smiled. 'I should have known this would happen.'

'My Lady?'

'Just to see you talk to him would make one suspect,' Isabelle said, 'but the sword? And the *favour*? And do not deny them – there is very little that gets past me in this keep. I doubt you even realised it yourself, Johanna. I have never known you to act so unthinkingly.'

Isabelle's words were chastising, but there was a smile on her face.

'I remember myself, so long ago . . .' She sighed. Jo watched, as her expression turned wistful. 'I always tried to be sensible, but he made me be so *rash*. All he had to do was look at me, and there was this *feeling*—' She pressed her hand to her heart. 'It was like I was drowning, but burning, too, like there was a *beast* in my chest, clawing to get out.'

Isabelle caught herself, lowering her hand.

'I am not reprimanding you,' she said. 'To do so would make me a hypocrite. Merely . . . advising more caution. At least I've realised

how wrong I was to suggest your suitor was one of the Barden sons.'
She came to stand beside Jo, voice just a whisper. 'Now I have seen
him, it is quite clear that he is neither of them. Did you know he
was coming?'

Oh. Jo's apparent northern lover. Isabelle looked very pleased
with herself.

Jo froze. 'I . . . did not.'

It was not entirely a lie. She had no idea that Cecily would be
forcing her way into the tournament. The rest, she told herself,
was irrelevant.

'Was he very badly hurt?'

'I think . . . quite badly, yes.'

Isabelle looked sombre for a moment. 'Then you should go to
him.'

'I – what?'

Isabelle glanced at the basket in Jo's hands. 'Go to him,' she
repeated. 'I will ensure your absence is not missed. What did you
tell Lord Adam? I must be aware if he asks too many questions . . .'

It was another kindness. Jo didn't know what she'd done to
deserve it, and felt guilty at misleading her stepmother so blatantly.
But she had no way of telling if she would even be allowed such
lenience if Isabelle knew the truth, or how terribly wrong her
assumptions were. She had become lost in her own happy memories
of love – ones which Jo could barely understand, let alone share.

She hastily explained the story about a letter from the north.
When she had finished, Isabelle laughed.

'At least this is a better way to ensure you will be able to visit
Dunlyn again before you are wed,' she said. 'No man could deny
his wife visiting her sick brother.'

Jo had not even considered that. She'd spoken without thinking, desperate to make Lord Adam leave.

'Thank you,' she breathed. 'Truly, Isabelle, I—'

Isabelle gave a smothered laugh. 'There is no time! Go!' She practically shooed Jo away. 'But be *quick*. I do not know how long I can delay your husband.'

Jo gave her a tight smile before slipping through the side door and out across the courtyard. She headed not towards the gatehouse, but the smaller entry used by staff, then into the camp that stood around the edge of the keep. It was almost entirely deserted as she crept through it.

In the low moonlight, she could see a shield painted with stars leaning against a tent. There was a light flickering inside.

Jo moved the basket to her other hand, readying herself. This was dangerous. If she was caught seeking out the Knight of Stars, her reputation would be ruined. If they were *both* caught, Cecily could face punishment.

But she had not appeared for the feast. She was wounded, and had vanished, and she *needed* her. And – Jo would not forget – she had chosen Cecily as her champion, regardless of her match with Lord Adam. She owed her this.

She approached the tent and peered around into the darkness. She was alone.

She edged closer, brushing the tie of the canvas with her fingertips.

'Cecily?'

Chapter 9

Lily froze. The damp cloth in her hand oozed bloodied water, dripping pink rivulets where she tended to the cut across her arm.

' . . . Jo?'

The canvas was wrenched aside. Jo, framed in darkness, stared down at her.

'Cecily.'

In the shadows, Lily couldn't read Jo's expression. She thought of the moments they had shared while Lily had worn someone else's name – the laughter, the moment in the field, the *favour*.

'Jo—' She finally found her tongue, dropping the linen to the ground and struggling to her feet. 'Jo, I—'

She took a desperate, hasty step forward. Too hasty: her legs gave out beneath her. She staggered forwards.

'Cecily!'

She had been ready for another collision with the hard ground. Instead, she was caught in Jo's arms.

Leaning against Jo, she allowed herself to be moved back to the pallet and lowered down. Jo placed a basket beside her, then hurried to the flap of the tent and tied it shut. She looked down at Lily with an expression of panic.

'Are you all right?'

Lily nodded, although her head throbbed and her chest was squeezing horribly.

'I am,' she breathed through the pain.

'I thought—' In the flickering rushlight inside the tent, Lily could see Jo's face, now. Fear, raw and real, scarred her face. 'I was so scared, Lily, I thought . . .' She choked on her words. Guilt rose in Lily's chest.

'Jo, *no*, I am—' Her ribs jarred as she twisted on the pallet, but she forced the lie through anyway. 'I am fine, truly. Just . . . cuts and bruises. I am *all right*.'

Jo stared down at her for a long moment. Finally, her shoulders slumped.

'You could have been *killed*,' she said, defeated. 'I know you said you wanted to ride in a tourney, but I never thought you would actually *enter*.'

'I *had* to!'

'Whatever *for*?' Jo cried. 'For pride? Because you wanted it so much?'

'No! I came to – to—'

'To *what*?'

Saying it out loud for the first time, to the woman for whom she had made this choice, Lily suddenly felt very foolish.

'To save you,' she finished quietly. 'From being forced to marry.'

Jo stared at her, aghast. '*What?*'

'Your last letter—'

'What of it?'

'You said . . .' Lily hesitated. Her conviction that Jo's last missive had been a cry for help faltered for the first time. 'That is, I *thought* . . .'

'Thought *what*?'

'I thought you needed me. You said you hoped to see me again, and it was clear you are being forced to wed, and I thought . . . I had to stop it. I had to *help*. I could not let you suffer through it alone, not if I could prevent it.'

'What in God's name did you intend to do? Enter and win the tourney, and . . . what, Cecily? You could not have offered me your hand.'

Lily sniffed. Under Jo's scrutiny, her weak plan seemed even more fragile.

'Cecily, *no*—' Jo caught her guilty expression. 'You did not *truly* think you could?'

'No!' The force of the word made Lily's ribs grind against each other. She gritted her teeth. 'I . . . I simply thought, perhaps if I *won*, or even just made the others look foolish, then the scandal of having to allow a nameless knight to marry you would be so great that in the chaos I could, um—'

It *had* been a foolish plan. She'd done it anyway. She remembered lamenting her uncertainty of Jo's own romantic preferences. When Jo glared down at her like *that*, she thought she knew. That expression – all frustration and incredulity and *anger* – made Lily wonder how Jo could even tolerate her as a friend, let alone anything more. But she had to keep talking, had to try to make Jo *see*, at least, and not push her aside.

'I hoped I could free you from this. I'd reveal myself to you and whisk you away and you would be *free*, Jo. And no one else would even have to know that I had been here.'

Jo stared at her in horrified disbelief. 'You did not *truly* believe that would work?'

Lily forced a shrug. 'I thought it might. You must admit that I unsettled things.'

'That much I *can* agree with.' Jo sighed. 'But *this*? This is madness! If you had been caught, you would have been punished, and if you'd been injured more severely—' She took a steadying breath. 'Either could have led to your death. You could have been killed! What about your *family*, your brothers? What about—' She cut herself off again. 'What about *me*, Cecily?'

The guilt returned, churning Lily's insides.

'I just wanted to help you achieve your freedom,' she said, quietly.

'You wanted me to achieve *your* freedom!'

'Jo—'

'I am not like you! I do not want the same things you do! You have found freedom, and I am glad that you have, and I am glad that it brings you happiness, but you *must* understand: that is *your* freedom. Not mine.'

'Being forced into a marriage you do not want is no freedom.'

'I am not being *forced* to marry Lord Adam.'

'But you admit that it is not what you want.'

Jo shook her head.

'What I *want*? Cecily, I want a place that is my own. I want to be away from here, and all the awful memories behind these walls. I want to work, and be good at the work I do. I want to be with someone I can trust. I want to be *safe*, from . . . from starving, or illness, or—' She swallowed. 'Or someone like my father.'

'But you do not wish to marry?' Lily pressed, staring up at her.

'You think this is a *choice*? Cecily, what I *wish* is to be safe, and well! Does a lord wish to attend meetings? Does a chamberlain wish to balance books? Does a peasant wish to dig the fields or a farrier wish to shoe horses? Who among us – any of us – would choose a lifetime of work over a lifetime of rest? But that is the way of things, and I have to give myself the best life possible in any way I can. And marrying is how I can achieve that. A farrier does not begrudge the horse. The unwed sister of an earl cannot begrudge marriage.'

Lily could only stare at her. Jo was *wrong* – Lily herself was evidence of that – but she was *furious*, too. And however much Lily wished she could still rescue her from a life she couldn't choose for herself, Lily could sense now more than ever the huge weight of what she had been attempting to do.

More than that – the weight of what Jo was about to do. Lily would rather face down a thousand knights and feel the sharp pain of defeat a thousand times than submit to a marriage. Yet Jo had taken this nightmare and turned it in on itself. It was unspeakably brave. As the pain in Lily's ribs flared she considered how, compared to Jo's choices, the bruises had cost very little.

'You are—' Lily took a breath, staring down at her feet. Still, she did not quite wish to admit that Jo could be right. 'I apologise,' she said instead. 'I didn't . . . I *don't* understand. I can't. But . . . I am sorry.'

It wasn't enough. But to her surprise, Jo gave her a soft, sad smile and then sat beside her on the pallet.

'It was very brave,' she said, in a conciliatory tone that Lily half-suspected she used with Ellis. 'But *unimaginably* foolish.'

Lily snorted through her nose, wincing as the movement jarred her ribs.

'Perhaps. I did not even do what I set out to achieve,' she said. 'You *are* still being married off.'

'I am.'

Lily stared down at her fingers. There was a horrible churning in her gut that was little to do with her injuries.

'I suppose you will be very happy with *Lord Adam*,' she said bitterly. 'I hear that the women in court find him very handsome.'

Jo pursed her lips. 'I suppose? I cannot say I have noticed. Ros has been telling me how *fair* he is but—' She shrugged. 'He is just . . . a man. I know I should feel *passionate* about my husband, yet . . .' she trailed off, eyes low. 'Perhaps, with time . . .'

She looked terribly unsure. More unsure than Lily had ever seen her.

'Well, *I* think that he's a buffoon,' she said boldly, shooting her a look from the corner of her eye.

Jo peered at her. Her lip was twitching. 'Oh?'

'I admit that I would not approve of *any* man you were forced to marry, but Adam seems particularly irksome. He did not leave me with fair feelings after the joust.' Lily shook her head. 'I feared that he and Lanval had worked out who I am. *What* I am. But after I fell . . .' She slumped. 'If he had known I was a woman, he would have revealed me then. I understand now that he thinks I am some grasping, useless boy. But he is supposed to be a *lord*. One would expect better behaviour when approaching an injured man of low rank.'

'Hmm.'

'I suspect,' Lily continued, enjoying the way Jo's smile was growing and puffing out her chest, 'that he was jealous. Which is another trait that goes against him, of course. Perhaps he realised he was in the presence of one who could best him on the field.'

Jo gave a true laugh at that.

'Be serious,' she said. 'You could not defeat him.'

'We will never know,' Lily said with an exaggerated sigh, her hand placed over her heart. 'As he is too cowardly to fight me, and I—' She paused. It hurt to acknowledge the defeat so plainly. 'I must return home. I cannot compete like this.'

Her shoulders slumped. Even *that* small movement made her wince, and she gasped as her chest throbbed, her hand wrapping around herself instinctively. Jo leapt forwards, hands hovering over Lily's arms – not quite touching.

'Cecily—'

'It is nothing. Just – just a twinge.' She breathed carefully through her mouth. There was a sharp, hot pain above her eyebrow once more.

'Oh—' Jo looked shocked. 'You are bleeding, wait—'

She must have reopened the cut above her eyebrow. Jo shuffled closer, reached into the expensive-looking pouch hanging at her hip, and then... she laughed. It was a low, quiet sound, barely more than a puff of air. Before Lily could ask what had amused her, she pulled out what she had found.

She was holding the handkerchief, the one that she had sent to Lily after the duel. She rubbed the silk between her fingers.

'It does not feel right for me to keep this,' she said finally, as if surfacing from deep thought.

Lily watched her carefully, but said nothing.

'It is *yours*, after all. I gave it to you, whatever my arrangement with Lord Adam.'

There was a sour twist to the end of that statement. It made Lily's heart beat faster, and she held back a cocky smile. Before she could speak, Jo appeared to have made a choice.

'Here.' She thrust the handkerchief towards her. 'Take it. Please. *You* earned it, no one else.'

Lily did. She knew that she should refuse and hand it back – Adam and the rest had been right, it *was* too precious a token for a knight-errant – but, God above, she wanted it: especially if this was the last gift Jo would give her before she wed.

She held it carefully between her fingers, as if it were made of spider web. The silk looked like it belonged in her hands, even though her knuckles were scuffed and bloodied, her skin mud-stained, her nails bitten-off stubs.

She traced the embroidery with one finger. She wanted to shove the handkerchief beneath her tunic and press it against her heart. Keep it there, forever.

'Thank you,' she muttered, not trusting herself to say much else. She had to push that feeling down. She had to *smother* it, lest it set her alight. 'But—' She looked up, catching Jo's eye. She, too, looked a little lost. Lily swallowed. 'What *is* it?'

'*Excuse me?*'

'Is it a cow?'

'It is a deer!'

Lily looked again at the misshapen brown blob.

'Jo,' she said, spluttering out the words, 'you are good at a great many things, and far more skilled than I at even more, but—'

'*But?*'

'It has too many legs!'

'That is a *tail!*'

Lily peered at it. 'Do deer have such long tails?'

'If you hate it so much I shall just have to take it back.' Jo huffed, although her eyes were sparkling.

'Oh, no.' Lily teased, holding the handkerchief to her chest. 'You gave it to me, it is *mine*. Your five-legged deer will protect me, I am sure of it.'

'I am lucky that my Knight of Stars is *you*,' Jo said, the words spat out with no malice at all. 'A lord or knight would have laughed at me if I had given them such a thing.'

Lily smiled, trying to stamp out the spark that had ignited in her chest when Jo had called her *mine*.

'A lord or knight would not know fine embroidery if it was stitched into his own backside,' she countered. 'And he would be too desperate to court you to tell you that your deer resembles a plague-stricken cow. That would *certainly* not win your goodwill.' She tucked the handkerchief into the pocket of her breeches. 'You are deeply unlucky to have gifted this to the only competitor who knows anything about embroidery at all.'

Lily pushed her hair from her eyes as Jo laughed. As she did, she realised the cut above her eye was still weeping.

'Ah—'

Jo noticed, too. 'Oh, Cecily, I had forgotten . . .' She grabbed the linen that Lily had been tending her arm with, examining it. 'Have you anything *clean* in here?'

Lily gestured with her head towards her pack. Jo quickly found a scrap of fresh fabric, dampening it and then advancing upon her.

'This could be worse,' she mumbled. 'But we'll need to see to the rest of them, too. Turn this way . . .'

Lily did as she asked. 'Thank you,' she said, keeping her eyes low. 'And—'

Jo hesitated, her fingertips warm against Lily's temple. 'Yes?'

'For God's sake, Jo. Call me Lily. Please?'

She could hear Jo swallow.

'Of course,' she said. 'Now, *Lily* . . . hold still.'

✳

Lily's skin was warm, patched in mingling reds and purples. Jo gently wrapped a linen strip around the cut on her arm, careful not to press too hard. In truth, the cut was not all that deep, but it felt important to keep her hands busy.

It was that, or cry. The fear that Lily had been wounded had coalesced horribly into anger at her plan, a feeling easier to hold and wield. Now she felt strained, as if she were a sodden sheet pulled taut and wrung out.

The tingling that had erupted in her fingertips and surged down her arms when Lily had taken her hand filled her, now. It swirled in her chest, emanating from the place where her palms brushed Lily's bruised skin.

'You *really* did all this for me?' she said at last.

Lily shrugged, nose crinkling. 'Of course.'

Her voice was far too casual. It didn't match the bruises that spread across her back and disappeared beneath the collar of her tunic, or the rattling noise that came from her chest when she breathed too deeply.

'I wish you would see the physician,' Jo said, leaning back.

'I cannot,' Lily countered. 'I would be immediately discovered.'

'So what will you do?'

Lily lowered her gaze.

'I am going home. I must leave and hope I can make it to Dunlyn Castle without further harm.'

Jo considered this for a moment. It was too risky.

'Tomorrow morning I shall return for you with one of my dresses, and we can go to the physician together. He doesn't know who you are. We can claim you are a . . . a lord's sister, or a lady's maid.'

Lily laughed, then hissed as the movement jarred her chest. 'And be subject to his questioning about how a lord's sister was so wounded?'

'We could say you and a few other girls had decided to walk towards the nearest town while your fathers were distracted. Claim that you were beset by bandits – that would make sense, as the tournament has drawn so much attention – and that your friends ran but you were attacked.'

'And you think no one will question that? Or the physician?'

Jo shrugged. 'We may have to send some men into the forest on a pointless hunt. They'll return empty-handed, of course, but we can spare them. And Alsen . . .' She drummed her fingers against her knees. 'I trust him to be discreet. He tended to Raff, after all, and I am *sure* he must have noticed what was happening between him and Penn.'

Lily seemed unsure. 'Jo . . .'

'*Please*, Lily. For my own peace of mind, if not your health.'

'I . . .' Lily looked at her. She held her gaze. Relented. 'Very well,' she said, sounding like a put-out child. 'I suppose you are correct. But I think you are worrying unnecessarily.'

'Then it's set,' Jo said, going to stand. 'Tomorrow we will—'

Lily grabbed her arm. 'Wait—'

Jo hesitated.

'Please . . . stay? Just for a while? Eat with me, at least. Or must you go back?'

Jo thought of the celebrations waiting for her. She had told

Isabelle that she would only be gone for a moment, but she was likely so distracted that she would not notice her absence. And Lord Adam would be too busy with Sir Lanval and their conspiratorial whisperings to care.

'I can stay a little while.'

The food Jo had managed to beg from the kitchen was good, the meat cold but rich, and cooked enough to be falling from the bone. There was more than enough for them both, and Lily was adamant that Jo share some of the feast.

Wounds tended to, Lily had slipped back to the buoyancy that Jo had grown so familiar with – and so fond of – during her brief stay at Dunlyn Castle.

'I cannot believe you made it so far without being discovered,' Jo said, giving the wine a sip. 'You must have ridden for *days*.'

Lily shrugged. 'I did. But I was alone for most of the way, and I am well-practised at sleeping outside so I could avoid inns and rest stops. *And*,' she continued, ripping off a hunk of bread and shoving it into her mouth, 'I taught myself how to piss standing up.'

Jo snorted on her mouthful of wine, coughing as she attempted to regain her composure. 'Lily!' she choked out, finally, as Lily thudded her on the back.

'What?' Lily said, clearly enjoying herself. 'It was a crucial skill for the journey.'

'You said you travelled most of the way alone,' said Jo, wiping her mouth.

'Yes,' Lily agreed, '*yet* I was not always alone, and nor could I guarantee I would always be.'

Jo shot her a shrewd look. 'I think you taught yourself simply to say you could. As a *challenge*.'

Lily smirked. 'Perhaps.'

'And what of the tournament? Did no one question you?'

Lily shook her head, mouth full. 'They did not,' she said, voice muffled, before swallowing. 'I have been told *dozens* of times that I am too young to compete, but no one has even suggested I may not be what they think I am.'

'I suppose none of them would dare to think that a woman could defeat them so easily.'

'That is precisely it. They'd rather think me a wyvern than a woman.'

'You have done extremely well. For all your talk of *rescuing me* . . . you have enjoyed it, I am sure.'

Lily grinned at her. 'Of course I have enjoyed it. I have never felt anything like it before: the thrill of it. I am beaten and battered and I have bruises in unspeakable places but, my God, Jo: I have loved each moment. Had I not been wounded, I would have continued until they threw me from the grounds.'

'But it is so dangerous!'

'Exactly!' Lily's eyes sparkled. 'It's *incredible*. Did you never watch your brothers sparring and attend your father's tournaments and wish that was *you* out there?'

Jo stared at her. She thought of Henry and Leo's play fighting. She thought of the boy and his broken neck.

'No.'

'Truly? Never?'

'No!'

Not for the first time, Jo was aware of the gulf between them: an impassable difference.

'You are *mad*,' she said, fondly.

'*And* I am your champion,' Lily countered. 'And you cannot deny I am skilled. I won that tilt, after all.'

Jo raised her eyebrows. 'That is not how I recall it,' she said. 'Or is lying flat on your back and bleeding *winning*, now?'

Lily continued undeterred. 'My opponent fell first. I fell soon after, I grant you. But he fell first.'

'And does that count as a win?' Jo said, clearly unconvinced. 'Surely that is a draw?'

'*He fell first*,' Lily repeated. 'I won.'

'You are as stubborn as you are reckless,' Jo said. 'Fine, then. You won. Does that make you happy?'

'It does.' Lily grinned. 'Although I have been cheated of a prize.'

Jo was suddenly aware of how close they were sitting on the small pallet bed. Their legs and hips were pressed together, their arms linked where they had traded food and drink so often.

'Lily . . .'

She turned. Lily's face was only a hand's width from her own.

'Yes?' Her breath was tinted with wine and meat.

'I – that is—'

There was a noise from beyond the tent. It was so quiet that she could have missed it – but something about it made the hairs on the back of Jo's neck stand on end.

'Did you hear that?'

Lily glanced at her. 'Hear wh—'

There it was again. Louder. And then – a sniff, quickly stifled.

Lily threw herself across the tent to grab her gambeson, pulling it back on over her undershirt. She tied it tight, obscuring her figure. Now Jo knew her, it was impossible to think she was anything other than a young woman, but likely only she would be able to see that. Being caught in the private tent of William Dale, the Knight of Stars, unknown man with no retinue and no familial name, could ruin her.

'I cannot be seen here,' she whispered. 'I must—'

Lily scuttled towards the back of the tent in silence, then lifted the canvas. Jo immediately realised what she was doing, and scrambled beneath it, sliding on her knees across the dirt. The tent was close to the keep, and she stood to face the thick outer wall, heart thundering.

The celebrations were continuing inside, the sound muffled by the stone. She took a breath to steady herself, then crept around the side of the tent.

There was a man lurking just in front of it, the gloom obscuring his figure. When he glanced around, Jo caught a glimpse of a pair of dark eyes hidden beneath a low hood.

She swallowed.

She should head back to the keep. Run the other direction on light feet and return tomorrow morning ready to sneak Lily to the physician. But something compelled her to stay.

The figure hadn't called out or made his presence clear. He just *stood*, as if waiting for something. Jo hoped that he was just another knight – a lost man, likely drunk, trying to find his own tent.

And then he moved into the moonlight. His surcoat flashed red and yellow.

Jo *knew* those colours. She had seen them, she was sure, not hours ago. And then she remembered the joust, the argument, the disapproving faces of Lord Adam and Sir Lanval. The eye-catching clothes the Wyck retinue wore. She heard Sir Lanval's voice in her head once more: *I will not have our plans ruined because of some green boy.*

He stepped forwards.

Jo reacted without even thinking. It was a white, blank blur as she grabbed the bone-handled knife strapped to her hip and leapt.

The man yelled. Lily's startled, pale face appeared through the flap of the tent, just as the man groaned and toppled forwards into the canvas.

'Jo . . .' Lily gasped, throwing herself to her side.

'He was going to—' Jo was shaking. Her lungs constricted. She couldn't breathe. Her throat was closing and her mouth was dry and she *couldn't breathe.* 'Lily— What have I *done?*'

The man sprawled facedown at her feet, groaning, wrapped in the quickly staining canvas. At least he was alive, she thought, vaguely. At least she wasn't a murderer. Her ears rang as her hand, hot and wet, slid on the hilt of her knife.

She thought of the lash and the cell. Lord Adam's face. Her father's.

The knife slipped from her grip.

Chapter 10

Blood was spreading across the canvas of Lily's tent. Jo was frozen to the spot, her face a stony picture of shock, staring at the man tangled in the sheet.

'What *happened?*'

Jo finally looked up. 'I—' Her voice shook. 'He was looking for you,' she managed at last. 'He – he was *waiting* out here, and I—' She took a breath. Tears shimmered on her cheeks. 'I did not even *think*. I didn't—' Jo stared down at the blood on her hand as if seeing it for the first time. '*God*, Lily—'

'*Why?*' The word was out of Lily's mouth before she could stop it.

Jo stared from her hands to the man. 'His colours . . .' she muttered.

The man groaned from the floor. It was too dark to really see, but—

'Red and – yellow, is that? I do not—'

'Red and gold. Lord Adam's colours. I should have *known*—'

It was like ice slipping down Lily's back – like a handful of snow shoved down her tunic. She took a hasty, automatic step back. She was well aware that she had earned the ire of Adam, but *this?* It was unthinkable. He must have decided that Lanval's threat in Hartswood had not been enough.

He was *correct* to think that. Jo was to be his wife, but she was *here*, in the darkness, with Lily. Jo had stabbed one of her would-be husband's men for her.

But Jo would be safe. She had the protection of her brother and stepmother, and besides: she was *Jo*. Who in their right mind would believe she could have stabbed a man?

Lily grabbed the new sword, still in its sheath, and quickly strapped it to her belt. She hesitated for only a moment before scooping down and grabbing her pack, the sack in which she had shoved her armour, her helmet and then – after regarding it for a handful of seconds – her shield. She leapt over the fallen knight as she shoved the helmet onto her head.

'I must go.'

Jo came back into herself. 'What?'

'I need to go, before anyone discovers him. Jo, you are the sister of the Earl. You have Isabelle's trust. You are *safe*.' She gave a bitter half-laugh. 'They would not even believe you could do such a thing.'

'But—'

'I cannot be caught. I *cannot*. If they need someone to blame for this – it will be me. Especially given Adam's . . . *distaste* for me.'

Jo took a long breath. Her hands were still trembling, but she straightened her back.

'Come, then.'

Keeping to the shadows, close to the tents, they hurried in the direction of the stables. If they could just reach Broga, Lily could ride out into the darkness and escape.

It was a wild stroke of luck that the stables were empty, save for the gently snorting horses. She found Broga easily, pulling the first saddle she could grab down from the wall and slinging it over the horse's back. Even the effort of that was too much, making her gasp in pain when she raised her arms.

Jo appeared beside her, a bridle gripped in her hands. There was blood on her fingers.

'Thank you—' Lily went to take the bridle, but Jo held firm.

'I am coming with you.'

Lily's heart dropped. '*What?*'

'I am coming with you. I am not letting you ride off into the night while you are so wounded. You will be *killed* if you do not seek help.'

'Then I promise that I *will* seek help.'

'And how can I trust that? I am coming with you, Lily. You cannot very well stop me.'

'But—'

'I will ride with you to the nearest safe town. I will hand you to a physician or a healer *myself*. And then I will return to the keep.'

Lily needed to fight her. But her lungs were burning and her head spinning and she had no way of telling how much time they had. Adam's man would be discovered eventually, or would heave himself from the ruined tent and struggle back to the keep to raise the alarm.

'*Fine*,' she hissed. 'Fine, but – how? Do you intend to steal a horse?'

Jo looked around nervously. 'If I must. I have already—' She gave a high, startling laugh, then clamped her hand over her mouth. She took a breath. 'I *stabbed* a man,' she muttered. 'I am already damned. Horse theft is not so great a crime.'

Lily watched Jo choose a horse at random and prepare it.

'Anyway,' Jo continued, 'I will be back in a day at most. I will return the horse. I am merely . . .'

'Borrowing it?'

Jo gave the final strap a tug and turned. Lily could swear she was smiling.

'Exactly.'

✳

Shouting. Far away, the eerie red glow of torchlight bouncing from the tents and walls. Lord Adam's man must have been found.

Jo's heart, at least, had stopped thundering. The churning in her stomach calmed. The memory of it now was like an untouchable dream: the only evidence of it the faint bloodstains still on her hands.

They were taking the longer route from the grounds, but riding the opposite direction to Lily's tent. Any soldiers or guards out on watch were all heading away from them. They rode in strange, heavy silence, both too afraid to speak, moving slowly so as not to attract attention.

Dressed once more in her men's clothes, with her sword at her hip and her shield hanging from one arm, Lily looked again like William Dale. The Knight of Stars. If they *were* caught, it would be ruinous for more than one reason.

Even the horse beneath Jo – an animal she did not know – was tense as they finally passed into the shade of the border of Hartswood Forest and onto the covered path that twisted beneath the trees. They stopped there a moment, listening.

And then, the decision entirely unspoken, they both spurred their horses on into the darkness of the forest.

Jo didn't know how long they rode for. They took the lesser-used roads, and while Jo was familiar with the main routes through the woods she became more lost the deeper they went. When they finally burst through the treeline, she barely knew which direction they were facing, let alone where they were.

Free of the press of the trees on the wide road, they could keep better pace. But the horses were tiring, and soon they were riding side by side, the animals huffing. Lily was sagging in the saddle. Jo could hear her wheezing even over the sound of the horses.

'Lily—'

'I am fine.'

Lily pulled her helmet off. In the darkness, it was hard to see her face, but her hair was sweat-sodden and stuck to her skin. She took a deep breath which caught in her chest, making her cough.

'I am *fine*,' she repeated breathlessly, before Jo could ask.

They rode on. There were many towns nearby, but so turned around, Jo's sense of direction had failed her. She kept one eye on Lily, watching her constantly. She was obviously in pain, and several times Jo feared she might simply fall from the saddle, but on they went.

The darkness sucked at them. Clouds had rolled in, obscuring all but an outline of the moon.

Hours or minutes could have slipped away. Finally, the dark sky began to bruise, the sun threatening to rise. Lily's head was low, shoulders slumped.

They would never reach a town like this. Lily needed to rest her aching limbs and bruised chest. If she collapsed or fell from the horse, Jo would be unable to get her to a settlement alone.

Ahead was a building, merely a shadow in the encroaching dawn, likely a stable or farmstead. Jo couldn't bring herself to care: it looked *safe*, and that was what they needed. Typically, Jo would never have risked something so bold. But Lily needed her, and the fear of discovery and the panic of the bloody crime she had committed was *nothing* compared to that.

She leant from her saddle and grabbed Broga's reins from Lily's unresisting hands, then tugged both horses around. She pulled them into the patch of woodland beside the road and tied them loosely to a tree before urging Lily down from Broga's back. She left Lily's things with the horses, hoping no one would steal them in their absence.

'Come on,' she muttered as Lily wobbled uncertainly beside her. 'We must find you somewhere to rest.'

They approached in silence through a wide, gated yard. There were two buildings: a small cottage, and a larger, barn-like structure. The door to the barn opened easily, and Jo quickly pulled Lily inside before peering around. The air was thick and close and smelt of heat and grains. As Jo's eyes adjusted to the dark, she could see sacks leaning against the walls. To one side were four wide tubs. It was a brewery.

It was as good a place as any to rest, if just for a few hours. A brewery this size meant there must be a town nearby. Hopefully in the dawn light Jo would better recognise where they were.

She pushed Lily into the far corner behind a stack of crates, then after only a little searching she found a tub of water and a hefty wooden tankard. She passed it to Lily with such haste that water sloshed over the sides and down her fingers, before shuffling in beside her.

For a long while, neither of them spoke, Jo pressed against the wall and Lily drinking until the cup was finally empty.

'Pass me your knife,' Lily muttered when she was done. 'We will need to clean it.'

Jo reached instinctively for her hip. Her knife wasn't there. Renewed panic seized her.

'I – I do not have it. I must have dropped it, *God*—'

Lily leant against the wall. She looked refreshed for the water, although her skin still looked clammy.

'Will they know it is yours?' she asked.

Jo felt as if she was going to vomit. 'A stranger would not,' she said, 'but Isabelle or Ellis would be able to identify it *immediately*.'

She groaned, placing her head in her hands. She had damned herself.

'I should return and hand myself to the guards,' she mumbled against her palms. 'And save them hunting me down.'

'Do *not*,' Lily said, her tone sure even at a whisper. She paused, and shifted slightly. 'If it is found by someone who knows you, that may work in your favour. They will be more likely to deny the knowledge to protect you. Or it could be found by someone who does not know it, someone from the Wyck retinue. Are you *sure* those were Adam's colours?'

Jo shuddered. 'I was.' She swallowed. 'I *am*.'

'Afterwards . . . you said you should have known. Jo, what did you mean by that?'

'I . . . overheard Lord Adam and Sir Lanval. When I left the feast to find you, I heard them talking—' She shook her head wryly. '*Arguing*, really. About me. About the marriage.' She swallowed. 'About *you*.'

Lily stiffened. 'About me?'

'Sir Lanval seemed concerned that your presence could ruin the match, but Lord Adam did not take him seriously. Perhaps they decided that it would be best for the threat to be removed from the tournament entirely.'

'Or Lanval may have acted alone.'

'What?'

Lily paused, then slipped into a story about an encounter with Sir Lanval in the forest. The terror which had been swirling in Jo's stomach solidified, hardening into rage.

'How *dare* he,' she spat. 'Lily, you *know* I value you, and I care for you, but you – but *William Dale* . . . is nobody!'

'That is as I told him.'

'And Lord Adam did not send him to you? He was not acting under his lord's command?'

'He did not seem to be.'

'God . . .' Jo said. 'It would make sense, I suppose. He was far more concerned about your presence than Lord Adam was. What could he have been planning?'

'As you said, he could have been removing the threat.'

'Without his lord's permission? Why? What could Sir Lanval stand to gain from our union?' Lily shrugged, so Jo continued, trying to work it out. 'Lord Adam is newly titled, yes, but it is not as if the family is poor, or risks ruin. They are popular wherever they go. Lanval had no reason to fear his lord's ruin, or for his own position within the household. It doesn't make *sense*, Lily!'

'Perhaps he was attempting to pre-empt his lord's command,' Lily suggested. 'He wishes to remain Adam's favourite, and saw me as a threat. I was wearing your favour when I fell, after all. To do so was an insult to Adam. But Adam is a *lord*, he cannot be seen chasing off knights-errant and wanderers. It would ruin his reputation.'

'So Sir Lanval acted for him?'

Another shrug. 'It seems likely. They are – close?'

'They seem to be, yes.'

'Then perhaps this is not even a knight protecting his lord. This is a man ensuring his friend marries well and achieves happiness.'

Jo stared at her. 'An enormous risk to take for a friend.'

Lily stared back, intensely. 'Indeed.'

Jo finally looked away. 'Even if that *was* the case, it does nothing to lessen my guilt. I might have killed that man.'

'Do not feel guilty.' Lily shuffled closer. 'We have no way of telling what his intentions were. If he *had* meant to harm me . . . you did the right thing.'

'It is not as if I *intended* to hurt him,' Jo muttered. 'I just . . . acted. I did not even think.'

'That is not always a bad thing,' Lily said, thoughtfully. 'You struck him well, but not fatally, and your instincts were correct. Those are keen skills to have if you are attacked. My brother would praise you for them.'

'Wonderful,' said Jo cynically. 'Perhaps *I* am the one who should have sheared off my hair and ridden in the tournament. Tilted for my *own* hand.'

'Hmm . . .' Lily seemed struck with an idea. 'With a little training, that would—' She looked up. Jo stared at her, eyebrows raised, *daring* her to finish that thought. 'Or not!' Lily quickly amended.

Jo shook her head at her. She *wished* she could be like Lily – all boldness and fire. But she wasn't: she was dutiful, and *scared*.

'When you are settled, I will return and set things right . . .' she said. 'I just hope that he is not – that I did not—'

She couldn't finish that thought: couldn't bear to think of herself as a murderer.

'He will not be dead,' Lily said, tone firm. 'Jo, do not allow yourself to think like that. You will be all right. Ellis's rule is *more* than enough to protect you, even if they somehow connect you to the crime.'

Jo clenched her hands tighter. She had never been so lost, so damned by her own behaviour.

'Our family are cursed to be troublemakers,' she said. 'Are we all so burdened? First Leo, then Penn, and now *me* . . .' She took a breath that twisted into a sob. 'I only wished to be *good*, Lily.'

Lily squeezed her hand. 'You are the least troublesome person I have ever met,' she said. 'And you saved my life.'

Jo sniffed, but didn't let go. 'We do not know that.'

Lily held her tighter. '*I* know that. And I shall inform you of it regularly so you remember it. Every day, if I must.'

'But he may not have—'

'You saved my life!' Lily's voice grew louder. 'You saved me with no more than an eating knife!'

'Lily, *hush*—'

'Johanna de Foucart saved my li—'

'Lily!' Jo pressed her palm over Lily's mouth. '*Silence!*' she muttered, although she was suppressing laughter. 'We are supposed to be *hiding*.'

'No one is—' Lily's words were muffled, and she grabbed Jo's hand, forcing her back. 'No one is even here!' she said. 'You should *know* what you did for me. I should shout it from the mountains.'

'You are *mad*.'

'I am *alive*. Because of you.'

Jo relented with a sigh. 'Very well,' she said, shaking her head.

'I cannot compete with your cursed stubbornness. But say what you will, I *did* injure him.'

'And no one will ever know that,' Lily said. 'Aside from *me*.'

They lapsed back into silence. Jo needed to stay awake and alert, but now her heart was calming, she was exhausted. In the gentle warmth of their hiding space, she began to drift.

Lily wriggled closer, trying to get comfortable. When she leant her head on Jo's shoulder, Jo could hear her ragged, shallow breathing.

Jo wrapped an arm around her, and said nothing.

Chapter II

Lily opened her eyes. It was warm, and light, and—

Her heart froze. They were still in the brewery. They must have fallen asleep. She reached for Jo, quietly shaking her awake.

Jo's eyes slid open slowly before she, too, realised where they were. She looked as if she were about to be sick as she stared around in horror, her mouth open in shock.

'What—'

'We fell asleep. We must go . . .'

Lily peered around. The sun had risen, the light filtering through cracks in the roof. Jo reached out and wrapped a hand around Lily's wrist. The touch went some way to calming her, or, at least, it made her heart beat in a way that could help her forget the situation they found themselves in.

In the humid air of the brewery, Lily felt her chest constricting. She was horribly warm: *too* warm, her skin sweaty and her hair plastered to her forehead. It was the enclosed space and the risk of being found. It would make anyone feel unwell. She tried to speak again, but her throat was parched, and all that escaped her lips was a spluttering cough.

Jo was on her in an instant, gripping her shoulders. She examined Lily's face for but a moment.

'Wait there—'

She grabbed the discarded tankard where it lay on the floor, then after a quick look around dashed out of their hiding spot and away. Lily wasn't sure where Jo had found the water the previous night – she had been too tired to focus – and pressed herself against the wall, waiting for her to come back.

'Jo?' Lily shocked herself with how hoarse and crackly her voice was. 'Where have you—'

The brewery door opened. It creaked horribly, and the brewery was suddenly flooded with sunlight.

'—still waiting on the barrels from the keep,' came a woman's voice, 'but we can sort the rest before then . . .'

Lily snapped her mouth shut, pressing herself even harder against the wall, willing herself to somehow meld into the stone. She listened as the woman walked around the room, talking to someone Lily could not see.

'—might have some back here—'

Lily's skin went ice cold. Before she could react, the crate she was hiding behind was shoved aside.

A woman stared down at her, perhaps around thirty years old. She was plump and broad-shouldered, with strong-looking arms and a face reddened by the sun. Her hair burst around her face in fuzzy curls.

She gave Lily a long, assessing look.

'Everything all right, Ma?' came another voice from the other side of the brewery.

The woman spun around.

'Fine, Harry,' she called over her shoulder. 'Do me a favour – can you let the hens out while I work in here? And clean the hen house, too.'

There was a grumble – Harry, apparently, did not relish the

idea of cleaning the hen house – but the brewery door shut again regardless. Finally, the woman turned back.

'So,' she said. 'What have we here?'

Lily didn't think, heaving herself to her knees. Pain flared up and down her side, but she forced it back, ignoring it.

'Please, my Lady, we didn't – we were—' Her words were lost. To tell her that they had been hiding would be to immediately paint them as guilty. 'It is . . . it is complicated, my Lady, we truly do not mean you harm. *Please*—'

'We?'

Lily snapped her mouth shut. The woman hadn't even realised Jo was there. Lily was about to excuse it as a slip of the tongue, when Jo emerged from behind the tub at the other side of the room. She was shaking, the tankard still gripped in her hands. The woman's head snapped around.

'I – I am sorry, my Lady. We did not mean to . . .' Jo's voice faltered, trembling as much as her shoulders.

'*Please*,' Lily begged. 'Please, we were just trying to find somewhere safe. If you would just let us leave, we will do so quickly. You will never know we were here.'

The woman turned back to her, weighing her up. She looked again at Jo. Something softened in her expression; she appeared to have made a decision.

'What's your name, boy?'

Of course. Lily had forgotten her disguise. She straightened her back.

'William,' she said. 'William Dale.' She gestured towards Jo. 'This is my sister.'

The woman gave a slow, silent nod.

'Your sister, is it?'

Lily attempted to draw herself up even taller. 'Yes.'

The woman took a breath. She looked between them.

'Get inside.'

'What—'

'Get inside the house, both of you. And we will discuss what is to be done with you.'

Jo sat stiff and straight-backed at the long kitchen table. She wondered if the brewster was one that the de Foucart keep had employed to ensure there would be beer and ale enough for their many guests. Jo had only ridden out to visit a handful of them herself, which at the time had felt like a failure on her part. Now she was glad for it: it meant that she was unlikely to be recognised.

She'd been expecting the house to be empty, but as the brewster ushered them inside, they came face to face with a lad no more than thirteen years old whose curly hair immediately painted him as her son. He shot them an inquisitive look, but the brewster gave him no time to question them, instead shooing him out to work in the garden at the back of the house.

The bulk of the home in which the family lived was taken up by a single large room – a kitchen and a living space combined. There was a hearth to one end, with tightly woven rush mats upon the floor and a long table in the centre. The shelves on the walls were packed with bottles and jars and little whittled figures – animals and people – and there were herbs hanging from the ceiling to dry. It was a well-loved, lived-in space that smelt slightly of bread and ale.

As they sat at the table, a girl with long dark hair and huge brown eyes had emerged from a side room, with a baby no older than eighteen months toddling behind her — these must have been the brewster's other children.

The home would have been a cosy, familial space if Jo had been able to appreciate it. But all she could feel was fear.

Fear and *anger* simmering behind her stinging eyes. She was so *stupid*. She had been hanging on by a single thread since their flight from the keep, and their discovery had snapped it.

She'd been sent hurtling back between the walls of the castle, to the years of fear and darkness. To her father's shouting, the crack of the lash, the threat, always, that it would meet her skin next. He'd never hurt her in a way that had left a mark — not a *permanent* mark, at least — but often his words were all that he had needed to keep her in line.

All the explanations and arguments and defences she should have mounted to explain her and Lily's impossible situation stuck in her throat. Her words, which were often all she had, died. They fell apart like dandelion seeds, fluttering to nothing.

She *hated* it. She thought she had been rid of that fear. Her hands were *still* shaking, even now with Lily's leg pressed firmly against her own beneath the table.

She had no way of telling what the brewster would do to them — if she would send them away, or hand them over to the authorities, or see fit to punish them herself. Jo balled her hands into tight fists, unthinkingly picking at the loose bit of skin beside her thumbnail.

It wasn't until Lily placed a hand over her own that she realised she had made herself bleed. That too made her feel foolish, and she quickly hid her hands on her lap beneath the table, staring down at the wood.

'So.' The brewster sat herself opposite them, arms folded. 'Runaways?'

Jo swallowed. She looked up. There was something intense about the way the woman was watching her.

Finally, she found her tongue. 'Just travellers looking for somewhere safe to rest.'

The woman raised her eyebrows at them.

'William is wounded,' Jo continued. 'But he was too exhausted for us to reach the next town. Truly, we had only meant to rest a moment, but . . .'

'But?'

'But we fell asleep,' Lily cut in, voice clipped.

Jo winced. That was far too curt, especially when they were at this woman's mercy. But the brewster burst into laughter.

'William, was it?'

Jo glanced at Lily from the corner of her eye. Lily nodded.

'You look as if you've been in a war, William.'

'I *feel* it, too,' Lily replied, smoothly.

'I would ask how you came to be so wounded,' the brewster continued, 'but I fear I will not like the answer. Is that correct?'

Lily gave her a half-hearted shrug, then winced. Jo reacted at once to the motion, reaching out and placing her hand on Lily's arm. The brewster watched them with interest.

'When I was a girl—' she started, then stopped herself. She peered towards the children. The boy was clearly listening to them, although he was pretending not to. She sighed. 'I know what it is to be a runaway,' she said. 'And to be desperate. Your only crime, as far as I can tell, was hiding in my brewery. I will not throw you to the law for stealing a single night's sleep.'

Jo's heart froze in her chest. 'You won't? But we—'

'You what? Slept in my brewery, took a mug of water? It is poor luck alone that meant I found you, and you did no harm to me or mine.'

'. . .Thank you,' Jo breathed. 'You should . . . by all rights, you should turn us in. Or . . . or—' She couldn't get out the words.

'Or worse?' the brewster said, eyebrow raised. 'Punish you myself?'

Jo didn't say anything.

'I will not raise my hand to you,' she said. 'Your brother is wounded, and *you* are shaking like a leaf. I am not going to throw you to the wilds.'

The stone in Jo's stomach didn't disappear, but the weight of it began to lessen. It still felt wrong – like this was a trick, somehow, and soon the kindness would shatter – but she was beginning to calm, the feeling coming back to her hands and toes.

'Thank you, my Lady.'

It was all she could say, her words muttered like a child's.

'Please, call me Mabel.'

Mabel extended her hand across the table, as if to take Jo's. Then she seemed to remember herself, swiftly pulling back.

'Well,' she said, standing quickly as if it had never happened. 'You both look half-starved. Let me see what I can fetch for you to eat.'

Mabel offered them a simple meal of dried meats, bread, and eggs from the chickens in the yard. It wasn't until the plate was placed in front of her that Jo realised she was ravenous.

Mabel sat across the table with the baby on her lap, juggling the child and her own meal. Now they were all sitting together, Mabel finally introduced the children properly. Her son's name was Harry, and the younger girl, who was nine years old, was Matilda. The baby, banging on the table with a wooden spoon, was Nora – apparently the loudest of the little family.

'And is it just you?' Lily asked, far bolder than Jo would have ever dared. 'Or have you a husband?'

Jo stared at her. It was an outrageously candid question, the sort that would have found her swiftly removed from court. But Mabel didn't seem to mind.

'I do.' She laughed. 'Or do you think these little beasts were granted to me by magical means? No, I have a husband. But he is presently . . . away.'

'Away?'

'He has gone to visit his sister,' Mabel explained. 'I own this place, so it is no hardship without him, but I will admit we are wanting for extra hands.'

Lily laughed. 'I can see why.'

'He'll be back soon enough,' Mabel said. 'I expect his return in the next few days, if not sooner.'

There was a slight wistfulness in her tone that Jo didn't miss. It was such an unbidden thing that it made Jo's heart ache; she forgot, sequestered as she was in the keep, that not everyone married for titles and power. It made a pain flare in her chest to know that she would likely never speak of her own husband in such a soft way.

'You sound as if you miss him very much,' she said, aware that she was talking out of turn.

Mabel gave a coy smile, as if caught doing something she should not.

'I do,' she admitted. 'I am eager for his return. It is very odd without him here.'

Silence fell as they ate. It was some time before Mabel spoke again.

'Not to pry,' she said, 'but I have noticed you appear to be travelling light, Johanna. I can fetch a spare dress for you if you need one, I am sure I have some that are suitable.'

'Thank you,' Jo said, chewing on a mouthful of gamey meat. 'That is very—' She hesitated. 'How did you know my name?'

Mabel gave no pause at all as she handed the heel of the bread to the baby to gnaw on.

'I heard William say it earlier.'

Jo froze. She was *sure* that Lily hadn't used her name – certainly not where Mabel could overhear. But Lily was not as cautious as she was, and it could have easily slipped her mind. Or, more likely, she had not even realised the danger of giving Jo's true name in the first place. Lily was so engrossed in her meal – and making faces at the baby – that she hadn't noticed.

'I see,' Jo said, a little stiffly.

'I apologise,' Mabel added, quickly. 'I should have asked, but with the state I found you in I did not want to pry.'

Jo immediately felt guilty.

'It is quite all right,' she said, determined to push the anxiety from her mind. 'But . . . do, call me Jo. I much prefer it, and—' She paused. It was *safer* to be called Jo, when anyone who knew her as *Johanna de Foucart* would be sure to question her involvement with William Dale. 'And—'

'Of course,' Mabel said, before Jo could attempt to further explain herself. She shot a quick look towards Lily. 'I understand.'

Jo blinked. 'Thank you.'

Mabel gave her a smile, before standing. 'I will see to this,' she said, gesturing at their empty plates. 'Harry?'

The pair cleared the table then headed back outside. Jo suspected that Mabel had left to give them some much-needed space, and again couldn't help but wonder why she was being so kind. She voiced her fears to Lily as they sat at the table after Matilda and Nora had gone to play in the yard.

'You fear that she is being *too* kind?' Lily said, aghast. 'Jo, I had never thought you would be so suspicious of someone.'

'I am not *suspicious*,' Jo began, ignoring the snort of disbelief that escaped Lily's mouth. 'Just . . . we are strangers to her and her family! And she has been so *good* to us . . .'

Lily's expression softened. She reached out, taking Jo's arm.

'Kindness is not unusual,' she said, softly. 'I hate that you think it is, Jo.'

Jo wanted to argue. She wanted to deny it – insist that her fears were founded in more than just her own troubled past. Jo was still sure Lily hadn't called her by her full name.

She fiddled with the sleeves of her gown. She tried to relax, attempting to force her limbs to loosen. It was futile, her head racing, her ears still ringing with the sound the man had made when she'd run her blade into his side.

She relented, twisting around, desperate for some familiarity – for some comfort.

'Lily—'

'Jo . . .'

They'd spoken at once. Lily, of course, spoke right over her.

'Oh, come here—'

Lily slung an arm around Jo's shoulder. She winced as she did – she must have pulled one of her injuries – but she didn't relent or back away. Jo stiffened, but Lily was not letting go, and her closeness was as irresistible as the heat of the summer sun.

Jo melted into her, leaning her head against her shoulder with a long sigh.

'What happened to the woman who has been running her family's keep for years, and single-handedly organised and hosted a tournament all while juggling the opinions of a dozen suitors?' Lily said.

'She stabbed a man in the dark.' Jo sniffed.

Lily snorted. 'Oh, *well*,' she said. 'In that case it is reasonable for her to not be herself.'

'What in God's name will become of me?' Jo muttered.

Lily squeezed her tighter. 'I cannot say,' she said at last. 'Perhaps you can decide that yourself, for once.'

It was meant to be reassuring. But now, under the roof of a stranger, it felt far too large a task. Besides, what decision was there for Jo to make? She would ensure Lily found a physician and return to the keep. Within a few weeks, she would be married.

She didn't voice that out loud, knowing that it wouldn't help. It would only leave Lily feeling inadequate, and frustrated with Jo's acceptance of the life Lily had rejected.

She sniffed against Lily's shoulder.

'Perhaps.'

Chapter 12

Lily could have laid her head upon the table and fallen asleep instead of moving on again. She could not believe their luck at being discovered by someone who had seen fit to treat them well, and as she peered around the little home she felt surprisingly safe. She was exhausted, and while she'd been fiercely hungry the food they had eaten had settled poorly in her stomach. Her chest was horribly tight beneath her gambeson. Every time she breathed – which was becoming more of an effort – there was a sharp, stabbing pain in her side that she was doing her best to ignore.

It was another worry she was refusing to heap upon Jo, and part of her resented how accurate Jo's worrying had been. She needed help.

She really *had* been close to falling asleep when Jo spoke, jerking her awake.

'We are being watched.'

Lily sniffed and opened her eyes. Staring at them from a few yards away was an enormous orange cat. It narrowed its yellow eyes at her. It did not move.

'So we are.'

Lily sat up properly with a yawn. The movement made her chest twinge, but Jo was still peering at the cat and didn't appear to have noticed. Lily extended a hand towards it, making the little sounds that she had used to lure the cats in her father's keep.

The cat stood and turned its back on her, walking away. Jo burst out laughing.

'I do not think he wishes to be your friend,' she said.

'Don't mind Gilbert.'

They both turned. Mabel had appeared in the door to the yard, flushed from work.

'He's a foul little man,' she continued, as Gilbert stalked past her legs and outside. 'But he's part of the family. He's supposed to keep the rats out of the barley, not that he seems to know that. Now . . .' She wiped her hands on her apron. 'What can I do for you?'

Jo quickly got to her feet. They needed to move on.

'Thank you for your hospitality, Mabel. But we really must be leaving. We left our horses in the woods and I must take William to a physician. Which is the closest town?'

'Oh—' Mabel seemed surprised. 'The closest is Astmere, but there's a good man in the next town over. I would not recommend the ride, though. It is not a short journey.'

'I am not sure we have much choice,' Jo said. 'William must be seen to.'

'True enough,' Mabel said. 'But please, stay here. I can fetch the physician myself, and William will not be forced to travel.'

Jo glanced at Lily. Lily could tell that she was nervous: that this was another kindness she didn't trust.

'We couldn't force ourselves upon you like that . . .' Jo began.

'You would hardly be forcing yourselves,' Mabel countered, 'if I have invited you to stay.'

Jo's resolve was faltering. Not, Lily could tell, because Mabel had convinced her, but because she was struggling to say no to this person who wielded power over her. She glanced again at Lily, then straightened her shoulders.

'Thank you, Mabel, truly,' she said, 'but we really must move on.'

Mabel's face was unreadable, but she nodded anyway, moving aside so Jo and Lily could make their way outside.

In the middle of the brewery yard, a delivery of empty barrels had just arrived. As they passed, Harry pulled a barrel from the pile. His grip was loose, and before he or anyone else had realised what was happening, he slipped.

Lily didn't think, just leapt forwards, grabbing the barrel just in time to prevent it from crushing him. It should have been an easy weight – she'd often helped in the kitchens, and weeks of training with sword, shield, and lance had strengthened her arms thrice-fold. But it was too much, pain flaring in her chest, squeezing around her lungs.

She dropped the barrel at her feet with a groan, coughing as she fell to her knees beside it. Spots popped in her vision as she struggled to breathe. There was a pressure on her back. A hand.

'Lily . . .'

Jo's voice was low – a whisper only for her, her true name.

She wanted to wave Jo away, to tell her she was fine, but the breath – and so the words – would not come. Her lungs burnt as she took deep sucking breaths that collapsed in on themselves before she could find relief in them.

All she could do was fight it, keeping her eyes shut, trying to breathe around the pain. Finally, the fit subsided, and she slumped in exhaustion against Jo's side.

After a moment, something wooden was pressed into her hands. She opened her eyes. A mug of water.

'Drink,' Mabel commanded. 'We need to get you seen to.'

At first, Jo maintained her resolve that they would ride into town to find the physician themselves, fetching their horses and things. But when Lily attempted to mount Broga, she couldn't even make it into the saddle. She leant against the horse's neck taking shallow, difficult breaths.

Mabel commandeered the horses into the family's stable and Jo and Lily back into the house, sending Harry to fetch the physician. Before he left, Mabel grabbed him, muttering something that Lily didn't catch into his ear.

Once she had seen to everything, Mabel joined them inside. She had a set expression on her face, then gestured for them both to sit at the long kitchen bench. For a long while, she said nothing, bustling about in the kitchen fetching three rough-hewn mugs and a pitcher of fresh ale.

Mabel handed one to Lily, filled it, then sat opposite her with Nora in her lap.

'William,' she said at last. 'I told Harry to be vague with the physician. I did not tell him why. Let him think you are a runaway, or a thief, or a man escaping the law. I do not care. I care that you receive the best treatment you can. So. I am asking you, *not* accusing, or seeking to harm you . . . is there anything you must tell me before he arrives?'

Lily blinked at her. 'What? I do not—'

'You are hurt. Badly.' Mabel drummed her fingers on the table, and her sure expression slipped. She looked as if each word was a question; one she wasn't sure how to voice. 'I am no expert, but

I would wager you've at least one broken rib. When the physician arrives, he will want to examine you. He will want to examine your chest.' Mabel gave her a long, pointed look. 'William. Is there anything you must tell me before he does that?'

Oh. Lily suddenly understood what she was asking. She was still *William*, here. She had forgotten. No wonder Mabel was concerned: the physician would arrive expecting to examine a young man, and instead find *her*. The disguise would fail immediately.

At Lily's silence, Mabel handed Nora to Jo, who took her with a look of abject fear, before turning back to Lily.

'Let me tell you of a woman I used to know. Lived down the way—' Mabel gestured with her head. 'Her name was Sibyl. She was the best midwife for *miles*. The other women used to tell us how a countess rode for a full day in the back of a hay cart – in labour, mind you – so Sibyl could see to her.

'When Sibyl died the village *wept*. Half of us had been brought into the world by her and the other half had been assisted by her. We went to lay her out; my mother, two of her friends, and me. I was still a child, really, but I *knew* her. Everyone did.

'It was my first laying out. It was like Mother had been waiting for the right one, so I'd learn how important it was. I watched as they began to strip her down, right down, and then—'

At this, Mabel paused. She looked thoughtful, choosing her best words.

'Let's just say she had a few extra parts that none of us knew of. Not the sort of parts one would associate with midwifery. Not at *that* end of the process, anyway.

'These women – my mother, too – agreed as one. No one would know. We cleaned her body, wrapped her in a shroud, and then in her bed sheet. The next day we buried her in the grave beside her husband. None of us told anyone. I don't even know if Mother told Father. She spoke to me, after, on the way home. She told me she knew I'd known what I'd seen, and that I wasn't to breathe a word of it. That Sibyl had been a good friend, and a good midwife, and she had done what she had to do. That it didn't matter.

'I didn't understand, then. *She did what she had to do.* But I listened to my mother, and kept it close.

'I realised, later, what Mother meant. It was different, of course, and I was a grown woman by then.' She stopped – caught herself – and laughed self-effacingly. '*Barely* a grown woman. Sibyl stuck with me. And when I saw you, in your ill-fitting men's clothes, I wondered if your story was not unlike hers.'

'Oh.' Lily wasn't sure what else she could say.

Mabel reached out across the table, taking Lily's hand.

'You gave me a name, and I will call you by that name. I believe that's right. *You* know who you are, and I trust you to tell me who that person is. But not everyone may see it that way, and while the physician is a good man, I cannot guess at how he may treat you. If you want—' She stopped, frowning, then began again. 'If you *need* to take on a woman's name and woman's dress while he is here, then I understand, and I will help you. And afterwards, once he is gone, you can be William again. If that is what you need.'

Lily realised what Mabel was saying. The idea of taking on another name – of your own name not really being yours – was an entirely foreign concept to her, one she could not understand. But one that she could sympathise with. For her, William had just been a costume to pull off and on. The Knight of Stars was a *tool*, like her shield or her sword or lance. He was a convenient way to achieve her goals.

When she was alone, she was *Lily* once more. When she and Jo had talked and laughed, sharing wine and bread in the tent that by all rights belonged to William Dale, the man himself was no more than a shadow. He didn't exist. It didn't sound as if it had been that way for Sibyl. She was Sibyl, all the way down, all the way through to her bones.

'William is just . . . a mask,' Lily said, finally. 'I took on the name as a disguise, so I could—'

She paused. Mabel didn't need to know the details of her flight from her father's keep or her misguided attempt to save Jo. And, if Lily had gauged Mabel correctly, she wouldn't push for those details either.

'So I could achieve what would have been blocked to me as a woman,' she finished, vaguely. 'Lily is my name. That is what you can call me. But—'

'Yes?'

'Thank you. For telling me. It feels like a relief.' She looked up across the table. 'To know that there are others who are . . . different.'

'Are you *different*?'

Lily glanced at Jo, still awkwardly holding little baby Nora. Mabel spotted the movement. Her eyebrows raised as Lily quickly fixed her gaze back.

'Sometimes I fear I do not fit,' Lily said.

Mabel didn't say anything for a moment, merely topped up Lily's mug.

'No one fits,' she said at last. 'Not in the way we want to, at least.

But we find our *own* places. We carve them ourselves, in the work we do, in the people we love. Sybil did it. I did it.' She patted Lily's hand. Her skin was rough. 'I'd wager you can do it, too.'

Lily took the full mug with a thankful smile. She looked at Jo again. Nora was now asleep in her arms, and Jo was sitting stiff and straight-backed, looking utterly alarmed.

'I hope I can.'

'And when the physician arrives, I'll tell him I've a young woman named Lily injured and in need of help in my home? And that will not be a lie?'

Lily shook her head. 'It will not.'

'All right. Let's find you a place to rest while we wait.'

It was late by the time Harry returned, joined by the physician. Mabel allowed them use of the family bedroom, shooing out the younger children, where Lily found herself subject to the physician's intense attentions.

He treated her kindly as he examined her cuts and bruises. He unwrapped the bandage around her arm, assessing the wound, before expertly rewrapping it. He prodded at her sides and ribs in a way that made Lily curse, and listened to her chest. He hummed to himself, tutting occasionally. Lily wondered what he could hear that she could not.

When he was finally done, he observed her with a concerned, clinical gaze.

'You are very unwell,' he said. 'Truthfully, I am quite amazed you are even able to sit up and talk. Most of your injuries are superficial, but your ribs are cracked. Your lungs are flooding. I am sure there is bruising and bleeding of the tissue that we cannot see beyond that. It is only for God's good favour that you are still alive. Do not waste that.'

Lily fell silent, turning pale.

'You must rest,' he said, turning aside. 'Even riding poses too much of a risk.'

'But—'

'You cannot argue this, my girl,' the physician said, expression severe. 'Sleep, and rest. I will leave something for the pain with Mabel, and I shall return tomorrow with a tincture you must mix and take three times a day. And if I hear you have been attempting to work or ride, I shall strap you down to a bed myself. Do I make myself clear?'

Lily flushed like an angry youth. 'You do.'

'Very well. I shall speak to Mabel.'

Lily sat on the edge of the bed after he left, catching her breath, before pulling her tunic back on over her thin undershirt. Even *that* action left her winded, making her pulse race, and she immediately regretted it: she was far too hot to keep it on. Mabel let herself in soon after, standing beside her with her hands on her hips.

'So,' she said. 'It seems I cannot let you leave quite yet after all.'

'What?'

'I spoke to the physician. He informed me you are too sick to leave, and *far* too sick to travel. You surely do not expect me to allow you to go?'

'But—'

'But *nothing*. If I allow you to go off on your own, how am I to know you'll take care of yourself? I will not have your death on my conscience.'

Lily's shoulders sagged. She didn't *want* to stay, and certainly didn't want to be *forced* to stay. She wanted – with a sharp, sudden pang – to go *home*. She was wounded and unwell. Her ribs were cracked and her heart still battered from her failure to save Jo, who would soon return to the de Foucart keep and her would-be husband. Lily wanted her home, and her bed, and her brothers, even if they barred her from swordplay for the rest of her life.

'I don't know where you came from,' Mabel continued, sensing Lily's hesitation. 'And I shall not ask. But whatever you are running from – if it *is* that you are running from something – will not be so bad a fate as choking on your own lungs.'

Mabel was right. Lily tried to swallow back the feeling of homesickness, and the grief of losing Jo.

'I see I have no choice,' she said, sighing. 'Thank you, Mabel.'

'You are welcome,' Mabel said, 'although I do not need your thanks. What sort of brewster would I be if I did not extend hospitality to travellers? There *is*, however, the matter of where you are to sleep. We've no spare beds in the house, but there's a loft above the brewery that should suffice.'

Mabel led her back to the kitchen where Jo was nervously lingering beside the door. Upon seeing Lily, her face split into a wide smile of relief and she rushed over. When she took her arm to help her walk, Lily tried to brush her away, but quickly realised that her legs had turned weak, and allowed Jo to help her across the yard.

The loft was a narrow space in the roof of the brewery up a sloping ladder. Lily eyed the ladder nervously, suspecting that she would struggle with the climb. But the space was ideal: cosy and out of the way.

Jo and Harry were sent up first, each carrying a bundle of blankets. Lily was forced to wait below, listening to the occasional thud and, once or twice, a half-muffled curse, as they arranged the space. Between them they managed to haul a wide pallet bed up there, too, followed by armfuls of fresh straw. Finally, Jo went up with Lily's things: the sack that contained her armour, her pack, the gifted sword, and her shield.

By the time they were done, Jo was red faced and breathless, but she looked pleased with herself.

'There,' she said, panting. 'That should do.'

Lily had been right, and it *was* a struggle to get up the ladder, but she managed it, wheezing the last few rungs before hauling herself up and peering around. The roof was low, and Lily could only reach her full height when standing directly in the centre of the loft. There was a window to the far end – little more than a gap in the wood – curtained with a scrap of faded wool. The fabric had been pulled back, allowing golden twilight to illuminate the space.

Pushed to one side were a number of crates and barrels, many covered in a thin layer of dust, behind which Jo had placed Lily's pack and sword, as well as the sack which contained her armour. Lily looked around, then spotted the final thing she had been searching for: the shield, hanging from a high beam. Jo must have hooked it on a nail sticking from the wood.

Against the other wall Jo and Harry had arranged the pallet, transforming it into a passable bed.

Lily allowed herself to drop onto it with a wheeze. They had piled up straw and fresh blankets in such a way that, while it wasn't as fine as the expensive bed she had left behind in Dunlyn Castle, it was certainly comfortable.

It was also, she noted, large enough for two.

Jo's head emerged at the edge of the loft, peering in.

'How is it?' she asked, hauling herself up. 'Will it do? I know it isn't much, but—'

'It's wonderful,' Lily said, laying her hands across her chest. 'Really.'

Jo looked thrilled – and relieved.

'Are you sure?'

'I am. Really, it's lovely. And it's more than enough for what I need.'

Below, she heard the door shutting. She gave Jo a curious look.

'Mabel and Harry are returning to the house,' Jo explained. 'I asked if we could have some time to speak.'

'Oh.'

Lily braced herself. This was it. Now she was safe, and unlikely to injure herself further, Jo would return to the keep and her husband.

'Does anyone know you left Dunlyn?' Jo asked.

That was not what Lily had been expecting. 'In . . . a way.'

Jo stared at her, eyebrows raised. 'In what *sort* of way?'

'I told the steward that I was visiting the convent,' Lily confessed. 'I told him I would be gone for some time.'

'And your brothers? Your father?'

'Ash and Father are visiting a neighbouring lord, some dispute about trade, I believe. And Raff is across the border with Penn.'

'So they have no idea you came south? Or what you intended to do?'

Lily shook her head, feeling distinctly like she was being reprimanded.

'You *must* write to them.'

'I— What, Jo? I cannot!'

'You are injured and unwell! If they could get here, or send someone to fetch you, they could safely take you home and you could—'

'Jo, they *cannot* know. Please. Promise me you will not send word to them.'

'Lily . . .'

Lily grabbed her hand. '*Please.*'

Jo seemed to be fighting herself. But Lily's will was stronger.

'*Fine,*' Jo relented. 'I will not. But if your condition worsens then I will have no choice.'

It was agreement enough. 'Thank you,' Lily said. 'I . . . I *do* want to see them, I admit. But they will only worry about me. They'll lock me away if they realise how injured I am.'

'I am amazed you even thought you could disappear without them realising.'

'I would have,' Lily insisted, 'had I not been wounded. They will all be absent for *weeks*, plenty of time for me to ride to Oxford and back. If I had not been thrown, I would have been home before any of them had realised I was gone.'

Jo sighed. 'I suppose that means I must stay, then.'

The shock was so great that it catapulted Lily into another coughing fit. When it finally passed, Jo beside her with a hand to her back, she managed, breathlessly—

'You *cannot.*'

'I can.'

'You said you would return to the keep! You are to be *married*, Jo! What about Adam?'

'Did you not *hear* what the physician said? You could have died! Yes, I am worried about Lord Adam, but I am *far* more worried about you.'

'But surely staying here just makes that worry worse?'

'Of course it does, but what else am I to do about it?'

'What I am telling you,' Lily said, quietly, 'is that if you have to leave . . . you can, Jo. Do not stay here on my account.'

Jo stared at her. 'I will not leave you.'

'But—'

'I am not going to leave you here, wounded and alone. Not when you did this to yourself to save me. Because I am a *fool*, I promised you I would not entangle your family in this mess, and so I am the only one who can look after you. And I *will* look after you, until you are well enough to travel. And when you *are* well enough, I will return to the keep.'

'And what about Adam? He will realise you have gone.'

'Ah—' Jo looked abashed. 'I . . . may have already seen to that. Not purposefully!' she quickly added. 'But it was a stroke of luck. He caught me leaving the feast and I gave him a story that I had received a letter about Penn being unwell. And—' She looked as if she was about to say something else, before stopping herself. 'Anyway.' She set her shoulders. 'He will think I have gone to ensure my brother is all right. He could not demand I return, not when we are still unwed. My family must come first, until I am his wife.'

'How can you be sure of that?'

Again, Jo looked guilty. 'It will be seen to,' she said, sharply. 'I will not leave you here alone. If it makes you rest easier, think of it as repaying a debt. You came to ensure I was well, and now I am doing the same for you.'

Lily wanted to argue. But the hot, jealous core of her flared. Jo had chosen *her*, not Adam. She had won, even if Jo's feelings did not mirror Lily's own.

'I must return to the house and explain things to Mabel,' Jo continued, slipping back into her natural pattern of busyness. 'Will you be all right?'

'Of course I will.'

The look Jo gave her betrayed that she did not believe that was true, but she left regardless, ensuring Lily was comfortable on the pallet before climbing back down the ladder. Lily remained in the loft for the rest of the evening, slipping in and out of sleep and disturbed only when Jo came to bring her something to eat and drink. She hadn't realised how *tired* she was – not the simple tiredness of sleeping too little and not well enough, but a bone-deep exhaustion that she recognised as a symptom of a true sickness.

She drifted through strange, repetitive dreams where she chased shadows and fell from her horse. Sometimes Jo was there, her hands stained red, her face an image of shock. She was roused from one of these unplaceable visions by Jo returning, the sky outside now entirely black.

'Mabel offered the kitchen for me to sleep in,' she said, sitting beside the pallet as Lily stirred. 'But . . . I did not wish to be alone, and I thought you might . . .'

The unspoken question hung between them.

'Of course,' Lily said. 'Let me—'

She went to shuffle closer to the wall, intending to make room for Jo to lie beside her, but the movement jarred her ribs, making her wince.

'Curse these *stupid* lungs!' she mumbled. 'Give me just a moment . . .'

'Lily, *no.*' Jo put her hand to Lily's shoulder, stilling her. 'I just need to . . .'

Awkwardly, she placed a hand on the roof to balance herself, picked up her skirts and attempted to step over Lily to get into the space beside her, next to the wall. Despite still being groggy with sleep, Lily had to bite back a rib-shaking laugh as she watched her, all the poise and assuredness she usually moved with gone. When she finally managed to get beneath the covers, she faced Lily with a huff.

'Just be grateful I did not stand on you,' she said. 'Mabel would have a *fit.*'

'I *am* grateful,' Lily said, unable to turn onto her side to properly look at her, and instead straining her neck to twist around. 'I do not wish to add any more injuries to my collection. The ones I have are more than enough.'

'More than enough for both of us,' Jo added, with a brief laugh.

'Jo . . .'

'Yes?'

'Thank you. For staying. You really do not need to—'

'I do.' Jo cut her off. And then added, thoughtfully, 'You are still my champion. Even if you are Lily again, instead of William. That makes me *your* lady, which means it is my duty to care for you and tend your wounds. I should be standing vigil by your bedside.'

Lily raised her eyebrows at her across the blankets. 'You are doing a very poor job of it,' she said. 'You are *in* my bed. That is not very ladylike.'

Jo pursed her lips. 'It would be unladylike if you were still William,' she said. 'But as Cecily Barden, daughter of an earl and one of my brother's allies? I am sure it is allowed.'

'Fine, then,' Lily said – although relenting to her was no pain when Jo was staring at her from only inches away. 'I accept your care.'

Jo's eyes flashed in the dark. 'Good,' she said. 'For you could not very well refuse it.'

Lily yawned. The conversation, brief as it was, had tired her endlessly. Pain flared in her chest once more.

'Go back to sleep,' Jo said, softly. 'I am sorry for waking you.'

Lily attempted to tell her that it was all right, but all that came out from between her lips was a mumble. She heard Jo laugh as her eyes slid shut, and the edges of her mind became fuzzy.

'Goodnight, my Lady,' Lily managed, as the darkness overtook her.

There was another soft noise. The last thing she heard before falling asleep was Jo's gentle voice.

'Goodnight, my champion.'

Chapter 13

Jo had never expected to see Lily so *still*. That was what truly worried her — what made her realise just how dire the situation was. In the days they'd spent together, Lily was always moving and laughing. She was incapable of sitting still, and when forced to do so she'd bounce in her seat and tap her feet and chatter endlessly.

But now she was quiet. She slept. It was unsettling to see her bed-bound, and it strengthened Jo's resolve to stay with her until she healed. Yes: she had promised Lord Adam her hand. But her promise to Lily meant more. She would not leave her, not yet.

She hoped that Isabelle had found a way to explain her sudden absence. The lie Jo had fed to Lord Adam about Penn being taken ill would make a fair excuse, but Jo had no way of knowing if Isabelle would have thought the same. She wished she could get a letter to her, but to send a note to the de Foucart keep would immediately betray who she was. For now, it was safer to be no one, *not* the sister of the new earl.

She couldn't spend all day in the loft by Lily's bedside, but she was loath to leave her alone, too. She especially could not stand the idea of Lily waking to an empty loft and no one beside her — Jo could only guess at how frightening that would be when she was still so feverish. She needed some way to let Lily know she had not left her.

She found a thick ledger and quill in the brewery, used for keeping stock, then pulled a page from the back. She scribbled a quick note, leaving it beside the pallet where Lily would be sure to see it should she wake.

Lily,

I am assisting Mabel downstairs. You are safe, and you are not alone. Do try to rest. I know you will likely be tempted to rise and entertain yourself, but you must let yourself heal.

I will return shortly.

Jo

When she was done, she crept quietly down the ladder, doing her best not to make too much noise despite knowing full well that it would take the building falling down around Lily to wake her. The brewery was empty, so she wandered into the house to find Mabel and Matilda leaning over the table, kneading out dough. Beside them, Nora sat on the floor, playing with one of the whittled figures.

'I see you're awake,' Mabel said, glancing up. 'How was the loft?'

In truth, Jo had struggled to sleep, resting lightly and jolting awake every time Lily so much as sniffed. She'd been too tense to properly relax, and while the loft was warm and surprisingly comfortable, she suspected that even on a feather tick with linen sheets she would have stayed resolutely awake.

'It was very comfortable, thank you.'

Mabel leant back from the table properly, wiping her hands on her skirts.

'Was it, now? Then I suppose that is why you look as if you've been sleeping upon a rock all night?'

Jo's exhaustion must have been clear on her face. 'Ah—' she said, feeling like a terribly ungrateful guest, 'truly, it *was* comfortable up there, I just . . . I am anxious for Lily, and I found myself unsettled all night.'

'Of course.' Mabel looked at her sympathetically. 'How does your sister fare?'

'My sister?' Jo's first thought was of Ros. And then she remembered far too late that yesterday they had told Mabel they were siblings. 'I – she—'

Mabel only gave her a smug smirk.

'I knew as much. No—' She spoke over Jo's attempts to weave another lie. 'It doesn't make a jot of difference to me *what* you are to each other. I swore to help you, and I shall. But how *does* she fare?'

'She is still asleep,' Jo said, relieved that Mabel had not taken offence at the untruth.

'She *needs* that sleep,' Mabel said. 'The physician was clear enough on that.'

'She does,' Jo agreed, 'but it is unusual to see. I've never known her to rest for so long. She is always doing *something*, always rushing about, and now . . .' She sighed, picking at her finger. 'I do not like to see her so unwell.'

Mabel walked towards her. For a moment, she looked as if she was about to embrace her, then thought better of it.

'It always hurts to see the ones we care for in pain,' she said. 'I have faith that she will heal, in time.'

Jo gave her a tight, wry smile. 'If she *lets* herself heal,' she said. 'Currently she has no choice, as she is too ill and exhausted to do much more than sleep. But once she wakes I fear she will be difficult to convince.'

'If she will listen to anyone, I'd wager it would be you,' Mabel said. 'You'll be staying with her, then? I would be happy to have you both.'

Jo nodded. 'I cannot leave her. Not like this.'

Mabel smiled at her, as if she understood.

'Come, help us with these loaves. The work will go quicker with three.'

Jo threw herself thankfully into the work. Mabel was correct: soon the loaves were baking, filling the kitchen with the smell of fresh bread as Jo washed the dough from her hands in the water butt in the yard, feeling rather aimless.

'If you're looking for work, I am sure I can find you something to do.'

Mabel appeared behind her, washing her hands too as Jo moved aside.

Of course: Jo couldn't expect Mabel to allow her to sit around the house while Mabel and her family worked, especially when she was providing them with such hospitality.

'Oh, yes,' Jo began, standing to attention. 'Please, tell me how I can help.'

As it transpired, there was an endless amount of work to be done, particularly household errands, and Mabel relished having an extra pair of hands about the place. Jo worked hard, keen not to make it known that she had never actually had to attend to most of these daily chores herself. Mabel spoke her through each job, and while thankful for her guidance Jo couldn't help but be annoyed that her inexperience was so obvious.

Lily remained in bed. Around midday, Jo crept up the ladder with a waterskin and a simple plate of food, only to find her still soundly asleep. The note had vanished, and it was only when Jo ducked closer to gently shake her awake that she noticed it was crumpled in Lily's hand. Lily had refused the food and only drunk a little water before lying back against the haphazardly placed cushions, the note still clasped in her hand. Unsure what else to do, Jo had left the food and drink with her before heading back down the ladder.

The physician returned as promised, bringing with him pouches filled with the ingredients needed to ease Lily's illness. He instructed Jo on how to prepare the medicine, and she returned to the loft at dusk with one of the tinctures and more food. The meal she had brought that afternoon had barely been touched. Jo nudged Lily awake, but Lily only managed to drink a few spoonfuls of broth before pushing her away. Lily's skin had taken on a sickly colour, and Jo felt terribly guilty as she poured the medicine between her lips, forcing her to take it all. She did not push her to eat more food – she didn't want Lily to vomit, after all – then finally left her to sleep. That night, she barely noticed when Jo finally headed to bed herself, twitching only a little as Jo tugged the blankets closer around them both.

It took Jo a long time to sleep, and when she did, all she could hear was the sound of Lily's coughing.

✳

Lily was woken by the trill of singing birds. The loft was bathed in sunlight. She must have slept for an age, although it seemed as if she had only shut her eyes a few moments ago.

She turned on the pallet, blinking away the last wisps of sleep. There was a scrap of parchment on the boards beside the mattress.

Lily,
> *I am outside. I hope our noise has not woken you.*
> *Rest well.*
> *Jo*

Lily smiled to herself. This was the second of these notes, and it was clear that Jo was worrying about her. She folded it and placed it in her pack before shrugging out of her clothes.

Mabel had given them a handful of her old dresses, but Lily felt a little discomforted at wearing one. She had got used to wearing the breeches and tunics she had stolen from her brothers, and didn't wish to return to skirts *just* yet, even though her ruse was behind her.

Finally dressed, she gingerly made her way down the ladder and into the brewery. Finding it empty, she headed outside to seek out Jo. Even opening the doors took immense effort, and still out of breath she walked slowly towards the sound of voices coming from the garden, her lungs rattling and wheezing.

Jo spotted her first, looking hugely relieved to see her awake. She'd pulled up her sleeves to work in the vegetable patch, her skirts pinned above her knees, her hair in disarray about her head.

'Jo—'

Lily had only taken a single step forwards when a coughing fit gripped her. It was as if her lungs were burning, and each cough ripped through her ribs like a saw, making them grate together. She stumbled, reaching out blindly until she found the wall to lean on.

She realised what the physician had meant when she said her lungs were flooding. Jo was by her side in an instant, her hands around Lily's arms.

'I am fine,' Lily gasped.

'You are *not* fine.'

Sweat beaded on Lily's forehead. Her stomach roiled: she was going to be sick. Before she could say anything else, she grabbed Jo's arm, bent double, and vomited against the stone. Jo placed a calming hand to her back, saying nothing.

When she finally stopped, Jo led her away from the vegetable patch towards a tree at the edge of the garden, heavy with glossy green leaves and tiny, budding apples.

'Stay here,' she commanded, as if Lily could even stand. 'I will fetch you a drink.'

Lily leant heavily against the tree, her eyes half shut. Jo returned quickly with a waterskin and Lily drank gratefully, easing the sting in her throat and swilling away the awful taste of vomit. Jo sat beside her, then began to rub up and down Lily's back until her breathing calmed. The touch was so gentle that for a moment it all felt worth it.

'How do you feel?' Jo asked, finally.

Lily leant her head on Jo's shoulder. 'Foolish,' she said, after a moment. 'Bored. Entirely frustrated with myself and my useless, broken body.'

'You must give yourself time,' Jo said. 'Once you're feeling a little better we will find you something to do.'

Lily snorted derisively. 'There is nothing I *can* do,' she said. 'I shall go mad.'

Jo lowered her head atop Lily's, resting there. 'You are already mad.'

She was so close. Lily could hear her breathing, mingling with her own ragged, laboured breaths.

'Jo . . .'

'Yes?' Jo didn't move.

'Are you *sure* you do not need to return to the keep?'

The pressure of Jo against her was suddenly gone. She was staring at her aghast, as if Lily had suggested something criminal.

'I am not leaving you,' she said. 'Not until you are better. *Truly* better.'

That brought the conversation to a swift close. Lily didn't press: she didn't want to dwell on the thought of Jo leaving either. Jo settled herself back against the tree, tugging Lily close. They sat in comfortable silence, listening to the leaves shuddering above them. After a while, Jo shifted, peering at her.

'Your hair . . .'

Jo reached up and pushed a few strands out of Lily's face and behind her ear. Her hand was pleasantly cool on Lily's feverish skin, but her closeness only inflamed that heat. Her gaze, however, was critical.

'You disapprove?'

Lily couldn't hide the pain in her voice. Her hair was *unwomanly*, now. She had sliced through it with wild abandon to ensure she remained disguised, and while *she* was very pleased with the new length, to everyone else it would seem odd at best and ugly at worst. Lily didn't bother herself overmuch with the opinions of others – they could hang their thoughts on her hair, which was hers and hers alone – but she hated to think that Jo might not like it.

'No,' Jo said with a sigh, lowering her hand. 'No, it is not that. I just . . . Do you wish me to be honest with you?'

'Of course I do.'

Jo gripped her hands together in her lap. 'You look as if you cut this yourself with your knife while spurring your horse to a gallop,' she said, finally.

'Ah, *well*—' Lily began, guiltily.

'*Lily.*'

'I was not riding!'

'But you *did* use your knife?'

'Of course. Did you expect me to find shears on the road?'

'You could have at *least* sharpened the blade. No wonder it is so uneven. Will you let me fix it?'

'Have you cut hair before?' Lily said, raising her eyebrows.

'Once or twice.' Jo shrugged. 'Or do you believe that you can do a better job of it? Would you like me to fetch you a blunt kitchen knife and your horse?'

Lily snorted. 'Very well,' she said. 'Fix it, if you insist.'

'I do not *insist*,' Jo contended. 'If you wish to leave it as it is, you can. I am sure the local children would enjoy having a jester in the town.'

Lily's gasp of outrage was entirely false. It made her cough, too, and Jo gave her a reprimanding look and another pat on the back before heading back into the house. She returned with a pair of shears, probably used for making and mending clothes, settling herself behind Lily, her calves brushing against Lily's back. There were several layers of linen between them, yet Lily was sure she could still feel the heat of Jo's skin; or perhaps it was just the lingering warmth of the hot summer's day and the horrible fever.

She could feel Jo staring at the back of her head. And then her fingers were in Lily's hair. As her fingertips brushed against Lily's scalp, Lily shuddered – then wriggled as sparks tingled down her spine, over her nape, dancing around her ears. Jo huffed out a small laugh, carefully took a section of hair and then – after a long moment – grabbed the shears and made the first cut.

Soon, there was a neat pile of bright red hair beside them, catching in the grass and blowing away on the summer air. The wind on Lily's nape cooled her with gentle, breezy caresses.

'There,' Jo said at last. 'That will do. How do you feel?'

Lily wanted to lean back, to rest her head on Jo's breast and linger there in the sunshine and the pleasing breeze. She didn't.

'Better,' she said. 'Much better.'

Jo gave a pleased-sounding hum. Gilbert, who had been eyeing them from the shade of the garden wall, swaggered over, taking a swipe at the strands of hair as they buffeted upwards. Lily giggled at him, then extended a hand towards him, calling him over.

He regarded her for a moment before slouching towards her and knocking his head into her hand. Behind her, Jo gasped.

'I am impressed,' she said. 'He *hates* me.'

Lily grinned as Gib rubbed against her fingers. 'He wants to be my friend, don't you, Gib?' she said. 'He is—'

Gib sunk his claws into Lily's arm. She wrenched it back with a shout.

'You *cursed* beast—'

The cat scrambled to his feet and dashed away, sending hair

scattering. Jo laughed, leaning forwards and taking Lily's arm in her hand.

'Oh yes, I can see that you are firm friends,' she said. 'It must be because you are kindred spirits: both fiery red devils.'

Lily huffed, but allowed Jo to examine her arm regardless. Gib hadn't left too deep a cut, but it *was* bleeding.

'Come.' Jo moved away, standing up. Lily immediately missed her closeness. 'Let's see if we can find something to clean this with.'

They explained what had happened to Mabel, who also laughed, then led them into the kitchen and pulled a basket of rags from a chest in the corner, finding a clean scrap of wool. Lily dampened it and wiped away the blood, peering into the chest. It was full of fabric and old clothes.

'What is all this?'

'Mending,' Mabel said, with a scowl. 'I have never been one for sewing, but it needs to be done. I have been putting it off for far too long, and now there is too much for one person.'

Jo reached in, then pulled out a pair of ripped breeches. 'Lily could do it,' she said.

Mabel gave Lily a doubtful look. 'Can you sew?'

'I *can*, yes,' Lily said, unsure. 'But—'

'I have seen your sewing.' Jo cut her off. 'You are skilled, certainly more skilled than I. This may give you something to do.'

Lily peered into the chest. She *did* have a talent for embroidery, and the prospect of days of sitting doing nothing but resting and healing was already making her feel jumpy and bored. There was unspent energy twitching in her fingertips. Perhaps Jo was right.

'I can certainly try.'

'I am sure you will do a better job of it than I,' Mabel said, pulling out a bundle of clothes as Lily sat at the bench. 'Thank you. I'll admit that it is not a job I enjoy.'

Lily smiled. 'I find it calming,' she said. 'At home, I often—' She snapped her mouth shut. She couldn't give too much away, she reminded herself. 'It is a skill I've often been forced to use,' she said instead.

'Then you are an invaluable addition to the house,' Mabel said. 'Do not worry yourself on making them look grand: as long as they are mended, that is what we need.'

'I shall see what I can do.'

Mabel and Jo returned to the garden, leaving Lily alone. She took the first item in the pile, turning it in her hands. It was one of Matilda's dresses, torn across the bodice. The rip itself was severe, and would take more than a single row of stitches to mend — certainly more if it was to be usable. The fabric seemed costly, and Lily suspected that the dress had been one for special occasions before being damaged. Improperly mended, it would be good for only work and play, and the fine fabric would be wasted.

The edges of the tear were already frayed, which would make it harder to stitch them together while maintaining the size. If Lily could find a scrap of spare fabric, she could add a patch beneath the rip to ensure it could stay true to size, but then the mend would be more obvious.

She mused on it as she placed the dress aside and picked up the next piece in the pile. This one was far easier — one of Mabel's skirts with a neat rip a few inches from the hem. It looked as if it had caught on something, a tear that started small but was left for too long.

It was as good a place to start as any. Lily leant into the chest again, looking for needle and thread. Mabel had some embroidery supplies, too, and where Lily had been expecting to find simple undyed thread she found a whole rainbow of vibrant colours.

However tempted she was by the colourful strands, she grabbed the undyed one instead, keen not to waste the more expensive materials. She mended the rip in no time at all, doing her best to hide the stitches.

'How did you manage that?'

She jumped when she realised that Jo was leaning over her shoulder. She hadn't even noticed.

'Traditionally one starts by threading the needle,' Lily teased.

'No, I mean—' Jo leant closer, running a finger over the mend. 'You can hardly tell it was ripped at all. How did you do it?'

Lily shrugged. 'It is simple enough. You start on the inside of the fabric, and fold it in on itself, and make the stitches run side by side, almost, ah . . .' She thought for a second, tapping her fingers on the table. 'Almost like a ladder, I suppose? In rungs? And then you tug it, and it closes the rip.'

Jo stared at her.

'It really is very easy,' Lily said, feeling as if something more was expected of her.

Jo laughed. 'If you insist.'

She wandered off again, leaving Lily with a pat on her shoulder as she did. Warmly pleased, Lily put the skirt down and picked up the next garment: a red woollen apron with a hole in the chest nearly entirely worn through. This would require darning, but none of the threads in Mabel's basket matched the well-faded colour of the fabric. Lily considered it a moment, then chose the green, thinking that if the colours were not a match, at least they would pair well.

When the fix was complete, she peered at the green stitching, nibbling on her bottom lip. The shape tapered to either end, like a leaf. So, perhaps . . .

She continued to work, extending the shape, adding a curling, twisting line – then another, then beside that another of the leaf-shaped patches. She reached into the basket mindlessly, grabbing for the yellow thread, then got to work again. She hadn't realised how much time had passed until there was a creak behind her and a small gasp of shock.

'My word.'

Lily finally lowered the needle. Her back ached where she had been slouched over the fabric, and as she moved pain flared down her side, across her chest. She hid it as best she could as she turned to face Mabel, who was now standing beside her.

'Mabel—' she said, 'I did not hear you enter.'

'I am not surprised,' Mabel said, impressed. 'You were quite distracted. Jo, come and see this.'

Jo was by her side in an instant. She was wiping her hands with a rag, her hair pulled back from her face and her skin flushed and sweaty. Lily realised how much time must have passed while she was engrossed in her sewing.

'*Heavens*, Lily,' she breathed. 'That is beautiful. Are those buttercups?'

Lily blushed. 'You can tell?'

'Of course I can tell. They're wonderful.'

Mabel took the apron from Lily, examining it.

'My— Good Lord, Lily, is this my old apron?'

Lily shrugged. 'It was in the pile, and I – ah, should I not have used the coloured threads? I am sorry, I am sure I have coin to replace them—'

'No, my girl, do not apologise. This is quite lovely. I feel remiss wearing it, now . . .'

'Oh, do not,' Lily quickly said. 'It was no work at all. Do not feel as if you cannot wear it . . .'

'Everyone in town will envy me,' Mabel said, with a glint in her eye. 'You'll find your services in demand, Lily. It's a fine way to make a living, you know.'

Lily looked down at the bundle of clothes, the needles and thread. In the keep, it had only been a passing hobby – a fancy that she could pick up and put down when she needed to. She had never considered there being any monetary or trade value in what she did: she had never had to.

'Perhaps,' she said, in a conciliatory tone. 'You truly like it?'

'I do. It seems as if we have found your role in the business, Lily.'

Lily couldn't help but smile. Jo's hand came to rest on her shoulder.

'I'm warning you,' she said, 'I will be deliberately ripping my dresses for you to mend now I know you can do *this*.'

Something in Lily's chest squeezed – something that wasn't the horrid illness or her broken lungs. She imaged how she could darn and embroider one of Jo's gowns, the colours that would best suit. An entire bouquet of flowers, just for her.

Buried in her pocket, Jo's handkerchief took on a new weight. Lily's cheeks heated as her mind raced with a thousand precisely embroidered petals.

Chapter 14

After Lily had returned to the loft to sleep, leaving the bundle of sewing behind, Jo pulled Mabel aside and offered her help in the brewery. She was determined to repay her kindness beyond laundry and tending the vegetable patch.

'I will admit I am not experienced at *all* in brewing,' she said, 'but please, if there's anything I can do . . .'

Mabel didn't even appear shocked at the offer. She smiled, wiping her hands on her skirts, then led Jo towards the brewery. She spoke through the process — from malt to mash — and Jo tried to take it all in, quickly learning that it was not as simple as she had assumed.

After an afternoon of lessons, Mabel left Jo alone with instructions on making mash. Jo eyed the tub warily, but got to work anyway, determined not to let Mabel down. But even that apparently easy job proved finnicky, and the result was more of a thin gruel than anything else.

She stared down at the ruined mash, burning with embarrassment and frustration. She was about to attempt to fix her failure, when the door behind her swung open. Mabel had returned. Jo gripped the wooden edge of the barrel tighter. Her stomach heaved, head suddenly tight, heart thundering. Mabel would be furious.

She would come down on Jo like a *storm* for wasting resources and being so stupid.

But Mabel didn't. She sidled beside Jo, looked down at the ruined mash, and *laughed*.

'The first time my husband did this,' she said, 'he added hardly any water at all. When it came to boiling it, he burnt a hole through the tub. Let's give it another go.'

This time, with Mabel beside her, Jo made it perfectly.

Within a week, they slipped into an easy, regular routine: Lily either resting or sewing while Jo helped in the brewery, both becoming part of the day-to-day running of the business and house. Jo felt at her best when she was busy, and while at first she aided Mabel as a way of repaying her and Lily's shared debt, she quickly began to enjoy the work, too.

Mabel's brewery was extremely popular. She brewed in huge batches, and there was always something to do. A week after their arrival, she announced that the batch already brewing was ready to sell, dipping a hewn tankard into the ale and testing it herself.

'Harry,' she said with a pleased expression, 'what day did Hamet say he'd next be passing town?'

'Tuesday,' Harry said, barely looking up from where he was mending a crate.

'That's tomorrow,' Mabel said, placing the lid back on the tub and wiping the tankard on her apron. 'I'll send you out first thing, you're to wait in the square for him.'

Harry groaned at this, but agreed anyway.

'Who is Hamet?' Jo asked, intrigued.

'The ale conner,' Mabel said. 'He tastes the ale before we can sell it on. If he doesn't agree that it's ready, or thinks it's of poor quality, he won't let me sell it. Not that he ever has, mind. He's never turned down our supply, has he, Harry?'

Harry looked smug. 'Not once.'

He set out with the dawn the next morning, and returned before midday with the man who could only be Hamet. He had tightly curled black hair and dark brown skin, wearing official-looking garb with a belt so heavy with tools and keys that Jo wondered how it didn't slip down around his ankles as he walked. He was pleased to see Mabel, and she him: clearly they had been working together for quite some time.

'And who is this?' he asked, looking at Jo with interest.

'I've had to seek help with my husband away,' Mabel said. 'This is Jo. She is my – she has agreed to lend a hand until he returns.'

Hamet gave Jo an assessing look. 'Are you looking to become a brewster?'

Jo gave him a polite smile. 'It is certainly very interesting,' she said. 'I, ah—' she stumbled, trying not to lie too much. 'I have recently suffered a – a familial loss. And I am looking for purpose.'

Hamet nodded sympathetically.

'My condolences,' he said. 'I hope you can find it. Now, let us take a look at this batch, Mabel. I expect great things, you know . . .'

As anticipated, Hamet declared the batch of ale to be of exceptional quality, congratulating Mabel on yet another fine job. They immediately launched into discussions of the best price to sell her stock – both to traders and to visitors.

'I had not realised selling beer was so complex,' Jo said, after Hamet had left.

'It *is*,' Mabel agreed. 'But I would not trade it for anything.'

'How can you even tell if the ale is ready?' Jo said. 'I would not even know where to *begin* with such a task.'

'Would you like me to teach you?'

Jo had not been expecting that. What was more: she hadn't expected to *want* to learn it, either. Yet she did. The process seemed magical – a secret that she desperately wished to be privy to. It made her feel wrong – like a traitor to her own future. She did not *need* to know. When Lily was well, Jo would return to the keep and marry Lord Adam. She would be a lady, *not* a brewster.

She supposed, at least, that understanding how brewing worked *may* serve her in that role. It would stop her household from falling prey to those who cared less about the trade than Mabel did, and who would sell them poor product at too high a cost. That thought soothed the sense of treachery: it would not be *wholly* wrong if it meant another arrow in her quiver when she was the lady of a keep.

'If you have the time?' she said, knowing she ought to refuse. 'I do not wish to burden you . . .'

Mabel shrugged. 'It is a useful skill to have if you are to stay awhile. I should have thought of it sooner, in truth.'

She led Jo back towards the tubs and offered her a tankard of fresh ale before talking Jo through the process, assessing the colour, smell, and taste of the drink. She even went so far as to insist Jo try a batch that was not yet ready – letting her describe the differences herself – then passing her a smaller mug of what Jo realised far too late was from a batch long past its best. It tasted *foul*, an acrid sourness that reminded Jo of bile, and she spluttered in shock after taking far too large a mouthful.

'*That* ale is bad.' Mabel laughed as she handed her a cloth. 'You'll not forget that taste in a hurry.'

Jo tried not to vomit as she cleaned herself up. At least she really *would* be able to detect bad ale, she thought – although anyone foolish enough to spend good money on *that* deserved to be robbed.

Apparently satisfied that Jo had learnt enough, Mabel moved on to the next job of separating out which of her stock would be being sold when the alehouse opened, and which would be traded with neighbouring businesses. Stock for Geoffrey – the owner of the single inn in Astmere – came first, and she had their cart loaded and Harry sent off with the delivery within the hour.

The rest of the stock would be sold over the next few days to other merchants, as well as locals and travellers. Jo listened to it all with real interest – in the keep, each day was the same as the last, the only real change coming with the weather as different crops or game slipped in and out of season. The brewery worked to its *own* seasons, a different kind of rhythm that meant there was always change, always some new challenge.

Jo mused on it as she helped Mabel ensure the brewery would be ready. She swept the floors before covering them in straw while Mabel hefted rickety chairs out into the yard. When they were finished, the space had been transformed: it looked like a place for socialising and drinking rather than a place of work.

'Here.'

Mabel held a broom in her hand. This was not the one Jo had been sweeping with – the bristles looked fresh and new, and there were pretty little patterns carved into the handle.

'What . . .'

'We hang it above the door.' Mabel gestured with her head, and Jo looked up – there were indeed a pair of empty hooks above the frame. 'To show we're open for business. I thought you may wish to place it for us? You have done truly excellent work here, Jo. It's a small thanks, I know, but I feel it is right for you to do this for us, today.'

'Oh . . .' Jo felt like she was being granted a huge honour. 'Thank you,' she muttered. 'But, really, I have not done *all* that much, and not nearly enough to repay you . . .'

Mabel waved away her thanks. 'You *have*,' she insisted. 'Accept my thanks and my compliments, Jo. You are a talented young woman.'

Jo blushed awkwardly. She wanted to deny it, to claim again that the work was no hardship, but she felt very sure that Mabel would not allow it.

'Thank you,' she mumbled again like a child. 'Um . . . how do I reach?'

How she reached, it soon became clear, was by balancing on the very points of her toes on an upturned crate. She was tall, but it was a struggle to hook the broom in place as Harry and Mabel giggled below her, keeping the crate steady. When it was done she was flushed but pleased, and she stood back with her hands on her hips to admire her handiwork. It felt *good*.

'Now what do we do?'

'Now we wait,' Mabel said. 'Word will spread fast, it usually does.'

'Then I should wake Lily,' Jo said. 'I would hate for her to be disturbed by the noise . . .' She thought, for a moment. 'Or to miss all the fun. I suspect *that* would pain her more.'

As expected, Lily was snoozing on the pallet, a pile of half-finished mending beside her and Gilbert curled by her feet. Jo gave her shoulder a gentle shove, and then a stronger one when it became clear that gentleness was not going to wake her. Lily roused with a snort, which quickly became another coughing fit. Jo hauled her up, used to these now, and rubbed her back as the coughing petered out.

'Thank you,' Lily managed, as Jo passed her the waterskin she kept on hand for these occasions. 'Is everything all right?'

'Fine,' Jo said. 'We did not wake you?'

Lily shrugged: when she slept, she was all but dead. As she regained control over her breathing and properly woke up, Jo told her about Mabel's intentions to open their doors to customers.

'I best get up then,' Lily yawned. 'Pass me that dress, will you?'

Lily had been choosing between Mabel's dresses and her stolen men's clothes since their arrival, flitting between them at random. Jo had asked her about it once, questioning if now she had no need for a disguise, she would continue wearing men's clothes.

'I see no reason not to,' Lily had responded. 'They are comfortable enough, and not worn through quite yet.'

She had said it so matter-of-factly that Jo had found no suitable reply. Besides, she *knew* Lily, and if she wanted to wear men's clothes then that was exactly what she would do. And the longer Jo stayed by her side the more she questioned why she should even *care*. Lily was Lily, no matter what she wore, and underneath both breeches and bodices she was exactly the same. Even when dressed in the garb of the Knight of Stars, Jo had been drawn to her, and she knew that she would have *remained* drawn to her even if Lily had maintained the disguise.

Jo passed her the dress as Lily rose with a wobble from the pallet, supporting herself on the beams above. She was wearing only a thin slip which clung to her body, revealing her long, toned legs, covered in freckles and fuzzed with light orange hair, making it look as if her skin was glowing. Jo tugged her gaze away as Lily pulled the slip down and the dress over it, oddly loath to look away.

The broom above the brewery doors did not go unnoticed, and what began as a trickle of single customers quickly became a steady stream. By the evening, the yard was full of people, many with corked jugs to fill and take home. The blacksmith had arrived with *five*, handing over an absurd amount of coin while Jo hurried to fill them. Mabel was in her element, running around, ensuring everyone was seen to, and more than once getting into arguments with men who tried to underpay her for her services.

In a moment of quiet, Lily pressed up against Jo's arm.

'She is *formidable*, isn't she?' she whispered as they watched Mabel remove a man from the premises who had not paid his debts. 'I wonder what her husband is like.'

'He must be marvellous,' Jo replied. 'I cannot imagine Mabel would settle for anything less.'

Mabel turned and spotted them. Lily burst into laughter before grabbing Jo's hand and tugging her back into the yard where they were to collect discarded tankards. It was growing late, and the sky was lit in a slew of pinks and oranges as the sun set below the treeline. It was a balmy, perfect evening. The air smelt of wheat, full of laughter.

By the time Mabel declared it time to shut the doors, the sky was a deep, thick black. It took some convincing to get everyone to leave, and it was Lily who shooed away the more persistent customers using language that would have made her brothers blush – although Jo had been forced to hold her back when one of the men had insulted her diminutive stature and foul mouth.

It wasn't until everyone had left and they were alone in the yard, leaning against the wall with a mug of ale each, that Jo realised Lily's chest was wheezing.

'Are you all right?'

'I am fine.' Lily dismissed her. 'I have done too much work, that is all.'

Jo tried to swallow back the urge to worry over her, or insist she return to bed. It had been a long, wonderful day. She didn't want to ruin it.

Instead, she rested her head on Lily's shoulder, rolling the mug in her hands, listening to the sound of her breathe.

Chapter 15

Lily's chest was still tight and unpleasant, even though the fever had finally ebbed. When they had arrived nearly three weeks ago, Jo had claimed that she would look after her, her wounded champion. She had taken those words to heart. Jo watched her with concern, always a little too close, always observing a little too hard. Lily was discomforted at being the subject of such scrutiny, but she had to admit that the attention was not entirely unwanted.

Mabel, far less doting, quickly took advantage of Lily's skills with needle and thread, and when Lily was not resting she was busy with mending and sewing. She had found a scrap of spare fabric to mend Matilda's dress, hiding the seams beneath intricate flowers, and Matilda was so pleased that she wore the dress to market. There, it caught the eye of the innkeeper's wife, and suddenly Lily's services were not only useful, but in demand, too.

Embroidery had been one of the few things expected of a noble lady that Lily truly enjoyed, and she threw herself into the work. At home, she was always leaping between new ideas – taking inspiration from the wilds around Dunlyn Castle, her brothers, or stories they brought back with them when they travelled further afield. She struggled to hold on to any one idea for long enough to see it to completion, but in the brewery she *had* to, and found distraction coming less often away from her brothers. Besides: having so many things to do stopped her from growing too bored too quickly.

She was searching through Mabel's chest for the thread she'd lost when her fingers brushed against a scrap of parchment. Her heart leapt, and she abandoned her search to read it.

Dearest Lily
I understand that he is your friend, but do tell Gib he is to cease bringing
mice to the kitchen table.
Jo

Lily grinned then tucked the note into her pocket. Often, Lily would find a note from Jo sequestered amongst the sewing or beside the pallet – at first, short missives which let Lily know where she had gone, but quickly becoming jokes or well wishes or teasing lines about whatever had amused Jo most while Lily remained abed.

Early into her recovery, Lily had managed to acquire a few sheets of parchment and a quill, and had begun to send notes back. Hers were often far simpler – *I am right where you left me, asleep in the loft* – or shared jokes, always dedicated to *my Lady* and signed from *your Champion*. She quickly scribbled one of these notes down now.

My Lady
You cannot expect me to deter such a fearsome knight from his duties.
Sir Gilbert is far too seasoned for me to question him.
Your Champion

She placed the note where Jo would be sure to find it, before locating the thread and heading into the brewery.

Here, the hours slid into one another – not in the long, painful way they did at court, but like butter melting on a hot pan. Lily had never been wanting for time at her father's keep, but neither had she had *enough* things to fill that time.

She had work to do – good work, that people thought was important. She and Jo worked not together, but in tandem, never really apart. The sewing gave her time to consider what would become of her once Jo left and she returned to Dunlyn. She was enjoying being useful and didn't want to let that go – but nor did she relish the idea of sewing for the rest of her days.

It was the first time she'd had any inclination to consider her own future. As a woman, she would never be granted the title of knight, but she wouldn't be the first noblewoman to enter a chivalric order. If she could hide the true extent of her injuries, perhaps Ash would allow her to stand beside him as a fighter rather than a sister when he became Earl. But she *would* have to hide them: she would never convince him if the family discovered how close they had come to losing her.

It seemed a hopeful future, and a pleasant distraction from her slowly healing wounds.

It was not the only pleasant distraction. Lily often found herself watching Jo as she passed, as she worked in the brewery, as she sat beside her at the kitchen table. Her eye was caught more than once by the movement of Jo's hips as she walked or the curve of her backside beneath her skirts, placing a stitch in the wrong place as her eyes were dragged from her work.

From the first day they had met, Lily had thought Jo beautiful. It had been laughable that the sister of her would-be husband was so captivating, and she had inwardly cursed the irony of it. She had quickly learnt that Jo wasn't *only* beautiful – and the more time they'd spent together, the more she'd seen of Jo's inner spark shining out.

She was confident and clever and funny, unafraid to tease Lily just as much as Lily teased her. She was stubborn, in an *entirely* different way to Lily's own stubbornness. She was brilliant.

It was that brilliance that had urged Lily to respond to her letters. It was what made her ride in the tournament to save her. And now it made her work, pouring herself into the gift she was determined to give her.

She shot a look at Jo as she drew her knees up to hide what she was working on. She had begged the gown from Mabel, bundling it away so Jo wouldn't be able to find it. Mabel herself had been immediately drawn into the secret – it would have been difficult not to, given that Lily needed her to acquire materials – and had found a gleeful charm in it. She had even fetched Lily spools of brand new, brightly dyed threads, handing them over with a smile so knowing that it had made Lily blush.

Lily had never toiled so hard on a single project, but neither had she ever had such a lofty goal. It took more focus than she had channelled in her *life* to stop herself from becoming distracted, and she was determined that *this* would not become another abandoned project. Often, her focus was *too* strong: more than once she had remained in the loft after Jo had woken, needle in hand and her head filled with flowers, only realising that the sun was setting outside when her eyes began to sting. But she did not care. For Jo, she would do it.

It was impossible for the gift to be as brilliant as her, but Lily had to try.

As Lily stitched, Jo and Harry began to clean out one of the tubs, scrubbing the wood until their fingers turned red and raw with the effort of it. Jo hauled herself inside the giant thing while Harry kept it steady, her feet lifting from the floor and her laughter echoing from within.

When she emerged, her face was bright red, her eyes sparkling. Her hair – which had been tied into her typical, severe plait – was bursting from the weave in wild strands, sticking to her sweaty skin. She'd rolled her sleeves up to work, but still there were stains on her dress.

Lily had never seen her look such a mess. And she had never seen her look so *free*, either. Jo spotted her staring, and gave her a sharp smile which wrinkled her nose.

The dress felt heavy in Lily's hands. She tried to return to her stitching, but her fingers were clumsy, her palms sweaty. Her heartbeat was racing, her lungs empty, and *this* she could not blame on her illness.

She looked again at Jo. The sun spilling in through the open doors illuminated her, making the loose strands of hair around her head light up like a crown of golden sunlight. When she leant back, setting her shoulders, the glow shifted, outlining her.

And, *oh* – she was wonderful.

Lily clasped the dress harder, pinching the slender needle between her fingers just to feel something else: something that wasn't this overwhelming, burning feeling.

She couldn't. It was *unbearable*. She gathered her things, rose to her feet, and without bidding farewell dashed out into the yard, stumbling over her own feet in her haste. At least she could breathe out here, where the air was cooler. She headed towards the garden, settling herself at the foot of the tree where Jo had cut her hair – where they had spent many long evenings since, leaning against the trunk and laughing.

Gilbert, who had been sunning himself in the vegetable patch, opened his eyes and lazily sauntered over to her. As he bumped his head against her legs she scratched behind his ears, eliciting a low, rumbling purr.

Lily knew that she was walking a narrow path in her relationship with Jo, always tiptoeing between friendship and something more, and these long days with Jo attentively at her side had tipped her over the edge.

The feeling that had spurred her to try to free Jo from marriage still simmered within her, still tingled beneath her nails and bubbled in her stomach. She'd told herself – and Jo – that she only wished to help Jo win her freedom. That had felt like a lie at the time, and now she *knew* it was.

She *did* want Jo to be able to grasp her freedom. But, more so – she didn't want her to wed. She had no claim over Jo, no right to her feelings, yet the thought of her sharing her life and bed with another made jealously hiss in her chest. She *wanted* her – and she would never have her.

Lily needed to let her go. But she couldn't.

If Jo had returned to Adam and left Lily in Mabel's expert care, Lily would have been able to unhook herself from her. But Jo hadn't – she'd stayed – and Lily had stuck. She was a teasel clinging to the skirts of a queen.

Gilbert flopped onto his back beside her, demanding to be pet.

'I envy you, Gib,' Lily said, tickling beneath his chin. 'You do not have to fear falling in love.'

Gib only blinked at her. She leant against the tree, watching as his fine hairs floated up into the air around them.

'And Jo asks you to stop bringing mice to the table.'

Gib continued to purr, apparently ignoring her request.

Lily was leaning half-asleep against the tree, her fingers brushing through Gib's fur, when a noise from the house made her start awake. Mabel had been seeing to a trader from a nearby keep. They must have reached an agreement.

She made her way to the yard to see an official-looking man swinging himself up onto a finely bred horse. He was wearing an expensive tunic and was peering down at Mabel with an expression that had very little to do with his elevated position on his mount.

As he turned the horse around, Jo appeared from the brewery, also alerted by the noise.

'And you are sure you can fulfil this?' the rider spoke *at* Mabel rather than *to* her.

'If I have assured you we can, then we can.' Mabel folded her arms across her chest as she spoke.

'You understand that you have signed an agreement, yes?' he said, unsatisfied. 'And if that agreement is not fulfilled, my master will go down on you. Hard.'

Mabel shrugged. 'I am sure he will.'

The man bristled. Lily watched, amused.

'Have you any more demands for us?' Mabel asked. 'Or do I have your lord's leave to begin work on his order?'

The rider scowled. 'Please do. Are you sure you have enough materials on hand to complete this? Enough people?'

Mabel stiffened and stood straighter.

'If I require anything, I can easily find it,' she said. 'And we are well staffed here. We will deliver it to you when it is ready, as agreed.'

'Very well,' he said. 'I shall inform my master. Good morning.'

He twisted the horse's reins around and pulled the creature from the yard.

'What did he want?' Jo asked, as soon as he had gone.

'Enough strong ale to drown a village.'

'Who sent him?'

Mabel rolled her shoulders. 'Some lord,' she sniffed. 'Wickham? Wright? His name does not matter, only his coin. It's a large order, and we must prepare it properly. His keep is in Glendale, that's two days' ride away.' Mabel tapped her chin as she thought. 'I'll need to make sure the batch keeps for the journey. It is a *complication*, but not one I haven't faced before.'

'Why so far? Why not engage the services of a more local brewster?'

'Because,' Mabel said, 'I am the best. Go and fetch Harry: we need to see how much barley we have left.'

Chapter 16

Over the next two days, Mabel arranged for several sacks of grain to be delivered. They hauled them into the brewery, ready to steep. The weather had turned, and the sun baked down through the roof, making the building oppressively hot. It was perfect for steeping the grains and encouraging them to sprout, but by the third day the air was thick and sticky, like walking through broth.

Work was slow, the humidity made worse by the steeping grain. Sweat beaded on Jo's forehead as she ground malt, pausing often to rest. Lily had joined her, perched on a crate with a stack of discarded embroidery at her side. It was too hot even for such gentle work, and instead Lily leant back against the wall with her eyes shut, her hair plastered to her head.

It was barely midmorning when Mabel pushed open the door of the brewery, peering around at them all. She had been baking, her face shiny and red and her skirts covered in flour.

'Curse this heat,' she said. 'There's no good work to be done in this. Have the afternoon for yourselves.'

'Are you sure?' Jo asked, rising from where she was sitting on the floor.

'Quite sure. There's a lake down the way; take yourselves there. It will suit in this weather, and you both deserve a rest.'

The offer, made entirely in kindness, made Jo's skin cold regardless. She *had* been working hard, mostly to make up for the inconvenience Mabel must have felt at having two unexpected guests in her home. It had also become a way to atone for the transgression she was committing by not returning to Lord Adam: when she was working in the brewery or tending to Lily, she was needed. Being needed made her invaluable, which meant she did not need to return.

But a day of rest and relaxation would be for no greater cause than her own amusement. There would be no barrels to scrub or malt to grind and Lily certainly seemed well enough for the excursion. And if Lily was well enough for that, then surely she was well enough to return to Dunlyn, too? Jo had sworn to stay with Lily until she was recovered, and to accept Mabel's offer was an admission that the time was upon them.

The realisation was like a slap. She did not want to return.

She rejoiced in Lily's recovery, but with it came the need to go back to the de Foucart keep and the arms of the man who would be her husband. Before, she would have done so. But now something had shifted.

Working at Mabel's side and spending long, lazy evenings with Lily felt like gasping for the first time after a long-held breath. Like stumbling into sunshine after a day locked indoors. She had been ignoring the fact that she had to return, pretending that she was too busy to think about it.

She needed to refuse. She needed to thank Mabel for her hospitality, send Lily on her way to Dunlyn, and go home.

But the sunshine was intoxicating, the weather hot, the air sweet with summer. Beside her, Lily had immediately lit up at the prospect of going somewhere which was *not* the brewery. Her illness had trapped her, and Jo could only imagine what sort of toll it took on a woman so used to doing as she pleased, when she pleased.

Jo's mind was made up. 'That sounds wonderful.'

Harry gave Lily directions – Jo carefully listening, positive that Lily would not remember them – as Mabel helped Jo pack a basket with food and drink.

'Oh, and here—' Mabel handed Jo a sticky parcel. The little bundle was still warm, smelling of sweet honey and wine. 'Almond fritters,' she said. 'I know they're your favourite.'

The parcel was suddenly too hot, the smell overwhelming and sickly. Jo was assaulted with the memory of sitting beneath the tree at the edge of Hartswood Forest, covered in honey, laughing until sticky tears rolled down her cheeks.

There was a chill to that memory, now. How in God's name had Mabel known?

'—and a bottle of beer' – Mabel was still talking, placing things in the basket – 'but watch it doesn't leak—'

'Mabel—'

'—on top of the bottle, so they don't bruise. Jo? What's the matter?'

Jo realised she was crushing the fritters. She loosened her grip. Genuine concern spread across Mabel's face.

'Jo?'

Jo placed the fritters in the basket, mind racing. She was being absurd. She was being cruelly suspicious again, when Mabel had only been kind. She had nothing to fear from her, she *knew* that.

'. . . Nothing.'

She followed Lily outside in silence. Lily, buoyed with the

prospect of a day out, had not seemed to notice. A neat line appeared between her brows as she looked up and down the road.

'Which direction did he say to take?'

It was hard to linger on the sense of unease with Lily by her side, humming and whistling to herself as they walked, pointing out swooping birds of which she did not know the name or blurs of fur as rabbits dashed through the fields that flanked the path. They turned from the main road to the less worn lane through the woodlands, and after a short walk soon came upon the sound of lapping water.

'Thank *God*,' Lily breathed as they broke through the treeline and onto the sunny lakeside shore, 'I can finally be rid of this thing . . .'

She tore off her head covering, which Jo had insisted she wear to protect her from the baking heat, and tossed it carelessly onto the pebbles before making quick work of the ties of her dress, pulling it over her head and throwing that aside as well. It landed heavily, scattering stones.

Next came her shift, clinging sweatily to her skin. She pulled her arms from the sleeves and tugged it down to reveal her freckled back, still marked with tender-looking yellow bruises. They captured Jo's gaze. She couldn't help but stare at the way they nestled against her ribs.

Lily didn't seem to notice. She flashed her a genuine smile over her shoulder, then tugged the shift down over her hips, swiftly kicking it aside.

Now completely naked, Lily set her shoulders and threw herself into the water with a colossal splash. Jo tiptoed closer, toeing off her shoes and lifting her skirts to stand at the very edge of the lake. The ripples where Lily had leapt in lapped gently around her ankles.

'Well?' Lily turned in the water, her face flushed. 'Will you not join me?'

Jo hesitated for just too long, cheeks reddening. 'I, ah—'

'Come.' Lily pushed her wet hair from her eyes. 'You are not *shy*, surely?'

'*No*.' Jo spoke too fast, too *loud*, and quickly corrected herself. 'It is just—' She swallowed, feeling the smooth pebbles beneath her feet. 'I was never taught to swim.'

Lily looked shocked. 'Truly? Whyever not?'

Jo shrugged. 'It was never something I needed to know. I suspect swimming is not required of a dutiful wife.'

Lily's silence only lasted a few seconds. 'Do you wish to learn?'

Jo pulled her gaze away from her feet. Lily was watching her. Lily who, despite their similar roles at court, did only as she pleased. When their eyes met, Lily's lips pulled into a devilish grin.

Something squeezed in Jo's chest. Her dress felt too tight.

'Do you think you could?'

Lily's grin widened. 'Of course.'

Jo imagined stripping off her clothes and leaping into the water. She imagined how it would feel against her skin, how close she would be to Lily beneath the gentle surface. She *did* want it. She wanted just *this*, just for her.

Before she could change her mind, Jo reached for the ties of her dress. She managed the laces swiftly, tugging the long gown up and over her head, stroking out the creases and folding it neatly on the shore beside Lily's pile of discarded clothes.

As she pulled off her shift, she noticed that Lily was still watching her, her face low.

Jo folded the shift and placed it beside the dress before gingerly stepping into the water. It lapped past her ankles, then her calves, then up and over her stomach.

'It is *freezing*,' Jo said, teeth chattering despite the hot weather.

'It will feel warmer once you are in,' Lily said. 'Put your head beneath the surface and you won't feel the cold.'

'That sounds *dreadful*.' Jo gave her a look of horror. 'I will freeze.'

'No, you won't.'

'I am not sure if—'

Before she could back away, Lily grabbed her, tugging her down into the water beside her. With a huge splash and an undignified scream, Jo tumbled into the frigid lake. She righted herself, spluttering, her hair plastered to her face as Lily cackled beside her.

'*You*—'

She jumped forwards, placed both of her hands on Lily's shoulders, and pushed as hard as she could, dunking her beneath the surface. They descended into splashing, and soon Jo's fear was replaced by laughter. She wasn't sure the last time she had laughed so much, or so long, although she was sure it was at Lily's side.

Drunk on mirth and sunshine, Jo took too confident a step forward. She stood on something slippery beneath the water and staggered, stumbled, and fell directly into Lily's arms.

Lily held her tight around the middle as if she had no weight at all. Her skin was warm and soft, her grip sure, her arms strong. Below the surface of the water Jo could feel all the places their bodies touched; the way their legs brushed against each other, the smoothness of Lily's back where Jo clung to her, the heat between their bodies where their breasts pressed together. It *was* a heat, too – nothing that could touch the chill of the lake, but one that seemed to boil inside her skin, sinking lower, nuzzling into the space between her legs.

So distracted, Jo didn't notice that she had fallen into deeper water until Lily loosened her hold, and Jo realised she was floating.

Another surge of panic gripped her. The hot feeling shattered, and she instinctively clung tighter to Lily.

'You are safe,' Lily said, turning them both gently in the water. 'I am with you.'

She sounded so sure. She showed Jo, without letting go, the way to move her feet to keep her head above the surface, and soon they were peacefully floating together.

Now more confident, Jo loosened her grip until only their hands were linked. Lily smiled at her, her wet hair lit up like fire by the summer sun, her freckles dancing as she laughed, spinning then gently around.

'You need to *relax*,' Lily said, happy that Jo was no longer panicking, 'or you will never be able to swim.'

She placed a hand to the small of Jo's back, moving her through the water until she was lying on her back, staring at the sky above. Jo's heart pounded, her body caught with the urge to thrash, but Lily was there, soothing her.

'*Relax*,' she said, laughing. 'You're all right. Trust me.'

Jo closed her eyes, focusing on her breathing, on Lily's voice, on the pressure of her hand on her back. The water lapped at her bare skin.

'*There . . .*'

The pressure was gone, and Jo was floating. She opened her eyes to see the cloudless sky above, stretching on to infinity. A pair of birds darted across the blue. The water was gentle against her ears, muffling them.

She took a low, long breath before righting herself. Lily was watching her, looking pleased, then swiftly ducked once more beneath the surface.

She swam in neat circles around Jo, kicking her legs and splashing her every time she drifted close. She dived under the water, turning neat tumbles beneath the crystalline surface as Jo watched on. She was showing off, but Jo could hardly blame her, not when she was so enraptured.

Lily moved in the water as if she was born to it. Jo wondered how many hours – how many *days* – Lily must have spent swimming in the lakes and rivers near Dunlyn Castle. Her body seemed built for it, strong but lithe, slipping through the water like it were made of air. Typically, Lily was always tripping over her own feet, as if she was never too sure of the confines of her own body. But in the water – or, Jo thought, when Lily had been the Knight of Stars – all that clumsiness was forgotten. She moved with purpose, her boundless energy channelled.

It could not last, and soon Jo's stomach was rumbling and her legs were beginning to ache. Lily, too, was tiring, her resilience worn down by her illness, and together they made their way back to the shore, Lily leading the way.

When Lily emerged, standing confidently from the water, Jo's breath gave out. The sunshine lit Lily up, making her glow. Droplets clung to her skin in sparkles.

Before he'd left, Penn had spoken at length about his lover's freckles as Jo half-listened to his rhapsodising, comparing them to the stars in the sky. Jo had *seen* Raff's skin – it was impossible not to, given how regularly she would watch while Penn changed his bandages – but all *she'd* been able to see was skin.

Jo had found it laughable, although she hadn't allowed Penn to know that. She'd assumed he was being typically dreamy, as far from the reality of their situation as the stars were from themselves.

But as she watched Lily rise from the water ahead of her, she was struck with how right he'd been. The freckles across Lily's shoulders and creeping down her back *were* like stars: a dazzling array of dots like the shimmering sparkles that sliced across the night sky.

Given a day, Jo could trace her finger across them and turn them into constellations, linking the individual freckles to make them animals, mythical gods, fantastic creatures. They looked as if they'd been painted deliberately onto Lily's skin, each one placed just so. It was almost a wonder they hadn't washed away in the water of the lake.

The thought made Jo's heart skip, her muscles tightening. Her skin felt warm, heat once again curling in her belly.

Lily strode forwards, dripping water, her pale skin made pink by the chill of the lake. Jo hadn't realised till now how broad her arms were, how strong they looked. As Lily stretched her tired limbs, Jo watched her muscles move, bunching in her shoulders. Even her shoulder blades seemed as if they had been carved there, framing her freckled back.

There were matching symmetrical dimples in the space just above her backside. Jo wondered what it would feel like to press her fingers there.

Oh. The unexpected thought sent a shiver down Jo's spine, igniting the heat in her core even further. But she couldn't name it, couldn't place it.

It felt like it had when she had imagined kissing William Dale.

Lily paused. She turned, staring at Jo over her shoulder with a smile and a nod – an indication to hurry up. Her eyes were the colour of the lake, shimmeringly bright.

Caught staring, Jo forced herself to look away as Lily splashed through the shallows towards the shore.

✳

Lily's hair was slowly drying in the summer heat, her shift clinging to her body. She'd pulled it back on after heaving herself from the water more through caution than modesty; there were some places she truly did *not* want to catch the sun.

Jo, too, had hastily dressed, pulling her shift back over her head before her skin had even begun to dry. Lily suspected that Jo's haste really *was* through modesty. She had noticed her blushing, even in the chill of the lake. They retrieved the basket then walked along the pebbled shore, heading for the shade where they could rest and eat.

At the far side of the lake, the shore was cut off by a steep outcrop of tree-covered land, hemmed in with heavy brambles. They were groaning under the weight of what must have been hundreds of plump, shining blackberries.

Lily reached through the thorns and grabbed one, eagerly popping it in her mouth. It was not quite ripe, but juicy enough that she didn't care. The taste burst across her tongue, so shockingly tart that she laughed, and suddenly Jo was at her side, reaching for a berry herself.

Jo was not so used to the flavour, and immediately grimaced. Lily couldn't help but giggle at her as she took another, this time controlling her expression. Soon they were both at work gathering as many berries as they could, Jo tipping them into Lily's cupped hands.

'This is terribly unfair,' Lily said, as she struggled to contain them. 'Now I cannot eat any of them.'

Jo grinned. Her lips were stained purple. 'More for me.'

Lily huffed at her, but before she could form a proper response Jo pulled a berry from the bush and nudged it past Lily's lips, effectively silencing her. Jo's fingers, those too stained, brushed against Lily's mouth for just a second. It felt a lot longer.

Jo seemed to realise what she had done as she did it, quickly pulling her hand back. Now she really *was* flushing, her purple-tinged lips caught beneath her teeth.

Lily said nothing, just smiled, thanked her, and desperately wished she would do it again.

When Lily's hands were full, they retired to the edge of the pebbled shore beneath the shade of the lakeside trees. Lily let the blackberries fall into the scoop of her skirt as Jo dug through the basket for something to eat them with.

Lily rolled pebbles beneath her bare feet, mindlessly making her way through their harvest. She was truly happy, and her lungs were clear for the first time in *days*. The sparkling water had reminded her of home, of long, hot days spent with her brothers when they were all children, before the world had happened to them.

The cool summer breeze rustled through the trees behind them: slender silver birches, the leaves rattling and whispering like gossiping maids chattering to one another about the women below them. As she tongued at a blackberry seed caught between her teeth, Lily wondered if she really *was* the subject of gossip: if the legend of the Knight of Stars was still being told in the de Foucart keep, or if anyone had yet noticed her absence from Dunlyn Castle.

She had been gone longer than she intended. But even if Ash and their father had returned, they would assume her at the convent, and Raff and Penn were likely still away.

'They can't have left Scotland yet,' she said aloud.

'What?'

Jo was staring at her. Lily retraced her thoughts, then realised belatedly that she had finished her musings out loud.

'Raff and Penn,' she explained, as Jo blinked at her. 'I was thinking about – how long I have been gone,' she admitted at last. 'If my absence has been noted.'

'Oh.'

'I hope not,' Lily quickly added, leaning back and letting the sun warm her. 'I cannot remember the last time I felt so content.'

'I am inclined to agree,' Jo said, expression easing as she took one of the blackberries from Lily's lap. 'I had not expected to feel so peaceful here.'

'And look,' Lily added, gesturing to the blackberries. 'We *have* managed blackberry picking and lakeside walks after all.'

Jo laughed, her eyes sparkling, as she tucked a strand of still-damp hair behind her ear.

'Indeed we have,' she said. 'And do you still believe that the berries near Dunlyn are tastier?'

'*Far* tastier,' Lily said. 'Although I think it would be difficult to have had a more wonderful day. Imagine, had you stayed in the keep, you might be married by now. We would have never even had a chance for something like this.'

A small frown appeared on Jo's face. 'I suppose I would be.'

'Do you think you would have had such a day with Adam?' Lily urged, cheekily.

Jo's face fell further.

'No,' she said, looking at her feet. 'I do not think I would.'

Lily couldn't stand that expression. 'He probably would have brought Lanval with you,' she teased.

That managed to snap Jo from her reverie. She grimaced. 'As his dearest friend, I am sure he would.'

'When you are wed, he will be *everywhere*.'

'If I even—' Jo faltered. 'He will, I suppose,' she said with a shake of her head. 'Perhaps I should tell him that it is only fair that I, too, am surrounded by my friends. We could make a lady's maid of you.'

Lily pretended to consider this. 'Are lady's maids permitted to wear armour and enter tournaments?'

'I suspect they are not.'

'Then I will have to reject your offer. I cannot be both your lady's maid *and* your champion.'

'I think you make a finer champion.' Jo smiled. 'If it is any consolation.'

'I quite agree,' Lily said, taking another blackberry. 'I will admit, I am not even sure what it is that a lady's maid *does*. I have not had one for—' Lily paused, remembering exactly *what* had happened with her last lady's maid, before she moved on to marry a low-ranking lord. 'For some time,' she finished, coyly. 'What do they even do?'

Jo shrugged. 'Help one dress, bathe, tidy one's hair . . .' She sighed. 'I admit, I, too, have not had one since my nurse retired when I was a girl. It was the one thing I refused entirely. I hated to think what she might see in the keep, with my father . . .' She blinked the memory away. 'Regardless, it is not as if I needed one. I am perfectly capable of dressing myself. I gather at my age they act more as . . . confidantes. Advisers.'

'Advisers?' Lily paused with a berry to her lips. 'Whatever for? For the best coloured ribbons to wear in your hair?'

Jo snorted. 'No, I think – matters of marriage. God knows I would need it.'

'What? Why?'

'I fear I may be . . . bad at it.' Jo was looking down again. There was a flush on her cheekbones.

'*You?*' Lily couldn't hold back her shock, the berry dropping back to her lap. 'How could *you* of all people be bad at marriage? Your work in the brewery is exemplary, and you ran a keep for *years.*'

Jo shot her an arched look. 'Marriage is not just about running keeps, Lily.'

It took Lily a moment to understand. And then she realised: it was similar to her *own* concerns around marriage. Or at least, marriage as she would be forced into it, with a man.

'Oh,' she said. 'I see.'

'Any man will have *expectations* going into a marriage,' Jo continued. 'And – I do not think I could meet them.'

'I am sure—'

'I have never even *kissed* someone, Lily!' she suddenly cried, hands in the air.

Oh. Lily wished she could reach for her. She didn't.

'Come,' she said. 'That cannot be true. Surely you have kissed someone before?'

'Oh, *yes,*' Jo conceded sarcastically, 'but . . . family, friends.

I have never kissed someone in the way a wife is supposed to kiss her husband, I fear.'

'Never?'

Jo gave her a pointed look. 'Do you think all of my father's children were as troublesome as my brothers? As keen to court danger and disgrace? No, unlike Leo and Penn I never found myself in dark corners of the castle with locked lips . . .'

Lily stared at her. 'Did you never wish to?' she asked, slowly. 'For . . . I mean, that is quite all right, Jo. There are many people who do not desire to kiss at all.'

'It's not that,' Jo said, waving her off, 'just . . . I've not had *time* for such thoughts, especially after Mother's death, and I was always so aware of Father's expectations.'

'He needed you to remain marriable.'

'He did. And more so; he needed me to remain a faithful and diligent child. With two troublesome brothers and one ghost . . .' She sighed. 'It was easier to acquiesce. To behave. I have never been as brave as Penn or Leo, and I wished nothing more than for him to leave me be. He *did*, but . . . he was always there. Always watching.' Her shoulders slumped. 'He feared my slip into disgrace more than he did Penn's, I think. He had more to lose from me following Leo's path. I am . . . *quite* sure that many of my movements in the castle were being watched while he was alive.'

'You were chaperoned?'

'Not explicitly. Not all the time. But Father's eyes were everywhere. Had I entangled myself with someone . . . he would have known. I would have been punished.' She looked at Lily, keeping her gaze. 'You know, I assume, of what he did to Penn?'

Lily swallowed. She had seen the lash marks on Penn's back only once or twice.

'I do. You feared he would treat you similarly?'

'I did. I think it would have been unlikely, given how he needed to ensure I remained pure and beautiful for any potential suitors . . . but I feared it. I had been so cowardly when he punished Penn, and I was terrified that one day his ire would touch me, too.'

'Jo . . .'

'It is of little import, now. I stayed free of punishment. I cannot complain when I know how much pain I managed to avoid. And even *without* Father, there was so much to do, and I was so *busy* . . . besides' – she was trying to smile – 'urge or no, I never found anyone I really *wished* to kiss.'

'No?' said Lily. 'Did no one catch your eye? None of your father's knights?'

Jo shrugged, keeping her eyes down.

'. . . and . . . and none of their ladies?'

Jo didn't respond, just stared down at her hands.

The silence was huge, and cavernous. A horrible pit opened in Lily's chest. She had said the wrong thing, spoken *entirely* out of turn. At least Jo wasn't furious with her, as many women might have been, assuming the question was an accusation. She just sat, staring down, saying nothing.

Lily didn't want to push, not after they'd spent such a wonderful day together. She edged closer, and the remaining blackberries spilled from her skirt.

'I am sure one day you will learn,' she said. There was an ache in her chest: one she didn't want to touch. 'And when you do, I know you will be very good at it.'

Jo snorted. The terrible silence shattered around them. 'I wish I was as certain as you, Lily.'

'It is just a matter of practice, I am sure.'

'And finding someone to practise with, of course,' Jo added doubtfully.

'. . . of course.'

Lily didn't voice out loud the words in her head, the ones that were painful in both their sincerity and the risk that they carried with them. The ones that made her heart sing and weep in equal measure.

I would kiss you, if you asked.

Please ask.

Saying nothing, Lily took Jo's hand, and stared out across the lake.

Chapter 17

It was late in the afternoon by the time they headed back to the brewery. Lily walked beside Jo in uncharacteristic silence: likely she was just tired from swimming, overexerting her healing lungs. Jo, too, was aware that she was being quiet as they walked. It had been a wonderful day, and with the sun setting ahead of them she felt genuine loss that it was ending. She peered across at Lily, who had removed her head covering and was twirling it in her hand as she walked. She thought of a constellation of freckles, of warm skin pressed to her own. Of perfectly symmetrical dimples.

That hot feeling bubbled low in her chest, seeping downwards, warming her.

As she kicked loose stones beneath her feet, she recalled the moment at the tournament when thoughts of Lord Adam had transformed into the imagined shape of William Dale. Now, William melted away as well, shifting like ripples into the image of Lily.

William had been ephemeral and unreal. She hadn't even known his face. But Lily was solid and terrifyingly touchable. Lily was the one whom she spent her days with, whom she slept curled around in their shared pallet bed, who'd held her naked body as they'd floated together in the lake.

As they sat together on the pebbled shore, discussing Jo's future as if it was never going to happen, Jo had wanted to kiss her.

It all coalesced into one, the confusion and the doubt and the strange lurch in her stomach when Lily had mentioned wanting to kiss ladies. Jo couldn't unpick it, couldn't peer through the tangle. All she knew was that she had wanted to close that gap between them. Away from the opportunity, she regretted that she had not.

No doubt it was for the best. She could only guess at what sort of reaction it could have garnered, especially given her own inexperience. To do something so bold would have ruined their friendship.

Yet still she glanced at Lily from the corner of her eye, wondering.

Mabel was busy when they entered the house, sweeping the kitchen floor with Matilda as Harry shook out the mats in the yard. Nora was sitting by the fireplace, playing with a discarded rush as Gilbert watched the flicking shape with interest. Mabel paused when they entered, leaning on the broom and looking up.

'You look well,' she said. 'You found the lake, then?'

'We did.' Jo smiled, refusing to let her swirling thoughts show on her face. 'It is lovely down there.'

'I headed into town after you'd left,' Mabel said as Jo put the empty basket down, 'to take Geoffrey's wife that dress Lily mended. They're putting up some musicians in the inn. Turned up late last night, they said, and they're giving them free board if they play this evening. You should go, it'll do you good.'

Before — before the brewery, and the escape, and the weeks at Lily's side — Jo would have said no. It would have been unsuitable.

She would not have been *allowed*. But now, with her hair damp and her skin tingling, she couldn't. She wanted to stretch the evening out and snatch even more of that bubbling feeling.

'Oh, Jo, *yes*.' Lily was at her side. 'Let's go.'

Even if Jo *hadn't* wanted to go, it would have been impossible to refuse her.

'I suppose I shall have to find something suitable to wear . . .'

Lily's face split into a familiar, cheeky grin – one that Jo had become painfully fond of – and then it slipped, as if she was remembering something.

'Wait, Jo, there is something . . . rather, I have something for you. Um . . .' The tips of her ears had gone pink. 'In the loft?'

Intrigued, Jo followed Lily up the ladder, watching as she ducked down behind the crates. After searching for a moment, Lily pulled out a bundle of purple cloth.

'It is not much, really,' Lily said, her cheeks reddening. 'But I had the idea, and I couldn't shake it, and I considered, since you had *asked* . . . or, you had *joked*, so – here.' She thrust the bundle into Jo's arms. 'It was one of Mabel's, so I've had to take in the seams a little, but it should fit, and I—'

Jo unrolled the fabric. 'Oh, *Lily*.'

'Is it all right?'

Jo stared at the garment in her arms. It was a simple surcoat, designed to wear over a linen dress, in a rich violet colour. But that was where the simplicity to it ended. Lily had stitched a whole *field* of flowers onto the fabric. They began at the shoulders and cascaded down the bodice in a shower of colourful petals. She could pick out a dozen different kinds, twisting and linking and bursting over one another. Lily must have used every colour Mabel had, the delicate blooms linked with finely stitched green vines from which burst perfectly round blackberries.

'This is *wonderful*,' Jo breathed, brushing her fingers over the threads. 'I cannot believe you did this for me.'

'You said that you would have to tear your skirts so I could mend them,' Lily said, fiddling with the cuff of her sleeve. 'This way, you do not need to.'

'I did not truly mean that.' Jo laughed.

'I know. But I . . . I wanted to make something beautiful.' Lily paused. 'For you.'

Jo's heart stuttered. The last time she had been gifted a dress it was from Isabelle. Those dresses had been very fine – and devastatingly expensive compared to this – but they hadn't been for *her*, not really. They had been to make her suitable, to make her more appealing to Lord Adam. But this was for her and her alone. Each stitch had been placed for no greater reason than the fact that Lily thought she would like it.

It was marvellous. Jo's eyes filled with tears.

'I know it is not as fine as the dresses you had in the keep . . .' Lily began, 'but, I thought—'

'Lily, *no*.' Jo hugged the dress to her chest. 'It is far, far finer than any of those gowns. I love it.'

Lily's unsure expression broke into a wide grin.

'I have never seen anything like it,' Jo continued. 'How did you *manage* this?'

Lily shrugged. 'It is just a matter of practice.'

Jo held the dress tighter. She thought of the lake and sparkling sunshine. Of Lily's smile and broad arms and soft, dangerous lips.

'Indeed,' she said, as her stomach flipped.

The dress was a near-perfect fit. Lily must have spent an *age* assessing the size of it, ensuring it was just right. Jo wondered if she had surreptitiously stolen one of Jo's other gowns to measure against it, or had judged by eye alone – a thought that made that stomach-twirling feeling return. There were no mirrors in the brewery, so Jo couldn't see what the dress looked like on her, but it *felt* wonderful. When the fabric brushed her legs or her fingers drifted against the edge of a stitched flower, her heart soared. It was entirely, wholly *hers*. It didn't matter how it made her look.

The brewery was on the opposite edge of town to the inn, but it was an easy walk down the wide, uneven road. The summer evening was mild, the sun hanging above the treetops, throwing Jo and Lily's shadows long and large ahead of them like striding giants.

Jo had never seen the inn so busy: clearly the prospect of an evening's free entertainment was too tempting for the residents of Astmere. They managed to find a pair of seats near the wall, and Jo left Lily happily chatting to a couple while she sought out something to eat and drink.

Geoffrey gave her the food free of charge, thanks to Lily's work on his wife's dress: a soft, fresh-baked loaf of bread, some salted meat, and a chunk of hard cheese. As Jo sliced through the cheese, Lily laughing beside her, she couldn't help but think how much *richer* it all tasted than the extravagant meals she had grown used to in the keep.

The inn was packed by the time a scraggly crew of musicians made their way to the area that Geoffrey had cordoned off for the event. It wasn't a stage like the ones Jo had seen in her father's court, or the courts of his allies, just a corner of the room marked out with benches to ensure there was enough space to play.

The troupe, which seemed too grand a word for them, was composed of four people. They were led by a man carrying a lute with a mess of shaggy, straw-coloured hair that flopped haphazardly across his face. He appeared to be the leader of their group — or at the very least, the one most confident in capturing their audience's attention, smiling at the meagre crowd.

Behind him the rest of the musicians were a rag-tag bunch. One was a woman, which surprised Jo, with brown skin and voluminous hair barely contained beneath a brightly coloured wrap. She was carrying a short pipe, fidgeting with it as she walked. Behind her was a pair of men: one round and broad with a drum hanging around his neck, the other lithe and short and very young, carrying a fiddle. His youth and shortness were exacerbated by the size of his companion, but he carried himself surely, looking out confidently across the audience.

'My grand guests!' the leading man called, his low voice silencing the crowd. 'My Lords and Ladies, my masters and mistresses. How pleased I am that we can be here to entertain you today, at the hospitality of your friend and mine . . . ah—' He faltered.

From behind him, the boy with the fiddle cried out, 'Geoffrey!'

'Geoffrey!' the man continued, without missing a beat. 'What a glorious evening it is to make so many new and wonderful friends. I am sure you will all remember this evening for many years to come!'

The woman behind him laughed, amused by his bloviating.

'Hush now, Noll,' she chastised. 'No one is here to hear your voice.'

'I thought that was precisely why they were here?'

'They are here to hear you *sing*,' she said, loud enough for the whole room to hear. 'Not to listen to your thrice-damned boasting.'

'Are they not one and the same?'

They laughed again, and with that, the leader – Noll, apparently – launched into the first song. His voice was low and loud, carrying with ease around the room, rattling from the rafters above. It took no time at all for the crowd to become enraptured, some singing along, some dancing, many stamping their feet in tune to the drum. During the third song, the fiddler placed down his instrument to sing in tune with Noll, his voice surprisingly high and clear. The sound was melodious, and the little troupe sounded better than the expensive minstrels Isabelle had hired for the tournament.

After a few songs, there was a brief lull in the music. Noll plucked at the strings of his lute a few times, picking out a soft half-melody, before pausing.

'This is a song I learnt in France,' he said. 'While I was visiting that fair country.'

This, apparently, was a shared joke, and the larger man behind him gave a low, sardonic chuckle before they launched into the tune. It wasn't one Jo had heard before, the melody slow as the man's fingers drifted up and down the lute strings.

When he began to sing in French, Jo found it difficult to parse exactly what he was saying. He spoke like one who had heard the lyrics but had never been taught what they actually meant, memorising the sounds rather than the words themselves.

The few phrases she could make out made it seem like it was a soldier's song – one sung in a group to entertain oneself around a campfire. There was a sense of sadness to it, and she wondered what, exactly, the singer had encountered across the channel.

But it was soon over, and those thoughts were pushed aside as the troupe swung into another popular drinking song, Lily singing tunelessly along beside her.

Lily's loud, off-key singing made a laugh bubble up Jo's throat. She was so *free*. Jo watched, Lily's face illuminated by the torches on the walls, her hair falling around her face in red wisps. Her freckles danced around her face in the shadows, her nose crinkling, her crooked smile made even more so.

When she laughed, she snorted like a little hog, and it was desperately endearing.

Soon the troupe's performance was over. They left the stage with exaggerated bows, but the crowd – now plied with food and good, strong drink – did not appear to wish to stop the revelry. Their place was taken by Geoffrey's son with a mandolin, and their expert singing was soon forgotten in place of his more rustic melodies.

Now the more exciting entertainment was over, several people took the chance to drag themselves or their partners up from their chairs to dance, a space opening in front of Geoffrey's son to make room. Lily stood, too, extending her hand towards Jo.

'Come,' she said, 'dance with me?'

Jo hesitated, looking at her outstretched hand, her calloused palm.

'Oh,' she said, her tongue suddenly feeling too large for her mouth, 'I am not . . . I don't know . . .'

'Oh, *come*,' Lily urged. 'Please, my Lady?'

As if powered by some outside force, Jo took Lily's hand. Lily did not, as Jo had expected, help her up, but lingered for a second before placing a kiss to the back of her hand like a suitor at a banquet.

There was a storm of butterflies in Jo's stomach. Lily sparkled at her, then hauled her to her feet.

The space cleared to dance was small, and Jo was crushed as people pressed against her. Lily didn't care at all, pulling her into the middle of the room and placing her other hand upon Jo's waist. Jo felt the heat of Lily's palm through her dress, the twitch of her fingers against her side as she moved her. It was *all* she felt. She thought of Lily's amused tutelage in the lake, her hands slipping against Jo's naked skin. She thought again of the desire she had felt to kiss her.

Something tight rumbled inside her.

Lily led, being more confident, although she was not a keen dancer. She had enthusiasm but no grace, not that it was stopping her. Jo's nervousness was no match for Lily's exuberance, and soon she was laughing with her as they spun around each other. It was as if nothing else existed – just them, and the music, and Lily's sparking eyes and the way she smiled all the time, even when she tripped over her own feet.

Jo couldn't help but stare at her as they moved across the room. She looked so *happy*, and it set a private thrill in Jo's chest to realise that it was *her* that made Lily happy.

Lily executed an imperfect twirl and staggered into Jo's side. Jo caught her – it was impossible not to, given how close they were standing. Lily floundered in her arms for a moment, and when she righted herself her face was split into a huge smile. She was panting with the effort of the dance, her skin *shimmering*, her breath quick and hot.

She was so close. The dance and the crush of the crowd had forced them together, face to face. Lily was but a whisper away.

Jo *could* kiss her, she realised. She could kiss her, and find out what it was like.

The urge took her with such shock that she thought her heart might give out. It was too much, it was all too much, and she was entirely out of her depth, drowning in hitherto untested waters.

'I—' she said. 'Excuse me, I—'

She extracted herself from Lily's arms and stepped back. She barely felt the people part around her as she pushed her way across the room, out of the door, and into the wide yard of the inn. There were people lingering *here*, too, and she hurried out of the gate to the path beyond, leaning against a twisted tree while her breath returned to her.

Her face was hot. Her whole *body* was hot, like she was on fire, like she was back in the baking sunshine and not out here in the cool, night-time breeze.

She took a huge, gulping breath. Her heart began to slow, the heat ebbing from her cheeks.

'Jo? Jo!'

Lily rushed across the yard. She didn't slide through the gate as Jo had, but vaulted easily over the low stone wall – much to the amusement of the people gathered outside the inn.

'What happened?' she said, breathlessly. 'Are you well? One moment you were there, and then—'

'Yes,' Jo said, attempting to regain her composure. 'I am fine, I just—'

'Did the crowd overwhelm you? Or was it the food, the drink?'

Jo grabbed at the excuse. 'It was the crowd, I think,' she said. 'And it was so *warm* in there, I felt quite shaken. I don't know what came over me.'

Her voice wobbled uncharacteristically on the last few words. Lily, of course, caught the tremor immediately. She looked worried but unsure, then reached into the pouch at her side and pulled something out, handing it over.

'Here,' she said. 'I – if you feel as if you need to . . .' She was so lost that Jo could nearly laugh. 'If you feel you are going to cry? Or . . . if you wish to . . .' She gestured at her own, sweaty face. 'Dab at yourself?' She grimaced. 'God damn it, I sound like an idiot. Here.'

She thrust out her hand. She was holding the handkerchief – the one Jo had given her. Jo was aware that she had taken to carrying it around with her, but rarely did she see her actually use it. Lending it to Jo was a sweet, courtly gesture; likely one Lily had heard of in tales as the thing expected of noble ladies but had never had a chance to put into practice herself.

She couldn't help but smile. Even now, even after that strange, hot moment in the inn, Lily was like the tide, pulling her away from her own worries. She was irresistible.

'Thank you,' Jo said, taking the kerchief.

She wasn't entirely sure what she should *do* with it, twisting it around in her hands. Her skin was rapidly cooling now she was back outside, and while her heart still pounded she was quite sure she wasn't about to burst into tears. Still, she wouldn't refuse the gesture, and self-consciously dabbed at her dry cheeks with the silk, feeling a little silly.

She caught Lily staring at her from the corner of her eye. And then, something snapped. They both burst out laughing.

'We are very poor at this, I fear,' Jo said, shaking her head.

'Quite,' Lily agreed. 'When my brothers are struggling with

their feelings I either shout at them or goad them into a fight until the mood passes.'

Jo laughed even louder. 'I *do* hope you do not intend to try either tactic with me?'

'Why not?' Lily retorted, bumping their shoulders together. 'It may work. How would you know how you would fare in a fight if you have never tried?'

'Lily Barden, I *despair* of you.' Jo sighed fondly as Lily giggled. 'You are no more likely to get me to wield a sword than I am to force you to see through that arrangement and marry my brother.'

Lily gave an exaggerated shudder. 'Do not even jest, I cannot bear it.'

'He is not *so* bad.'

'Indeed he isn't! I am happy to have him as one of my dearest friends, and if Raff's opinion is anything to go by he is extremely fair to look at. Yet he has one fatal flaw that I am afraid I cannot overlook.'

'And that is?'

'That is that he is a *man*.' Lily gave another of those fake shudders. 'And therefore unsuitable.'

'Unsuitable?'

'Unsuitable for my needs, for my purposes. For *me*,' Lily said cockily. 'I would not wish to be married to him or any other man.'

Jo laughed. 'And do you not care for men's company?'

It was a simple question, and the obvious one. But Lily's expression had turned serious. She gave Jo a searching look.

'I do not,' she said at last. 'Do *you*?'

Jo opened her mouth to respond, then quickly shut it. She felt very sure that she was being asked a different question. She twisted the kerchief even more between her fingers, sure there was a new tension in the air – something betrayed in the intensity of Lily's stare.

'I . . . tolerate them well enough, I suppose,' she said. 'I *had* intended to marry one, after all.'

'I see.' Lily chewed on her lip a moment, then straightened, pulling her shoulders back. 'Jo . . .' she said. 'I need to tell you—'

'Oh—'

There was a sudden breeze, a shake in Jo's hands, and the handkerchief slipped from her grip. It fluttered to the ground between them, and the tension – if it even had been there to start with – dissolved as Jo stooped to catch it.

Another hand snatched it first. She righted herself to find herself eye to eye with Noll – the man with straw-blond hair who had sung in imperfect French. His face was covered in tiny scars, his right eye a little unfocused.

He shot her a wide, charming smile as he handed the handkerchief back to her.

'My Ladies.'

Jo took it and quickly shoved it into her pocket.

'Thank you,' she said. 'Your performance was very good, sir. We heartily enjoyed it.'

'I am glad,' Noll said dutifully. 'It is rare we get to perform for such a crowd.'

There was something about his demeanour that set Jo on edge. He seemed perfectly charming, his smile easy and his nature relaxed, but beneath that simmered something she couldn't name.

'Will you be staying for long, sir?' Lily asked, unfazed.

'Alas' – the man sighed, placing a hand to his chest – 'we are bidden to move onwards early tomorrow. We are planning to travel north, and the road is very long. A shame, for this town has welcomed us with open arms. Not everyone is so amenable towards travellers.'

'That is sadly true,' Lily said. 'Although I must say Astmere has greeted us extremely well.'

'Is that right?' He raised his eyebrows.

'Indeed,' Lily continued. 'We are staying at the brewery, down the way—' She pointed down the road. 'The owner is a marvellous woman, and kind. I hope that you find fortune and similar kindness on *your* journey.'

He gave them both another grin. That sense of *wrongness* stirred in Jo's chest again. It must just be her already elevated heartbeat, the lingering effect of the fit that had taken her in the inn.

'Thank you, my Lady. And I hope you are similarly blessed, wherever your paths take you.'

He gave them another of those exaggerated bows, then turned on his heel and walked away. The rest of the troupe were lingering on a roughly hewn bench outside the inn, and as he approached them the younger man passed him a slopping tankard, which he took with a grin. His laugh echoed boldly into the night air.

When Jo looked back to Lily, she had her arm extended towards her.

'Shall we? Mabel will worry if we return too late.'

The sky had faded to a deep purple, stained pinkly around the horizon. The first stars were trying to emerge, tiny pinprick holes in the velvet above them. Behind them, Jo could still hear the low chatter coming from the inn. A pair of birds twirled over their heads, their tiny, pointed tails twisting as they flew.

She took Lily's arm.

'Let's go home.'

Chapter 18

Lily lay resolutely alert and sleepless in the roof of the brewery, staring up at the cobwebbed ceiling above her. She was thinking through the best way to dispose of the webs – a broom handle, she supposed, wrapped in cloth. The webs were not particularly bothering her, and she hadn't even noticed them until that night, but now she was fixed on them, itching to remove them.

She hadn't suffered a sleepless night like this in *weeks*. At their peak, they would plague her, night after restless night interspersed with endless, fogged days. Often, the sleeplessness wasn't caused by worrying or anxiousness or even anything as easy as being *not tired*: her thoughts simply refused to let her go, and she clung to the edge of wakefulness until the sun finally rose.

It came more often when she *was* worrying, though, and tonight, staring up at the webs, anxiety bit at her nape.

Do you not care for men's company?

It was a question that Lily had known the answer to *years* ago, barely even twelve years old, utterly enamoured with the girl who worked in the kitchens.

Jo hadn't realised what question she'd been asking. And the more Lily thought of it, the more she was certain that Jo didn't even realise it was a question she *could* ask; of anyone else *or* of herself.

When Lily had asked if there was no one she wished to kiss – man *or* woman – Jo had seemed confused, not offended.

Lily had wanted to tell her where, exactly, her preferences lay. But despite Jo's steadfast support of their brothers and her unending care for her, Lily was still terrified of how she might respond. It would not be the first friendship ruined for it, and she loved her too much to lose her. As they'd sat at the lakeside, sharing blackberries, something had almost passed between them. It had happened again as they'd danced, before Jo had fled. *Had* those moments been there, or had they just been her own, tragic infatuation making her believe that Jo could ever feel more for her than friendship?

Beside her, tangled in the woollen blanket, Jo rolled over with a deep snort. Lily wondered how late it was – how *early* it was – and if it would be worth slipping from the bed and getting to work now instead of lying there until dawn finally broke.

It was a tempting thought. The sleeplessness was infuriating, and the anxiety unpleasant, but more so: such nights were *dull*. At least if she got up and snuck downstairs, she could find some way to occupy herself.

But more tempting was the comfort of the bed and the warmth of Jo beside her. Lily's lungs and limbs had finally stopped paining her, although they still twinged, and she'd been able to sleep undisturbed these past few nights. It was *bliss*, and when Jo sniffed and shuffled even closer, she was loath to break the spell of it.

Lily rolled onto her side, pulling the blanket up to her chin, when there was a noise from below. She froze, listening. No doubt it was just Gib after rats. There it was again: louder, coming from outside. It sounded like the gate opening.

There were *always* noises in the brewery or the house beside it.

The road was often busy, even late at night. But as Lily stilled, straining her hearing, she immediately knew something was wrong. The fine hairs on her arms suddenly stood to attention despite the warmth.

There was a *clunk*. The gate shutting. A metallic scraping. A door opening.

Heart in her throat, she gave Jo a shake, hoping she could wake her silently. Jo frowned and allowed Lily to roll her over, before slipping back into even deeper sleep with a rattling snore. Lily winced and immediately relented. She rose from the bed, thankful that she had fallen asleep in her shift, and keeping low with her stomach pressed to the wooden rafters, peered over the edge of the loft into the brew below.

There was a figure down there, obscured in the darkness.

Lily quickly ducked back so she wouldn't be seen. Moving swiftly, she snuck to their packs, and as quietly as she could slid the sack from behind the crates and straw. She could not fully armour herself: it was impossible in the cramped space of the roof and would take far too long. But she still had the sword, and her padding would provide her a *little* protection, at least.

She tugged her gambeson over her slip, then waited until the figure was at the other end of the room before slipping down the ladder, sword in hand.

She landed quietly, scrambling behind a tub before the man could turn and see her. He was searching through Mabel's stock: a thief, looking for what he could take.

Anger flared in Lily's chest. How *dare* he? How dare he take what he had not worked for, from someone who had only been good and kind to them?

She tightened her grip on the sword, edging towards the shadows. She stilled. She didn't breathe, afraid that the gentle noise would alert him to her presence.

The thief stepped from the shadows. He had a heavy-looking sack slung over his back, which rattled as he walked with the distinct sound of pewter.

Instead of heading outside, he shuffled along the far wall, heading deeper into the brewery. He was drawing closer to her hiding space. Too close. Slowly releasing her breath, Lily backed away until she collided with the opposite wall, then slid towards the door.

The door. If she could position herself there, she could prevent him from leaving and cause enough noise that the rest of the house would be alerted. If she could trap him in the brewery, he wouldn't be able to get away with Mabel's things. Or, a more tempting thought: she could take him by surprise and cut him down. Punish him herself.

He'd moved behind the tubs, entirely out of sight. Lily took her chance, squeezing between the barrels and the wall.

She waited. It felt like an age had passed, although it could only have been a few minutes as she listened for the sound of his footsteps. She hoped she could hear them over her own frantic heartbeat.

There. A step. The clink of pewter.

She stepped into the open doorway.

'You will go no further.' The man stopped in his tracks. Not waiting for a response, Lily readied herself, raising the sword with both hands. 'Drop what you stole, and *leave.*'

The man hesitated for just a moment, then jumped forwards, grabbed her around the middle and shoved her out into the yard.

She stumbled, the man gripping her gambeson, and as they staggered into a pool of moonlight she realised that she knew his face and unkempt straw-coloured hair.

The singer from the tavern. Noll.

She attempted to swing her sword, but Noll was far too close. He threw a desperate, powerful punch into her gut, winding her. If he recognised her, he made no show of it, using the moment of confusion to attempt to dash away. Lily didn't even wait to catch her breath, but followed suit, the sword still gripped in her hand.

She swung at him wildly, unsure if she was trying to force him to leave, wound him, or kill him. The edge of the blade sheared his arm, blood blooming beneath his shirt.

'You—' he began.

She would not give him time to speak. She leapt, bringing the sword down in a wild arc over her head, as if she were back in the ring. He stepped back to avoid the blow, the blade missing his face by a hair's breadth, the tip of the steel nicking his cheek.

Lily had become unbalanced from the swing, and taking his chance Noll leapt forwards and shoved her back. Lily tripped over her own feet, landing with a heavy thud as her sword slid away. Noll landed on top of her, pinning her. He looked *wild*, and Lily realised that she didn't even know if he was armed. She tried to push against him, but he was too heavy, even unbalanced with the sack still grabbed in one hand.

She needed to yell for help, but her voice was stuck in her throat. All she could do was stare up at him, waiting for the final blow.

There was a shout. Running footsteps. A shadow detached itself from the darkness and slammed heavily into Noll's side, sending him flying.

Lily heaved herself up to see Jo standing over him, looking furious. Her long hair was in wild disarray, her expression set. Both of them glanced towards the discarded sword. Jo's hand flexed at her side, and for a moment Lily was sure she was going to reach for it – but she hesitated too long, and Noll moved first.

Taking her chance, Lily scrambled to her feet, grabbing the sword before Noll could take it. She stood beside Jo, their hands brushing, the tip of the bloodied blade at Noll's throat. Lily's heart stuttered in her chest.

'*Leave*,' she growled.

They stared at each other. Lily edged the blade closer. The moment hung in the air, ready to snap.

Noll relented first. He heaved himself up, and without another look vaulted over the low stone wall of the yard and off into the night.

The relief came slowly, like waking from a nightmare. Lily sagged, the sword slipping from her hand into the dirt, and then Jo was on her, grabbing her, wrenching her back to the present. She ran her hands up Lily's arms, cupping her face.

'Lily—' Jo gasped – and Lily realised how close she was, how warm her hands were, how her breath tickled against her lips. 'Are you all right? I saw, I *thought*—' Jo gripped her harder. 'I thought you were—'

Lily was going to reassure her, to tell her that she was fine, that Noll had only winded her. Before she could, Jo surged forwards, and kissed her.

Lily's heart *soared*. It was a brief, chaste kiss – closed lips pressed clumsily together – but it thrilled her anyway. Jo broke it in seconds, and when she pulled away her eyes were shimmering with tears.

'My *God*, Lily, you are—'

'Incredibly foolish, I know.' Lily laughed. 'You do not need to remind me.'

'If you would not interrupt me,' she muttered, 'I was going to tell you that you are *brave*. Not that I would expect anything else from you.'

'Oh.'

'Although you *are* foolish. Damn your overconfidence. If anything were to happen to you . . . I don't know what I would do without you.'

There was a noise from the building behind them. Jo immediately released her, leaping back like she'd been burnt. The door to the main house burst open, and illuminated by torchlight in the doorway stood Mabel and Harry.

'What is going on?'

'There was a thief—' Lily tried to focus. 'He was in the brewery. He was . . . God, Mabel, he was one of Geoffrey's musicians. He took off that way . . .' She gestured limply the way he had gone.

'Christ . . .' Mabel turned to Harry. 'Go and fetch the alderman,' she commanded.

'But Ma, we cannot just let him—'

'I will not risk any of you chasing him,' Mabel said. 'Go!'

Harry rushed off in the opposite direction as Mabel jogged over.

'Are you all right?' she said. 'Did he hurt you?'

'No,' Lily panted. 'I am fine.' She grinned – she couldn't help it. Her heart was singing, now, a triumphant thing. 'I injured him, though. Twice. And we scared him off. He will think again before attempting to rob you, Mabel.'

Mabel sighed as Jo rolled her eyes.

'Come, both of you,' she said. 'Inside. Before any more of those bastards show up.'

Lily sat at the long bench that ran the length of Mabel's kitchen, one of the rescued pewter tankards clasped in her hands. Mabel had pressed it to her, and upon her first, spluttering sip she had realised that it was full of strong, potent mead – to calm her nerves, Mabel said. Lily thought that it was pointless, her nerves were *fine*, but when Jo slotted their fingers together she realised her hand was shaking.

The excitement of the fight and the elation of the kiss were wearing down, sloughing away, leaving the fear she should have felt when she first spotted Noll lurking in the dark.

She only spoke to give Jo another reassurance that she was unhurt, and explain to Mabel exactly what had happened, before all three of them lapsed into silence. Harry reappeared sometime later, but not with the alderman.

'It wasn't just us,' he explained breathlessly. 'Many others were robbed. The alderman said he'd send someone this way to see if they can catch him, but he's needed elsewhere, with those who had things stolen.'

'What was taken?' Jo asked, not letting go of Lily's hand.

Harry sat across from them at the bench, gladly taking a mug of ale from his mother.

'Tools,' he said, 'goods that were small enough to carry. Jewellery, food. The farrier had two horses taken. The town is awake, everyone is furious, old Geoffrey at the inn is beside himself, claiming it is all his doing . . .'

Mabel placed a hand to his shoulder. 'No wonder the alderman is busy.'

'Look, Ma,' began Harry. 'We have no way of knowing when he may send people this way. If I could just—'

'No,' Mabel said, sternly. 'I will not have you run off into the dark after a thief. Your father would never forgive me for it. I would not forgive myself should some harm befall you. You stay here, where we need you.'

Harry scowled, but stayed where he was. After they'd all finished their drinks, it became clear that the alderman would not likely be arriving any time soon, and Mabel had insisted they all retire to bed.

Lily and Jo returned to the loft, the once safe space now feeling wholly wrong. Lily didn't put the sword away, leaving it near the pallet so she could grab it quickly if she needed to. Noll's shadow seemed to lurk in every dark corner.

It hadn't been like the tournament. She thought that it would be, that all fights were the same, but out there in the dark there had been no rules. There had been no onlookers, no announcer. Just her against a desperate thief with no reason to leave her alive. Had Jo not pushed him off her, she had no way of telling how far he would have gone to escape.

With her heart calmed and the house – and the people within it – safe at last, she realised that it was *her* words that had sent him to the brewery. It was her fault.

She felt very small, and very lost. She was back in the sparkling lake, but now the water was as deep and dark as the sky, and she was drowning.

'Jo—'

Her voice shuddered. Jo was on her in an instant, pulling her close.

'You are all right,' she muttered, soothing her hand down her hair. 'You are safe. It's all right.'

Lily took a gasping breath, and realised with shock that she was crying. Usually, she would have attempted to school herself or distract herself: anything to avoid giving in to the hot, shameful feeling. Tonight she didn't, and let Jo hold her, stroking her hair and muttering soothing nonsense into her ear.

'It was my fault,' Lily managed. 'I told him about Mabel, and the brewery, and he—'

'Lily, *no.*' Jo spoke over her. 'Do not blame yourself.'

'But I *am* to blame,' Lily insisted. 'Had I not spoken to him . . .'

'He may have found us anyway,' Jo said. 'Or he may have found someone easier to rob, someone who would not face him down with a sword. *He* is to blame for this, not you.'

Lily sniffed into silence again. Jo didn't let her go, and after a while, spoke again.

'I was so scared,' she whispered. Lily didn't respond, just let her speak. 'When I saw you out there on the ground, I thought . . .' Lily felt her swallow. 'I thought I had lost you. And I have come so close to losing you already, that I—'

Jo didn't look up. She didn't move.

Lily couldn't bear it any longer. She edged backwards, gently cupping Jo's jaw and turning her to face her, moving her as if she was as delicate as a baby bird – a fragile thing that could shatter beneath her clumsy hands.

She heard Jo exhale as she touched her. She allowed Lily to move her until they were face to face.

Lily brushed Jo's cheek with her thumb. She was so close, her huge eyes black in the dark, her hair falling loose and long around her face. Lily's heart skipped over itself. Moths swirled in her stomach.

It would only take a single, tiny movement to brush their lips together. It would be as easy as breathing, as easy as slipping into a dream. If it were anyone else, she would — she would give in now and accept the consequences later. But this was *Jo*, Jo who, by her own admission, had never been kissed like *that*. Jo who had kissed her — and Lily didn't know why. Lily couldn't break her trust while she was still so unsure. She refused to push her towards something she didn't want.

Still, Jo hadn't moved away. Her expression seemed lost, but as Lily gazed at her, it hardened. It was the expression she wore while working: the expression that made her look like the lady of a keep.

Her lips, dark and chapped in the low light, parted.

'Jo—' Lily began, ready to soothe her.

'Kiss me.'

Lily's heart nearly gave out. Her ears rang. '. . .What?'

'I want you to kiss me.'

She shouldn't. Both of them were scared, alert from the near miss with Noll. This was just fear, just desperation, just an attempt to banish the shadows. It was *confusion*, just — just a *test*. To see what it was like. To chase an impulse. Jo didn't care for Lily in the way Lily did for Jo: in that hard, bone-deep, half-in-love way that drove her to madness.

But Lily was *weak*. She had prayed for Jo to ask. And now she had.

It really *was* as easy as breathing to close the space between them. They were back in the lake, Jo's feet barely brushing the floor, and Lily there to hold onto: to guide her, to keep her afloat.

Their lips met, and Lily's heart screamed in her chest.

Jo's lips were dry from the heat of the summer, but soft, too. She moved slowly, but even that gentle movement was enough to make Lily's heart race even harder, to make her stomach twist and flutter. She wanted *more*. She wanted to open her mouth, to taste her, to press her hands into Jo's hips.

She couldn't. She had to be *restrained* for once in her life, and not give in.

One of Jo's hands made its way to Lily's waist. Lily shuddered; she couldn't help it. Jo smiled against her mouth. Lily intended to push a little closer, but Jo shifted first, and suddenly her other hand was on the back of Lily's head, tangling in her hair, her mouth opening beneath the kiss. Lily lit up at the touch, her breath catching, bottling up in her lungs. A quiet, breathy noise escaped Jo's lips – a gentle, pleased sound that lit a curling pressure in Lily's core.

She wanted to hear it again.

She moved her lips against Jo's, opening them wider, the smallest exploration of a new land. She felt Jo's chapped, warm lips with the very tip of her tongue. Jo shuddered, so Lily repeated the movement, but didn't intensify it – merely let it linger.

Jo slid her hand down Lily's back, coming to rest at the very base of her spine. Her fingers twitched against Lily's skin, searchingly, curiously. Heat bloomed between Lily's legs. She sighed against Jo's lips, waiting.

But Jo froze. Her breath stuttered. She pulled away. In the darkness, she was flushed, but uncertain. She looked as if she had been startled from a deep sleep.

'Jo?'

'I just—' Jo took a deep breath. She lowered her head, resting their foreheads together.

'What is it? Do you want to stop?'

'*No*,' Jo breathed, quickly. 'But— But I—'

'*Jo*.'

Jo finally released her, leaning back. She laughed, the sweet sound echoing around them.

'It is . . . a little overwhelming,' she confessed, tucking a strand of hair behind her ear. 'I did not expect . . . I don't know *what* I expected.'

Lily remembered the first time she had kissed another girl – she'd been so young, and back then it really had just been *practice*, as she'd said to Jo as they sat by the lake. It had been some time later when she'd first kissed someone she really, truly wanted to kiss: the daughter of one of her father's allies with jet-black hair and matching eyes. Lily had been so awestricken that she'd fumbled the whole thing entirely, laughing at the worst possible moment and fleeing from the room in red-faced embarrassment.

It wasn't like that for Jo. This wasn't the culmination of months or years of bottled-up feelings. Jo had never kissed *anyone*, and was obviously troubled by her lack of experience. She'd built it in her head into something vast and terrifying: a challenge to be conquered. No wonder she was overwhelmed when it finally came to pass.

Moving slowly, Lily reached out and took Jo's hand.

'It can be, at first,' she said, attempting to not sound patronising.

'I suppose that is what you meant by needing *practice*.' Jo laughed, shaking her head. 'I . . .' She looked up. Her eyes were dark. 'I suspect I shall need more of it, yet.'

Her expression was eager. Lily swallowed, flushing.

Be good, she reminded herself. *Be good.*

'I suspect you shall,' she agreed, smoothly. Then she realised what it was she had said: what she had *implied*. 'Wait, that is—' she stuttered. 'I am not saying that you *need* practice, or that you are unskilled – you are not *bad* at— Oh, God's *teeth* . . .'

She lowered her head to her knees with a soft groan. She heard Jo chuckle beside her, then felt her hand on her back, resting gently between her shoulder blades. When she peered around, Jo placed her finger beneath her chin and gently raised her back up.

She didn't speak, merely pressed a single, light kiss to the corner of Lily's mouth.

'Thank you.'

Chapter 19

It was a bright, clear day as Jo stirred from heavy dreams. Shafts of light, sparkling with dust, flooded through the cracks in the roof, lighting the loft in glimmering gold. Outside, there was movement in the yard, and the rooster that ruled the garden was already crowing. They must have slept late – no wonder, after being woken at such an early hour by the intruder, and then, afterwards . . .

It had been some time before she had fallen asleep, curled around Lily.

The yellow morning light had banished the shadows that had crept around the edges of the brewery, the darkness in the corners transformed back into crates and sacks and straw, no longer lurking shapes or waiting intruders.

Beside her, Lily was still fast asleep, her mouth open and one long, freckled arm flung above her head. As Jo moved beside her, her face crinkled into a slight frown, her nose wrinkling. Her lips were a pleasing dark pink colour, like overripe berries.

Jo hadn't been thinking when she asked Lily to kiss her. All she knew was that she had wanted it, that she had *needed* to kiss her. The moment in the yard after Noll had fled had been brief and fuelled by relief – it had been a celebration that Lily was all right. She had considered it for no longer than she had considered throwing herself at Noll: which was to say, she had not considered it at all.

But back in the safety of the loft it had been different. Lily's lips had looked so soft, her face so close, and suddenly the feeling that Jo had been struggling to name became something solid – a desire that Jo could touch.

Had she been anywhere else – had she been *home* – she would have ignored it. She would have pushed it down and stamped it out and smothered it until it was only ashes. But here she could breathe. She could choose, for once, what she wanted. There was a prickling sense of unreality to the whole place, like a dream, and Jo didn't want to wake, not yet.

The air had been warm, and Lily was safe: she *was* her champion. She would never hurt her. Jo had regretted immensely not taking Lily's sword and running Noll through for even *daring* to lay his hands on Lily. She would not regret another inaction.

It had been as easy as falling to ask, and easier still to kiss Lily back, to marvel at the way their lips played together, the feeling of her skin, the way Jo's body lit up when Lily touched her in return.

Lily's response had been immediate and enthusiastic, but she hadn't baulked or complained when Jo had pulled away, either. It had been too much. Jo's mind was racing, her body lighting up in a way that was so good – yet so terribly unfamiliar – that it had overwhelmed her. But Lily had accepted it, slipping back into laughter and later slipping between Jo's arms as they fell asleep, tangled around one another.

Jo reached for the surcoat she'd left folded over a crate, pulling the handkerchief from the pocket. It truly *was* stained now, but still soft to the touch. When she brought it to her face, it smelt of Lily. Her heart thudded, skin aflame.

Rubbing the kerchief between her fingers, Jo watched as Lily snuffled in her sleep. Lily was healed, now – her attempts to see off Noll were the final proof that Jo needed. But she didn't want to leave her. She didn't want to return to the de Foucart keep or tie herself to Lord Adam.

She wanted to stay. She wanted to kiss Lily again. She wanted to kiss her a hundred times, until that strange, too-hot feeling tempered and ebbed away.

Lily rolled over, her lips curled into a smile. Perhaps the feeling never *would* ebb, and kissing her would always feel like that.

Jo wanted to find out. She didn't understand the feeling – she couldn't even *name* it – but she was going to. She was contemplating waking Lily to at least *talk* about what had happened, if not continue it, when her ear was caught by a noise from outside: raised voices in the yard.

The alderman must have finally arrived to discuss the attempted robbery. She quickly dressed, hastily pocketing the handkerchief to return to Lily later, then followed the sound outside. She found Mabel standing in the road beside a man on horseback.

When Mabel turned at the intrusion to the conversation, Jo realised she had been wrong. This wasn't the alderman. Mabel looked pale as snow, her sternness and surety gone from her face.

'Mabel?'

'It is— My husband.'

The lightness died in Jo's chest at Mabel's tone. 'I thought he had gone to visit his sister?'

Mabel's mouth opened and shut wordlessly before she gathered herself.

'He had,' she managed. 'But he – he was hurt. Some time ago, in fact, but they struggled to find a messenger and—' Her words faltered.

An icy lump settled in Jo's stomach. 'Is he alive?'

'He is,' Mabel breathed. 'But they do not want him riding. I *must* bring him home, but I *cannot*—' Her shoulders shuddered: it was a sob she was doing her utmost to hide. 'It will take a day to reach him on the cart, and another day to return, and God only knows if they'll let him go right away . . . and I cannot leave the brewery.'

Jo hesitated. She had never seen Mabel like this.

'We will look after it,' she said. 'Lily and I can take care of the business, and Harry and Matilda can help where we require it. If one of the neighbours could take Nora, I am sure we could manage.'

Mabel stared at her. 'I cannot ask that of you, Jo.'

'You do not need to. I am *offering*. And I am sure Lily would agree.'

'But—'

'You have done so much for us. You have given us shelter and food and made it so that Lily does not come to any further harm. Let us do this for you in return.'

'Are you sure you will be all right?'

'I am,' Jo said, surely. 'Besides, I am sure we cannot cause such a great disaster that you won't be able to fix it upon your return.'

A small smile managed to crack through Mabel's fear.

'Thank you,' she said. 'This is too much. I have only done what any person would do.'

'You have done more than you needed to for strangers,' Jo said.

'You do not even know us, and you have given us hospitality and – and *kindness*.' Something about the last word made it stick. 'Let me repay that. Please.'

A small furrow appeared between Mabel's eyebrows. Her lip quirked – a word, swallowed.

'Strangers indeed,' she said. 'Thank you, Jo. I will talk to the children – I can you ready the horse? I will have to take the cart so I can bring my foolish husband home with me.'

'Of course,' Jo said.

'And, Jo?'

'Yes?'

'Go and wake Lily. You should inform her you've given her new employment.'

By the time Jo returned to the loft, Lily was awake, blearily blinking in the sunlight while Gilbert nudged at her arm.

'I heard voices,' she said, struggling to rise. 'And the cart being readied. What's happening?'

Jo sat beside her, pulling her knees up to her chest. 'We appear to have been given run of the brewery.'

'*What?*'

'It is Mabel's husband. She has received word that he has been injured, and she must go and fetch him. I have offered our help. I am sorry, Lily, but I could not see another way.'

Lily sat up properly, now. 'And she accepted it?'

'She has, reluctantly. I *am* sorry, really. I should have asked you first—'

'I would have offered myself,' Lily said, cutting her off. 'God knows we are in debt to her, especially after what happened last night.'

'*Lily*, for the last time, that was *not*—'

252

'It *was* my fault. If this goes some way to repenting for that then I am glad for it.'

Jo stared at her. She wanted to discuss what had happened last night – she wanted to apologise for ending it so soon, to talk about what would happen *now*, if things would change . . . if the way Lily saw her would change. But there wasn't *time*.

'Are you—' she started, twisting her hands together. 'Are you all right?'

She could have been talking about the kiss, or the robbery, or the fight. She could have been talking about Lily's illness or her mending bones.

Lily stood. Her shift wrinkled around her body, slipping over one arm.

'I am,' she said. For a moment, Jo feared that something had changed – that Lily's regard for her, once solid, had crumbled. And then Lily extended her hand with a smile, the expression sympathetic. 'Come,' she said, as Jo took her hand. 'We must get to work.'

Jo hurried after Mabel as she bustled through the house, gathering things. She had sent Lily off with Harry and Nora to beg her neighbour to look after the baby, and Matilda was following them around the house, carrying items her mother thrust towards her.

Mabel spoke the whole time, talking through what exactly needed to be done in her absence. She reassured Jo again that her husband was not too long a ride away, but she had no way of knowing when she would be able to bring him home. It could be *days*.

She told Jo when the ale was due to ferment, how long the mash had been sitting, which tubs would need herbs added to them. They needed to ensure the large order to Glendale would be ready in time.

It sounded *exhausting*. Running the keep was *nothing* compared to this, yet Mabel spoke as if it were no hardship at all. However much work it was, Jo felt sure she could see to it: the encounter with Noll had left her feeling strengthened, as if she could face down *anything*. Ensuring the mash did not turn was far easier than facing down a bandit. And, a small, selfish part of her whispered: the busyness had won her a few more days. She could not return to the keep when she was so sorely needed here.

When Mabel finally left, Jo leant against the wall of the brewery, trying to make sense of it all.

'Jo?'

Harry stood beside her, looking worried. He was on the cusp of adulthood, that tentative age when everything felt overly serious. He'd been taking on the role of the man of the house since his father had left, and now his mother had followed him. The child that he really was threatened to crack through his stoic exterior.

She took a breath and stood straighter.

'Let us get to work.'

The rest of the day passed in such a blur that Jo had no time to stop and talk to Lily about the previous night's kiss, or think about her aborted return home. Even their midday meal was a quick affair, and one which added more tasks to their seemingly endless list: they would need to restock the pantry, harvest or trade vegetables, and acquire some meat.

By the time the sun had set, they were all drained, and it was clear that Matilda especially was worrying for Mabel. She had never been parted from her mother for longer than a day – the time it took for Mabel to make deliveries and return home – and now she was *gone*. She pressed close to Jo's side as they ate their supper in uncertain silence.

They sent the children to tidy once the meal was over, more to distract them than anything else. Jo pulled Lily into the corner so they could talk with at least a small sense of privacy.

'We should not leave them in the house alone,' Jo said. 'Matilda is anxious for her mother, and Harry . . .'

'He is just pretending to be brave.' Lily sighed. 'We should sleep in the house with them until she returns. I am *sure* Harry will complain that we are treating him like a baby, but he needs someone else here. Especially after Noll.'

As night drew in, Jo returned to the brewery to fetch a few of their things and ensure the doors were locked. Lily brought her sword into the house, too, slipping it beneath the wide bed they would all be sharing in Mabel's absence. It was unlikely that Noll or his gang would return, especially now the whole town was alert, but it made Jo feel better regardless.

They sent the children to bed, with much complaining from Harry, then sat together in the seats tucked into the corner of the room beside the banked fire. Lily even grabbed the half-full bottle of mead that Mabel had opened the previous night, pouring them both a generous helping.

She sat beside Jo with a yawn. There was exhaustion on her face that mirrored how Jo felt: likely even more so, given how Lily had thrown herself into the physical labour of running the brewery while only just recovered, and unused to the work after so long resting.

Jo needed to finally mention what had happened between them.

She should ask what it meant, what it *could* mean, in the future. She should return the handkerchief, with a new understanding about what it meant. But she was so tired, and there was already an ache building between her temples – a throb like a blacksmith's hammer upon an anvil. The mead, sweet as it was, was tempting her to give in to her tiredness, making her eyelids heavy.

There was a creak beside her. And then a hand in her own. Lily was watching her, with a soft, unutterably fond smile on her face. The conversation could wait.

She twined their fingers together, returning the smile. When they retired to bed not too long later, Jo was asleep within moments, Lily's arm wrapped around her middle and her nose buried in the crook of Jo's neck.

✳

Time, which until now Lily had had in abundance, was suddenly in short supply.

It had been only two days ago that she had felt *well* for the first time in too long. It had been two days ago that they'd lazily drifted in the sparkling water of the lake, two days since everything had changed. Two days since Jo had kissed her – and had asked Lily to kiss her back.

Lily had fallen asleep that night with such a lightness in her chest she could have floated up into the roof. She had dreamt of those kisses and imagined a future full of them: amongst other, even sweeter diversions. But she had awoken to panic, and the day had been a blur of preparing and working and all thoughts of kissing had to be forced aside.

The panic pricked something *else* in her mind, too. A different fear. Jo had lamented her lack of experience, citing her need to *practise*. What if that was all that night had been?

Were it anyone else, Lily wouldn't have minded. She would have happily accepted that she was a means to an end if it meant she got to kiss a beautiful woman who wanted to kiss her back.

But Jo was *Jo*. She was different. Lily would *accept* being an experiment, but it would pain her. Lily had never been able to school her tongue or dam her opinions, and she wished they had a scrap of time where she could *ask*, or at least better gauge where Jo's interests in her really lay. But the moments they had alone were brief, and both of them were so busy that there was little time for such tender talk. They continued to sleep in the huge family bed, too nervous to leave the children alone.

She contemplated writing Jo a note and leaving it somewhere she would be able to find it. Her first attempt — *We must talk* — sounded so vague and terrifying that she immediately scribbled it out. Her second became so long and rambling that it barely made sense when she read it back to herself, and she realised that any attempt to write down her feelings instead of say them out loud was doomed to fail.

In the end, she settled for something familiar.

You have still not yet learnt how to swim. Shall we return to the lake when Mabel is home? The blackberries must be ripe now.

It didn't say *nearly* enough, but it was better than nothing. Several hours later, while cleaning the kitchen, she found a little rectangle of parchment.

I should love to. I have missed the taste of blackberries.

Lily's heart skipped as she read it. A heavy heat curled low in her belly. Did Jo mean what Lily *thought* she meant, or did she truly just wish to swim and eat blackberries?

There was no time to dwell on it, and no time to ask, working hard and unable to rest. Mabel may have been absent and her husband wounded – or worse – but the order from the smug man on horseback needed to be ready soon. Jo talked her through the brewing process, and Lily's embroidery was abandoned for the more pressing work.

The fourth day after Mabel left, Lily was working at Jo's side in the brewery, crushing malted grain. It was good to be doing something which required real muscle again, her sleeves rolled up as sweat beaded on her skin. It had taken her several attempts to crush the grains to Jo's exact specifications – too fine, too coarse, *too much pressure, Lily, for God's sake stop* – but now they were sitting and laughing, a sack Lily had sewn slowly filling with grain ready to mash.

Jo sat back on her heels with a huff, blowing a strand of hair out of her eyes.

'We're doing well,' she said, pleased. 'I see no reason why this should not be done in time.'

There was a little fleck of grain stuck to her cheek. Without thinking, Lily reached across to brush it away.

Jo's skin was warm. She did not flinch back, Lily's thumb gently resting against her cheek. She blinked, her mouth slightly open, her tongue wetting her lips.

'Lily . . .'

Lily let her hand drift lower, cupping Jo's jaw, fingers pressing softly at her nape. She took a breath. She felt Jo breathe, too, so close that the puff of air kissed Lily's lips.

She was about to close the gap between them, when there was a noise from outside – the rumbling of a cart. Jo leant back with a disgruntled sigh.

They weren't expecting a delivery, but neither could a visitor be ignored. Swallowing down her disappointment, and unsure of what she could say to soothe it, Lily got to her feet and headed out into the yard.

As she stepped into the sunshine, she realised that it wasn't a trader or merchant. It was Mabel, her hair bursting around her head and her nose burnt bright red in the sun.

'Mabel!'

Mabel tugged at the driving reins, pulling the cart around into the yard as Lily ran forwards to heave open the gates. There was a blanketed bundle in the back of the cart: no doubt Mabel's husband, wrapped up for the journey. She hurried over to aid Mabel down.

'Are you well?' she said. 'And your husband, is he—'

'He is,' Mabel breathed. 'Thank God, he is alive. And in the best place, now.'

Despite her reassuring words, Mabel still looked distressed.

'Where is Jo?'

'She is in the brewery, but—'

'I must speak to her. Urgently. Will you see to him?'

'What—'

'*Lily.*'

Lily relented, although she wanted to know what had caused such fear. 'Of course.'

Mabel leant towards the cart. 'This is Lily,' she said, speaking towards the hidden man in the back. 'She will help you. And be *polite* for God's sake. None of your cursing. You're around women again.'

Lily bit back a laugh but was unable to say much else before Mabel hurried past her into the brewery. Wondering what Mabel could possibly need with Jo, she grabbed one of the crates leaning against the brewery wall, dragged it towards the cart and used it to heave herself into the back beside the blanketed bundle.

'My – ah—' She hesitated. She had never really paid too much heed to etiquette. 'Sir?' she hazarded. 'Mabel has asked me to assist you . . .'

The bundle groaned and rolled over. Mabel's husband finally sat, pulling down the blanket that had been obscuring his face.

Lily nearly fell from the cart.

'John?'

John stared at her, his face pale, his eyes deeply bagged. *'William?* What are *you* doing here?'

'I – *we* were taken in by the brewster, Mabel. I, that is – she is your wife? *You* are Mabel's wounded husband?'

John sat up with a wince. He seemed whole, but his hand went to his side – that must be the location of his injury.

'I am.'

'I was under the impression that you were a – a lord! With land, and a title, and a retinue!'

'And I was under the impression that *you* were a man,' he said, looking her up and down and taking in the dress she wore. 'Lily, is it?'

Lily's throat tightened. 'It is.'

He shuffled to the edge of the cart, clutching at his injury with a hiss as he did. 'Come, help me . . .'

Lily did as he asked, grabbing his arm to assist him as he clambered gracelessly down.

'I fear we have much to discuss,' he said. 'And . . . So long as we are being forced to be truthful with each other, John is not my name. You may as well know that, seeing that I find you beneath my roof.'

'Oh.' Lily wasn't sure what else to say. 'What do I call you, then?'

John — the man who had called himself John, all those days ago — gave her a smile and a short bow.

'You may call me Leo.'

Chapter 20

Jo sat amongst the piles of grain, rubbing a piece between her fingers.

She had spent the past few days in a nervous desperation unlike any she'd known before. At first, she'd needed to speak to Lily plainly, to talk about what had happened. But the more time passed, the more that need transformed into something different, and far more urgent: she didn't want to *talk* about it. She wanted to kiss her again.

It was such a new, strange feeling that she barely knew what to do with it. She had *never* felt this way before, and now it was engulfing her, inescapable.

They'd been so *close*. She bitterly looked down at the grain on the mat in front of her with a scowl.

'Jo!'

The familiar voice startled her from her thoughts. 'Mabel?'

Jo scrambled to her feet as Mabel entered, shutting the brewery doors behind her. Her expression was tight. Scared.

'Are you all right?' Jo ran to her. 'What is the matter, is it your husband, is he—'

'He is well. He is *home*, which is what matters most. But I must speak to you. Now.'

There was a chill down Jo's spine. That was a tone she recognised. It was similar to the one the steward had used when he told her that her father had finally passed.

Mabel took her hands but failed to meet her gaze.

'Jo . . .' Her voice was far too quiet. 'I am sorry,' she said, at last. 'But I have not been truthful with you.'

'What?'

'I . . . I know who you are.'

Jo's insides turned to stone. Weeks ago, she had stamped out the embers of suspicion she had felt when Mabel had used her real name. She'd done it again, when Mabel had baked fritters just for her.

She should have fed them, instead.

'*What?*' she repeated, feeling foolish.

'Johanna de Foucart. Daughter of the late Marcus de Foucart, sister to the new Earl, Ellis. Second eldest daughter, fourth child. I *know* you, Jo.'

'But . . . *how?*' Jo's voice caught in her throat, strangling her.

'Do you trust me?'

Jo hesitated. She *did*, curse her own idiocy. 'Yes,' she said, weakly.

'I have someone who very dearly wishes to see you.'

Jo allowed Mabel to lead her from the brewery and into the main house. They walked in silence – Mabel serious and sombre, Jo drifting. Mabel pushed open the door to the kitchen, and Jo was hit at once with the warmth and comfort of it, the smell of straw, the waxy pop of the rushlights on the walls.

A figure was hunched over the wooden bench, facing away from them. Lily hovered beside him, her gaze snapping up as Jo and Mabel entered. She looked pale.

'Jo . . .'

She hurried over.

'I am here,' she muttered into Jo's ear. 'I am *always* here.'

'What is—'

The man at the bench – Mabel's husband, Jo could only pre-sume – stood. He turned, the air around them suddenly thick, tar-like and slow.

He faced her. The air *choked* her now, her lungs empty. The very tips of her fingers tingled. Her head swam, ears rushing. Her legs shook.

'Johanna—'

Leo. He pulled her into an embrace. He was tall and solid and entirely, *impossibly* alive. Jo's arms went around him of their own accord. He was so warm.

'Leo . . .'

It came pouring out all at once, like a dam bursting, like a wooden door shattering under a siege. Jo's resolve – which she had held for so long, patched over and mended but never, ever broken – splintered outwards, leaving only the remains.

She sobbed into Leo's shoulder until her chest hurt, the tears that had refused to come when she had stood dutifully by her father's casket finally released. He didn't say anything, just held her, waiting for the shaking to stop.

'Johanna,' he said at last, pulling back but not letting her go. '*Jo.* I am so sorry. I should never have left you with him, I—' His voice cracked, too. 'I told you I would look after you, and I failed in that.'

'You did not—'

'I *did*. You are my little sister. I remember when you were *born*, and I left you with that . . . that *brute*. I left you with him for far too long. I'm so sorry I was too late.'

'Too late?'

When he next spoke, Leo's words were heavy, his voice thick with unshed tears.

'I nearly came when I heard about Father's death,' he said, 'but I was sure no one in the household would want to see me. What if you thought I was only returning to reclaim the title? What if they *forced* me to? So I remained, and then later, we heard them talking in the inn – about a tournament, and a competition. They were *laughing*, Jo, saying that *you* were the prize. I had to find you. So long as I knew you were *safe*, and were all right, and weren't being married off to a bastard . . . I would be able to live with myself a little better.'

'You were at the tournament?' Jo gasped.

'I was. No one even realised. I just needed to see you. I had intended to finish the tournament, ensure you were well, and return home, but I was wounded, and trapped.'

'How? Was it the joust, or the duel? The melee?'

Leo looked abashed. Jo hadn't seen him in twelve years, but even then, she recognised that expression. It was one she had seen on *Penn's* face, too, and the familiarity of it shocked her.

'What is it?' she asked. 'Leo, what *happened*?'

To her surprise, Leo turned to Lily.

'I was coming to find *you*,' he said. 'Or rather, I was coming to find *William*. It was after you fell during that joust. Your absence at the feast did not go unnoticed, and I was concerned for you. But when I approached your tent and I heard voices . . .' He laughed, rubbing at his face. 'Truthfully, I had assumed that you had a serving girl in there, or a lady's maid. It would not have surprised me, especially after all the attention you garnered during the tournament.'

'Oh, Leo,' Jo stammered, suddenly realising what had happened. '*No*—'

'Yes indeed,' he said, biting back a laugh. 'I had not even realised it was *you* in there until I heard you talking together, and then . . .'

He grabbed his pack from the table and reached inside.

'I believe this is yours?'

He was holding Jo's knife.

'Leo . . .' Jo's eyes were burning, tears threatening to spill even though the well of them was spent. 'Leo, *please*, I am so sorry—'

'You do not need to apologise,' Leo said, swiftly. 'Call it retribution, if you like, for my abandoning you.'

'No—'

'It is not as if you knew who I was,' Leo said, his voice enragingly calm. 'Although I must ask . . .' He looked genuinely curious. 'Why did you do it?'

'I thought . . .' Jo gripped her hands together. 'I thought you meant to harm Lily. William, I mean.'

Leo frowned at her. 'Why would you think that?'

'Not *you*,' she clarified. 'Of course I would not suspect you, but . . . we both had reason to be cautious.'

She picked at the loose skin beside her thumbnail. She didn't want to slander Lord Adam – not now she knew that he had never been as great a threat as she had assumed – but Leo needed to know the truth.

'I overheard some men speaking when I left the feast,' she began. 'They were talking about William, and my marriage, and – and their plans, ruined. One of them was calmer, the other furious.

When I heard you outside, and saw you lurking . . . I could only assume the worst, especially as you were wearing similar colours. Then later, Lily told me that one of them had threatened her, and that was enough to confirm it.'

'Who did you think I was?'

Jo stuttered. 'I am not sure—'

'Jo.'

She relented. It was impossible not to. 'One of Lord Adam's men,' she said, quietly.

'Lord Adam?' Leo gasped. 'My God. I saw Sir Lanval the previous day, and I felt sure he had been harassing William, but to assume *that* of them?'

'There was little to assume, from what Lily has told me,' Jo quickly explained. 'Sir Lanval held a *knife* to her throat. If it *had* been one of Lord Adam's men and not you—' She bunched her hands in her skirts, making fists. 'Then I would have felt no remorse in harming him. Not if it ensured Lily stayed safe.'

Leo stared at her. 'My God, Jo.' He breathed.

'Wait—' Lily cut in, stepping forwards. 'Did no one question how you were wounded? You told us that you were a lord, or at *least* a man of means. Surely that was enough to send men to find the people who had injured you?'

Leo looked sheepish again. 'Ah,' he said, '*well* . . .'

'What did you do?' said Jo.

'As I said, I recognised your voice,' he said. 'And your knife confirmed it. But I could not believe that my little sister would purposefully attempt to kill someone. When they found me, I told them the same tale I told you: that I had been concerned for William and gone to find him, only to find an empty tent. As

I set off to return to the keep, I was attacked. It took very little to convince them that I'd been wounded by a criminal who had fled. They took me to the infirmary, and I repeated the story to Countess Isabelle. Told her that by the time I had gone to find William, he had vanished. And *she* asked if I had seen *you*.' He nodded at Jo. 'I could not tell what she wanted, or what would happen to you should I admit you had been there . . . so I told her I had not.'

'What—' Jo took a single breath. 'What did she say?'

'Very little.' Leo shrugged. 'But she did not seem surprised, if that is what you mean; nor was she surprised that William, too, had vanished.'

Jo swallowed. She thought of Isabelle's promise to let her return north, and to hide her absence from Lord Adam at the banquet.

'Do you know what happened when I did not return?'

'No one told me anything directly, of course,' Leo said, 'but I was laid up in the keep for so long that I caught the gossip. The Countess put out a story that you had been suddenly called north.'

The lie she'd given Lord Adam. Isabelle had mentioned they could use it in Jo's favour, although neither of them had expected to need it so soon. Jo's stomach swirled guiltily: Isabelle was taking a huge risk for her, especially if Lord Adam discovered the lie.

'And . . . did no one question it? Lord Adam—'

Leo gave her an assessing look. 'Lord Adam, the man who is to be your husband?'

Jo flushed guiltily. 'I—'

Before she could defend herself, Leo burst into laughter. He wrapped an arm around her shoulder, and the sudden touch made her feel as if she were finally safe.

'My Jo,' he said, chuckling. 'What sort of hypocrite would I be if I chastised you for running from your duties?'

'I *had* intended to return . . .' Jo began lamely.

'Of course you had,' Leo said, with a disbelieving laugh. 'In any case . . . he seemed to accept the news, although I did not see very much of him. I was there for an *age*, and only ever saw him or his men in passing.'

'Why *were* you there for so long?' Lily put in.

Leo shrugged. 'No one knew my true name. It took a week before I could find anyone who I could trust to send word to Mabel, and longer still before they could even set out. In truth, I had not planned what I would do if I were injured.'

Jo stared at him, aghast. 'You had not planned what you would do if you were injured at a *tournament*?'

'I may have been overconfident in my skills, unpractised as they are.'

Jo rolled her eyes. 'Why is it that I am beset with—'

The words died in her mouth. She had been intending to chastise him, to tease both him and Lily for their foolhardiness: for the pride that felled them both. And then she realised what had happened, how absurd the whole thing had been – two people, unknown both to her and each other, had taken on a disguise and ridden to fight. For *her*.

The thought was too much. She had never asked for anyone, never needed anyone. She had ensured that she could rely on *herself*, and no one else.

And yet here were two people who had thrown themselves into danger for her, without *needing* to be asked. Who had acted foolishly, yes, and rashly – but for her.

She sat down heavily on the bench. Lily was beside her in an instant, reassuringly close, not quite touching. When Jo looked up, Mabel was watching them.

'Lily,' she said. 'Would you come with me to fetch the children?'

Lily hesitated for just a moment, her hand hovering over Jo's shoulder. 'Of course.'

When they were gone, Leo sat at Jo's side on the bench in silence. Jo didn't know what to say, didn't know what to *do*. Now the shock of his return had worn away, all that was left was a strange, ringing emptiness – like a drained well.

She reached out and took his hand, just to remind herself that he was there.

'I thought you were dead,' she said, voice small.

'I am so sorry, Jo.' He squeezed her hand. 'I – I betrayed you. But I had to choose, and Father . . .'

Their eyes met. The memory of their father passed between them, one for which they didn't need words. Jo thought of Leo's dismissal again, the way their father had forced both him and Mabel from the keep. It had been so long ago. Long enough to—

She paused, quickly working it out.

Harry.

'Mabel was with child when he removed you, wasn't she?'

Leo stared at her. 'Christ above, you're clever. Yes, she was.'

'And it was us or them?'

Leo nodded, looking ashamed. But Jo knew what sort of man their father had been.

'You made the right choice,' she said. Leo seemed to be about to argue, so she spoke over him. 'You *did*. It was impossible, but you did it. God knows what he may have done to her . . .'

She peered around the room. The brewery had become a home these past few weeks. Looking at it now, she could see her brother in it; in the steadfast way Harry loved his siblings, in the whittled figures on the shelf, in Mabel's almond fritters. *This* was his freedom; one he had been forced to build. It was no wonder he had never returned. Who would have sacrificed all this for the horrors of the de Foucart keep?

A shard of jealousy lodged between her ribs. She wanted it, too. Her first, angry thought was that it had been so *easy* for Leo and Penn to go – as men, they were not burdened under as many expectations. But that was wrong. Both had been the heir, if only for a short time. Neither was suitable for rule. Leo had chosen Mabel because he had been *forced* to. Had their father allowed the relationship, he never would have gone. Penn's newfound freedom only stretched as far as the boundaries of Dunlyn Castle.

She stared at the rush mats beneath her feet. When they first arrived, Mabel had told them then that the business had been hers. It did not belong to Leo, or Mabel's father, or some distant male relative. That jealousy was misplaced: she didn't want what Leo had, or Penn. She wanted what *Mabel* had, what she'd built for herself with hard work and dedication and years of stubbornness.

Leo's return was shedding a new understanding on her own desire, tentative as it was, not to go back to the keep. Leo had left them all behind. Penn had left *her* behind. With Ellis as the Earl and Isabelle a formidable supporter of his, there wasn't anyone left for Jo to abandon. They would fare well without her: that was why they were marrying her off. Besides, she could not very well anger a ghost.

'Are you all right?' Leo's careful words broke her thoughts.

'Yes,' she said, slowly. 'Yes, I am. God, Leo – I have missed you so much.'

He slung his arm around her shoulders.

'And I have missed you.'

It did not take long for Mabel, Lily, and the children to return. Harry came first, pushing through the door with that typical look of scepticism on his face. It dropped as soon as he saw Leo, dashing to reach him.

'Pa!'

Matilda immediately rushed for him, too, nearly knocking Lily over. Leo was on his knees at once, pulling them into a tight embrace. Harry did his best to appear stoic, while Matilda clung to Leo's arm, laughing through tears. At last, Leo extracted himself from Matilda's grip and stood to take Nora from Mabel's arms. He held her up as she squealed and giggled at him.

'My little Eleanor.' He gasped. 'You have grown!'

At that, Jo gasped. 'You named her after Mother?'

Leo placed the baby on his hip. 'We did,' he said. 'It seemed right. I – I am sorry, if that was—'

'No, Leo.' Jo was beside him, her hand on his arm. 'It is lovely. She would be so happy for you.'

Leo gave her a damp-looking smile. 'I hope so,' he said. 'I really do. You . . .' He hesitated, looking again at Nora. 'You look so much like her. When I saw you come in . . . it was like she was back.'

Jo gripped his arm harder. Tears prickled at the corner of her eyes, which she quickly brushed away.

Once the children had settled, they all gathered around the kitchen table to celebrate Leo's return: one that had taken far too long. Mabel took herself away to the kitchen with a furtive glance, and so distracted by Leo, Jo didn't realise what she was doing until the sound and smell of frying dough filled the room. When she deposited a plate of hot almond fritters onto the table, everyone hurried to grab one.

'As fine as ever, love,' Leo said, tugging Mabel closer. 'I have missed these.'

Mabel swatted at him. 'If you had not got yourself wounded, you wouldn't have gone without.'

Leo took another fritter. 'Jo,' he said, 'do you remember when we took that plateful—'

'Yes!' Jo laughed. 'It's one of my fondest memories. I thought I would be sick we ate so many. I am amazed we were never caught.'

'Penn was so cross when he found out we didn't include him.' Leo grinned. 'He didn't speak to us for *days*.'

Jo giggled. 'Oh, *yes*. Until you stole him another one to make up for it.'

Leo, for some reason, blushed. Jo put down her half-eaten fritter to regard him. 'What?'

'I told you both I stole it to make Penn laugh. What I *really* did was charm a kitchen girl into giving me one.'

'Lying is a *sin*.' Mabel ruffled his hair. 'You did not charm me, you brute.' She looked at Jo. 'I'd only been in the keep a week or so, and in comes the *heir* looking for fritters. I could not well refuse him, could I? And then his *lordship* keeps coming back, and I realise he's not so frightening after all. Great overgrown boy looking for sweets.'

Leo grinned up at her. 'Still am.'

'You know,' Mabel said fondly, 'he tells that tale every time I make them for him. Even the children know it by heart.'

Jo wondered how many of Leo's stories were about her, or their siblings – how he'd ensured that under this roof, she would never truly be a stranger. It was why Mabel had brought them in, she realised: she was family.

'This was why you let us stay,' she said aloud, looking at Mabel. 'Because you knew who I was.'

Mabel looked abashed. 'It is,' she admitted. 'I recognised you from the keep, even though you had no idea. Leo had gone looking for you, and yet here you were, in our *home* . . . I could not have forgiven myself if I let you go and he never even realised you were here. I should have been more truthful with you. I really did think Leo would be only a day or so behind you. And then it was too late, and I had no idea if Leo even intended for you to know who he was . . .'

'You have nothing to apologise for,' Jo said. 'I can understand why you did it.'

Mabel gave her a weak smile, before Leo moved the conversation back to the family, asking after Ros. Jo quickly described her husband and children as Leo listened on.

'I cannot help but wonder how it is you were not wed as well?' he said with a frown. 'After Ros, I had assumed Father would be keen to tie you to someone wealthy. I was shocked to hear that you would be married after the tournament.'

Jo paused. 'He had started to enquire,' she explained, 'but he was forced to deal with the more troublesome son first. He knew that I would remain dutiful, yet . . .'

Leo's eyes widened. 'Of course,' he said, 'Penn – forgive me, Jo. We heard rumours of . . . of kidnapping, and murder, and I intended to come but it was the same time our Nora was born, and—'

Jo placed her hand to his arm. 'Leo,' she said, calmly. 'Do not worry yourself.'

'What happened? We had heard that he returned, but was stolen away again—'

Jo sighed.

'It is . . . complicated,' she settled on, finally.

'Oh?'

Lily leant around Jo's back. She extended her hand, as if she intended for Leo to kiss it.

'Cecily Barden,' she said, bowing her head. 'The sister of the man who stole your brother away.'

Leo looked between them, baffled.

'Complicated seems to be correct,' he said. 'Mabel, love: find the mead. I refuse to have this conversation without a drink in my hand.'

*

Drinking by Leo's side felt like being back in the de Foucart grounds, eating and carousing with the other knights. Lily struggled to marry the two men in her mind: the easy-going, friendly Sir John, who had taken her under his wing at the tournament, and Leo, who was a father and husband and – most importantly – Jo's brother.

Her boldness felt quashed with him there. Even as John he had seemed discomforted at the idea of her courting Jo, and now she knew that it was because he was so protective of his little sister. Why else would he have put himself in danger for her?

No doubt it was the same reason *Lily* had. For the hope that Jo's future could be better, and for love – although a much different kind of love.

As Mabel passed out cups of mead, Jo told the story of what had happened with their brothers, and how she and Lily had come to be friends. Leo and Mabel watched, their eyes wide. When they were finally finished, Leo shook his head – although his eyes were sparkling with poorly suppressed mirth.

'I cannot believe this,' he said, draining his mug. 'Is all of our family mad?'

'Mine certainly is,' said Lily. 'Or perhaps it is just that the de Foucart children drive us to madness. Ash is certainly thankful that there are none of you left of age: he has avoided being stricken with the same curse.'

'And is that madness what drove you to enter the tournament?' Leo asked.

Lily put her cup down. Jo's leg was pressed against her own: she didn't feel bold enough to take her hand, not in front of her brother.

'It is,' she settled on. 'I had to make sure Jo was all right. But . . . I may have been over-enthusiastic.'

Lily told as much of her story as she could, becoming bolder the more she spoke. It was good to finally tell Mabel the whole tale of how they had arrived in the brewery, and she chose her words carefully, emphasising their friendship and her inability to understand how Jo could have accepted her fate so easily, leading to her decision to ensure Jo would not need to wed.

She couldn't be sure that she could say anything that would reveal her true feelings. Their reactions to the news that Penn had absconded with another man made her sure that they would not judge or demonise her for a relationship with a woman, but what she feared most was Jo's reaction. There was no name for the thing between them, and Lily could not voice her own feelings out loud lest they alarm Jo in their intensity.

When they finally retired, long after the sun had set and the children had fallen asleep at the table by their father's side, they returned to the loft. As Lily heaved herself up, pulling Jo after her, she mused on how much she had missed it: this small, comfortable space that was just for them.

Jo was quiet as she settled herself on the edge of the loft, looking down towards her dangling feet. No wonder: it had been a long, emotional day after several full days of continual hard work. She was probably overwhelmed and exhausted.

'Jo?' Lily sat beside her, their fingers brushing. 'Are you all right?'

Jo stared down. Her brows were knitted together.

'I—' Her voice sounded hoarse. She stopped, gathered herself. Began again. 'I *am*, Lily.'

And then she burst out laughing. The sudden noise took Lily by surprise.

'What—'

'This all has been so *much*. I fled the keep, I found Leo, and *you* . . .' She shook her head, overwhelmed. 'I suppose at least I can take some solace in the fact that I did not injure one of Lord Adam's men. I keep thinking that I ought to return. I *know* I ought to, now that you are well and no longer need me.'

Lily's breath caught. Jo was right: she *should* leave. Now Lily's wounds were healing, Jo could return home and finally marry Adam. The thought made a stone calcify in Lily's insides, blocking her throat.

'Oh.' She choked. 'I suppose . . . in that case, it is good that you have been able to—' It was a bitter thought. It was unfair to Jo. But she said it anyway. 'Practise.'

Jo stopped swinging her legs. 'What?'

'You said that you were worried that you would not be able to kiss a husband as you ought, and now, with *me*—'

Jo's expression cracked. Her eyebrows twisted into guilt.

'Lily, *no*—' She grabbed Lily's hand. 'I did not . . . I do not think of what we shared as *practice*,' she said. 'The other night, I meant—' She was babbling. 'I only meant that I wished to do it again. And I – I felt foolish asking.'

Lily could have laughed. 'You felt *foolish*?' she repeated.

'I did. I did not know if you felt the same, and I did not want to *demand* anything, and I—' Jo sighed, then wrenched her hand away, placing her head in her palms. 'I have ruined it, haven't I? Truly, Lily, I barely understood *myself*, and – and you were not practice. I swear. I have not spent the past few days desperate to kiss you again just so I could ensure that I would be better prepared for a husband. A husband that I do not want!'

Lily floundered in the sudden flood of Jo's emotions. Her first thought – which inflated her chest with smug satisfaction – was *you have been desperate to kiss me again?* But Jo was more important than her own pride.

'You do not want him?'

'I do not. I swore I would return to the keep and marry once you were well. And now you *are* well, and I have realised . . . I do not want to go back. I don't want that, Lily.'

'You don't?'

'I don't. I really don't. Being here is *freedom*. All I wanted was to escape the memory of my father, and all he brought with him, and

I thought that the only way to do that was to marry. But now . . . now I am not so sure. Now I wonder if I can take it myself.'

Lily stared at her. She didn't speak, too scared that to interrupt Jo would be to break this new, fragile resolve.

'You said yourself that you thought little of Lord Adam,' Jo continued. 'What if he *is* just like my father? What if I was willingly walking into another nightmare? I thought that I would be content, if he was different. But these past weeks . . .' She took Lily's hand again, finally meeting her gaze. 'I have been *happy*, Lily. I had forgotten how.'

'So what will you do?'

Jo carefully threaded their fingers together. 'I do not know.'

It was a fair answer. Lily thought a moment, finding the right words.

'What do you *want*?'

Jo stared at her. Her eyes flicked down, taking her in, lingering on her lips. 'I want to kiss you.'

There wasn't anything else Lily could do but acquiesce. It was pointless to tell Jo that she, too, had been just as eager to kiss her again when she could *show* her, instead.

Jo hummed against her lips, and Lily realised how real Jo's desperation had been. She was bolder, now, and Lily wondered where her mind had led her during those moments where she was desperate to kiss her again. Jo moved more surely, deepening the kiss, and while Lily was eager to reciprocate she was also terribly aware of their perch at the edge of the loft.

Pulling away – Jo made a low noise of complaint that shot down Lily's spine like sparks – she guided her back towards the safety of the pallet. Jo eagerly reignited the kiss, barely giving Lily room to breathe.

She didn't *want* to breathe, either – not when Jo's lips were on hers, her mouth soft and pliant.

Moving cautiously, Lily wrapped her hands around Jo's waist, gripping her tight. She was soft beneath her hands, and she longed to feel more of her. She longed to *taste* her, to suck that soft skin into her mouth.

Jo's hands, too, were roaming, enthusiastically but inexpertly. Her palms went to Lily's back, holding her in place. Lily kissed away from her lips, down her jaw to her neck.

'Tell me what you want,' Lily whispered, lips brushing Jo's skin.

Jo huffed a silent laugh through her nostrils. 'I don't know what there is *to* want.'

Lily smiled, melding it into another kiss. 'Then you shall learn.'

However much Jo had insisted that Lily wasn't practice, she *was* inexperienced, and Lily didn't want to push her too far or too fast. Lily had been with women in Jo's position before – she had been one herself, once – and she took pride in the fact that she could guide her. She started slowly, trailing her hands up Jo's side, the fabric of her dress catching beneath her fingers.

'Do you want to take this off?'

Jo nodded. Together, they managed to pull Jo's dress over her head, leaving her only in her shift. Remembering her actions at the lakeside, Lily took a moment to place it down carefully before turning back to truly look at her.

The hazy dark made it hard to see, but Lily could still pick out the way the shift clung to Jo's body, the way it hugged her hips and the generous shape of her breasts. Lily went to kiss her again, when Jo stopped her.

'Now you,' she said, eyes dark.

Lily was suddenly very glad that she had chosen a dress that morning. It was far easier to remove, and she tugged it off with such haste that she tumbled off the pallet.

They both burst into giggles as Lily righted herself, her thin shift tangling around her legs, and Jo pulled her back onto the makeshift mattress. Lily kissed her, laughing against Jo's lips, her hands brushing her jaw, down her neck, down her arms.

Jo's skin was warm through the fabric of her shift. Lily moved slowly, aware that Jo had never been touched like this before. When she smoothed her hands over Jo's shoulders to her breasts, Jo let out a small, hot gasp. Her nipples pebbled beneath Lily's palms, making those sparks of desire flare, the place between her legs aching.

'Is this all right?'

Jo answered that with a kiss. 'Yes—' she muttered. 'Yes, Lily, I—'

Her words stuttered into another sigh as Lily gently pinched her nipple between her fingers. The sound was *delicious*. She moved a little harder, guiding Jo down so they were sprawled together on the pallet. Facing one another, she moved her hand from Jo's breast and slid it down her body, over her stomach, across her hip. She let her hand rest there, a moment.

Jo's shift bunched around her legs. Her bare skin was so *close*. Lily twitched her hand down lower, feeling the soft warmth of Jo's thigh beneath her palm. Jo made a gasping sound but did not pull away. Lily let her hand rest there, fingers playing in the hem of Jo's shift.

'You should—'

'Would you prefer if I—'

They spoke over one another, words mingling between them. Jo spoke again first.

281

'You could remove it?'

Oh, how Lily wanted to. But she had to be sure, first.

'Do you *wish* me to remove it?'

Jo kissed her. 'Yes.'

Lily slid her hand up Jo's thigh beneath the linen. Jo hummed, urging her on, then Lily gently took the fabric and lifted it over Jo's head, revealing all of her.

Lily wished it was the middle of the day so she could see her properly: the curve of her hips, the roundness of her breasts, the darkness of her lips. Lily reached out automatically, dragging her hands up Jo's body. Without the fabric between them, she could feel how soft and plush Jo's skin was, take the weight of her breasts in her hands. Seeing all of her – *feeling* all of her – was too much to resist, and Lily bowed her head as if in prayer to suck Jo's nipple into her mouth.

The noise Jo made was like a prayer, too, as Lily flicked her tongue over the berry-hard point. The taste of her skin was somehow sweet, almost addictive. She released her nipple with a faint *pop* then tugged her into another kiss, fingers digging into her warm, supple flesh.

Jo's hands were moving again, now too, sliding up Lily's sides and then, in a bold movement that made Lily gasp, she reached up to cup Lily's breasts.

Jo really *was* a quick learner, pressing her palms against Lily's nipples, rolling them beneath her hands. Lily's body was tightening, the ache between her legs becoming urgent and slick. Jo moved with such surety that Lily was momentarily shocked, but that shock quickly vanished beneath Jo's touch, beneath her desperate kisses, her yearning lips.

Lily's fingers dug instinctively tighter into Jo's thigh. Jo moaned softly against Lily's mouth, twisting around on the mattress, catching Lily's leg between her ankles. Lily was only happy to comply, happy to let Jo move them as she wished.

It took her entirely by surprise when Jo urged Lily closer then ground herself down against her thigh. It seemed to take Jo by surprise, too – she stuttered a little gasp, then her eyes snapped open, as if realising what she had just done.

'Lily . . .' Her voice was low and hoarse. 'I . . . I did not . . .'

'Do you want me to touch you?' Lily shifted her hand, nudging inwards.

Jo's lips parted. She was so *close*.

'Yes.' It was no more than a whisper.

Lily moved slowly, *reverently*, feeling Jo shudder beneath her. She moved one hand to Jo's shoulder, tangling in her long hair, then slid the other across her leg. She teased along the crease of Jo's thigh, brushing her fingers lightly against the thatch of curls she found there.

Jo kissed her – urging her on.

'If it's too much . . .' Lily muttered, remembering the way Jo had backed away the first time they kissed, 'you must tell me. If you want me to stop, tell me to stop.'

Jo made a soft hum of assent. Lily brushed their lips together, a ghost-kiss, then moved her hand to slide her fingers between Jo's thighs. Jo's legs tensed. Her grip tightened. Lily shifted a single finger lower, down between the soft folds of skin. She brushed against the nub she had been searching for, and Jo arched back with a hiss, rolling onto her back. Lily grinned against Jo's mouth, kissed her harder, then repeated the movement.

Jo was already slick and eager beneath her hand, so Lily pressed harder, rubbing her fingers against her, drawing her out. Jo shuddered, twitching against the straw. Lily edged lower, and with a heated kiss she slid her tongue into Jo's mouth and a finger inside her.

Jo *moaned*. Lily gave her a moment to get used to the feeling before quickening her speed, expertly moving her hand, drinking Jo's moans and mumbles and curses into her mouth.

'Lily—' Jo breathed it, voice breaking. 'Lily, *ah*—'

Lily smiled, moving quicker, surer. Jo gasped again, letting a string of wordless sounds into the warm air, tightening around Lily's finger. Sensing she was close, Lily pulled from her, once again placing her attentions to the sensitive bud just above her entrance. Jo bucked against the mattress, hands gripping the sheets below. Lily worked her harder, and with another low moan Jo's pleasure peaked. She slumped back against the pallet, shuddering breathlessly.

Lily leant back, propping one leg to either side of Jo's hips, looking down at her. She was dishevelled and panting, her hair spread around her head in wild, dark strands. Lily was about to snatch a kiss, when Jo pushed herself up, grabbing Lily around the waist before she could topple from her lap. Like this, Lily was taller, and Jo cupped the back of her head, pulling her down and kissing her greedily.

'Can I—'

Jo paused. Their lips did not part. One of her hands snuck lower, fingertips again flicking over Lily's nipple, down her chest, over her stomach. Jo's hand came to rest in the fabric bunching between Lily's bare legs, fingers softly playing in the linen. Lily's body was lighting up, every nerve flaring towards the throbbing point between her thighs.

Jo kissed her again. She licked her tongue into Lily's mouth, exploring her. Tasting her. She moved her hand lower, bunching in the fabric.

'Can I?'

Oh. Lily hadn't been expecting that. She hadn't been thinking of it, either, despite how urgent her own arousal was growing. But Jo was *offering*, and her voice was so sweet and her touch so gentle that Lily could barely gather her words to respond.

'Please, my Lady.'

Jo smiled against her lips. But she didn't move yet, still fiddling with the fabric.

'And this?'

'*Please*, my Lady.'

Jo swiftly pulled Lily's shift away, letting it drop carelessly to the ground. She took a moment to take Lily in – even the touch of her eyes enough to make Lily shudder – before leaning in to place a kiss between her breasts. Lily felt her hand shift, but she could barely register the movement as Jo placed her lips to the tip of Lily's nipple. Lily gasped again as Jo opened her mouth, *sucking*. There was a low, warm pressure in her stomach, coiling in her core.

Finally, Jo's hand made its way into the hot, desperate place between Lily's legs: searching, brushing against her skin, tangling in her hair.

'Here—'

Lily reached down, taking Jo's hand, guiding her to the best spot. She didn't speak, eyes lightly shut as she moved Jo's fingertips. The pressure was nearly too much, taut and ready to snap like a bowstring, and when Jo finally brushed against her, Lily cursed into the air.

They moved together, Lily rubbing against herself with Jo's fingers, showing her the best way to move, the best speed. Jo was as quick a learner in this as she was everything else, and soon Lily released her hand, letting the pleasure shudder over her as Jo stroked her. She let out a hot breath as Jo moved, her lips still hovering over Lily's breasts.

This was *marvellous*, and all the more marvellous for it being Jo between her legs, Jo's hand on her, Jo's lips skimming her skin. She could have stayed like this forever, could have peaked with just this gentle movement, but Jo shifted, brought her hand to the small of Lily's back, then slowly slid a finger inside her.

It was so unexpected that Lily gasped, tensing. Jo froze, and anticipating what she was about to do, Lily managed to stutter two words:

'Don't stop.'

Jo didn't. She moved slowly but intently, and Lily allowed herself to tense and writhe and sigh under her movements, making sure Jo knew what felt best. She only said one more word, lost in a whisper.

'*Another.*'

Jo did as she asked, licking again at Lily's nipple, moving their bodies closer together. The pressure in Lily's core grew, expanding, pressing down. Her legs tensed, gripping Jo tighter as Jo eased into her. With a cut-off, strangled gasp she buried her face in the crown of Jo's head, fingers tangling in her hair. Stars burst in front of her eyes as her climax broke, clinging to Jo with shuddering limbs.

Jo hesitated for just a moment before moving her hand. Lily slumped down, as if all her bones had turned to butter, letting Jo take her weight. They fell backwards onto the pallet, Lily sliding from Jo's lap to lie beside her.

In the shadows, Jo's eyes were wide and sparkling. Her lips were red and plump and begging to be kissed again.

Lily did, then pulled the woollen blanket up and over their heads, cocooning them in the warm dark.

Chapter 21

Lily lay staring up, once again unable to sleep despite her leaden limbs and satisfied body. She had stirred from pleasant dreams after only a handful of hours, unable to slip away again. She could not stop thinking about what Jo had said.

She did not want to marry Adam. She didn't want to return to her family's keep. But what *would* she do?

Marriage had been a way for Jo to achieve her freedom. She'd said so herself, hiding in Lily's tent on the edge of the tourney grounds. But it wasn't the same freedom that Lily sought – the ability to do as she pleased or go where she wanted. It was freedom from the memory of her father, the trauma he had left carved into her body, as much a part of her as her bones.

It was the pain Jo was trying to escape, not the keep. The nightmare that she still lived every day, just by existing in the space that had once been his, amongst the people that had been impacted by him.

Lily was one of those people. Her friendship with Jo and her dissolved betrothal to Jo's brother had only come about through the interference of the late Marcus de Foucart. Without him, they never would have met, and the burden of Jo's brother's flight and the pain she had felt when she thought him dead would never have happened.

Jo was determined, and strong, and she achieved the things she set her mind to. If she intended to find a new way to escape her father's memory and achieve her freedom, she would.

But where did that leave Lily? Was she, too, not a part of that memory?

Jo would go, and Lily would lose her.

Lily had parted ways with lovers before. Her previous relationships came with the knowledge that they could not last, and many of the women she had been with had left her for marriage. That knowledge made parting easier, and while the feelings were still intense, her broken heart mended quickly. Lily would not deny loving several of the women she had been with before, but they were impermanent, and she had accepted that.

Jo was different. Lily had wanted Jo for so long, and Jo's reciprocation was so strong that it made Lily feel faint. She was not like the rest.

If Jo left – *when* she left – Lily would be shattered like a lance on a shield. She would never be able to right all those pieces. She could feel the cracks already beginning to form.

Beyond the window, the sky was lightening. Sick of lying and worrying, Lily carefully rose from the pallet, dressed, and headed into the house.

To her surprise, the kitchen was already occupied. Leo hunched at the table in the glow of a single rushlight, a little wooden block gripped in his hand. He was whittling. He looked up when she entered, then his gaze focused.

'Are you all right?' he said with a frown, putting the knife and block – still just a rough-hewn figure – down.

'I cannot sleep.' Lily came to stand beside him. 'I have been . . . worrying.'

'Worrying?'

Lily hesitated, trailing her fingers through the wood shavings on the table. This was Leo: Jo's elder brother. Talking to him about her would be speaking out of turn. But he was *John*, too, John who had been friendly towards her at the tournament, who had dragged her into their celebrations. She could see why he'd done that, now: he was an eldest sibling with a gaping hole in his heart where his little brother and sister had been ripped from it.

'About Jo,' she finished, not meeting his gaze.

'Ah.' A light silence draped over them both. After a moment, Leo gestured to the bench beside him. 'Sit. Please.'

He didn't sound angry, or as if he were about to reprimand her, so Lily complied.

'At that tournament,' he said, apropos of nothing, 'I *knew* there was something between you and Jo. It was so obvious. But I assumed you were just a young lad dazzled by a pretty girl. It was *sweet*, even if I found your attentions on my sister worrying.' He paused. 'They do not worry me anymore.'

Lily let him speak, watching him carefully.

'I have lost twelve years at Jo's side,' he said, 'so I do not know her as well as I ought. As well as I would *like*. But I see her, and you, and I know, Lily. She is safe with you. And . . . and that is all I ever wanted for her. Safety.' He picked at the skin around his nails. 'It is the very least she deserves.'

Leo seemed to realise that he had taken over the conversation. Fixing himself, he turned to her. 'What about her worries you?'

Lily's nerves were fraying.

'That—' She took a breath, forcing the frayed edges back together. 'That she may leave,' she said at last. 'She wants her freedom away from the memory of her – of *your* father. If she doesn't return to the keep, she can have it. And I will be—'

Lost. Alone. Left. There wasn't an end to that thought, not one that she dared say out loud. She looked down at her hands, trailing off.

'Did Jo ever tell you what happened to Mabel and me?'

Lily frowned at the redirection.

'Only a little . . . She said that you had fallen in love with a servant, and your father had removed you from the keep.'

Leo twisted his hands together.

'We were both so *young*, and reckless,' he started, staring forwards at nothing. 'When Father found out, he was not even *angry*, not at first. He thought it amusing; his eldest son having his way with serving girls. It was a sign of *virility*.' Leo grimaced. 'He said I could do as I wanted so long as it didn't stand in the way of marrying a *suitable woman*. When I told him I wanted to marry Mabel, he laughed at me. Told me I would do as I was told.'

'But you didn't.'

'But I did not. We carried on for a while, and then we learnt Mabel was with child. I told Father, idiot that I was. *Still* he wasn't angry. He told me he would deal with the situation – send Mabel away so I would avoid the indignity of having a bastard live beneath my own roof. But I refused.'

'You refused?'

'I did. I told him that I would not have Mabel sent away. I would marry her, and legitimise the child. *That* is when he became angry. He—' Leo shuddered. 'When I refused him, he sent a man after Mabel while she was working in the kitchens. Let me just say that it is a poor idea to sneak up on a woman when she is chopping vegetables with a knife longer than her arm.'

'My *God*, Leo—'

Leo suppressed a laugh. 'Indeed,' he said, eyes sparkling. 'She was strong, even then. After that, Father could tolerate me no longer. He told me I would leave Mabel and wed one of his allies' daughters, and that he would have Mabel and the child *dealt with*. I fought. There was an argument, it turned violent . . . and he had me removed.'

'Removed?'

'He escorted us from the keep with half a dozen guards. When we were through the gates, he set the dogs after us.'

Lily was rendered speechless. She knew that de Foucart had been cruel, yet still somehow his cruelty surprised her, even after his death.

'That is *horrific*,' she breathed. 'Leo, I am so sorry—'

Leo sighed. 'It was a long time ago,' he said. 'And because of that, I have Mabel and Harry. I would not trade them for *anything*. It was a year or so after Harry was born that Mabel's aunt died and left her the brewery. After that, we settled, the family grew . . .' He ran his hand through his hair. 'I am *happy*, here. I feel peace that I never knew in my father's keep. I regret abandoning my siblings, but – God, Lily. I could not have stayed. And Father knew that. He knew he was making me choose between them and Mabel, and the baby. I had to hope they would be strong enough to cope without me.'

'It is a cruel choice. Your father—'

'Was a bastard. But he's *dead*, and I am alive. Not everyone can make the choices I made. I left my home behind because I had a *new* family. Because I had a wife and a child and they needed me more. I would rather have *died* than abandon them. From what I've heard of Penn, he left because he would have rather died than stay. But those choices had consequences. When I left, Father's grip on my siblings became tighter, his punishments crueller. When Penn left, Jo no doubt felt that grip tighten even more, and *worse*, Father's true nature threw the family into ruin. Jo is the last of us who bore witness to him. I cannot imagine the toll it took on her.'

'But she is so *strong*,' Lily muttered. 'She carries it all so well.'

'She does. And she has done for far too long.'

Lily fell silent. Leo gave her a conciliatory smile, clapping his hand to her shoulder.

'Many of us forge our own paths. Some of us are . . . are *rocks*, thrown into a pool. And we do not care about the waves that we cause. But Jo *does* care. That is what makes this choice so hard for her. She knows what can happen to those left behind. But the family is broken, now. They will manage without her.'

'And me?' Lily asked, feeling horribly selfish.

'You stole your brothers' armour and rode into battle for her. You fought men three times your size and a hundred times more practised. You faced down a thief in your nightgown. Jo knows that you are strong, too. If she chooses to leave, it will because she knows you will manage without her, not because she does not care for you.'

'But—' Lily's eyes stung. They felt hot, and tight, and she pressed the heels of her hands against them. 'But I do not wish her to go.'

'And I do not think she wishes to leave you. I think she cares for you, Lily, truly. Do not forget that, whatever happens in your future, together or apart.'

Lily took a shuddering breath. 'Thank you, Leo.'

'It is the least I can do,' he replied. 'After all *this*—' He made a gesture, encompassing it all: his life, his past, the long table with Lily sat beside him. 'It's probably not enough.'

She gave him a small smile. 'What do we do now?'

Leo looked around.

'We get to work before anyone else wakes,' he said, 'and when they *do*, we accept their praise for how hard working and dedicated we are. Come, help me see to the chickens.'

Later, when the rest of the house was finally up, they *did* get praise for getting to work so early. Lily shot a smile to Leo, who winked at her behind Jo's back.

She hoped he had been right.

✳

In all the ways Jo had imagined finding her brother, it had never been like this. It had been so *easy*, as if destiny itself had led her to him. She thought of all the letters she had sent, all the women she had spoken to. She wondered how close she had come to him without even knowing, bitterly realising that she had been searching in all the wrong places.

When she had first started her unsuccessful hunt, she had

worried what a reunion might be like. If Leo would be so changed by the horror of their father that he would be a different man. That the large, kind youth who had left would have hardened into a fearful cynic. She worried too that if they *were* reunited, that the simple passing of time would have shattered the sturdy relationship they'd had as children.

But it hadn't. After the initial shock had worn for both of them, they settled into cosy easiness with each other. It *wasn't* like it had been when they were children – they had both seen too much for that – but his warm smile and sturdy presence filled a gap in her heart: one that she had tried to fill with good behaviour and busyness. Her only regret was that Penn was not here with them. He missed Leo even more than she did, and he would have been ecstatic to see him again.

With Leo's role in the brewery restored, and Jo's new resolve not to go back to the keep, she was bereft of purpose and granted free time that she'd never had before. It was less than a week after his return that she found herself sitting in the kitchen after rising late, completely at a loss for what to do with herself.

When Lily appeared at her side with a smile on her face and wordlessly placed the full basket beside her on the table, Jo immediately knew what she was suggesting.

They shared the weight of the hamper as they walked towards the lake. They settled in the sunshine beside the blackberry bush, the fruits swollen and ripe.

Jo felt no hesitance now in stripping off her clothes and stepping into the water. It was good against her skin, the coldness now familiar rather than startling. Lily followed, and soon they were floating together, Lily leading and Jo following. The water grew deep beneath her, but she was safe: she had never trusted someone like this before.

She didn't know which of them first turned guiding touches purposeful, or slow movements urgent. When Lily pulled her closer until they were pressed together, the water rippling around them, she could no longer feel the chill of the water for the heat of Lily's body. When she closed the tiny gap between them, tugging her into a deep kiss, it was as if the water of the lake extended for miles around them, making them unreachable.

It didn't take long for them to move back into the shallows, then gradually up and onto the grassy bank beside the pebbled shore. The trees above them shuddered in the breeze, covering Lily's wet skin in scattered shadows. Jo kissed her in every place she could reach, deftly pressing her lips to Lily's stomach, her fingertips, the edge of her knees.

So alone, here, time seemed endless. They were utterly exposed on the bank beside the lake, but neither had they ever seen another soul. There was no roof and no walls, yet still it felt more private than the little loft room above the brewery. They moved together, Jo's soft stutters and Lily's far louder curses mingling with the gentle sound of the water rolling pebbles on the shore.

Afterwards, sprawled naked on the grass, Jo watched Lily through her lashes, the gentle rise and fall of her freckled chest. The marks across her nose had darkened in the sun, even starker against her pale skin.

There was a hot ache in Jo's chest: one that felt as if it might split open her ribs and rend her in two.

Jo had always buried her feelings, pressing them beneath the soft, loamy earth of her mind. She hadn't known that burying them would make them grow, make them put down roots, and while she had plucked those thoughts when they *did* reappear, the roots remained, and grew stronger.

Now her feelings had bloomed like a flower bursting through winter frosts, battling against the snow to reach for the stars.

But beside those feelings came one that she did not know how to name. One which she hadn't even known *existed*, sweet and rich like the violets that used to grow in her mother's pleasure-garden. Kissing Lily – *being* with Lily – had made it spring forth, as if from nowhere.

She finally understood what Lily had meant when she'd turned Jo's question on her, asking if she cared for men's company. She wondered how she would have responded if she had known what Lily was really asking. She would have said *yes*, of course. But now she wasn't so sure.

The only man who had lit a spark in her chest – the only man that she had wanted to kiss – was the Knight of Stars.

Jo watched Lily breathe, content and sleepy. She thought of the shape of her smile, and the line of her hips, and those *damned* dimples just above her backside.

As if aware she was being watched, Lily stirred and opened her eyes. When she spotted Jo staring at her, she grinned, then lazily rolled onto her side and pulled Jo into a kiss.

It made Jo's heart expand, her whole body light up in flames. There was something in her chest trying to get out.

She chided herself for being so foolish that she had never realised it before. Penn had fallen in love with another man, after all. Surely it was possible for *her* to fall in love with a woman, too?

Lily pulled back, gifting her with that lopsided smile.

No: Jo was being foolish. It was *absurd*, and far too romantic. Jo recalled her fear that she would not be able to recognise love when it happened, when she was set on marrying Lord Adam. Now she was finding it where she was sure it didn't exist.

Yet she wasn't sure what else to call it, not when Lily kissed her like that. She didn't know what else to call it when Lily took her by the waist and floated in the water beside her, or laughed by her side as they worked long, slow days. There was no other way to describe it when she watched the perfectly embroidered dress pool at her feet as Lily undressed her, or when Lily moaned softly into her mouth.

She remembered what Isabelle had said, all that time ago, about the man she had left behind. The feelings that Jo hadn't been able to understand. Not until now.

When Isabelle spoke of Jo's apparent northern lover, even *she* had been able to see it – before there was even anything to see.

Jo wanted to say it out loud. Perhaps if she did, she would know if it was true.

Or perhaps she would realise she was wrong. Perhaps Lily would baulk at the confession. Lily had told her of her previous lovers – all women, all temporary – and Jo had a sudden bite of fear that she was like them: a passing interest destined to fade. Eventually, Lily would return to Dunlyn, and no doubt would want to find another lover. Jo could not fault her for that, even if she jealously wished to keep her for herself: she was inexperienced and fumbling, with both her body and her emotions. Lily deserved someone more seasoned.

At least she was not *entirely* incompetent. It was with a smug smile that Jo remembered her fears that she would never be able to satisfy a husband in the way he would want to be satisfied. She had always been dedicated to learning new skills, and *this* was a skill that she was eagerly advancing in.

The first time Lily had used her mouth on her, her shock of messy red hair disappearing between Jo's thighs, Jo had cursed so loudly she thought she would wake the house. When, the next night, she told Lily in animated eagerness that she wished to attempt the same on *her*, Lily had blushed so furiously that Jo feared she would set the straw beneath her aflame.

She had not, but her own cursing had been loud enough to put Jo's to shame, and it had taken them the rest of the night to coax Gilbert down from the rafters where he'd hidden from the noise.

Jo thought back on it fondly, the memory once again stirring that heat in her core. Something had awoken in her for the first time: something so hungry it was impossible to satiate. When she shuffled closer across the grass, drifting a slow hand to Lily's thigh, the feeling reared up, eager.

Lily knew what she sought without a single word passing between them.

Later, they returned to the brewery with the sun nearly set, warm and loose-limbed with grass in their hair. As Jo held Lily's hand softly in her own, she thought again of voicing the feeling she had only just begun to define. But again it seemed too soon, too much. She still had the handkerchief in her pocket, and had taken to carrying it with her, waiting — but for what, she could not say. It *had* taken on a new meaning, now, and Jo was determined to find the best time to return it, and the right words to say when she did.

With Lily healed and Jo relieved of work, they slipped smoothly into the new routine. Their days were long and their evenings longer. They returned to the lake often, to the clear water and the brambles. The berries were ripening over time, each mouthful sweeter than the last.

Jo's skin was warm, and there were blackberry seeds caught between her teeth. Her heart was drowning, and she had never been so happy.

Chapter 22

'Ladies, wake up!'

Jo stirred from sticky dreams. Her arm was wrapped around Lily's middle, her head pillowed on her breast. She was growing fond of waking like this, falling asleep each night warm and satisfied in Lily's arms.

'Lily! Jo!'

Mabel was calling them. She heaved herself up as Lily also woke, blinking sleep from her eyes.

'What—'

'Just a moment!' Jo called down the ladder. 'We shall be with you in just – just a moment!'

Mabel could *not* climb the ladder and see them in such a state. Jo had no doubt that she would accept a union between two women, but she had no desire at all to have an awkward conversation with her sister-in-law.

They emerged downstairs as quickly as they could, and Jo could tell by the quirk of Mabel's lips that she knew why they had taken so long to heed her calling.

'I believe the ale is ready,' she said, the quirk splitting into a huge grin. 'Shall we?'

All four of them gathered around the tubs. Mabel dipped the

mug into the nearest one, filling it and peering at the liquid inside, assessing it. Deeming it suitable, she took a sip.

'My *God*—' she spluttered, spitting the ale to the straw at her feet with a string of curses. 'This is *foul*.'

Jo's stomach dropped. They had worked so hard to ensure the batch was prepared for the order. She was sure that she and Lily had handled the process in Mabel's absence to even the smallest detail – but there was something she had missed. Something she got wrong.

That familiar, sickening feeling of fear lurched in her stomach. But she caught it quickly, taking a breath. She would not panic. She could use this to *learn*, to use her mistakes to build a better future. With so much that had happened, Mabel would not berate her for their mistakes.

She hurried over and took the mug from Mabel, taking a cautious sip.

It tasted . . . fine. She swilled the ale in her mouth then took a larger mouthful, as Mabel watched on aghast. It tasted *better* than fine: it tasted good, especially for a batch that had been done in some part with the brewster absent. There was a bubble of pride in Jo's chest. It had *worked*. She had done a good job.

'Mabel,' she said, offering the mug back, 'this tastes perfectly normal.'

Mabel took it and gave it a sniff. She wrinkled her nose and then took another reluctant sip. She spluttered again.

'One of us must be wrong,' she said. 'Leo, Lily, settle this.'

The mug was passed between them. Lily did not know what tastes she was looking for, but deemed it pleasant enough. Leo even went so far as to call it a *very good batch*. Mabel looked at them all as if they had gone mad.

'It tastes spoiled,' she insisted. 'Can *none* of you taste that?'

Jo shook her head as Lily shrugged. Leo said nothing, watching his wife carefully.

'Mabel.'

Mabel looked at him. Something passed between them – although Jo could not tell what. Mabel blinked, then passed the mug back to Jo.

'Very well,' she said. 'But we'll need Hamet to agree to this before we sell it on, *especially* as it's going to a nobleman.'

'When is he next in town?' Jo asked, finishing off the ale.

'He should hopefully only be a few days at most,' Mabel said. 'He's often in these parts. The batch should keep till then. And then we can load it up and deliver it.'

'And until then?'

'Until then . . .' Mabel looked around. 'We rest, I suppose. We cannot begin a new batch until this is shifted, and there is no more work to be done with this one.'

They were lucky, in the end, and Hamet reappeared in Astmere only two days later. He was pleased to see them again – and thrilled to see Leo returned – and complimented them once again on the quality of the ale. When Mabel informed him how much of a part Jo had taken in preparing the batch, he praised her in such overblown language that Jo blushed.

'You really *do* have a future as a brewster ahead of you,' he said, as he bid them farewell.

Jo could only look at her feet, but his words made a flame of pride ignite in her chest.

With no time to spare, they quickly loaded the cart with the barrels, Mabel barking orders as Leo, Harry, and Lily heaved them into the back then tossed a sheet over them. These larger deliveries being sent further afield were often Leo's responsibility, Mabel explained, but with the wound in his side still healing they all saw the risk in sending him away from home again so soon. Mabel had said she would ride out in his place, but Leo had bristled.

'I . . . would prefer you stay here,' he said, his voice low. 'I do not wish— It is a long journey, and I—'

He stuttered self-consciously, shooting an awkward look at Jo and Lily. Jo could guess at his hesitance: he had been away from home for so long, he did not wish to part from his family again so soon. It was sweet, and it made her heart ache.

'I will go,' she said, stepping forwards.

'No, Jo—'

'Why not? I dealt with enough merchants in your absence. I am sure I am quite capable of delivering some barrels to a keep.'

'It is not that I think you incapable,' Leo said. 'Just I do not wish to send you off alone.'

'She will not be *alone*,' Lily cut in. 'I shall accompany her.'

Leo snorted. 'Forgive me, Lily,' he said, 'but I am not sure if two women unaccompanied on the road is any safer than one.'

Lily folded her arms across her chest. 'Perhaps not, but one woman and her guard would be perfectly adequate.' Leo looked as if he were about to refuse her, and Lily spoke over him before he could. 'I would not argue this, Leo. Do not forget I defeated you in the ring. You of *all* people should be confident in my ability to keep your sister safe.'

Leo's mouth hung open.

'Did she *really*, Pa?' Harry asked, looking between them. Jo had been about to ask that very question.

'Yes,' Leo relented. 'She did, curse her. Fine. Fine! You will accompany Jo. Tell everyone you are William Dale again. And keep her *safe*.'

'I swear I shall.'

Later, when they were alone again and preparing to set off, Jo approached as Lily dug through their shared things.

'Did you *really* defeat Leo?' she said, disbelieving.

'I did,' Lily said, sitting on her heels. 'Do you recall the sword fight you and Ellis watched? You approached, just after . . .'

Jo *did* remember. It was impossible to forget.

'My word,' she breathed. 'I never even realised . . .'

Lily smiled lopsidedly. 'Both of us were there fighting for you. It is like a story, isn't it?'

'It is a little . . .' Jo watched as Lily returned to her things. 'What are you doing?'

'Fetching my armour . . .' Lily said, voice muffled as she leant behind the straw and crates. 'I just – *ah!*'

She pulled out the sack, placing it down with a loud clank.

'You *cannot* be serious,' Jo said. 'You cannot wear *armour* on the road. It is far too conspicuous, and far too warm. Make do with a gambeson and your sword, for God's sake.'

Lily pouted at her. 'I may need it.'

'I cannot see how that would be true. We are travelling to a keep, down busy roads. We are not heading into *war*.'

'It pays to be prepared.'

'I cannot tell if you truly *are* worried that we will be beset by enemies, or if you just wish to play at being a knight once more.'

Lily stopped where she was searching through the bag, looking up and chewing on her lip.

'Is it so obvious?'

Jo tucked a loose strand of hair behind Lily's ear with a kiss.

'It is to me,' she whispered.

Lily grinned against her lips. Jo moved her hand lower, down Lily's neck, towards her shoulder—

'Jo! Lily! Be quick!'

The moment shattered. Jo sighed, leant back, and with a final quick look towards Lily clambered back down the ladder.

*

Lily placed the sack into the back of the cart. Jo's back was turned to her, taking directions from Leo, so she hurriedly tugged the sheet over her things and tied it down, keeping everything hidden.

She had dressed again in her brothers' stolen things. Her sickness had left them fitting even more poorly than they had before, but at least she looked like a man again. With her hair slicked back and her sword strapped back to her side, she felt as if no harm could possibly come to them on the journey. No one would even *dare* approach them: it was unusual to carry such a conspicuous weapon, after all.

Mabel approached with a leather pack. It was full of food, water, and ale for the road: more than enough for them both.

'Good luck on the journey,' she said. 'And ensure you return to us in one piece. I've no wish to tend to you for weeks on end once more.'

'I shall try.' Lily laughed. 'Besides, I hope we can make the delivery and be off again as soon as we may. If the man he sent to barter with you is anything to go by, I can only assume that his master is the devil himself.'

Mabel was forcing herself not to smile. 'Don't you allow him to hear you say that,' she warned. 'He'll have you locked away.'

Lily gripped the hilt of her sword. 'He may try.'

She quickly shoved the pack under the sheet then clambered up to the front of the cart. They'd hitched it to Broga, as she was more familiar to them than Mabel's horse, and Lily gave her a pat once she'd settled into the seat.

Apparently satisfied with her brother's directions, Jo soon followed, seating herself beside her. Up there, with Jo at her side, Lily really *did* feel like a knight once more: like *Jo's* knight, like her champion. It was a wonderful feeling to return to, and she swore to herself that she would ensure she was fitted for proper armour once she returned home.

She *did* need to return. Seeing Jo at Leo's side and the easy camaraderie they had fallen into made her miss her brothers, and Jo's departure would go easier on her if she was back with them. Once the delivery was complete and the physician had cleared her for travel, she would return north.

She had a plan, now: one that she was determined to see through. She would demand – not ask – that she remain in the keep and not be sent to a convent. Once Ash became earl, it would be easy to convince him to make her a part of his retinue.

She would ask Jo to go with her, if only until she left to find her own path. They could finally go back to the northern lakes, and the berries which Lily remained convinced were sweeter. Jo would like that, and she would leap at the chance to see Penn again.

Lily mused on it as they travelled, watching the scenery roll past. It would take two days before they reached their destination, and while Lily could think of better things to do than stare at passing trees, she couldn't feel *unhappy* about it, either; not with Jo by her side.

In lieu of anything to do, she started to sing. The noise startled Jo, who looked at her as if she were about to chastise her, then joined in. Their voices did not harmonise at all, the sound reminding Lily of Gib's squawking after being trodden on, but they sang and laughed until their voices turned hoarse.

They stopped late on the first night, pulling into an inn that Leo had recommended and storing the barrels and Broga in the stable. Jo saw to food and board while Lily hovered ominously behind her, keeping steady, direct eye contact with the landlord with her hand resting on the hilt of her sword.

The food was passable, and they were seen to a small loft room which they would be sharing with a handful of other travellers. Lily carefully placed herself between Jo and the rest of the patrons, insisting Jo take the pallet closest to the wall. It was a mild night, and despite Lily's concerns the other travellers seemed friendly – although not enough for her to drop her disguise. Lily once again claimed to be Jo's brother, and they were both blissfully unbothered by their companions until dawn.

They set off early, keen to be back on the road. It was another long, warm day of riding, and several times Lily jumped down from the cart to walk alongside so she could stretch her legs and ease the ache in the base of her spine. Beside the road grew thick brambles, and unable to resist she reached for a berry. She must have gone too fast, or too thoughtlessly; her hand caught on the thorns, leaving tiny, bloodied scratches across her skin.

The brambles here were wild and untended. She heaved herself back onto the cart with a dozen berries and hands covered in scrapes. One settled, she popped one of the berries into Jo's mouth. Jo laughed as juice stained her lips and Lily's fingertips, before she looked down.

'Lily—' She reached out to stroke the torn skin. 'Are you all right?'

'The danger of blackberries.' Lily shrugged. 'What's a little pain for all this sweetness?'

Evening was beginning to draw in as they spotted the keep looming on the hill upon the horizon. It was not as large as Dunlyn, but it looked well-kept, and they were soon riding through tracts of precisely managed farmland. Back on the busier road, Lily had to straighten her back again – she was a *knight*, here. She needed to look the part.

She peered at the keep as they drew closer. There were banners flying from the tallest battlements, although at such a distance she could barely make out their colours, let alone their coat of arms. As they approached the keep something about them prickled a memory in the back of her mind.

They turned at a fork in the road, and the glare of the setting sun was suddenly blocked by a little copse. She realised how she knew those colours. Those shapes.

She gripped the hilt of her sword.

'Jo?'

'Yes?'

'Those colours . . .'

Jo turned to look. 'What about—' Her breath gave out. 'No . . . Lily, surely not?'

So Jo recognised them, too. They were unmistakable, now, even with the setting sun threatening to blind them. A red field split by a golden chevron, a flaming heart beneath.

They were the banners of Lord Adam Wyck.

Chapter 23

Jo's heart was in her throat as they approached the towering outer walls of Lord Adam's keep. The unremarkable castle was now vast and imposing. A trap. A *prison*.

It was growing dark by the time they reached the huddle of houses at the foot of the hill upon which the keep rested. It was a simple hamlet: a few homes, a farm, what sounded like a blacksmith from the relentless hammering coming from beneath the roof. Jo pulled the cart to a stop.

'We should turn around,' Lily urged, keeping her voice low.

Jo wanted to agree. They needed to leave. But she had a *job* to do.

'What about Mabel?' Jo hissed back. 'I refuse to disappoint her like that.'

'Mabel will *understand*,' Lily pushed. 'Of course she will, if we explain . . .'

Still Jo was unconvinced. 'I do not—'

'My Lady!'

Jo's words died on her lips. She turned, fixing her face into a keen smile, to see a man wearing a surcoat in Lord Adam's colours, pulling a heavily laden handcart. Her smile stuck in a rictus as he approached.

'Is this the ale from Astmere?' he asked, cheerily. 'Mabel's brew?' Jo nodded an assent. 'Wonderful,' he said, ignoring her silence. 'I'll inform the housekeeper you've arrived. My Lady, Sir.'

He ducked them both a curt nod before hurrying up the hill towards the keep. Jo's spine remained stiff.

'They know you're here, then.' Lily sighed.

'They know I am here.'

'What do you intend to do?'

Jo set her shoulders. 'I intend to make my delivery,' she said, gripping the reins tighter. 'Lord Adam will not come *himself* to greet traders, do not be absurd. We will gain entry, get Mabel's pay, and we will *leave*. Quickly.'

Lily shifted beside her. 'I am not sure—'

'I am,' Jo said, shocking herself with how true that was. 'He will not even know we were here.'

She thought of the last time Lily had confronted Lord Adam or one of his men. The incident in the field, after she had been thrown. She hesitated. It would be far more dangerous for Lily to be recognised as the Knight of Stars.

'Did you bring a dress?' she asked.

Lily frantically shook her head. 'I did not.'

Jo took a breath. She took another, attempting to calm her heartbeat. She peered around the hamlet.

'I will go in. You stay here.'

'Jo—'

'I will not risk him recognising you, Lily. They will not harm me, just—'

'Just berate you? *Trap* you?'

'And if they find *you*? If they see you as William, not as Lily?

You'll be condemned for being with me. They'll claim you—' Jo grimaced. 'They'll claim you defiled me.'

Lily gave a nonchalant half-shrug. 'Well,' she began, 'I *did*—'

'Lily.'

'I am merely saying, *Jo*, that if he *did* claim that, then he would not be entirely—'

'*Lily!*'

Lily threw up her hands. Her flippancy was an act, Jo suspected, hiding real nerves beneath.

'Please,' she said. 'Just . . . wait for me. I will be quick.'

Lily gripped her hands together, shot her another doubtful look, then slid down from the seat.

'Wait—'

Jo watched as she hurried to the back of the cart, reached under the canvas sheet and pulled out a sack. Jo's fingers twitched nervously on the horse's reins.

'What—' The sack made a familiar metallic clanking sound. Jo realised at once what it contained. 'I thought you said you were not bringing your armour?'

'I said I would not *wear* my armour . . .' Lily reached back under the canvas, this time pulling out her shield. 'You did not tell me I could not bring it with us.'

Jo sighed. Lily was correct, she supposed, and besides: she did not have the inclination to argue with her.

'I had been intending to tell you to stay safe,' she said, glancing at the sack and shield, 'but with *those*, I doubt I need to.'

Lily gave her a cocky grin. 'I will stay safe.'

'And *I* will be swift,' Jo assured her. 'It should not take too long to unload some barrels. Wait here for me.'

Lily performed a low, exaggerated bow. 'Until your return, my Lady.'

With a fond shake of her head, Jo spurred the horse onwards, towards the keep.

It was a short ride up the hill, but by the time she reached the gates her heart was pounding in her chest. She took a deep breath to steady herself as she approached the guards stationed outside. She spoke before they could question her.

'I am here with a delivery,' she said. 'Ale, from Astmere.'

The guard closest to the gate nodded to his partner, and they both stepped back in tandem, allowing her entrance. She headed beneath the low stone archway, her stomach swirling. This was far too risky. Still, she had a job to do, and she would see it through.

A woman approached who could only be the housekeeper.

'I have a delivery,' Jo repeated, speaking around a thick tongue. 'From Mabel, in Astmere.'

'Ah, yes. This way. . .'

Jo pulled the cart around, following her to a wide doorway which must have led to the basement and kitchens. Jo jumped down from the cart as the housekeeper pulled away the canvas sheet.

'This all seems in order,' she said, wiping her hands on her skirts. 'I'll fetch some boys to assist with the barrels.'

Jo watched her scurry away, then got to work. As she folded the canvas sheet into a more manageable shape, she peered up around her. From the inside, the keep was just as imposing, and a dozen narrow windows peered down at her. She repressed a shiver: this would have been her home, had she chosen to marry Lord Adam.

She was sure the eerie air of closeness that permeated it was more to do with the dark sky above and her own nerves, yet still she was glad she would not be forced to stay.

Soon she was joined by a couple of strong-looking lads, and together they began to heave the barrels from the cart. She kept close to Broga, out of the way.

'Look out, miss!'

She jumped aside just in time to avoid a horse and rider, going at such speed that it nearly knocked her from her feet. The lad who had shouted whistled through his teeth as the rider vanished through the gates, scattering servants.

'What *was* that?' Jo breathed, brushing down her skirts.

'Messenger,' the lad said simply. 'Wonder what's got Lord Adam sending out missives at this hour.'

The other lad shrugged, and they quickly got back to work.

When they reached the final few her chest began to loosen. She had done it. She would leave, collect Lily, and ride through the dark to the nearest town with an inn.

But not *yet*. In the haste of unloading and her own bubbling fear, she had forgotten that the housekeeper had not returned with Mabel's money. Jo had no desire to enter the keep and risk running into Lord Adam or Sir Lanval, so she would have to wait by the cart.

She was helping the lads with the last barrel when there was a call from behind her.

'My Lady—'

She sighed in relief, recognising the voice of the housekeeper.

'Miss—'

Her heart dropped. The housekeeper *was* approaching, but

close behind her were a pair of figures that made dread sink in Jo's chest. Lord Adam, flanked closely by Sir Lanval.

No.

Jo sat, watching as Lord Adam busied himself around the room. It was a surprisingly cosy space compared to the chill of the keep: flickering torches on the walls bathed it in warm orange light, keeping back the shadows of the lofty ceiling. She perched on a high-backed chair into which someone had carved an intricate harvest scene, stalks of wheat carved into the armrests. They were worn almost entirely smooth, and she realised that she was not the first person to find comfort in rubbing their fingers along them.

Finally, Lord Adam seated himself at the table opposite her. She could sense Sir Lanval lingering by the door behind her: a guard, to keep them safe. Or keep her in.

'Lady Johanna,' Lord Adam began, his hands pressed to the tabletop. 'I am so glad to see you returned to us.'

'Thank you, my Lord.'

'Is your brother well?' He gave her a smile. It didn't reach his eyes. Jo wondered if he had worked out the lie.

'Yes, my Lord,' she said. 'Quite well, thank you. Much better than he was.'

'I am pleased to hear it. He has been in my prayers.' Jo very much doubted that, but she did not say so. Lord Adam continued. 'And now you are returned, we can finally see through our plans to wed.'

Jo's grip on the chair tightened. She did not want to marry him. So much had changed since the tournament. But her throat had seized, her lungs empty, jaw locked. As he approached, it was as if his face flickered like a candle flame – all at once both Lord Adam and her father, long dead.

'We are lucky so much was arranged before your brother was taken ill,' he continued. 'I have sent a rider to the church already. The priest is a – *was* a friend of my father. He will happily perform the ceremony, likely the day after next.'

So that had been the messenger, sent in haste. Lord Adam must have been watching her from one of those towering, skinny windows.

'So soon?' she said, finally finding her voice. 'What about the banns?'

Lord Adam waved a flippant hand. 'Simply a formality,' he said. 'Our union has been arranged for some weeks, now. The priest will be willing to make an exception. I would prefer we are wed sooner rather than being forced to wait.'

'I see,' she managed. 'But—'

'But?'

Tell him no, she begged herself. *Refuse him. Curse his name and go!*

She said nothing, fused into the carved wood of the chair.

'Come,' Lord Adam said, getting to his feet and extending his hand. 'Let me take you to your chambers. It is late, and I am sure you are tired.'

Every facet of Jo's soul screamed at her not to take his hand. Her body thrummed with the urge to run.

But she was back. Back within a keep. Back as a noblewoman. A wife.

She took his hand, and let him lead her out.

✳

317

It was taking far too long for Jo to return. Lily rolled the mug in her hands, staring into the coals of the blacksmith's fire.

She had been approached by the blacksmith a little while after Jo had left her. She'd been worried, fearing that he'd demand she move on, but instead he offered her a drink. At first Lily had assumed he'd thought her a woman and been attempting to woo her, but it became clear that he had fallen for her disguise and had concluded she had been left behind by her erstwhile lover after watching Jo ride off without her.

The assumption was not entirely incorrect, Lily conceded, and accepted his hospitality gladly. He had been fine company, and Lily had a true interest in the smithy, even if she had no skill in it. He'd seemed happy to have someone to talk to about the role, and his wife gave Lily a fond smile with a roll of her eyes as she handed her a mug of ale.

But even the warmth of his home and the fine ale did not soothe her fear, and as the evening melted into night that fear only grew.

It should not take this long to make a single delivery.

She slid outside. Lily had been waiting for *hours*, and the purplish sky above had turned a deep black. Clouds had rolled in over the afternoon, and she couldn't even see the moon above. Leaning on the blacksmith's fence and looking upwards, she shuddered.

It was far too dark.

She ducked back inside.

'If I could . . .' she said, 'I must find my . . . my friend. Could I leave my things with you?'

She headed up the winding footpath to the keep. She was thankful for the clouded sky as she slunk through the shadows, keeping close to the wall. There would be an entrance somewhere: all keeps had a door in the outer wall for servants and traders. Tonight, she needed to look like just another castle boy, *not* a knight.

She found it with ease and pushed inside.

The inner courtyard was small but busy. Jo should be here with the cart and ale: but Lily could see neither her nor Mabel's cart. There was a tense grip in her stomach. *Where was she?*

Across the way, she spotted a lad carrying a barrel. She dashed over to him, hoping he'd take her for another servant.

'Hey—'

He turned to stare at her, saying nothing.

'Is the girl who brought the ale still in the keep?'

He continued to stare at her. Lily realised how suspicious she must seem.

'Housekeeper wanted to speak to her,' she added.

'She left,' he said, shifting the weight of the barrel. 'A while ago. What did the housekeeper want with her?'

'She wouldn't tell me,' Lily said quickly. 'Thank you anyway.'

Before he could work her out, she rushed away, not thinking about where she was headed. She found herself beside a stable on the far side of the yard and leant against a wall to catch her breath.

There was a snort behind her. She turned.

Broga.

The familiar face was enough to make her weep. She quickly pushed through the gate and gave the animal a pat, stroking her nose as Broga attempted to eat her hair.

The boy had told her that Jo had already left, but she couldn't have done: not without the horse. Lily had no way of telling what had happened to Jo, but she had to find her.

Taking the direction the boy with the barrel had gone, she walked into the keep. She followed the narrower servant's corridors, heading towards the sound of chatter. Kitchens were always a hub of gossip, and with luck she would hear more there.

She found it easily, packed with people and swelteringly hot. She lingered nervously by the table, waiting. It was intolerable: she needed to keep moving, and it felt as if her bones were trying to leap through her skin. Clinging to the sleeve of her tunic, she forced herself to stand still and listen.

Finally, she caught a snatch of conversation that could be useful.

'—the wedding, and I have no idea where he expects me to—'

The horrible weight in Lily's stomach hardened. A *wedding*. That all but confirmed it: Adam had her. But if he was forcing Jo or had convinced her to wed him, Lily could not say.

Trying not to focus on that latter thought, she sidled towards the woman who had spoken: severe and grey-haired, talking with ducked heads to an older lady who must have been the cook. She looked frustrated.

'—in the upper wing above the West Hall,' the cook was saying, as Lily approached.

The grey-haired woman sighed. 'I cannot spare the staff,' she said. 'If he had *warned* us of a guest—'

There was only one person they could be talking about. Lily raced through the kitchen, dodging around staff, then back out into the next corridor. Finding the hall they must have been speaking about was easy enough, as well as a twisting staircase heading up. She needed to reach Jo. If she *had* changed her mind and decided to marry Adam after all, the least Lily deserved was to hear it from her.

There was only a single door at the top of the stairs. This must be it. Lily approached on tiptoe, listening.

There was a muffled moaning sound coming from the room beyond. It sounded like crying.

She could stand it no longer. Bracing herself, she threw herself inside.

'Jo—'

There was a loud, furious curse.

Lily froze in the doorway. In front of her, framed within the canopy of an enormous bed and lit up in dancing firelight, was Lord Adam.

And Sir Lanval.

Lily had lived long enough to recognise at once what they were doing. In fact, after one encounter with Raff and Penn in the armoury, which she had been desperately trying to scrub from her memory, she knew *precisely* what they were doing.

Lanval attempted to scramble from his lord's lap at the same time as Adam tried to stand, resulting in Lanval tumbling messily to the floor. Adam stood as Lily tried to look *anywhere* else.

'How *dare*—' and then he hesitated. '*Dale?*'

Lily froze. He was on her in an instant, and Lily forgot his nakedness in favour of his hand forcing her against the wall.

'It *is* you, isn't it?' he said. 'William Dale?'

Lily swallowed. She nodded.

'Why are you here?'

There was no use in lying. She stuck her chin in the air.

'I am seeking Lady Johanna.'

Both men stared at her. Adam did not let her go. Her heart raced: she had no idea what he would do to her – how he would punish her for discovering his secret. He would need to silence her.

He moved closer.

'I believe—'

She did not let him finish. She threw her foot back and kicked him between the legs as hard as she could.

Chapter 24

Jo peered around the chamber she had been forced into. It was a beautifully furnished room, with a huge, richly canopied bed in the centre. There was a chest beneath the window. She had not opened it yet, but was sure it was full of expensive gowns.

It was a room for a bride.

She was trapped. The match had been agreed to weeks ago, and in that time it had passed into memory, like a child's dream. Now it was suddenly, horribly real.

She drummed her fingers on the tabletop and glanced out the window. It was dark outside: the sun had set *hours* ago. She hoped Lily was all right. She would have to find a way to remove herself from the keep and seek her out.

She was considering searching the room for an escape route when there was a sound in the corridor beyond. There was a brief, perfunctory knock before the door swung open.

Three people crowded the doorway. Lord Adam, Sir Lanval, and pressed between them, Lily.

Jo swallowed back Lily's name as Lord Adam shoved her into the room, remembering that she had intended to appear as William. Both Lord Adam and Sir Lanval looked flushed — an expression not of anger, but *embarrassment*.

'What is going on?'

'We need to—'

'I found them together.'

Lily spoke over Lord Adam, her words hot and quick. Sir Lanval's eyes went wide and he quickly slammed the door shut behind them.

'How *dare* you slander—'

'She has a right to know!' Lily shouted over him. 'You expect her to take part in this without her knowing?'

'She *cannot*—'

'Lady Johanna.' Lily forced herself away from him, rushing to Jo's side. 'I found them. Together.'

Jo looked from Lily to Lord Adam and Sir Lanval – their matching expressions, their flushed faces.

'Together?' she repeated, not quite sure she could believe it.

'In bed,' Lily continued. '*Together.*'

'. . . Oh.'

Jo didn't know what else she could say. But it made sense. Lord Adam's desperation for them to marry, and the conversation she had overheard during the feast. Even Sir Lanval threatening Lily made more sense now. They had been keen for her to wed Lord Adam *not* because she was a good prize, or a good match, but because she was *convenient*. They had intended to make her a shield behind which they could hide.

She looked between them. She did not care if they were lovers, although judging by the nervous way Sir Lanval was hovering beside Lord Adam, close but not quite touching, she could assume they were quite a lot more than that. It would be absurd of her to care, given her family, and her own relationship with Lily.

324

'Is this true?'

Lord Adam did not drop her gaze. She *knew* it was true: knew from their expressions, knew because Lily would never lie to her. But she wanted to hear him say it.

Finally, he looked away.

'It is.'

'Addy, *no*—' Sir Lanval grabbed his arm. 'Do not damn yourself like this.'

'But it *is* true,' Lord Adam snapped, wrenching his arm away. 'William is correct, damn him. Lady Johanna should enter this marriage with her eyes open. And do you think William would keep the secret? Forever? Do you think Johanna would not work it out herself?'

'But—'

'No, Lanval.' Lord Adam turned to Jo. 'It *is* true.'

'And what role did you wish me to play in this?' Jo demanded, unfazed.

Lord Adam gathered himself.

'I need a wife,' he said. 'I am the *Lord* of this keep, and as such, I need to avoid' – he took a breath – 'difficult questions.'

He looked desperate. Jo understood his desperation, and wished she felt sympathy for him. But she didn't. All she felt was anger, pounding in her chest.

She wasn't a *person*, just a tool – a way for Lord Adam and Sir Lanval to hide. Knowing that her worth was only as a bride had been bitter, but a bitterness she had accepted. Lord Adam hadn't even wanted *that*. He didn't want *her*, or the skills she had spent a lifetime honing for this very purpose. He didn't even want her as a friend or companion. He just wanted someone quiet and compliant enough not to notice where his real affections lay.

'This marriage will work for us,' he continued. 'For all of us.'

'What do you mean?'

'We have all broken the law. We will *all* face punishment for our crimes. If word spreads of Lanval and me, we will be killed. And if people learn of *your* relationship with William, he will be punished, and you will be ruined. And do not deny it—' he added, as she opened her mouth to protest. 'Why else would he be here? Why else would he have vanished the same night as you? I had suspicions that the tale about your brother's illness were not truthful. Be grateful I did not tell anyone of those suspicions.'

Jo held herself taller. His words felt like a threat, but they both held the power to damn the other. They were duelling in the ring, both with a sword glimmering above the other's neck.

She wondered who would swing first.

'This union benefits us *all*,' Lord Adam continued. 'We will be wed in name alone. All of us will be *safe*, and have what we want. I will not force you to share my bed, or act as my wife. I will allow you and William to remain together. You will not be forced to part, and – and it will ensure you beget me heirs.'

'Without your involvement?' Jo said, eyebrow raised.

'Indeed.'

He was offering them a lifetime together. A lifetime trapped in his keep. Lily would be beside her, yes: but they would be trapped nonetheless. She already missed the sun on her face.

Lord Adam took her prolonged silence as acquiescence.

'It is set,' he said, pulling himself straight. 'William, I will see that quarters are arranged for you. Come.'

Jo wanted to grab Lily's hand. She wanted to beg her to stay – or beg Lord Adam to *allow* her to stay. But it was already far too risky, and Adam's expression was severe. Behind him, Sir Lanval looked positively venomous.

Her fingers gripping at nothing, she watched as Lily was forced from the room.

*

Much to Lily's indignation, it was Lanval who guided her towards the chamber in which she would be staying. He seemed to have no idea at all that she was a woman, and they walked in stony silence to a tiny room on the opposite side of the keep. She barely noticed his presence beside her, too shocked and angry to bear him any mind.

She expected him to leave her in the chamber, but as she stepped into the room he quickly followed, shutting the door behind him.

'Lady Johanna and Lord Adam are to wed, then,' he said.

Lily swallowed. 'So it seems.'

'I need—' He sniffed, his nostrils flaring. 'I need your *help*, William.'

Lily's first thought was to refuse him. But there was that look in his eyes again – the glint of desperation that she now recognised. The same expression he had worn when he threatened her, drunk and panicking in Hartswood Forest.

'Lady Johanna is very sure of herself,' he said. It did not sound like an insult, although it could have been.

'You fear her rejecting Lord Adam's offer?'

'She *cannot* reject him. But—' His words were stony, but he seemed unsure regardless.

'You *do* fear it, don't you?'

Lanval did not speak.

'Does Adam?' Lily continued.

Lanval's shoulders slanted. 'Of course not.' And then – preposterously – he laughed. He looked *exhausted*. 'Adam does not fear rejection. Adam does not know what it *is* to be rejected.'

'But you do?'

They stared at each other.

'I do,' he said at last.

Lily wondered what had come before this – what had led him to Adam's home, and his bed.

'I think we understand each other,' Lanval continued. 'You and I. Surely you can see the sense in this match. This is a good choice, the *best* choice. For all of us. You must make sure that Lady Johanna understands that this is a way for us all to live in peace. Not just peace: comfort, too, and wealth. Lord Adam is an extremely rich man.'

'Is that why you threatened me for him? His money?'

Lanval looked as if she had slapped him.

'How *dare* you?' he hissed. 'I would do *anything* for him. Not because of his wealth or his title. Don't act like you cannot understand how that feels.'

She wanted to push him aside, to spit in his face and tell him to get out. She would not have her future *given* to her.

But it was not her choice to make. As she had stood in Jo's bridal chamber, silently begging for her to refuse Adam, Jo had said nothing. She had not rejected him. She'd let him speak. Internally, Lily had screamed at Jo to say something – say *anything* – but she hadn't.

Lily had lost her.

No doubt Jo saw the sense in it. Like this, they could be together, and safe, and Jo would be able to fulfil all those rigid, smothering expectations that she had of herself. Anger swirled around Lily's chest, trying to choke her. Perhaps Jo didn't even intend for Lily to stay. That felt suddenly, sharply true. Of course Jo wouldn't have chosen her and their fragile happiness, not over the safety that Adam had offered. She had changed her mind before. She could do it again.

Lily couldn't let Lanval sense that. She had to pretend that she still had some power over him.

'I cannot vouch for her, Lanval,' she said, deliberately forgoing his title. 'I cannot force her hand. I would not *dare* tell Lady Johanna what to do, on this or any other matter.'

'But she is *yours.*'

'She belongs to herself. Her choices are her own.'

'But you *must* agree with me?'

Lily just shrugged. This only angered him further.

'Do you love her?' he said, finally.

Lily froze. 'What?'

'*Do you love her?* It is a simple enough question.'

It *was* a simple question. And of course, Lily knew the answer. But she couldn't voice it out loud, not to *him*. It was too precious for that. She had not even voiced it to Jo. She refused for *this* to be the first time she said it out loud, especially now Jo had thrown her aside.

He could tell, though. He knew. He relaxed, as if he'd won.

'If you love her,' he said, 'you will tell her that she *must* agree to this.' He stepped towards the door. As he opened it, he hesitated. 'And if she loves *you*, she will.'

And then he was gone, leaving Lily alone in the tiny, empty room.

Chapter 25

Jo had never thought a wedding could be organised in so short a time. Tomorrow, she would be married.

It felt like a lifetime ago that she had been told she would be marrying Adam. She had been happy to tie herself to a man she didn't know, to run his keep and – even if she had never been keen to focus on the mechanics of the act itself – bear his children. Looking back, she wondered how she could have been so blind. So *naïve*. How she could have let them tie her to Adam without even seeking her permission.

It had been barely any time at all, and yet she had changed: like someone had reached into her chest and pulled her inside out.

She was being too cruel to herself. She hadn't been naïve: just trapped. She had never even imagined there could be another future for her. And now she had seen what her future *could* be, away from marriage and expectation.

She was desperate for it.

One thing she was thankful for: they had not barred Lily from the keep. Still calling her *William*, they had forced her into chambers on the other side of the castle but had allowed her the freedom to go where she pleased, presumably to ensure both of their compliance. She reappeared outside Jo's chambers just after dawn, looking exhausted. The bags under her eyes and her messy hair made it clear that she had not slept.

Jo was on her in an instant, grabbing her and pulling her into the room. She was the only thing in the castle that felt real.

'Are you all right?' she checked, running her hands up and down Lily's arms. 'I was afraid Lanval might have made some excuse to harm you . . .'

'I am fine,' Lily said, although her expression was closed-off. 'Just . . . tired. I did not sleep.'

Jo sighed. 'Nor did I,' she admitted. 'The bed is comfortable enough, but without—' She hesitated, feeling as if she were about to confess something she shouldn't, before remembering who she was talking to. 'It was odd sleeping alone.'

'Indeed.' Lily did not seem cheered by Jo's words.

Lily moved further into the room. Guided by Jo, she sat herself on the very edge of the bed, fiddling with her hands.

'Lily?'

Lily looked *broken*. More broken than she had appeared after the tournament, with her cracked ribs and bleeding head.

'Are you *sure* you are all right?' Jo pressed. 'Lanval did not harm you?'

'He did not,' she said. 'But he spoke to me. He is . . . concerned, about the match between you and Adam.'

'No doubt he is,' Jo snorted. 'I cannot imagine having to watch the person you love marry someone else.'

Lily kept her eyes low, saying nothing. Jo sat beside her on the bed.

'I should tell him he has very little to worry about,' she spat. 'I have no desire at all to marry Adam. I *refuse*.'

Lily stilled beside her. 'What?'

'I refuse,' Jo repeated, louder.

Lily looked aghast, like she couldn't understand what Jo was saying.

'But . . . his offer, Jo. It is reasonable. You *said* – you said you had to marry, and this will keep you – *us* – safe . . .'

'I know. I know!' Jo threw her hands in the air. 'I know that it is the right thing to do. That it is what I am *expected* to do, but—'

'But you don't want it? You *still* don't want it?'

Jo stared up at her. 'I do not,' she said.

'But you did not refuse him! You just – you just *stood there!*'

Finally, Jo saw why she was so broken.

'Lily—' Her lungs constricted, choking her. All she could do was pull Lily into a hug, trying to pour herself into her. 'Lily, *no*. I wish I could have said something. I know I should have. I should have told him to go, or told him I would rather die than marry him. But he just *looked* at me, and I—' She took a breath, knowing it was a poor excuse. 'He looked just like Father.'

Lily slowly wrapped her arms around her, the movement tentative.

'I am so sorry, Lily,' Jo muttered against her shoulder. 'Please believe me. I do not want him. I do not want this match, but I was so *scared*. I am sorry.'

Lily breathed against her. For a moment, she said nothing. Jo did not speak, terrified that to do so would only make it worse. When Lily finally pulled back, her eyes were red.

'I thought you chose him,' she said.

'Never, Lily. Never. I do not care what he offers me. I do not want to marry him.'

'You want your freedom,' Lily said, carefully. 'Away from . . . from all this. From keeps and cruelty and memories.'

She was right, of course. Jo *did* want to finally untie herself from her past. But that wasn't all she wanted, not anymore. Freedom would not be the same if she were alone.

'I want more than that.'

She said it so quietly, like a confession. She could sense Lily staring at her.

'What *do* you want, Jo?' she said at last.

'I want *you*.'

Lily's lips parted. She looked winded.

'Lily, I – I am sorry, if you don't—'

Lily silenced her beneath a kiss. It was heavy and awkward and desperate, and when she released her, Jo's skin was flushed, darkening her freckles.

'Do you mean that?' Lily asked, breathlessly.

'I do. And if you asked me to agree to Adam's demands, I *would*, but these past few weeks . . .' Jo reached out, taking Lily's hand and clasping it to her chest. 'I have never felt like this. I've never felt *free*, before. I hadn't known that I could want anything else. And now I *do* know, and I—' She shuddered, talking around a sob. 'I do not want to give that up. We *had* safety with Mabel. There are other ways of ensuring we will be well.'

Lily just stared at her. 'But you have already agreed to the match . . .'

'*Do* you think I should marry him, Lily? Do you think I ought to? As I said, if you wished it, I *would*. I would do that for you.'

'Of course I do not think you should marry him,' Lily said. 'But, Lanval—'

Jo sat up. 'What is it? What did he say?'

Lily hesitated before speaking. 'He was desperate. He begged me to convince you to go through with the match. In honesty, I dismissed him, I thought . . .'

'You thought I had already agreed.'

'I did,' Lily admitted, guiltily. 'It is the *sensible* choice, and you have always been dedicated to your duty. You could do your duty *and* have me, if that was what you wanted.'

'I don't,' Jo said, quickly. 'God help me, Lily, it has taken me far too long to realise. I don't. I only want you.'

A wobbly smile spread across Lily's face. She looked so relieved that Jo could not resist reaching out and pulling her into another kiss, holding her against her chest.

'I do not wish to marry him,' she mumbled into the crown of Lily's head, breathing in her smell, feeling her weight in her arms. 'I will *not* marry him. I need to remove myself from this arrangement. I just— I do not know how.'

Saying it aloud lifted something from her shoulders. She was lucky that it was Lily beside her; Lily who understood exactly how she felt, teetering on the brink of a marriage she did not want.

'I know you are sensible,' Lily said, extracting herself from Jo's grip, 'and I know you wish there was a diplomatic way to do this, but I don't—'

'No.'

'No?'

Jo gripped the coverlet.

'I do not wish I could rely on diplomacy for this. I do not wish to play the *noble lady* at him. The terms under which I agreed to marry him have changed. *I* have changed. I do not want to simply sit here and *simper* at him and let him decide what *my* future looks like!'

Jo abruptly realised that she was shouting. Lily was staring at her. She looked impressed.

'I *tire* of being an earl's daughter,' Jo said, schooling her voice. 'Of an earl's sister. Of a kind and courtly noble lady with no will of my own. I tire of being *nice*. I spent my life bending to my father's will so he would not punish me. I will not bend anymore.'

Lily sat up properly. 'Then what do you propose we do?'

'"We"?'

'Of *course*, "we". I am not going to sit here and let *you* have all the fun when *I* am the one who risked my life to prevent you marrying in the first place.'

Jo stood and began to pace the room.

'I cannot leave,' she said. 'I could refuse him, but he won't listen to me.'

Lily seemed to be thinking. She slumped onto her back, bouncing her foot where her legs were crossed over one another.

'You need a viable way to be out of the match,' she said.

'I do. And simply telling him no is not enough.'

'The only thing that would prevent this is if you were already married,' Lily mused.

'Oh, wonderful.' Jo rolled her eyes. 'I shall just go into the basements and find a willing serving boy, shall I?'

Lily sat up. Her eyes glinted.

'Lily, *no*, it was a jest—'

'No, but . . . what if you *were* already married?'

Jo stared at her. 'But I am not.'

'Adam does not know that. His *people* do not know that. Anyone can marry, Jo. Only nobility care about banns and papers and such things. Do you think Mabel and Leo married before a grand audience, or do you think they met in the church doorway and celebrated in the inn afterwards?'

Jo stared at her. 'What are you proposing?'

Lily slipped from the bed. She wrapped her hand around Jo's wrist, stopping her relentless pacing. She laced their hands together.

'That is what I am saying.' She gripped Jo's hands. 'I *propose*.'

Jo burst into startled laughter. 'Do not be absurd.'

'I am not!' Lily protested. 'Obviously Cecily Barden cannot be your husband. But William Dale?' She raised her eyebrows. Her lips took on that crooked smirk that Jo loved so much. 'He is not a good match for an earl's sister, I know,' she said. 'But he *is* a match.'

Jo finally realised what Lily was saying. It was a wild, impulsive idea. But it could work.

'So we claim that we – that William and I – wed in secret? A love match?'

'Exactly. Bring forth a witness if we must. Have them find Mabel and ask her.'

Jo nodded. Lily's hands were warm, her grip sure. It pained her to let her go.

'It could work,' Jo mused, resuming her pacing. 'I cannot marry Adam if I am *already* married to William. But how would I broach it? If I sought him out before the wedding and told him, I fear what he may do to you. As William, you have some use to him, but *only* if we can marry. And besides, if I speak to him alone, he will simply ignore me. We are breaking so many laws, what would one more be to him if it ensured his safety?'

'Then we need to ensure that *this* is a law he cannot ignore.'

They lapsed into silence. Jo peered out the window.

'I do not want to have to barter my future, Lily.' Lily approached from behind, placing her hand to her back. 'I want to *take it*.'

When she turned, Lily was staring at her. Slowly, without breaking her gaze, Lily went to one knee. She took Jo's hands.

'When we spoke at the tournament, I told you I would fight for you. That I would fight *beside* you. I stand by that.'

'Lily—' Jo breathed it out, no louder than a sigh.

'I *will* be your champion. Your Knight of Stars. I am not valorous or virtuous, and I am not a . . . a lord, or a nobleman. I am not even a knight. But I will be your champion, Johanna. *My Lady*. If you will have me. If you will keep me.'

Tension built behind Jo's eyes as Lily lowered her lips to the back of Jo's hands in a slow, deliberate kiss. It overwhelmed her, filling her, like her chest would cave in on itself with the pressure of it and something bigger and brighter than herself would come streaming out of the hole.

'Of course—' Her words shuddered as her voice broke. 'Lily, *of course*. You *are* my champion. You have been since that day at the tournament, since I—'

Oh. Of course.

She released Lily's hands and scrambled for the pocket beneath her overskirt as Lily watched on, looking faintly bemused. Then her fingers brushed something soft and silky.

She pulled out the handkerchief. Lily's eyes went wide.

'I had intended to give it back to you,' she said, 'but we were so *busy*, and then – I admit, I was waiting.'

'Waiting?'

'For the best moment.' Jo flushed. Lily bit her lip – stopping herself from laughing.

'And – is this it?' Lily asked, still on her knees, gazing up at her. 'The best moment?'

The silk crumpled between Jo's fingers. 'Yes,' she said, not breaking Lily's eye. 'It is.'

Lily rose to her feet. Her eyes – huge and startling and sparkling like stars – shimmered with tears. Jo handed the kerchief to her, letting their fingers linger over each other.

'Lily—'

Lily surged forwards and kissed her. Her lips were so soft, her touch so sure, and Jo melted beneath it. Lily wrapped her arms around Jo's waist, tugging her closer, and Jo reached out, too, moving her hands up Lily's chest, coming to rest at her shoulders.

Lily pulled away, resting their foreheads together. Her breath was hot against Jo's lips.

'My Lady,' she whispered.

Jo looked at her through her lashes. 'My champion.'

Lily smiled. She licked her lips. Jo was about to kiss her again when Lily spoke.

'Do you remember what I said to Ellis?' she said. 'Beside the ring?'

'You said a great many things.'

'Hah,' Lily chortled. 'I did. I told him that I should swear myself to you so you could guide me. So you teach me how to be less foolish.'

Now it was Jo's turn to laugh. 'I failed you, I fear. You have made *me* foolish. Love has made me foolish.'

It was only half a confession, but still the words tingled on Jo's tongue. Lily froze in her grip. She looked as if she was holding herself back: eager, but terrified.

'Jo—' she started, lips trembling.

'I love you.' Saying it aloud made the tingling grow, made it overwhelm her. 'Of course I do, Lily. Of *course* I love you.'

Lily's expression cracked into a dazzling smile. The tears flowed freely, now, shining down her face. She kissed Jo again, apparently too overwhelmed to do much else.

'Jo—' Another kiss. 'My Lady—' Another. 'I think I have loved you since the day we met.'

'But I was so *stern* . . .'

'Only when you had to be. And I know, now . . . you were scared. But beneath that . . .' Lily sighed. 'There is a reason I left you that letter.'

That *letter*. It had been so unexpected. Jo cherished it.

'I love you.' She said it again, just to feel the shape of the words.

'And I love *you*, Jo.' Lily hesitated. 'But that alone will not be enough to stop this marriage.'

Jo huffed. She did not appreciate the sudden slap of reality. She edged back, still not quite letting go of Lily's hands.

She thought of Lily's vow. She thought of the tournament, and Lily's absurd determination to prevent Jo from marrying. Even *then*, Lily had never had a plan, only an impulse and the madness to see it through. She had been a disruption, not a threat.

The idea struck her. Adam would need to be publicly refused: there was no other way to ensure he would be forced to call off the match.

'William,' she said, one eyebrow raised. 'I have a command for you. I need you to embarrass one more man in my name.'

Lily's grin was *devilish*.

'My Lady Johanna,' she said. 'I will.'

Chapter 26

The sky above was a dazzling, daydreamy blue. Tiny birds which Lily did not know the name of darted above her, twittering and singing. She felt as if she were flying up there with them, dashing above the treetops.

Jo loved her. Nothing else mattered.

They had discussed the best way to cause a disruption, and despite her assertions that she wanted Adam to feel her anger, Jo had seemed keen not to go too far. Lily suspected this was an attempt at self-preservation: she did not want to be the centre of attention.

Lily grinned. Jo would not be the centre of attention, of course. William Dale would be.

She rolled up the sleeves of her tunic as she walked down the hill towards the main road. When she had returned to her chamber after speaking to Jo, she realised that a chest of men's clothing had been delivered in her absence. Having lived with two boisterous brothers, she recognised that all the clothes within it were cast-offs, but at least they were clean. They were still not *quite* enough for her needs, and so she had snuck from the keep and set out towards Glendale.

She had shield, sword, and armour — even if it was old and

dented – but she could do *more*. In town, she purchased a needle and a thick spool of off-white thread from a spinster in the marketplace, along with oil and cloth with which she hoped she could at least remove some of the rust from her kit.

She returned by way of the blacksmith's home, where she had left her armour and sword. After pressing the last of her coin into his palm, he took her old, misshapen armour to hammer and bend back into shape. He even polished it for her and re-set the straps as Lily used his whetstone and the oil she had purchased to hone her sword; the one that Jo had gifted her.

Despite her desperation to stay by Jo's side, Lily was keenly aware that she ought to avoid Lanval and Adam, so it was late afternoon by the time she returned to the keep. She headed back through the door in the outer wall, her armour bundled in a sack, and hurried inside without anyone giving her a second glance.

She checked on Broga again, who appeared to be well looked after. That was ideal; the horse would be crucial for her plans the next day. Mabel's cart was nowhere to be seen, and with them both keen not to arouse too much suspicion, they had not been able to hunt for it either. That – along with Mabel's payment, which had never actually made it into Jo's possession – would be keen losses, but ones that could not be helped.

After giving Broga another pat, Lily made her way directly to Jo's chambers. They were empty. For a moment, she panicked. But her eyes fell on a small square of parchment on the table on the opposite side of the room.

My Dear William,

I have been called away in order to prepare for the wedding. It has become clear that one cannot size a gown without the person who is to be wearing it present. This is, apparently, a surprise. I look forward to seeing you later.

Yours, Johanna.

She was fine. She was still here. And likely having a terrible time – Lily could not imagine Jo would be keen to be under the scrutiny of a seamstress determined to make her into a bride. She shuffled back into the chamber they had prepared for her and threw her things onto the bed. At least she could use this time to better prepare. She heaved open the lid of the chest and quickly began to dig through the garments inside, looking for the dark blue gambeson she was sure she had seen in there.

It was late in the evening by the time she was summoned to Jo's chambers. Lanval appeared at her door – it seemed they had no desire to involve any more people in the farce than they needed to – and chaperoned her in complete silence.

Jo, at least, was pleased to see her, and shut the door on Lanval before he'd even had a chance to greet her. She apologised for having sent for her, clearly feeling awkward in the position of power she'd been thrust back into.

'You may summon me whenever you wish,' Lily said, cheekily. 'I am always at your disposal.'

Jo rolled her eyes at her, thrust a bowl of steaming stew into her hands, and began to complain at length about her day. She'd spent the morning with Adam's mother Lady Anne, being taken on a pointless tour of the castle and grounds. She had been introduced to Adam's many siblings, and Lily had been amused when Jo shrugged when asked to recall their names. Jo was *good* with names: she had memorised the names of even the most infrequent visitors to the brewery. To be so dismissive meant she really was intending to never see Adam again.

'Has he been kind to you, at least?' Lily asked, concerned.

Jo shrugged. 'It is hard to say, when he has removed himself so thoroughly from the arrangements. I have seen him, but I suspect he is deliberately avoiding me, lest I outright refuse him. Which I *would*, were I granted a moment alone with him.'

Lily held back a laugh as Jo continued to recount her day, her complaints growing more virulent. She told Lily how Lady Anne had insisted – 'Insisted!' Jo hissed, not concealing her annoyance – on Jo's assistance in arranging the wedding.

'Is it not traditional that a bride assists in arranging her wedding?' Lily asked, biting back a laugh.

Jo glowered at her, her bottom lip sticking out. Lily really *did* laugh at that, despite Jo's expression.

'It is my deep regret that it *is*,' she spat. 'I managed to pass on most of the decisions, thank God. But I demanded a few things.'

'Oh?'

'Flowers,' Jo said, giving her a soft, conspiratorial smile. 'If I am to be ornamented, I wish it to be with flowers. And in blue. That was my . . . that was Mother's colour. I know that this is not a *true* wedding, but . . . I do wish she was here, regardless.'

Jo very rarely spoke of her mother – almost never, in fact. Lily had come to know the late countess through Penn's stories of her, and she wished that she could have met her.

She took Jo's hand.

'God,' Jo said, tossing her spoon to the table. 'I cannot wait to be free of this place.'

'You will be,' Lily said. 'I swear it, Jo. With all I have.'

Jo stared at her. Despite her anger, there was a soft tilt to her brows.

The evening melted quickly into night, and they moved from the stiff, high-backed chairs onto the bed. The canopy above was stitched in intricate, swirling patterns which Lily traced with her eyes as Jo ran her fingers slowly through her hair.

'Has Adam seen to fit you with maids?' Lily asked.

'He *has*.' Jo sighed.

'Does that mean I will not be able to stay?'

Jo peered down at her. 'I am afraid it does,' she said. 'With so much to do, they will be here early, ready to dress me for the day. I expect Adam's mother to be with them, too. She is so excited.'

Lily watched her frown. There was still a sting of guilt there. It was no wonder: Lily wasn't sure if Jo had *ever* gone against someone else's wishes. If she had ever been anything other than the perfect, dutiful daughter.

Her temptation to tell Jo more of her plan fell away. She did not want to burden her with any more guilt, even if it was unwarranted.

'It seems we have no time at all, then,' she said instead.

'No time for what?' There was a neat, notched line between Jo's brows.

'For *this*—'

Lily reached up, tangled her hand in the hair at Jo's nape, and pulled her down into a slow, lingering kiss.

'Oh,' Jo said, when Lily finally let her go. 'Then we must make what we can of the time we have.'

*

The day had been long, and tiring. Exhaustion had settled into Jo's bones like an ache, mingling with an uneasy mix of boredom and guilt.

But with Lily's lips on hers, it all melted away.

Wordlessly, they sank back onto the bed. They shouldn't — it was far too risky — yet she didn't care, either. Part of her wanted them to be caught, just for the chaos of it.

More, she wanted Lily. *Just* Lily. She was a lighthouse in a storm, a rock in a vast ocean. Jo *needed* her. Lily seemed to sense that need, holding Jo close.

They began to undress each other with slow reverence, steps of a dance they had shared countless times. Illuminated by the torches on the high stone walls, Lily's skin glowed. The red hair furring her legs and arms and curling between her thighs made her look as if she were aflame. Jo pressed closer, laying a trail of kisses along her collarbone, across her broad, freckled shoulders, down her toned stomach. She nipped the peaks of Lily's breasts between her teeth, enjoying the way she gasped beneath her, the way Lily's hands trembled in Jo's hair.

Lily was *hers*, her champion, her knight. In the shadows beneath the rich canopy, she could forget Adam and his keep, his intentions to use her as a shield. Here, there was only Lily. Lily manoeuvred them around, pressing Jo onto the coverlet, leaning above her. She stared down at her, her eyes wide, her messy hair in disarray. She was *wonderful*, and handsome, and had guaranteed Jo her freedom.

Lily kissed her one last time before moving down her body, ghosting her lips over Jo's skin. She pressed her tongue into the dips of her hipbones, making Jo writhe. Jo *simmered*, that pressure which she was becoming familiar with growing like a great wave building.

Lily moved lower, trailing her lips. She smoothed her hands up Jo's thighs, easing them apart. Jo released a breath, letting her eyes slide shut, hands playing in Lily's hair.

When Lily kissed her, her tongue pressing hot and wet against her, Jo lost herself to it, tugging Lily's hair, breathing out a sigh. Lily moved so surely, so *expertly*, flicking the tip of her tongue over the most sensitive spot, closing her lips around it.

Jo cursed and muttered Lily's name. Lily *smiled* against her, quickening her movements. She smoothed one strong hand up Jo's thigh, then shifted up. Lily's fingers teased at Jo's entrance, and Jo made another low, needy noise, urging her on.

Lily's lips pursed around her, *sucking* her, and then at last she slid her fingers inside her. Jo arched back, eliciting a soft noise of amused surprise from Lily, who pushed a little harder on her thigh, keeping her still. Jo *couldn't* keep still, her legs twitching, hands grabbing at nothing. Lily intensified her movements, fingers and tongue and lips all working in tandem. A great, slick pressure built as Jo pushed back against Lily's digits, keening breathlessly.

The pressure became too much. It broke, washing over her in trembling currents like waves lapping on the lakeside shore one after another.

Lily licked at her again – the light touch making Jo shudder – before making her way back up her body. When they were face to face, Jo pulled her into a rough kiss until she was breathless. Jo's body was alight, her skin sparkling wherever they touched. Lily grinned at her, looking flushed and so *unbearably* smug that Jo could only laugh.

She trailed her hand over Lily's body. Her nipples were hard beneath her palms, and as she reached the place between her thighs Jo realised that she was eagerly wet and ready. She brushed her fingers over the shock of curls, enjoying the way Lily stuttered and jerked beneath her touch. Lily twined their legs together, and Jo urged her down onto her thigh, feeling the heat of her pressed against her skin.

Lily gave an unbidden, desperate thrust forward, her hips grinding heavily against Jo's leg. She made a low moaning sound as Jo moved with her, trying to match Lily's pace and movement as she ground down on her thigh. She was desperate to use her fingers on her, but there was no room between their bodies, so instead she placed one hand to her hip and the other to the small of her back, keeping her steady. Her fingertips pressed into the dimples above Lily's backside as if they'd been made for her touch. Lily keened in her grasp, and Jo nudged forwards, her teeth scraping against Lily's neck, her wonderfully carved collarbones.

She kissed every place she could reach as Lily quickened her speed, her breath catching in the air, until, at last, she shuddered as she reached her own peak, clinging desperately to Jo, breathing slowly and raggedly.

They lay together, their breaths mingling. Jo peered at Lily, taking her in, wondering at her. Her messy hair, her freckled skin, her sparkling, laughing, joyous eyes. She'd shared that joy with Jo, too, and Jo had become intoxicated by it. She had never known what this feeling could be like, and now she'd been brave enough to name it, it was all she could think of.

She nuzzled their faces together, noses brushing.

'I love you.'

Lily's response was little more than a whisper against her lips.

Chapter 27

A sky of endless stars. A clear, crystalline lake that reflected them back at themselves, creating an infinite, sparkling void. Jo floated within it, utterly content, Lily at her side.

She opened her eyes reluctantly. For a moment, Jo thought she was back in the loft, safe above the brewery. Then she remembered.

She sat up properly, looking around the bridal chamber. Lily was fast asleep on the bed beside her. The sky outside the window was beginning to bloom into dawn. It was lucky that she had woken when she did: there would be maids at her door soon enough.

She gently shook Lily awake.

'Jo . . .?' She yawned, eyes widening. 'Damn. I must go before anyone arrives . . .'

Jo wished she wouldn't, but she knew she must. 'Of course . . .'

She watched as Lily rose, hastily dressing in her discarded clothes. As she reached the door, Jo sat up.

'Wait—'

Jo slid from the bed towards the table, grabbing the wax-sealed letter she had left there the previous day. She thrust it into Lily's hands and pressed another quick kiss to her lips.

'I will see you soon?'

Lily kissed her back. Her breath was musty, her skin sleep-warmed. 'You will.'

It did not take long after Lily had snuck out for there to be a loud rap at the door. Despite the sudden panic gripping her, Jo rose, smoothed out her shift and then opened the door to see what felt like an army of maids, led by Lady Anne.

Jo set her shoulders and prepared herself for what was to come.

First was the bath, carried by four lads from the kitchen and deposited next to the fire. The water was only lukewarm, and the maids scrubbed at her skin until it was red. They coated her hair in sweet-smelling oil before twisting it into plaits.

When she was clean and dry, she pulled on a new shift. Before she could begin to dress, a lady's maid approached with a tiny, stoppered bottle of perfume in her hand. She dabbed it behind Jo's ears, at her neck, in the valley of her breasts.

Next they pulled on her underdress, dyed in a deep yellow. After that came the gown itself: a rich, silk dress in berry-red with voluminous sleeves that swept the ground at Jo's feet and a low, scooping neck. It had been embroidered with thick golden braids, and as Jo traced her finger across them she yearned for Lily's flowers.

Finally came her head covering. Lady Anne reverently draped a creamy silk scarf over her head, which cascaded past her face in rippling waves. She reached for a little box, and Jo knew at once that it must have contained the diadem she would wear atop it.

Jo held back a gasp as she lifted the lid. Dozens of gems inlaid into a narrow golden band sparkled up at her from the velvet cushion inside. It was a striking piece, the dazzling red stones flashing in the light. Within the narrow crown lay a brooch, that too ornamented with garnets and intricately carved with miniature flaming hearts. Their combined worth would have been enough to buy Mabel's brewery a hundred times over.

She reached for the brooch first, fastening it to her bodice, then lifted the diadem from the box. She turned it, watching it glint in the morning light.

It felt heavy in her hands.

Turning to the huge metal mirror in the corner of the room, she stared at herself. The women moving behind her no clearer than if they were shadows. Jo's requests – flowers, and her mother's colour – had been ignored.

For so long, she had buried her feelings. She had faced her father with acceptance. She'd bent to him so much she had snapped. She reached into herself, feeling for the hot well of anger that she'd smothered for so long. But no longer.

She took a breath, stared into her own eyes, and settled the diadem on her head.

Jo walked towards the great hall like an encroaching storm, head high. Adam extracted himself from the crowd, Lanval close behind him. He looked pale, but relieved.

'My Lady,' he said. 'You look beautiful.'

Jo smiled at him. 'Thank you, my Lord.'

The procession to the church began immediately. The gathered crowd – Adam's family and his court – went first, followed by the band of minstrels that Adam had somehow managed to corral at such short notice. Jo allowed Adam to lead her from the keep and out onto the road next, their hands linked.

Behind them came Lanval on his horse, dressed in sparkling, newly polished armour. He looked like a knight from a Romance, his chest plate blinding, an excessive plume blooming from his helm. He sat stiff and straight-backed, their single guard.

The church came into view, appearing from behind a row of trees. Beyond it, half a hundred people had gathered: peasants, servants, townspeople. Jo felt a stone in her stomach at how big of a scene they would create.

She wondered where Lily had sequestered herself. She may even be in the crowd itself, waiting, and for the first time Jo regretted not demanding the specifics of her plan.

They made their way in silence to the doors, where the priest — the oldest man Jo had ever seen — was waiting for them. Adam let go of her hand and gave her a last, desperate smile as the priest began to recite his words in a voice much louder than Jo had anticipated from such a tiny figure.

'Lord Adam,' he said at last. 'Do you freely consent to this match?'

Adam straightened. Lanval stared at him, eyes shimmering.

'Yes,' Adam called. 'I do.'

'And Lady Johanna,' the priest said, turning to her, 'do you consent to this match?'

Before Jo could even open her mouth, Adam spoke over her.

'She does,' he said. 'Freely and happily.'

Jo's stomach lurched. He had taken even that from her. Any remaining guilt she felt shattered in her chest as the priest — ignoring that she hadn't even spoken — launched into the vows.

Anger swirled in her gut, hot and tight, finally released. She barely heard the priest's words or her own muffled replies over the ringing in her ears.

She would *never* let Adam forget this.

'Stop this!'

The voice was loud and clear and familiar. Jo span as the crowd parted around a figure seated high on a snorting dun palfrey, looking down not at them, but at Jo.

Jo's heart stuttered in her chest. She forced herself not to laugh. *Oh, Lily.*

The Knight of Stars sat straight-backed and resplendent, his armour shining, his painted shield clasped in front of him in a steady hand. Beneath the armour he wore a startlingly blue gambeson stitched all over in a whorl of intricate stars. His sword swung from his belt in a buffed leather sheath, the hilt and pommel polished and glimmering in the sunlight. There was a scrap of silk tucked beneath his chest plate, fluttering in the breeze. Jo knew at once what it was.

Through the visor of his dazzling helmet was a pair of sparkling blue-grey eyes. Jo's heart soared, rushing upwards into her throat.

'This match *cannot* go ahead,' Lily called across the crowd. 'Lady Johanna cannot wed this man.'

Adam was frozen in shock. Lanval pushed past him, his sword already in his hand.

'What is this?' he spat. 'What are you *doing?*'

'Upholding the law,' Lily replied. 'Lord Adam cannot marry Lady Johanna, as she is already wed. To me.'

'*What?*'

The crowd broke into angry shouts. Lady Anne, who had been watching, gave a startled shout before fainting directly into the arms of one of the Wyck guards.

'Johannah—' Adam gasped. 'What is this? Is this true?'

She stuck her chin in the air. 'It is,' she replied, venomously.

His face crumpled. But the shock only lasted a second before it was replaced with betrayed rage.

'You— *No*, Johanna—'

'Yes, Adam.' She stepped away from him towards Lily.

'This will *not stand*,' Adam spat. 'I will not allow it.'

'You won't?' Jo said, archly.

From the horse, Lily stared down at him pitifully.

'You can challenge me if you wish, my Lord,' she said, coolly, 'but the law is immutable. Johanna cannot marry again. She may *re*marry, if her husband is dead. Or do you intend to kill me in front of all of these people? The decision is yours, Alfred.'

There was a ringing silence. Lanval was gripping his sword with a shaking hand. Adam looked between them – from Lanval, to Jo, to Lily.

And then the silence was split by the sound of Adam drawing his blade.

Lily leapt from Broga's back, her own weapon already in her hand. Adam advanced, fingers flexing around the hilt.

Jo cried out. 'Adam, *no*—'

He paid her no heed. He strode forwards, gaze fixed on Lily. Lily shoved Jo out of the way, pushing her aside as Adam swung. Jo's scream cut in her throat as Lily threw her sword up just in time to meet Adam's in a deafening *clang*.

There was only the briefest pause before Adam lunged again. Lily was quicker, spinning out of the way, and suddenly Jo was transported. She was back in the tournament at her laughing brother's side, watching the Knight of Stars fight in the ring.

But that had been little more than a show. Lily had been in danger, but never *true* danger. She'd watched with awe and excitement as William Dale had performed; now all she felt was fear.

This was not the ring. There were no rules, no marshal, no announcer to rip combatants away from each other. This was a man desperate to take what was his; by force, if necessary.

As Lily bound forwards, sword up, Jo realised there was no way she could win. Not against such a seasoned man. Jo looked around desperately, in search of a solution. She could not let Lily lose. She didn't care about her future, or about the trap she was desperate to escape. She only cared that Lily was all right. She could not let Adam hurt her.

Beside her, Lanval had also frozen. He should have been helping his master and lover, yet he'd become rooted to the spot, his face pale and his sword held limply in his hand.

Taking her chance, Jo leapt forwards and wrest the sword from his grip. He only had a moment to realise what was happening before she'd thrown herself between Lily and Adam, the stolen sword raised above her head.

Adam attempted to skid to a halt, but was too slow. His blade met Jo's in a horrible scraping screech, the steel sparking as he attempted to right his path. Jo's arms shuddered, the force sending waves of pain through to her shoulders.

Adam immediately dropped his blade. Jo gripped her own harder, refusing to let go.

'My Lady—'

'I cannot marry you, Adam.'

'You did not—'

'*You never asked!*' Her voice rang out across the churchyard. 'You never asked,' she repeated, breathlessly. 'I will not have my future given to me.'

'Johanna, *please*—'

'*No.*'

She dropped the sword. As if coming back into himself, Lanval scurried to grab it. When he righted himself, his face was red, eyes shining. Adam glanced at him as he moved out of the way, but the warmth that Jo had seen in Adam's expression before was gone.

'You cannot do this,' he said.

Jo tilted her chin. 'I can.'

She took a step back. For a second, Adam seemed to consider following. Then he stilled.

'*Please.*'

She ignored him. She ignored him just as he and everyone else had ignored her for so long. She pulled the diadem from her head, sending the white headscarf dashing away across the churchyard. For a moment, she paused, before handing it to Lanval, catching his eye as she did.

Behind her, Lily was heaving herself back onto Broga's back. She extended a hand to Jo.

'My Lady?'

Jo allowed her to pull her up onto the horse.

'Are you ready?' Lily murmured, quiet enough that only Jo could hear.

Jo wrapped her arms around Lily's waist, feeling the sun-warmed metal beneath her hands. 'I am ready.'

Lily spurred Broga with her heels, and they were off, laughing down the road.

Chapter 28

They rode for as long as they could, the blue sky above them flushing into pinks and yellows. They had decided to return to Mabel's brewery: it was the only place either of them *wanted* to go, the best place to gather their thoughts before moving on.

The journey which had taken two days with a heavy, awkward cart would take half of that by horse, but with two riders Broga tired more quickly and they were forced to call in early at a roadside rest stop. This was no inn – just the family home of an alderman with room to spare and a reputation for being welcoming.

He greeted them warmly after Jo slid from Broga's back, curtseyed, and by way of introducing them, said breathlessly:

'My name is Johanna, and this is William. We are recently married, and need somewhere to rest for the night.'

The alderman didn't ask about their state of dishevelment or their flushed faces – nor did he point out that Jo's dress was far finer than the ancient armour her apparent husband wore. Instead, he congratulated them, took them in, and fed them a hearty meal that they both sorely needed.

He allowed them to sleep in his spare room, chuckling over how popular his home had become after hosting a trio of northern travellers the previous night. Jo and Lily laughed along as he mused about changing professions to innkeeper, until finally they were alone again.

Dusk light poured in through the tiny window. Now coated in dust from the long ride, Lily's armour seemed to glow, as if the sunlight was trapped within the metal itself. She'd kept it on throughout the meal — Jo was unsure if it had been a deliberate choice or if she had simply forgotten that she still wore it — and now Jo stepped forwards, brushing her fingertips over the smooth surface, leaving clean streaks of steel in their wake. She pulled away the handkerchief, still tucked beneath the breastplate, before placing it carefully upon the bedcovers.

'May I . . . ?'

She trailed off, watching Lily carefully from beneath her lashes. Lily said nothing, trapping her bottom lip beneath her teeth with a nod.

Jo started with the vambraces, unbuckling the straps with care then sliding them from Lily's arms. Next came the buckles that hooked over Lily's shoulders and nestled in her sides, connecting breast and back plate. Those took a little more work, and when Jo undid the last buckle and removed the pieces Lily let out a satisfied sigh that warmed Jo to her core.

With the plates removed, Jo now had access to Lily's pauldrons, the leather straps tight against the star-sewn gambeson beneath. Jo brushed her fingers over the stitches as she removed the armour. The embroidery must have been done in haste, yet still the stitches were surer and more skilful than any Jo could have made. The low light illuminated them in bright, dazzling white.

When Jo went to her knees in front of her, Lily made a soft, startled noise. Jo looked up to see Lily peering down at her, face flushed, hair in disarray. Her hands were hanging loosely by her sides, so Jo took them, pressing reverential kisses to the lines etched into her skin by her armour.

She slid her hands around Lily's legs to release the straps of her greaves. They too were carefully placed aside with the rest of her armour, and now Lily stood beside the bed wearing only her gambeson, breeches, and boots. She heaved Jo back to her feet, tugging her closer, brushing their lips together.

'Thank you, my Lady.'

Jo kissed her – not enough for Lily's liking, who made an offended hum of complaint when she moved back – then stroked her palms down Lily's shoulders. She tugged at the ties of the gambeson, then that, too, joined the rest of the knight's garb beside the bed. Lily's nipples were hardening beneath the linen tunic, and Jo's body responded in kind, her thighs clenching, her heart racing beneath the detested wedding gown. Boldly, she slid her hand beneath Lily's tunic, cupping one of her breasts.

That was all Lily needed. With a noise somewhere between a purr and a growl, she shucked off her tunic and grabbed at Jo's dress. Then paused, her hand hovering above Jo's breast.

'Lily?'

'You forgot—'

Lily's fingers brushed against the golden brooch. Jo's insides turned icy.

'He'll come after me,' she muttered, 'I'm a *thief*. . .'

Lily ignored her, gently unpinning the brooch and examining it.

'*He* is the thief,' she said, placing it aside. 'He did not pay Mabel for her services, and her cart remains in his possession. Besides,' she added, 'this is a small price indeed for our silence on the nature of his and Lanval's relationship.'

'But. . .'

Jo's words were smothered beneath a kiss. 'Now,' Lily muttered. 'Where were we?'

The gown, however expensive it had been, proved to be little match for Lily's desperate enthusiasm to have Jo bare. In her haste to disrobe her, there was an almighty *ripping* sound, and the bodice tore in two.

Lily regarded the ruined garment with wide eyes. Jo, unable to help herself, burst into unconstrained laughter. Lily nestled her face into Jo's neck, shoulders shaking as she, too, giggled.

'I don't suppose you've needle and thread hidden amongst your armour?' Jo murmured into her hair.

'I do not.' Lily's mouth was hot against Jo's skin.

'A shame.'

The yellow underdress, at least, was spared, although tossed aside with such vigour that it caught on the upper canopy of the bed, eliciting another wave of giggling from Lily as they stumbled backwards onto the mattress.

'You were magnificent,' Jo said, pulling her close. 'My champion. You did wonderfully.'

Lily's response was to nip at her collarbone.

'As were you. When you took that sword' – the nip became a lingering, open-mouthed caress, teeth twitching against Jo's pulse – 'you were *glorious*.'

Jo blushed under her attentions. Before she could respond, Lily caught her in an even more desperate kiss, pressing her into the pillows.

The next morning they roused early, impatient to return to the road. The ruined wedding gown proved useful after all, tied to Broga's saddle with Lily's shod armour clanking within.

As they drew closer to the brewery, the familiarity of their surroundings made Jo's chest ache in a warm, pleasant way – especially as they rode past the little lane that led to the lake. Jo sighed in relief as the familiar walls of the brewery came into view, the clucking chickens, even Gilbert draped lazily over the stone wall of the yard.

She slid from Broga's back, marvelling at the steadiness of the ground beneath her feet while Lily pulled the horse around towards the stable. Jo was about to approach the house when she heard a noise.

A laugh. A *familiar* laugh, one she hadn't heard in far too long.

The door opened.

'Penn?'

Penn spotted her, and suddenly they were both running. He caught her in a crushing hug, lifting her fully from the floor, her feet dangling as he twirled her around.

She was *sure* he had never been able to do that before.

When he finally put her down, she couldn't help but stare at him. His face was sun-kissed, jaw stubbled, his curly hair pulled into a messy, tiny tail at the back of his head. His face had rounded out since she had last seen him, his arms broadened. He looked so *alive*, like the shell of himself had sloughed away to reveal something better and brighter beneath.

He gave her another hug, then pulled back, his eyebrow raised.

'I am *so* pleased that I am not the most troublesome child anymore,' he said, grinning at her toothily. 'Running away with a knight? And a *woman*, at that? Very bold, Jo.'

'It . . . is somewhat bolder than that,' Jo admitted, amused at the way Penn's eyebrows crept even higher up his face. 'I will need to explain, and to Mabel, too . . .' She peered around. 'Are the others here?'

'Of course,' Penn said, laughing. 'You have led us on quite a chase.'

Jo set her shoulders. 'Now you know how it feels,' she retorted.

Before he could properly respond, Lily appeared. She was brushing down her hands, lost in thought, when she looked up. She paused. And then she, too, was running.

'Penn!'

Penn grabbed her, pulling *her* into a hug as well, before holding her at arm's length.

'I am very cross with you, Cecily.'

Lily blanched. 'Penn—'

'You *stole my shirt.*'

Lily burst out laughing. The noise apparently alerted the rest of the party, and after a clatter from inside the house, Raff and Ash appeared in the doorway, looking hugely relieved.

'Lily!'

They were on her in an instant, and Jo stepped back automatically as both men grabbed her.

'You stupid creature,' Ash said, an arm wrapped around her shoulders. 'What were you *thinking*?'

'Bold to assume she *was* thinking,' Raff replied over her head. 'Damn you, Lily. We have been *sick* with worry.'

'*You* have been sick with worry,' Ash countered, letting her go. '*I* knew Lily would be well. She learnt from a skilled master, after all.'

Both Raff and Lily snorted at that.

'How did you find me?' Lily said, brow furrowed. 'I told the steward I was visiting the convent . . .'

'You are not quite as clever as you think,' Raff said, shaking his head. 'Come on, sit, eat, and we can talk about this mess.'

After quickly greeting Mabel, Leo and the children, they all sat at the long table. It was the first time Lily had seen every seat full, and it warmed her from her toes up. Being around her brothers again felt like being home, like a piece of her had been returned.

Jo apologised at length to Mabel for the loss of the money and the cart. When she handed Mabel Adam's brooch, Lily could have sworn that Mabel nearly fainted. What followed was a brisk argument which Jo won, insisting Mabel take the brooch as payment for the ale, cart and her kindness during their stay.

Together, their brothers told them the story of how they had found them, talking – and then shouting – over one another. Raff and Penn had returned to Dunlyn sooner than expected thanks to a rockslide on the road in Scotland and had found the keep empty – save for a vague, hastily written letter from the Countess Isabelle de Foucart, asking them to pass on word to Johanna and a man neither of them knew called William Dale.

When Ash had ridden to the convent upon his return, only to find that Lily wasn't there – that she had *never* been there – they realised what must have happened.

'We worked out at once that Lily must have gone to the tournament,' Penn said, sat beside Leo. 'Especially after we searched the armoury. But Jo hadn't returned to Dunlyn as Isabelle assumed, so we headed to the de Foucart keep trying to find you both. When we asked after William Dale, we were told he was a young knight-errant, overly confident, utterly mad and with fiery red hair. It was obvious who he *really* was, confirming our suspicions. But he – *you* – had vanished again, taking Jo with you.'

'We were unsure what to do,' Raff said, 'so we asked around the local towns. Penn complimented the dress of the innkeeper's wife in Astmere, and *she* said that the embroidery had been done by Lily, the new girl working with Mabel.'

'We told her we were looking for a gift for our sister,' Ash laughed, 'and she pointed us towards the brewery.'

It all slotted into place. Lily was silently impressed at her brothers' ability to track her.

'Why did you even enter in the first place?' Ash continued. 'What were you attempting to achieve?'

Lily shot a quick look at Jo. She nodded, just once. Lily took a breath, then told them all, starting with her foolish desire to ensure Jo was not forced to marry and ending with how she had achieved that desire after all.

Everyone stared at them. Even Harry, who didn't care for stories, was enraptured.

It was Penn who broke the silence first.

'I really *am* no longer the most troublesome child,' he said, laughing. 'I am impressed, Jo. Very impressed.'

'What do you intend to do now?' Ash asked, finishing off his ale. 'Will you return to Dunlyn?'

Lily again looked to Jo.

'I . . . am unsure,' she said. 'We have not discussed that far ahead, yet.'

Across the table, she noticed Leo shoot a look at Mabel. Mabel licked her lips before speaking.

'Forgive me if this is out of turn,' she said. 'But if you wanted to stay, you would be more than welcome. In fact, we will soon be in need of the extra help.'

'Why so?' Jo said. 'Are you expecting more orders? I was concerned that after the mess with Adam your business would suffer . . .'

'Oh, not *that*,' Mabel dismissed her. 'Rather . . .' She looked again at Leo. He nudged her with a sly smile. 'Oh, curse it. I am with child. And it plays *havoc* with my senses, and all the ale tastes like *piss*, if you'll excuse me, and we'll need the help sooner rather than later.'

The table exploded with congratulations. Penn – who was still reeling from being unexpectedly reunited with his brother – had tears in his eyes.

'If you do not wish to stay, that is fine,' Mabel quickly added. 'We can find help elsewhere. But as you are both so well-practised, I simply thought that it was *right* to offer it to you first. I'll pay you, of course, and you can stay up in the loft if that is what you desire.'

Lily looked again at Jo. Her eyes were wide and sparkling. She looked as if she were about to throw herself from her seat. Beneath the table, her leg was bouncing.

'I . . . I mean, Jo, it is your choice . . .'

'No, Lily,' Jo retorted, 'this is *our* choice. If you do not wish to stay . . .'

'No, I—'

'Oh for *God's* sake,' Ash snorted. 'Lily. Do you wish to stay here?'

Lily hesitated. She looked between her brothers.

'I . . . I think I do, yes.'

'And Jo? Do you?'

Jo swallowed. She nodded before she spoke. 'Yes.'

'There we have it,' Ash said, throwing his hands in the air. 'Fetch me more ale, we can celebrate your employment.' He paused, grinning. '*And* your marriage.'

Lily's head rang with the sound of laughter. She'd left their brothers in the kitchen, surrounded by empty bottles. She'd slunk from the room on quiet footsteps, only Raff looking up as she left and nodding her away with a soft, knowing smile. She stood at the foot of the ladder to the loft, then pulled Jo's note from her pocket and read it one more time. The parchment was stained red from the wax seal.

My dearest champion. My knight. My stars.
I remember the day we met. I think about it so often, and I still wonder why you chose me, all that time ago.

I love you. I love you. I love you — and I did not know what it was to love, before now.

I have no idea what you plan to do, but I know <u>you.</u> You are wild and free and utterly mad: this is why I love you as I do. Good luck. No doubt you will need it, for whatever you intend.

When you next see me, I will be a bride. And you will be yourself, as you always are, as you were always meant to be.

Stay brave, my champion. Stay strong. And for <u>God's sake</u> stay safe.

Your love, your lady —
Johanna

She folded it carefully before sliding it back into place and ascending into the loft.

'Are our brothers all right?' Jo asked, as she appeared.

'They are *drunk*.' Lily laughed. 'I left them in the kitchen. I hope Mabel has enough ale for them . . .'

She kicked off her boots, tossed off her tunic, then settled on the bed beside Jo. She was staring up at the cobwebs in the beams above the pallet.

'We need to deal with those webs,' Lily said, 'if we are to stay here.'

'I suppose we do,' Jo agreed, turning on the pillow. 'Are you *sure* you wish to stay?' she said. 'I just . . . I understand how close you are with your family, and I would hate for you to think you need to leave them for me . . .'

Lily shuffled closer. 'Jo . . .'

'And I know you had such *plans*, and I just—'

Lily smothered her words beneath a kiss.

'If I did not wish to stay here,' Lily said as she pulled back, 'I would not. But I *do*, Jo. I know I've always blathered on about freedom, but I think . . . I think freedom was too big for me. I *like* this. Now I know you want me, too . . . I will go where you go. And besides,' she added, 'I promised the miller's wife that I would sew forget-me-nots onto their daughter's wedding gown. I cannot possibly do that from Dunlyn Castle.'

Jo smiled. 'No,' she said. 'I suppose you cannot.'

She closed the tiny gap between them again. Kissing Jo felt like a dream. Lily had never dared to hope that it could feel like *this*. Tomorrow, she supposed, she would be starting a new life. They would be starting a new life together. But right now, under the dusty beams, all she knew was Jo, and the way she moved under her lips.

Jo slid her hands down Lily's chest, tangling in her undershirt, tugging it aside and smoothing her fingertips over the soft, warm skin beneath. Lily hissed into the kiss, then laughed.

'So bold, my Lady.'

She slid her hand down Jo's leg, pulling up her shift. Jo shuddered as Lily's palm brushed against her thigh.

'As are you,' Jo whispered, 'my champion.'

Lily's grip tightened as she pulled her closer, deepening the kiss. And then all there was were sighs as the sky through the tiny window deepened into black, and filled with stars.

Epilogue

One year later

There was a chicken in the bedchamber. Lily faced down the beast, her hands gripping tight around the handle of the broom she had been using to sweep away the old rushes.

It regarded her with its tiny, beady eyes. It did not blink. Lily was not even sure if chickens *could* blink – she could not remember if she had ever seen one blink. She would have to ask Jo, who would surely know, and—

The bird leapt from the unmade bed and flew at her, squawking and flapping. Lily stumbled back, righted herself, hit it squarely in the head, then in a deft move shoved it through the doorway and out into the kitchen. It landed with a soft *thud* and scuttled away.

'I see you are putting your swordplay skills to good use.'

Jo was watching her, arms folded, as the chicken scurried past her and out into the garden. Lily leant heavily on the broom, puffing a loose strand of hair from her face.

'Anything to keep you safe,' she said.

Jo sighed and walked over. She tucked the strand behind Lily's ear with a fond smile. Lily's hair was to her shoulders, now – long enough to pull into a tail, and certainly long enough to drive her to madness. She would need to ask Jo to cut it again.

'How is the brewery?' Lily asked, noticing the webs clinging to Jo's long, loose hair.

'It is a *mess*.' Jo slumped. 'Those tubs are disgusting, and I do not know if we should attempt again to clean them or accept the loss of buying more.'

'How much would new tubs be?'

'Too much.' Jo sighed again. 'And that, of course, is if we can even clean the room itself. *And* fix that leak in the roof. I can see now why they were keen to be rid of this place.'

Lily glanced around. They had come into the brewery by awkward circumstances: Mabel's cousin was the baker in the closest town, and the brewery had been owned by his friend before she had passed away. With no family, the brewery had passed into disrepair. The cousin had offered it to Mabel, who had in turn offered it to them.

Even with Mabel's support it was a risk. But it was *theirs*. And if they *couldn't* fix the leaking roof and the useless tubs and the infestation of chickens in the bedchamber, then they had the reassurance that Mabel would welcome them back, and the space in the loft would be waiting for them.

'I have managed *one* task, at least,' Jo said.

'Oh?'

There was a blush mottling Jo's cheekbones.

'Come . . .'

She grabbed the broom, rested it against the wall and then took Lily's hand, leading her outside.

'What have you— *Oh*.'

Lily stared up at the outer wall of the house. They had managed to repair most of the outside of the building – securing beams and patching holes — and had even managed to affix a couple of hooks above the door, ready to place a broom when they opened as an alehouse.

Beside the hooks, Jo had hung Lily's shield. The shield of the Knight of Stars. In the spring light, the white stars glowed. Jo had repaired the damage to it, too, and fixed the flaking paint.

'Jo . . .' Lily breathed. It was all she was able to say.

'Is it all right?' Jo asked, nervously. 'I know I should have asked, but I thought you might enjoy the surprise, and—'

Quickly looking around to ensure they were alone – which here, they almost always were – Lily tugged her into a kiss.

'I love it,' she said. 'Truly.'

'I know that I have rather taken over this place,' said Jo, apologetically. 'But this way we'll know that it's *yours*, too.'

Lily gazed back up at the shield. It looked *right*, there above the doorway to the crumbling building that had become their home. She took Jo's hand. Her fingertips were a little dry, a little calloused. She had been working hard.

Lily laced their fingers together.

'It's *ours*.'

Acknowledgments

They say that writing the second book is harder. I am happy to confirm that this is entirely, abundantly true. Oof.

What else is there to say?

Stars was an odd beast to wrangle, and an even odder one to write. It took me a little while to accept that, yes, I could create the story I really wanted to - even though I was worried it was tropey and nonsensical. But I do love a woman in armour.

I knew from the start that I wanted to write about knights, and beer. And Jo and Lily kissing, I suppose. For a while, the two ideas battled it out — would it be a story about a tournament, or a story about a brewery? In the end, I melded them together.

This is, ultimately, a story about women. Which is why the brewery felt so important. While Stars is *slightly* anachronistic (by this time, women were on their way to being forced out of the trade), brewing in medieval times was a *woman's* trade. It was run by women, organised by women, and the beer was sold by women. And women would indeed face punishments if they sold bad beer. Legislation about brewing from the time used female pronouns, rather than the standard catch-all of "he" that was typically used when describing "the human race in general". It's a little funny, now, that beer is seen as the realm of men, when we have women to thank for it.

The broomstick that Jo hangs above the brewery to show the beer is ready is real, too. In fact, it's why witches ride brooms. Sadly, I never got a chance to explore the magic as much as I would have liked – but I'm sure there's room for a Pratchett style AU in which Jo is a witch in training.

Thank you to everyone who has supported me through this process, and the unsettling position I found myself in of writing the second book while the first was being released. Thanks, as ever, to my family for supporting me, to my mum for believing that I could keep going, and to my partner for buying me chocolate on those particularly difficult days.

Thank you to the usual suspects - Inber, Dorian, and Conny – for your unwavering love and support as I tangled myself up in stress the likes of which I've never known before. Without you, I'd have gone utterly mad, and none of this would have happened.

Of course, thanks as ever goes to my publishers and editor(s), especially during my (many, many) moments of anxiety. Thanks again to Kate Oakley for her work on the cover, and to Diane J. Rayor for allowing me use of her translation of Sappho Fragment 31 at the start of the book.

Writing *Stars* was particularly odd, finishing drafts and edits as *Hartswood* was finally hitting shelves and finding readers. Thank you to everyone who *did* find *Hartswood*, everyone who loved it, and everyone who reached out to me to tell me that they loved it. I'd never realised how vulnerable releasing a book would make me feel – and how huge of an impact it can have on your mental health. To all my readers: thank you so much. Knowing you love my boys just like I do makes it worth it.

And, of course, thank you to everyone who left a review begging for a Jo/Lily sequel. I hope you've enjoyed their story just as much as you did *Hartswood*.

One Night in Hartswood

Oxford 1360

When his sister's betrothed vanishes the night before her politically arranged marriage, Raff Barden must track and return the elusive groom to restore his family's honour.

William de Foucart — known to his friends as Penn — had no choice but to abandon his intended, and with it his own earldom, when he fled the night before his enforced marriage. But ill-equipped to survive on the run he must trust the kindness of a stranger, Raff, to help him escape.

Unaware their fates are already entwined, the men journey north. But amidst the snow-capped forests an unexpected bond deepens into a far more precious relationship, one that will test all that they hold dear. And when secrets are finally revealed, both men must decide what they will risk for the one they love . . .

ONE PLACE. MANY STORIES

Bold, innovative and
empowering publishing.

FOLLOW US ON:

@HQStories